Praise for

THE THRONE
OF THE FIVE WINDS

"Intricate, elegant, and sharp as a blade—*The Throne of the Five Winds* is sweeping political fantasy at its finest."
—Tasha Suri, author of *Empire of Sand*

"With a deliberate pace and fine attention to details of dress and custom, Emmett weaves a masterful tale of court intrigues."
—*Booklist* (starred review)

"Brimful of thrilling palace drama and menacing court intrigue."
—Kate Elliott, author of *Black Wolves*

"Action and intrigue [take] place within a layered and beautifully realized fantasy world that will appeal to readers of Evan Winter's *The Rage of Dragons* and K. Arsenault Rivera's *The Tiger's Daughter*."
—*B&N Sci-Fi & Fantasy Blog*

THE
POISON
PRINCE

By S. C. Emmett

HOSTAGE OF EMPIRE
The Throne of the Five Winds
The Poison Prince

THE
POISON
PRINCE

HOSTAGE OF EMPIRE:
BOOK TWO

S. C. EMMETT

orbit

orbitbooks.net

Copyright © 2020 by Lilith Saintcrow
Excerpt from *The Wolf of Oren-Yaro* copyright © 2017 by K. S. Villoso
Excerpt from *The Mask of Mirrors* copyright © 2020 by Bryn Neuenschwander and Alyc Helms

Cover design by Lisa Marie Pompilio
Cover illustration by Miranda Meeks
Cover copyright © 2020 by Hachette Book Group, Inc.
Map by Charis Loke

Orbit
Hachette Book Group
1290 Avenue of the Americas
New York, NY 10104
orbitbooks.net

First Edition: November 2020

Orbit is an imprint of Hachette Book Group.
The Orbit name and logo are trademarks of Little, Brown Book Group Limited.

Library of Congress Cataloging-in-Publication Data
Names: Emmett, S. C., author.
Title: The poison prince / S.C. Emmett.
Description: First edition. | New York, NY : Orbit, 2020. | Series: Hostage of empire ; book 2
Identifiers: LCCN 2020015577 | ISBN 9780316453424 (trade paperback) |
    ISBN 9780316453417 (ebook) | ISBN 9780316453400
Subjects: GSAFD: Fantasy fiction.
Classification: LCC PS3619.A3984 P65 2020 | DDC 813/.6—dc23
LC record available at https://lccn.loc.gov/2020015577

ISBNs: 978-0-316-45342-4 (trade paperback), 978-0-316-45341-7 (ebook)

Printed in the United States of America

LSC-C

Printing 1, 2020

For Sarah, Nivia, and Angeline, with thanks.

AUTHOR'S NOTE

The reader is presumed to have read Book One of these adventures; certain matters will otherwise be somewhat opaque. Many terms, most notably in Khir, are difficult to translate, and much effort has been made to find the correct, if not the prettiest or simplest, overtones; footnotes have been discontinued due to uncertainty over their utility. Any translation errors are of course the author's, and said author hopes for the reader's kind patience.

Now, let us return to the center of the world, great Zhaon-An...

I must go,

My sleeve is caught.

—Zhe Har the Archer

A Strange Pair

O utside the ancient westron walls of Zhaon-An's bustling old city, a foreign princess was the second to be laid in newly built, bone-white tombs.

The traditional crumbling mausoleum of historical petty princes and ambitious, likewise historical warlords was to the north of the city's simmering, its borders hard pressed by ramshackle temporary dwellings spreading in that direction. The Emperor Garan Tamuron, however, had decreed a new, more auspicious site for the Garan dynasty just outside the walls facing the setting sun. His long-dead first wife's urn was sealed in a restrained, costly tomb-wall, and any in Zhaon could have reasonably expected that another imperial wife or concubine would follow—or, in the worst case, the Emperor himself.

Instead, it was Garan Ashan Mahara, daughter of the Great Rider of Khir and new bride to the Crown Prince of Zhaon, whose restrained and beautifully carved eggstone urn was immured next to the Emperor's memorialized spear-wife, and the interment had proceeded with almost unseemly haste but great pomp, honor, and expense.

It was considered wise to show a princess's shade, as well as her home country, a certain respect.

Thunder lingered over distant hills as a slight woman in pale, well-stitched mourning robes of unbleached silk put her palms together and bowed thrice. A small broom to sweep the tomb's narrow, sealed entrance and the dimensions of a Khir pailai was set aside in its proper alcove; the carved stone showing the name and titles of a new addition to the ranks of the honorable dead was marked first in Zhaon characters, then in Khir. Each symbol had the painfully sharp edges of fresh, grieving chisel-marks.

The mourner's black hair held blue highlights and a single hairpin thrust into carefully coiled braids, the stick crowned with an irregular pebble wrapped with crimson silk thread. Neither ribbon nor string dangled small semiprecious beads or any other tiny bright adornment fetchingly from that pebble, for Khir-style mourning did not admit any excess.

At least, not in that particular direction.

Komor Yala's chin dropped; her breath touched her folded hands. The hem of her pale silk overdress fluttered, fingered by a hot, unsteady breeze. It was almost the long dry time of summer, but still, in the afternoons, the storms menaced. The lightning was more often than not utterly dry as well, leaping from cloud to cloud instead of deigning to strike burgeoning earth. At least the harvest would be fine, or so the peasants remarked—softly, cautiously, in case Heaven overheard and took offense.

A bareheaded man in very fine leather half-armor waited at a respectful distance, his helm tucked at a precise angle under his left arm and a dragon-carved swordhilt peering balefully over his shoulder. He stayed motionless and patient, yet leashed tension vibrated in his broad shoulders and occasionally creaked in his boots when his weight shifted.

For all that, Zakkar Kai did not speak, and if it irked him to wait for a woman's prayers he made no sign. The head general of Zhaon's mighty armies had arrived straight from morning drill performed on wide white Palace paving-stones to accompany Crown Princess Mahara's lone Khir lady-in-waiting outside the city walls, and his red-black topknot was slightly disarranged from both helm and exertion.

Finally, it could be put off no longer. Komor Yala finished her prayers, her lips moving slightly, and brushed at her damp cheeks. She had swept the pailai clean before Mahara's wall, and gave another trio of bows. Her clear grey eyes, feverishly aglitter, held dark sleepless smudges underneath, and her cheekbones stood out in stark curves.

The Zhaon would say *grief is eating her food*; a Khir proverb ran *a slight woman carries poverty instead of sons.*

She backed from the tomb's august presence, pausing to bow again; when she turned, she found Zakkar Kai regarding her thoughtfully, deep-set eyes gleaming and his mouth relaxed. He offered his armored right arm, still silent.

The absence of sweetened platitudes was one more thing to admire in the man. Her brother would have liked a fellow who could refrain from polluting a serious visit with idle chatter; a slow smolder of hidden unforgiving fire, that had been Komori Baiyan.

But her damoi was struck down at Three Rivers, where so many other noble Khir sons had fallen. Yala could not decide if he had likely faced Zakkar Kai upon that bloody field, or not. She also could not decide how to feel about either prospect. It was not likely Kai would speak of battle with a foreign court lady, even if he had noticed a particular Khir rider during the screaming morass of battle.

Yala placed her fingers in the crook of his right elbow; the general matched his steps to hers. Finally, he spoke, but only the same mannerly phrase he used every other time he accompanied her upon this errand. "Shall we halt for tea upon our return voyage, Lady Yala?"

"I am hardly dressed for it," she murmured, as she did every time. Near the entrance to this white stone courtyard, in the shade of a long-armed fringeleaf tree with its powdery scented blossoms, her kaburei Anh leaned against the wall like a sleeping horse, leather-wrapped braids dangling past her round shoulders. "And your duties must be calling you, General."

"They may call." He never left his helm with his horse, as if he expected ambush even here; or perhaps it was merely a soldier's habit to carry gear. "I am the one who decides the answer."

A man could afford such small intransigence. Yala's temples ached. She made this trip daily; it was not yet a full moon-cycle since her princess's last ride. Yala herself had attended her princess's dressing upon that last day, grateful to be free of the dungeons.

Had she still been imprisoned, or had she not avoided the shame of a flogging, would Mahara still be alive?

"And I am not dressed for such a visit," Kai continued, levelly. "We make a strange pair." He halted inside the fringeleaf's shade as Anh yawned into alertness.

"Very." Yala's throat ached. The tears rose at inopportune moments, and she wondered why she had not wept for Bai so. The grief of her brother's passage to the Great Fields was still a steady, silent, secret ache, but Mahara...oh, the sharp, piercing agony was approaching again, a silent house-feline stalking small vermin. Yala forced herself to breathe slowly, to keep her pace to a decorous glide, to keep her unsteady limbs in their proper attitudes.

"There is a cold-flask tied to my saddle," Kai said almost sharply, his intonation proper for commanding a kaburei. "Our lady grows pale."

"I am well enough," Yala began, but Anh bowed and hurried off down the long colonnade. It would take her time to reach the horses, but her mistress and the general would still be in sight.

Zakkar Kai was careful of Yala's reputation, though it mattered little now. With her princess reduced to ash and fragments of bone by a pyre's breath, what *did* matter?

Nothing much. Except perhaps the small idea growing in Yala's liver, a painful, pricking consciousness that her duty to Ashan Mahara was hardly done.

Zhaon's great general fixed his gaze forward as if upon parade and set off for the horses, which meant Yala accompanied him at the mannerly pace of nobles retreating before the august dead. They walked silently through bars of sunlight and shade; Yala kept herself occupied with counting the columns, the numbers push-ing away a black cloud seeking to fill her skull. When her escort halted between one step and the next, half-turning to face her with a sharp military click of his riding boots, she did not look at him, studying instead the closest carven pillar.

So much room, so much stone dragged step by step from so many quarries, so many carven edges; Zhaon was a country of wastage and luxury, even with their dead.

Kai's gaze was a weight upon her profile. "Yala."

"Kai." Her hand dropped to her side, hung uselessly. *What now?* Was he about to observe that he could not after all accompany her here every morning? He had been silent well past the point of politeness, today.

"I must eventually ride to the North." His jaw tightened; the breeze played with his topknot, teasing at strands pulled free by the morn's activity. "The Emperor..."

No more need be said. "Of course," she replied, colorlessly. Khir, hearing the news of a princess's death, had reoccupied the bor-der crossings and bridges; no wains of tribute had reached Zhaon from its conquered northern neighbor, and merchants both small and large were uneasy. The entire court of Zhaon was alive with rumor, from the lowest kaburei to the princes themselves; even the Emperor must hear the mutters upon his padded bench of a throne high above the common streets. "He is your lord."

Obedience was due no matter how the heart ached, in both Khir and Zhaon.

"He is also my friend, and he is dying." Kai did not glance over his shoulder to gauge who might be in earshot, but here among empty apartments meant for shades and incense, who would gossip?

"Yes." There was no use in dissembling; the entire palace knew the Emperor's nameless malady was fatal. The rai gave up its fruit for eating and next year's crop, children died of fever or misad-venture before their naming-days, men rode to war and women retreated to childbed; every street was paved with thousands of smaller deaths—insects, birds, beasts of burden, and cherished or useful pets.

Death had its bony fists wrapped about the world's throat, and its grasp was final.

"I may speak to him before I leave, should I find opportunity." Kai's gaze, usually a jewelwing's weightless brush, was unwonted heavy today. "But not unless you tell me plainly whether or not I may hope."

What was there to hope for, with Mahara gone and unavenged to boot? Yala blinked, her gaze swinging in his direction. His features came into focus, swimming through the heavy water in her eyes. A single traitorous drop slipped free, tracing a cool phantom finger down her cheek.

She studied him afresh—long nose, deep eyes, the usual hint of a sardonic smile absent from full, almost cruel lips, mussed top-knot. His half-armor was in the Zhaon style, meant to provide both freedom of movement and some small insurance against bolts or sharpened edges; it was stiffened leather and waxed cords, buckles and straps, any lack of ornamentation belied by the quality of the materials. The heat-haze of a male used to healthy exertion tinged with a breath of leather enfolded her without touching the chill streamlets coursing through her bones.

She had suspected he might require some manner of answer today. "Should I ask you to be plainer in turn?"

"I've been *exceedingly* plain." A faint ghost of a smile touched one corner of his mouth, but he continued in a rush, cavalry with leveled weapons sweeping all before it. "I can offer you protection. I have estates; they are modest, but I could well and easily acquire more." The wad of pounded rai in his throat, meant to keep a man from choking on truth or its cousin—what he must say to survive—bobbed as he swallowed. "And…there is much affection, Yala, upon my side. Even if I am loathsome to a Khir lady."

Was that what held him back? She could not ask so plainly, even if he was paying her the high honor of directness. "*Loathsome* is not the term I would use, General Zakkar. Even if my Zhaon is some-what halting."

"Your Zhaon is very musical, my lady." The compliment was accompanied by a slight grimace, as if he expected her to bridle at it. Faint amusement lit his dark gaze for a moment before vanishing into somberness. "Dare I ask what term you *would*?"

"Kind." She thought for a moment; the complexity of her feelings demanded a balancing of one quality against another. "And deadly, when you see the need."

After all, who had killed the first assassin she had seen in Zhaon? This man, and no other. It was perhaps unfair to wonder whether he might be induced to move against a later attacker, one who had so far escaped justice.

"Another strange pairing." He did not look away, no surrender accepted or considered. "Yala, will you marry me?"

Finally, he had said it. She could now answer *I am still in mourning*, and be done. She could turn her shoulder and deliver the cut with the calm chill of a noblewoman well used to clothing a sharp edge in pretty syllables.

Instead, she watched his eyes, muddy like a half-Khir's. Within a single generation of admixture the gaze lost its directness; some held that the pale grey of nobility ran through the great houses because the Blood Years had forced them to marry their own more than was quite wise. Zakkar Kai's face was not sharp enough to be even quarter-Khir; he did not have mountain bones. Gossip spoke of some barbarian in his vanished bloodline, a common brat-foundling taken up by a warlord who became Emperor of this terrible, choking, luxurious land.

Barbarian or not, he was mighty among his fellows and measured in courtesy. His careful generalship—standing fast to bleed his enemy, breaking away to replenish his army and tire his foe with chasing—had broken the back of Khir's resistance, and the victory at Three Rivers had brought her princess to perfumed, hot-cloying Zhaon as matrimonial sacrifice.

That Crown Prince Garan Takyeo had been kind to his foreign

bride was beside the point. This country had swallowed Mahara and her lady-in-waiting whole, and now Yala, bereft, was a pebble in the conqueror's guts.

Another traitorous tear struggled free and followed its elder sister's path down her cheek. As Yala should have followed Mahara, had she not been gainsaid at the pyre.

Leather made a soft noise as Kai's callused fingertips brushed the droplet away. It was the first time a man other than her own brother had touched her thus, and Komor Yala almost swayed.

His was the hand wielding that antique dragon-hilted sword, cutting down many of Khir's finest sons. It was the same hand sending the sword's point through an assassin in a darkened dry-garden upon a wedding-night, defending Yala. That he had thought her the new Crown Princess was irrelevant; it was also Zakkar Kai who had brought her back to the palace complex after tracking a clutch of conspiratorial kidnappers who had *definitely* mistaken Yala for her princess.

How could she possibly put each event onto scales and find their measure? She was no merchant daughter, bred for and used to weighing.

"If I were free to answer," she said slowly, "I would marry you, Zakkar Kai." There was little point in dissembling. He was not the worst fate for a Khir noblewoman trapped in a southron court, and she—oh, it was useless to deny it, she rather...liked him. The more he showed of the man behind his sword, the more she found him interesting and honorable, until she could not be sure her estimation of his actions was from their merit or her own feelings.

A high flush stood along his cheekbones, perhaps from morning drill or the heat. Surely it could not be a surfeit of affection for a foreign lady-in-waiting. "But you are not?"

"I must write to my father." Was that why she continued to deflect a general's interest? How could she even begin to brush the characters that would explain *this*? It was craven and ignoble to think that as Zakkar Kai's foreign-born wife she would not have to face her father's disappointment at both her failure and her weakness.

"Of course." He nodded, a short decisive movement of a man well suited to command. "I will not speak to the Emperor until you have word." His throat worked again, and he did not take his rough fingertips from her face. A strange heat, not at all like Zha-on's sticky, hideously close summer, spilled from that touch down her aching neck, and somehow eased the terrible hole in her chest. *"I will wait as long as I must."*

It was the warrior's reply to the Moon Maiden. A smile crept to her lips, horrifying her. How could she feel even the barest desire to laugh or seek comfort, here in the house of the dead? "You are quite partial to Zhe Har, scholar-general."

"Only some few of his works." Kai still did not move, leaning over her to provide welcome shade, the rest of the world made hazy and insignificant by the mere fact of his presence.

Why had he not been born Khir? Of course, he would be dead at Three Rivers, or Komori Dasho might—as he had told his daughter once—have refused any suit for her hand. It did no good to wish for the past to change, or to ask uncaring Heaven for any comfort. A single noblewoman's grieving was less than a speck of dust under the grinding of great cart-wheels as the world went upon its way.

He leaned forward still farther, and Yala felt a faint, dozing alarm.

But Zakkar Kai, the terror of Zhaon's enemies, stern in war and moderate in counsel, merely pressed his lips to her damp forehead before straightening and stepping back, leaving her oddly bereft. "Come." He offered his arm again. "We must see you home, my lady."

Home. If her father sent word quickly enough, she could plead filial duty and escape northward. No doubt Crown Prince Takyeo would provide an escort to at least the border. She could be in Hai Komori's dark, severe, familiar halls by the middle harvest, facing her lord father's displeasure without the shield of distance, paper, or ink.

Komori Dasho would never be so ill-bred as to directly refer to her shame, but his silent disappointment would be that much harder to bear.

Yala bowed her head and once more took Zakkar Kai's arm. Her skull was full of a rushing, whirling noise but she held grimly to her task, placing one foot before the other on bruising, sun-scorched stone.

She had been sent to protect her beautiful princess, and failed. All else was inconsequential. The world was a cruel summer-glaring dream, and she was lost within it.

SUBMIT, REGARDLESS

The Jonwa, home to Zhaon's Crown Prince and hung with the pale paper bubbles of mourning-lanterns, was not much cooler than outside despite its stone floors and high ceilings. The massive sculpture of paired snow-pards in the entrance hall glowed, mellow speckled stone rubbed to satin in a pool of sunlight robbed of heat by a succession of several mirrors. The pards' flanks cast a somber reflection upon polished wooden flooring, but the statue's twin heads, facing each other in eternal deadlock, were both shrouded with unbleached linen.

Crown Prince Garan Takyeo, the first in succession to rule mighty Zhaon, sat at his study's great ironwood desk, staring blankly at an open book upon the ruthlessly organized surface. It was Cao Lung's *Green Book*, holding much upon the subject of mourning, but its block-pressed characters would not stay in their orderly falling-rain lines, wandering as the reader's attention did.

He had been staring at this particular page for some while.

There was a feline scratching at the door-post, and Third Prince Garan Takshin, in a Shan lord's head-to-toe black except for the pale slash of a knotted mourning-band upon his left arm, stepped through. "It won't change into an eggbird, no matter how long you look at it," he said by way of greeting, his scars—one vanishing under his red-black hair, another pleating his top lip into a sneer despite any attempt at pleasantry or even ease—flushed with morning sunshine. He had no doubt been at morning drill, and though the rest of him was freshly bathed his topknot was slightly rumpled.

"At least we would have the eggs if it did." Takyeo tried a smile, rubbing at his freshly clipped and oiled mustache and smallbeard. Perched upon this backless chair with his wounded leg stretched straight and wrapped in odorous, herb-smeared bandages, attaining a pleasant expression was a more difficult operation than he could quite believe. "And a bright good morning to you, too. Have you eaten?"

"At dawn. Which is why I came; it is well-nigh lunchtime, and none of your servants will brave this room to scold you into keeping your strength." Takshin's dark, leather-soled house-slippers whispered as he padded to the shelves of annals, treatises, and other spine-bound or rolled items necessary for a prince's intellectual exercise. He affected to study a shelf with much interest; the gold hoop in his ear gave a single savage glitter. "I am hungry too, so bestir yourself, old man."

A thin thread of amusement broke the shell of blank inattention Takyeo had spent the morning in. It was a relief. "You are like an old woman. *Come and eat, come and eat.*"

"We must look after your health." Takshin imitated an elderly maiden-auntie's quaver, accompanying it with a rude gesture often seen in the sinks of the Theater District or Zhaon-An's teeming slums. Usually, it was deployed when a brothel-keeper had not been paid her portion, or a gambling criminal wished to denounce dice for working against him without quite accusing his opponent's hand of sleight.

The juxtaposition wrung a weary laugh from Takyeo, who began arranging his robe and his leg for the task of rising. Zakkar Kai's pet physician swore the wound would heal true, but not if the Crown Prince placed undue strain upon sliced, violated muscle and bruised bone.

It was to Honorable Physician Kihon Jiao that Takyeo owed his ability to stand at all. The arrow that had almost crushed his femur was a heavy, barbarous affair of northern make, but many in outlying Zhaon provinces menaced by horseback bandits also used such things. The assassin's hiding place—a bramble-choked hedgerow just outside Zhaon-An on a road much used for pleasure-jaunts by prince and noble alike—held no clues, nothing more than a blurred shape in long summer-juicy grass where the man had taken his ease and a leaf-covered pile of droppings showing that he had frequented the spot, an adder lying in wait.

"Shall I steady your cane?" Takshin continued, solicitously enough to be sarcastic, and Takyeo waved an irritated hand.

"Stop fussing, or I shall tell the physician you have a cough." His hand felt strange without the greenstone hurei denoting princely status, returned to its owner by Zakkar Kai with a lack of comment and tucked carefully in the sleeve-pocket of whatever robe Takyeo wore. Even after dropping the ring upon the floor of the throne room and stalking away, Takyeo could not quite slip the traces of responsibility.

Gossip said the Crown Prince had flung the heavy greenstone band with its deep sharp seal-carving at his lordly father; gossip was wrong, and yet for once in his life Garan Takyeo wished it was not.

"He won't believe it; I am generally held to be too sour to take ill in summer." Takshin turned his back upon the study, staring at the shelves again. "*He* sent another letter this morning, Ah-Yeo." The childhood nickname, born of lisping younger siblings' half-swallowed attempts to honorably name their elder, brushed along paper and leather spines, touched the carved ends of neatly stacked scrollcases of segmented babu.

"Mh." Takyeo left the *Green Book* where it lay. After lunch, he would try again. It was merely a question of will, was it not? Like everything else. "Of course it was not a Red Letter." Those imperial missives, with their giant scarlet cartouches, could not be turned away. The Crown Prince's orders to his steward Keh were very specific—nothing from the Emperor but a Red Letter could be brought into Takyeo's presence.

Inside the Jonwa, *he* was the ruler—at least until his father ordered succession differently. There was no point in even hoping for such a change, since it would not alter the underlying battlefield.

Nothing would.

"Of course." Takshin ran a callused fingertip, scraped from near daily, always punishing practice with weighted wooden sword and blunted knife, along a shelf of classics, his head cocked slightly. "He expects you to submit, regardless."

"He does." Takyeo had submitted all his life. *Be princely*, their father always said. *You are my heir, and must behave as such.*

It was unexpectedly easy to refuse. Or, if not quite refuse, then to drag his half-lame heels and parry the expectations hung upon him from the cradle. Sometimes Takyeo wondered what his long-dead mother would say of all this, but the painting of her in the ever-lit shrine Garan Tamuron attended daily—as well as the portrait enclosed in his eldest son's own household shrine—merely smiled emptily.

The age of miracles, of painted mothers finding their voices to chide husbands and errant descendants, was long over, if it had ever existed outside of tales told to gullible children. No intercession could be expected, especially when Garan Tamuron, Emperor of Zhaon and Heaven-blessed father of many sons, had decided upon a certain course.

Takyeo paid his respects to his mother's portrait in the Jonwa's shrine daily too, like any good son. Since the wedding, his foreign wife had too. *She has a kind face*, his wife had said of his long-dead, barely remembered mother, and added her own shy smile.

An entire morning spent seeking to avoid thinking upon his grief was wasted now, and the strange buzzing inside his bones mounted another notch. He was no closer to discovering the source of that maddening, unsteady feeling. There was nothing about it in any of the medical treatises he had read in the course of a princely education, and he did not think Kihon Jiao would consider it a symptom.

Takshin half-turned, not quite glancing aside to regard his eldest brother. It was an unexpected mercy; either of them could say what they wished, not having to scrutinize the other's face for a reaction. "I am glad you will not," he said, finally, in a level tone stripped of his usual sharp sarcasm. "'Tis high time *he* learned what it is to be balked, and by you, no less."

"It is not disobedience." Takyeo found his leg was not overly stiff; the silver-headed cane propped against his desk took his weight admirably. "Merely disinterest."

"So I have pointed out, but I do not think he takes it as comfort." Takshin's smile was not gentle at all. He had been a prickly but soft-hearted child before his first trip to Shan, prone to flinging himself into battle to right every perceived wrong. Now he made no move to aid his eldest brother, a welcome change from everyone else's flitting and fussing.

Takyeo suspected any attempt to thank his younger sibling for such forbearance would be met with either indifference or a snarl, so he made none. "He probably suspects you enjoy my recalcitrance."

"He suspects correctly. I only wonder it took you this long." But speaking of their august father was not Takshin's sole purpose, and nor was baiting his brother to lunch, the gleam in his eye said. "Your housekeeper is beside herself. You have given some orders she does not think are quite wise."

Lady Kue was not given to gossip, but she could hardly keep such preliminary arrangements from the notice of another member of the household. Takyeo took a tentative step, found his balance and leg both held, and wondered how long the mercy would last. "I doubt she says as much."

"You are correct. Still, there is a proverb in Shan about a master's foolish wishes, and I would wager she is muttering it today." Takshin's chin almost touched his shoulder, keeping his brother in peripheral vision. Still, he did not turn, his broad back exposed. It was, like all his poses, only partly disdain, and wholly a message. And now Takshin, choosing his own course as usual, arrived at the heart of his business with his eldest brother. "Do you truly intend to withdraw to the countryside?"

Perhaps he was the only one who could—or would—ask in such a manner. Even Kai did not mention the rumors, though he was patently aware and had probably guessed Takyeo's departure date as well, though such information lingered only in the secret cavern of the Crown Prince's head-meat as of yet. "My household has undergone some changes of late, Taktak." Takyeo made certain his robe fell in its usual folds. Pale silk, both bleached and unbleached, strict mourning, though he could have chosen regular cloth and an armband three days after the pyre. A wife was not a parent, and yet he wished to mark the fact of her absence even more profoundly. "Surely you have noticed."

"Very well, we shall retreat to a country villa to lick our wounds." Takshin took no offense. His slight, ironclad smile stayed just the same, not stretching or diminishing by any fraction. "I'm certain Lady Yala could use a change of scenery as well."

"No doubt." Takyeo was equally certain that consideration weighed heavily in his brother's scales. It was not quite clear whether Takshin was simply fond of the Khir lady-in-waiting, or if he harbored other designs. If it was the latter, it would be the first time he'd evinced any real interest in a court lady, and it was just like Takshin to choose a foreign one. "I have not asked her plans or preferences. When her mourning is done, perhaps we shall find an accommodation for her."

It was, after all, the least a Crown Prince could do. His wife would have wished her friend safely placed.

"Perhaps." Takshin did not rise to the bait, unwilling as always to show his true feelings—and have them used against him. But he did turn to face his eldest brother fully, and that was an encouraging sign. "Well, are you ready to hobble to table, Eldest Brother? If we wait much longer I shall begin chewing your shelves."

Takyeo's grimace was good-natured, and only partly pained. "You travel upon your stomach like a merchant." A bird called in one of the Jonwa's gardens, a high sharp piercing trill, and he wondered, before he could stop himself, if his wife had heard the sound.

Did her shade linger? You were not supposed to hope for such a thing. It generally meant there were matters left unaddressed and a spirit could not rest. Such diaphanous presences rarely stayed beneficent.

"Or an army." Takshin's smile was that rare beast, a sliver of genuine amusement from the Shan-adopted prince. That barbarous land with its mad, now-dead queen had taken his bristling, heartsoft younger brother and returned this fellow, who showed only infrequent flashes of his former self. "Come."

For all that, Takshin could be relied upon, and not merely because his adoption removed him from the line of succession. Even if Zhaon's throne were offered him with both palms, Taktak might refuse with a sneer and a sword-cut, especially if the offer was made in a manner he considered impolite, pitying, or even merely jesting.

The Crown Prince took another experimental step. His leg held. Perhaps after lunch Takyeo could summon his wife's lone Khir lady-in-waiting and they could desultorily speak upon the classics. Discussing the Hundreds in fits and starts, Lady Komor visibly and audibly searching for safe subjects to converse upon, the occasional silences between them restful instead of pained... somehow, it helped.

Perhaps because Yala's clear grey Khir eyes were very much like Mahara's.

There. He had thought her name, too, and the unbidden image of his foreign wife's round, pretty, wistful face almost caused him to stagger.

Takshin pretended not to notice. He was proving to have far more discretion than Takyeo thought him ever capable of. That realization should have been a comfort, but in reality, there was none to be found.

Not with his lovely, decorous warrior-wife half crushed under a horse, her leg pinned to its side by a barbarous, heavy iron arrowhead.

HEAVEN WILLS

The Emperor was not upon the low, silver-padded Throne of Five Winds, nor at the business of rule elsewhere in his vermilion-pillared Great Hall with eunuchs and ministers shuffling, murmuring their assent, or broaching soft questions. He was not pausing before one of the Kaeje's gardens to admire the view, his fingers busy with satin-smooth kombin beads, or seated before a chessboard on the Scholar's Porch across from Zakkar Kai, Fourth Prince Makar, or any other—courtier, Golden, or eunuch—who wished to play.

Instead, the nerve-center of Zhaon's ancient and now united power reclined upon a wide bed in a hexagonal room bright with mirrorlight, its blank stone walls hung with tapestries. The Second Queen's fine needlework showed upon more than one of the hangings, and so did First Concubine Luswone's. The First Queen's wifely contribution was heavy, healthful ji-hao incense in great brass burners set upon the wide, balustraded porch looking over one of the Kaeje's two state gardens, the wide, curiosity-stuffed green spaces meant to awe visitors and comfort the captain of the country's wallowing ship. Two stone-lipped fountains played a counterpoint to the murmur of the crowded room, and a babu water-clock chop-clicked each daylight span into fractions.

Black-clad eunuchs and bright-plumaged courtiers pressed close, avidly eyeing the wide, crimson-caparisoned royal bed. The body upon it was still strong, many years' hard campaigning training bone, muscle, and sinew to resistance of luxury and illness both, but Garan Tamuron's cheeks had thinned alarmingly and his robe was too high-necked for comfort upon such a bright summer's day. His red-black topknot, though scantier now and holding visible grey, was caged with fine gold filigree and a sharp golden pin; though he was propped upon many square pillows his dark eyes were just as piercing as ever.

That fierce gaze softened as it bent upon a slight woman in dove-grey silk with a mourning armband upon her thin arm and a wide pinkish sash high at her narrow waist. Her wan, not-quite-pretty face was now visible because she had tucked her veil aside, her hairpin holding a shivering fall of fine, thin wooden segments mimicking the fall of a hau tree's branches from a nest of thin but neatly arranged braids. Her fine-boned hands were clasped tightly in her lap, and the dress, though the colors were perfectly appropriate, was far too heavy for summer.

No doubt she wore thick cloth in lieu of armor, for Second Concubine Kanbina rarely, if ever, left her bower in the Iejo, that palace built for noble consorts not possessing wifely status. The lady was held to be somewhat…delicate. Of course, the last concubine was either the most favored or the least liked, sometimes both at once. The First Queen often snapped her fan and remarked, *a creeping little mouse, nibbling in the house*; the Second Queen and First Concubine did not speak of her beyond platitudes, and they did not visit. Still, every holiday and festival, small, well-chosen gifts left her half of the Iejo, and likewise appropriate, tasteful gifts or replies arrived from the Second Queen and First Concubine. The First Queen did not lower herself to such niceties with a concubine who had not, after all, given her husband even a girl-child.

It was a wonder First Queen Gamwone did not choke on poison whenever she bit her tongue, and though a scullery maid might be able to mutter such a thing, the Emperor was wise to refrain from remarking as much. "It is good to see you," Garan Tamuron said instead, softly, and offered his hand.

Kanbina's veil would have reached below her waist had she not gathered it aside; she leaned forward and clasped his hand in both of hers, covering the great greenstone-and-silver ring upon his first finger. "I beg pardon for interrupting your business, husband." The words were scarcely audible, and a flush mounted from her neck, struggling up her thin cheeks. Her ear-drops were likewise restrained, thin hoops of beaten silver with tiny red stones caught inside the arc on rays of fine silken thread. Their ribbons were short, holding them close to her head, and they did not sway as much as another court lady's might. "I was not..." She glanced at Tamuron's expression, and finding nothing there but mild interest took heart to continue once more. "I was not certain you would wish to see me."

"And why not?" With another he would attempt bluff heartiness, but such a tactic would overwhelm this sensitive instrument. And it was, he could admit to himself, a relief to have a moment of relative quiet amid the bustle of the morning's cargo of decisions to be made, weighed, or deferred. "You are a much prettier visitor than these ministers."

"Hardly." But the lady of lost Wurei looked pleased nonetheless, and her flush halted. Her mouth relaxed, and the shadow of the soft-cheeked, bright-voiced girl she had been peered through an older woman's pale moon-waning face. "You are always so kind."

"Hardly, indeed." Tamuron gestured, a peremptory flicker, and the courtiers pressed farther back, spilling onto the wide wooden porch amid streams of incense. Some few were gog-eyed at a creature they had never, after all, seen—Kanbina did not leave her small corner of the Iejo for theater or market, or even to visit the Artisan's Home within the palace complex. The Head Court Eunuch, Zan Fein, opened his fan and made a short gesture to push the rest of his dark-robed brethren away; it was he who had bowed most deeply upon her arrival, forcing all those lower in rank to do the same.

Zan Fein, master of protocol and many less forgiving arts, had his own calculus for measuring prestige, and his only public—or private, for that matter—comment upon the Second Concubine was that she was a true noblewoman, and quite refined.

Kanbina now studied the Emperor's face even more closely, appearing somewhat at a loss for words.

"How is your son?" Tamuron inquired, gently. "Is he filial?"

"Very." At the mention of Zakkar Kai, newly adopted and raised to princely status as well, Kanbina's dark eyes lit and she ducked her head somewhat shyly. The soft glow suited her. "I must thank you again for granting him a hurai, my lord husband. He is well worth the honor."

Her official gratitude had arrived under her little-used ceremonial seal, beautifully shaped characters showing she had spent much time practicing with brush as a noblewoman should. Tamuron knew she played the sathron for hours at a time, as well. What else did a trapped princess forced to marry a conqueror have to spend her time upon, especially while bereft of children, that longed-for joy of any woman's life? "So speaks a mother in truth."

"Adoptive-mother." Kanbina dropped her gaze. It was best not to admit too much pride in children lest Heaven take offense, and she would be more cautious than most. "Is it very bad?" Her fingers, chill even in the close, thick heat, tightened upon his. "The pain? Physician Kihon will not tell me, he says I am to concern myself with my own health."

"The good physician is correct, Kanbina." Tamuron wore the first true smile in weeks under his sparse mustache and closely clipped smallbeard; the lines of strain at the corners of his mouth and eyes eased. Still, the memory—the blood upon the sheets, Kanbina's gasping apologies as if she feared he would hold *her* responsible for miscarriage—pained him. "Do not tell him I said so, though, or he will become insufferable."

"My own health is not worth the worry." She ducked her head again, her ear-drops arrested as they swung and her hairpin's decorations making small soft sounds. Her fingers moved slightly, and there was a slight roughness to the tips where sathron-strings would bite. The instrument was unforgiving even with its gentlest devotees. "It will not be long. That is why I came to visit."

"Do not say such things." Tamuron patted her hands with his free fingers, as if brushing an easily bruised fruit. The matching, heavy hurai upon that hand was a weight barely felt, but he took care not to tap too hard against her knuckles. "We shall both recuperate, and spend long days upon verandahs, watching our grandchildren play."

Her face fell, and Tamuron could have kicked himself, if the cursed malady wasn't robbing him of his strength like a thief in an abandoned house.

So, he waited patiently for her to gather courage, as a rider soothes a high-blooded, high-strung horse whose previous owners had whipped too frequently. Finally, she took heart and spoke again. "Are you jesting? My lord?"

"No, Kanbina." Tamuron let his own roughened fingers rest upon her softness. The sathron was indeed a harsh master, but not nearly as harsh as bowstring, swordhilt, or staff-wrapping. "Still, I have made provision for you. Zakkar Kai will be a good son, and your estates well cared for."

"Kai *is* a very good son; I thank Heaven and you for allowing me to have him." Her dark gaze turned solemn and serious, and she lost some measure of her diffidence. "But I am not worried, husband. I am ready." She leaned forward slightly, and her tone dropped further. "I . . . I wanted to tell you something. Or ask you."

"Then do." He had not dealt with her gently; he knew as much. It was one of the few times in his life he had underestimated an opponent, but then, a man did not oft suspect his own wife. Though he should have considered the possibility—perhaps a peasant could afford trust, but a warlord knew that coin was dear indeed. To an Emperor, how much more so? He could openly admit a misstep, faced with the one that failing had wounded. "You, of all people, may ask whatever you wish of me."

"The First Queen," Kanbina whispered. Her hands trembled, and he could scarcely hear over the murmuring of the court and the *thud-click* of the garden's water-clock. "Husband, please do not be angered, but...she does not send you...gifts, does she? Gifts of food, or wine...or tea?"

It was faint comfort that she had finally acknowledged the matter openly. Garan Tamuron had reached a summit of power and ambition, true—and found himself just as trapped by circumstance as a boy from an old but penniless family taking up a sword to make his fortune.

The world whirled, all things were mutable, and yet so little changed.

"You knew?" He might have stiffened, and his smile faltered a whit. Kanbina, ever sensitive, almost flinched, but he pulled gently upon her hands to steady and provide strength. If he had known how to handle such fragility in his middle youth, would she be less timid?

He would have been a better man, at least. There was no shame in admitting as much now and working to ease the burden he had thoughtlessly imposed, was there?

"I have ever been shy, my lord husband." Kanbina lifted a shoulder, indicating the court with a tilt of her head. The branches falling from her hairpin shivered, clicking softly. "Not stupid."

Tamuron nodded. His shoulders ached, and the long striped rashes upon his torso itched abominably. The malady was obviously not contagious, but that only made the affliction more perplexing to the physicians and apothecaries striving to cure, or at least arrest. "I never considered you stupid, Kanbina. I thought I could protect you."

"I thought so, too." The wistful prettiness of her youth bloomed again over her softening features. "*You* knew?"

"I..." Of course he had known. Too late, of course, and by then the damage was done. He hadn't known the method, of course, but it looked as if his Second Concubine did. No wonder she stayed inside her walls; the only wonder was, indeed, that she had not pursued a vengeance upon Gamwone. Tamuron could even admit he might have been relieved at the event, and might not have chastised his last concubine too harshly upon its success. *Or* failure. "Too late, it appears. I regret it."

But then, Garan Wurei-a Kanbina did not have much of revenge within her humors, and she was ever kindly. "I know you could not afford to chastise her openly. Yet I have often wondered." She nodded softly, but there was an unwonted gleam in her dark eyes. "Has she struck you down too, my lord?"

What courage she had, to ask him. It shamed even the conqueror of Zhaon's many recalcitrant fiefdoms to see that bravery.

"No." It was his own failing body to blame, the malady gripping his humors with bony fingers. "Heaven has done so, justifiably enough. I have been fortunate, but I have also been a coward."

"It is not so bad." Kanbina moved as if to draw her hands away. Her fingers had warmed against his, the coolness of a woman taking heat from burning male humors. "Heaven will forgive both of us any cowardice, do we bow with good will." She sounded so certain he almost believed the proverb.

"You are far braver than I have ever been." He let go reluctantly. "Will you have tea with me, Kanbina? Or a meal?"

"If Your Majesty commands." Her cheeks were ashen under their copper, now, and all sign of ease had fled. Her small shoulders stiffened. "I have always obeyed."

"So you have." Without a murmur, without any sign of recalcitrance—and yet, he wished he did not have to *exact* obedience. Not from her, in any case. Some men liked their congress perfumed with shuddering fear, but he had ever preferred to be matched, whether outside the confines of a bed or within. Shiera had been such a partner, and her loss still burned within him; he had hoped Gamwone...but that was beside the point. His business was the present, not an old man's nattering upon the past. "I would not press. I do not wish to cause you pain, Kanbina."

"There is none." Now she was decisive, for the first time in many years. "I have had a very quiet life, my lord husband, and I have a son after many years without. I am content." She moved as if to rise. A susurration slid through courtiers and sober-robed eunuchs alike.

They could be forced to withdraw, but their gazes devoured an emperor and his concubine without mercy.

"You came to warn me." Tamuron loosened his hands, arranging them upon his belly. At least he had not run to fat; the malady wasted him but did not make him soft.

"I did." Freed, and visibly gladdened by liberty, she reached for the bentpin holding her veil aside. "Forgive me, I know you did not need it."

If Heaven had willed it, he would have been glad to marry her in place of Gamwone, but Wurei had come last in his catalogue of conquest for many reasons and she was ill-suited to a queen's responsibilities. Not that Gamwone performed hers, wifely or ceremonial, with alacrity or even willingness these days. The Second Queen took on the ceremonial duties, but she did not exceed their compass. "Will you return?"

"If you command it," she repeated, and let her veil fall. She was probably relieved to have its blurring between herself and the world. And in other words, she would obey, but she did not mean to seek him out.

As ever.

He could hardly blame her, and yet. "I prize your peace, Garan Wurei-a Kanbina."

"So do I." She righted her skirts, distractedly. "And soon I will have much of it. I will beseech Heaven's blessing upon you daily then, husband, as I have for many years."

He granted her leave to flee with a simple nod. She gathered her skirts and glided from the room with a decorous rustle, her step still as light as that of the highborn girl he had taken last to seal the keystone of Zhaon's unification, the sole surviving member of Wurei's once-powerful, once-royal clan.

His lips tightened. Gamwone had much to answer for, indeed, but a husband was the head of the house as the Emperor was head of Zhaon. Tamuron had made his First Queen what she was, just as he had failed to protect a shy, terrified girl. Senescence was a time of reckoning, was it not? His succession was ordered, but what of other affairs?

His chosen heir would not speak to him. His second son was entirely his mother's creature; his third son disdained his presence unless it was to deliver a cutting, barely polite remark; the fourth was a scholar to be proud of, certainly, but uninterested in other affairs; his fifth was all but useless; his sixth still a boy. His first daughter, on her way to a queendom of her own to the south, was in histrionics; his second seemed amenable enough but who could tell what preening poison her mother poured into her not-yet-adult ears?

And what of the mothers of that clutch? His first wife was a poisonous problem, the second indifferent, his first concubine cold, the second wracked by his mistakes. War threatened from the north once more, and the hordes of pale Tabrak were restive as they had been before their last great swathe cut through Shan and the south of Zhaon before melting back into the Westron Wastes. And, to finish the list, Garan Tamuron was pissing strange colors, twisted with bone-pain, and scratching furrows in his own peeling, discolored skin.

If he had ever thought himself mighty, he was roundly punished for the misapprehension.

Tamuron beckoned Zan Fein forward. The eunuch glided much as Kanbina did, the usual clicking of his jatajatas absent in deference to the Emperor's condition. "A most charming visitor," he murmured, his sleepy eyes half-closed.

The Emperor, frowning, had no desire for pleasantries. "Where were we?"

Zan Fein acknowledged his master's mood with a slow flick of his fan and a draft of umu scent. He was drenched in the costly perfume, as usual. "The matters of taxation in Lord Yulehi's province, Your Majesty."

Yes, the First Queen's uncle was taking advantage of his half-year at court to fatten the clan's coffers. Some care needed to be taken to allow him just enough to whet a clan's natural appetites but not enough to produce overweening ambition. "Very well." Tamuron sighed as a scribe availed himself again of the chair by the bedside, arranging the implements of his trade. "Take this down, then. *In the matter of taxation*, list territories . . ."

Matters of rule went on, a runaway armor-cart with maddened horses rolling irresistibly upon a screaming, blood-drenched battlefield, crushing any wounded slow or unlucky enough to be in its path. So many battles fought, and now he could see the smallest, most ignored engagements were the only campaigns that mattered.

And the only ones Garan Tamuron had ever truly lost.

SAFEST COURSE

In another part of the Kaeje—that most royal of palaces within the great walled complex—a small breakfast-room was muffled with a double layer of embroidered hangings because the queen it held like a pearl in folded silk despised any chill. Every corner was rounded, there was no partition to a garden's free air, and a multiplicity of pillows for propping a royal body in any languid posture necessary to aid digestion crowded the table as well as the three royal bodies they were meant to aid.

It should have been a comfortable room, but Second Princess Garan Gamnae oft found it anything but. Especially lately.

"I did not *ask* you," Gamnae's elder brother said coldly, and the Second Princess of Zhaon almost gasped.

It was not unheard of for Garan Kurin to utter a sharp word at the breakfast table, but it had never been common for his ire to fasten upon his mother instead of his little sister.

Well, at least, it had been uncommon before now. Second Princess Gamnae, caught in the act of pouring fragrant jaelo tea, halted in astonishment. Amber fluid rippled inside her thick, expensively glazed balei-ware cup, and she hastily glanced in their mother's direction to gauge the effect of this strangeness.

"You have an ill temper this morn." First Queen Garan Gamwone, her round, pretty face patted with matte zhu powder, did not raise a manicured black eyebrow. Instead, she paused as well, dabbing delicately at her lips with a square of pressed-rai paper as she surveyed the arrangement of sliced fruit and sweetbroth that was her usual first meal of the day. "Did you sleep badly?" Her tone was cajoling, meant for a child who had overstepped and must be firmly reined.

"Mother." Kurin's eyes narrowed. His topknot, caged in gold-beaded leather and stabbed savagely with a dull-iron pin, was oiled today, but it looked a fraction too tight. Maybe that was why he was so irritable, but then, he had been exceedingly snappish lately, and not just to Gamnae. "If you open your mouth to speak again before I receive an answer from Gamnae, I may be forced to break your dishes."

"How *dare* you—" Mother began, but Kurin's fist landed upon the tabletop, hard. Every piece of pottery or glass jumped. Gamnae's eating-sticks trembled, their tips resting politely upon a tiny fish-carved stand.

"Be *quiet*," Kurin hissed.

The thin stream of tea descending into Gamnae's cup wavered. She'd overfilled the cup well past a mannerly two-thirds; she hastily set the pot aside, holding her sleeve just so. Perhaps Mother wouldn't notice and let loose that awful, withering scorn. *Do not guzzle like a greedy merchant's daughter, Gamnae. Really, you are old enough for manners now. You should display some.*

"Elder Brother?" she said, tentatively. Maybe she could halt the approaching storm, but it didn't seem likely. Neither the First Queen nor her precious eldest son could be diverted once irritation truly set in. Gamnae's pretty babu-patterned morning gown stuck to her lower back even through a thin linen modesty-shift. It was a hot morn, but those did not often make her sweat. "I do not understand."

"Don't pretend to be stupid, little sister." Kurin held his own orange silk sleeve aside as he selected a slice of walanir from the savories plate. His morning robe was familiar, patterned only at hems and cuffs with Gamnae's careful stitching, a Year's End Festival present he was probably deigning to wear only because he wanted something of her. "Or I shall slap you."

He meant it, and Mother would not stop him.

"Yes. Takshin saw me in the gardens." Gamnae risked a glance at Mother, gauging the effect such news was likely to have in that quarter. "He asked me to visit the Jonwa."

Two spots of bright crimson stood high upon the First Queen's cheeks. Her hair was merely drawn back in a sleeping-braid instead of lacquered in place by her chief maid Yona's dry fingers as it would be later in the day; a few stray strands touched her soft forehead. One plump, soft hand with resin-dipped nails was clutch-crumpling the stack of pressed-paper squares meant for couth touching of lips between courses; the filigree sheath over the nail on her smallest finger glinted.

Any mention of Gamnae's *other* elder brother put Mother in a bad mood. Takshin had been sent to Shan and come back scarred, silent, and difficult. Sometimes, Gamnae wondered if it would have been better to send Kurin instead. At least in Shan the Second Prince wouldn't be able to pinch or poke at her, though to be honest Kurin had largely ceased to torment her when he found other, more satisfying prey.

Now, though, he seemed eager to recommence. Everything was changing so quickly. It was hard to keep her balance when the world kept rocking like a small boat.

Gamnae *hated* boats. And at the moment, she almost hated Takshin for speaking to her in the gardens yesterday, too. Why couldn't he have found a less public place, or sent her a note? A note might have gone almost unnoticed unless one of Mother's big-eyed, scrawny maids thought news of it likely to win a prize from Yona.

But no, someone had seen her passing words with her second brother, Kurin had found out, and now whatever he wanted Gamnae didn't know, but it couldn't be pleasant.

At least *that* was the same as ever.

"Kurin." The First Queen's voice was deceptively mild, but Gamnae's stomach dropped with an entirely unheard splash. She knew that tone. "This is a revolting display at breakfast. You will apologize at once."

"The instant I do something meriting an apology to you, Mother, one will swiftly occur." Kurin didn't even glance at Mother, and *that* was a difference indeed. "So, Taktak wishes you to visit him at the Jonwa? Or does he think you'll sing lullabies to our grieving Eldest Brother?" A smile stretched his thin lips, crinkling the corners of his eyes, and for the first time in a few weeks he looked truly pleased. "Come now, little sister, do not be shy. Who exactly did he ask you to visit?"

"No one." Gamnae's throat almost closed up, and she tried, frantically, to think of what barbed mischief Kurin might be planning—and how to ameliorate it. Stopping was beyond her power, but perhaps something small could be done. "Well, no one of consequence. He just said, since I'd visited the Crown Princess—"

"Do not mention that foreign bitch at my table." It was not quite queenly to hiss, but Mother wasn't bound by rules like other people. Were there ears listening greedily at the hall partition? The servants withdrew while the family was at private meals, but it was silly to think nobody was waiting, large-eared, to carry tales all through the Palace's warren.

Gamnae, instead of glancing at Mother to gauge her mood more surely, watched Kurin. She'd seen this look upon him before, but never in front of their mother. No, Kurin did not let his eyes blaze or his mouth twist like this when anyone who mattered could see.

Her brother picked up a small, whisper-fragile blue sauce dish. Then, with a swift fluid motion that spoke of a prince's necessary training in the art of combat, he flung it across the room. The sound of its breaking was lost under Queen Gamwone's gasp.

"Shut *up*," Kurin said, in a low fierce tone Gamnae *also* knew very well, but had never heard him use before Mother. "Or the sweetbroth goes next."

"Kurin..." Gamnae all but gaped, her fingers still upon the teapot's handle. Words tumbled breathlessly out of her, half placating, a crownbird's fluttering to distract a predator from its true nest. "He just said my presence might be a comfort in a grieving household, that's all. You know how he is." She did not dare glance at her mother again, not at this point. If she could somehow escape, hide under the table perhaps, like she used to when she was much younger...but there was no retreat possible. She was a tiny creature caught between two mountains, neither caring what they crushed during a collision.

"You..." Mother had barely enough breath for the word. It was strange to see First Queen Garan Gamwone of Zhaon at such a loss. Why, she almost sounded as frightened as Gamnae, and that could not be possible.

Could it?

"Comfort in a grieving household." Kurin turned his head slightly, eyeing Mother sidewise like a caged cat. His long fingers curled loosely around the base of the second, smaller sweetbroth tureen, the one with spicy walanir greens wilting upon hot liquid. "A pleasant way of putting it, indeed." He smiled, baring a row of white teeth, one of his canines just slightly crooked. "Well, well. Little brother."

"It's really nothing." Gamnae tried again to press the rai smooth, like a cook with a troublesome dish. "I won't go, of course. There's no reason—"

"That's right." Mother straightened, and the two rosettes upon her plump cheeks glared from unwonted paleness elsewhere. The humors drained from her face seemed to have collected upon her morning-robe, which was a bright, fetching pink. "Now, Gamnae, you are finished with breakfast." Her left hand, lying upon the table, had turned into a round fist, dimples changed into white knuckles, and though she had let go of the stack of napkins, her other hand's fingers had curled into a spider-shape. "Run along, your brother and I have things to discuss."

It was a deliverance, and Gamnae gathered her skirts, preparing to rise. Once in the safety of her rooms she could call for a tray of something, if her stomach would unclench. A bright smear of pao sauce dripped from a hanging scroll; Kurin had flung the dish with a great deal of force to make it shatter so against heavy hangings.

"Gamnae," Kurin said, very softly. "*I* did not give you leave to go."

Who should she obey? Her brother was the man of the house, yes, but Mother was sitting right there. Gamnae hesitated, trying to decide which obedience would hurt less. Mother could punish her today, of course.

But Kurin...he would *wait*.

"Please," she managed, a dry croak masquerading as politeness. "I don't feel well. I should go to my room."

"Certainly. But"—Kurin raised an admonishing finger, his princely greenstone hurai glinting—"you will *also* visit the Jonwa regularly, and you will call upon that Khir girl Takshin's so careful of. You're going to be her very good friend. Do you understand me?"

Oh, no. "Lady Komor? But she's only a lady-in-waiting, and..." Objections died in her desert-dry throat when Kurin's chin swiveled in her direction. If he fixed her with that paralyzing glare, she might shame herself by vomiting. Or worse. "Elder Brother..."

"I expect to hear gossip about your kindness to such an undeserving creature, Gamnae. *Now* you are excused." Kurin turned his attention back to Mother, and Gamnae's legs were soft as gluey, pounded rai.

"To your own mother," Mother began, in a small, deadly whisper.

Kurin did not heft the tureen. Instead, his free hand flickered again with a warrior's speed, snatching up a plate of candied pearl-fruit. It went sailing across the room and Gamnae flinched, letting out a hopeless, mouselike squeak lost in the sound of breakage.

Neither Mother nor her eldest brother paid attention. The Second Princess found her footing and swayed for the partition, her house-slippers shushing against piled rugs; if she tripped someone would turn upon her for clumsiness, and they were both in a mood to cause some significant harm. Were there shadows listening behind the sliding, painted door? She did not care, if she could reach that uncertain harbor in time to escape more of this.

Whatever *this* was. The boat was foundering, and Gamnae did not know how to right it. She had never known.

"Yes, Mother." Kurin now sounded utterly bored instead of vengeful, and it was now he who was most dangerous. "How else will I make you listen? I am your son, not your soldier or your kaburei, and *I* am the head of the clan."

Gamnae's feet were numb. She halted only to arrange her skirts, hoping neither would notice such a necessary operation performed with trembling hands.

Mother hated being interrupted, and her tone was terrifyingly quiet as well. "Your uncle—"

"Lord Yulehi knows who holds his leash. I am head of this household now." Kurin glanced in his sister's general direction. "Didn't I tell you to leave?"

Gamnae fled. There was nobody beyond the partition; perhaps the servants sensed something changing in this part of the Kaeje. It wasn't until she reached her own familiar quarters that Garan Gamnae realized she had brought her cup along in her free hand, hot jaelo-fragrant tea slopping against thick glazed pottery.

Father was sick, Sabwone was gone to be married to the king of Shan, and now Kurin was making it very clear Mother was no longer the household god requiring greatest propitiation. Everything had twisted into a new shape overnight like Murong Cao's story of the fishes, and Gamnae's stomach revolved inside her, trying to catch up.

She did not drop her cup yet she heard, in the far distance upon the battlefield she had left, something else break with a musical tinkle. The halls were empty, another change. Even her own pale, whispering close-servant Mai was nowhere in evidence, probably in the kitchens swallowing a hurried first meal.

Gamnae decided not to call for a second breakfast, though her stomach was an empty knot. Instead, she locked the door to her sleeping chamber, peeled away her morning-robe, and crawled back into her wide, comfortable bed, setting the cup upon her night-table to cool. Expensive hangings all chosen by Mother and full of exhortations to maidenly obedience watched her from the walls, but at least the floor was cool and bare, and if she drew the thin curtains meant to keep stinging insects from her nightly rest she could imagine they didn't see her.

If she pulled the covers over her head, perhaps the world would cease moving like clay in fast water, too.

Huddled in her shift under a light cotton sheet—it was too hot for anything heavier—she trembled, and wondered just what Kurin wanted with the Khir lady-in-waiting. It didn't matter nearly as much as staying out of his way for a good long while, and Mother's too.

That, Gamnae decided, was her safest course.

FAIRLY ENOUGH

B athed, his cheeks scraped clean and a few cups of hot sweet
soldier's tea behind his breastbone, Zakkar Kai stepped into
the Emperor's presence; a murmuring ran through courtier and
eunuch alike. The head general of Zhaon's mighty armies paid little attention, pausing only to accept Zan Fein's bow with a slight
inclination of his upper body and scan the open slat-doors to a
porch choked with the robed, topknotted, and hopeful as well as
those with actual business.

Before, during, and after every battle, it was crucial to view the
terrain.

"There he is, my general." Garan Tamuron still had some
muscle-bulk to his frame, and his dark gaze was still sharp. The
hollowness of his carefully shaven cheeks was new, though,
and so was the set of his mouth, tight with pain as it had rarely
been even after the worst battles of Zhaon's most recent unification. His knuckles were slightly swollen, too, and though he sat
upon the edge of his bed he was not dressed. His robe was rich,
golden longbills worked with tiny stitches onto crimson silk, but it
was an invalid's wrapper.

All this Kai took in within seconds. Each time he saw the man
who had rescued him from childhood tragedy there was some new
damage to account for, like bad news during a fighting retreat.

"Have you eaten?" Tamuron continued in a ringing tone,

perhaps to make certain everyone present could mark Kai's position as unchanged. "Come, fruit and tea for my head general, and withdraw to your own meals. Sit with me, Kai. There is much to discuss."

Kai made the prescribed bow, restraining the urge to stamp as if he was booted and helmed, entering an army tent during heavy rain and knocking mud free upon a wooden clot-mat. It would be ridiculous in the slippers he was forced to wear for both cleanliness's and propriety's sake within the palace, since Zhaon was not at war and a man wearing a greenstone hurai was forced to better manners than most. "You are most hospitable, Your Majesty, but I have already eaten."

"Lies." Tamuron's grin was a shadow of its former self, but at least it was genuine. A kaburei close-servant with leather-wrapped braids hurried forward to offer a brawny arm, but the Emperor waved him away, determined to stride to the small ebonwood table, with its inlaid top, without aid. Perhaps he wished to remind the court he was not quite ascended to Heaven yet, merely watching the door he would exit by. "You were at early drill and have had nothing but soldier-tea, if I know you."

The general acknowledged his emperor's astuteness with a wry smile. "Drill keeps the blade sharp and the body fit, my lord, and one cannot perform if one is over-busy digesting." At least his lord's mind was still sharp and his senses just as keen, but Tamuron did not mention Kai's daily visits to the new tombs. "Have you not remarked as much several times?"

"If I have, I have forgotten it, though I will happily take a slight honor for the wisdom." Tamuron indicated the table, underlining the invitation, and settled himself upon a high-backed wooden chair. That was new; he usually preferred his meals upon a much lower plank. Struggling to rise from table would be injurious to royal dignity, perhaps. "Your mother visited earlier."

"Did she?" Kai waited as Tamuron arranged himself. Kanbina had said nothing of any plans to visit her lord husband. Perhaps it was a sudden urge, but she was not given to those, and it would have to be a caprice of startling power and durability to lever her from her quarters. "I am due at her house for dinner tonight." He was looking forward to it; much of the rest of his day would not be nearly as pleasant.

Yala in the morning, his adoptive-mother at dinner—he could stand a great deal in the tent between those two restful poles.

"A filial son." Tamuron's smile was ironclad, the expression of a man who found some little amusement in his own pain but still must look at ease despite it. "She thanked me again for your hurai."

"Any mother would be proud of such an honor." Did Tamuron wish Kai to thank him for the greenstone seal-ring clasping his first left finger, denoting princely status but no place in the succession? Its weight was not a kindness, and well Kai knew as much. "No matter how undeserving her son."

"Sit down." Tamuron finished settling the royal robes and indicated the only other chair, lapsing into silence as trays were brought and unloaded. The court moved into the garden, low conversation and slippery laughter, eunuchs treading the gravel or stone paths in their walking-pairs of jatajata sandals and courtiers in thin-soled ambling shoes, slippers nestling in perfumed bags at their belts. Some few would hurry to table in other parts of the palace complex, but those who wished for power—or suspected they might be called upon at short notice—would have to forgo a late-morning snack unless a hurrying servant or kaburei could fly to fetch a tidbit or two.

For a short while neither general nor Emperor spoke. The tea was fragrant siao; ripe pearlfruit, breadfruit, summer greenmelon, long thin musk-smelling aiju, and soft crumbling curd lay in pleasing patterns upon gold-edged platters. A ceremonial greenstone cup full of an evil-smelling brew was medicine prepared under Physician Kihon Jiao's unblinking attention, and the Emperor took it down in a single gulp as if it were sohju, grimacing.

"That looks unpleasant," Kai remarked. His own seat was a lower, backless stool, commensurate with a rank below the Emperor's but also thickly cushioned to soften the reminder.

"No more so than anything else." Tamuron selected his eating-sticks and rolled them together for luck, a soldier's habit. "Eat, and tell me. Are there dispatches?"

"Not recently." Kai selected his own sticks; he preferred the spear-tipped to the square. "I thought it best to move the Northern Army to Kutau." He could close his eyes and see the dispositions of the three great armies—south and west, and north the greatest of them all—but he knew where his lord would spend the most worry, and moved to answer a question not yet asked.

"A good choice. They won't fall for Three Rivers again." Tamuron's eyebrows, still deeply black, knotted in the center. "The official explanation should reach Ashani Zlorih soon."

Said official announcement of mourning—partly crafted by Zan Fein—called the Crown Princess's death a "hunting accident." The current rumor flooding Zhaon-An was that a cortege of black-clad acrobat-assassins had surrounded the Crown Prince and Princess, and that the latter had expired in her new husband's arms.

It was difficult to tell which story would inflame Khir more.

I must write to my father, Yala murmured in his memory, and Kai did not have the heart to tell her any missive would be opened before it left the palace to make certain nothing unfortunate was brushed upon its inward folds. The details of the Crown Princess's death were not of a manner to soothe her country's ire, and as Princess Mahara's only Khir lady-in-waiting, she was in a position to do Zhaon's diplomacy much damage by an inadvisable character or two.

Of course any letter of hers might not even leave the Jonwa; Takyeo would no doubt quietly move to insulate the only remaining Khir woman from charges of spying or inappropriate influence. The Crown Prince valued his dead wife's companion enough for that, at least.

Kai attempted to shelve his distractions, but it was a losing fight. He was in a mood he had rarely felt before, anticipation both pleasant and irksome riding his humors. After all, Yala had not said *no*;

perhaps that was why the heart and liver both sat so lightly within Zakkar Kai today.

If she did attempt a letter to her father, how long would she wait for a reply?

Tamuron had larger concerns, of course. Much depended upon the king of Khir's reaction to the news that his precious only daughter, sacrificed to the necessity of state marriage, had died choking upon her own blood deep in the conqueror's country so soon after the wedding's pomp and silk. "If the news has not reached Khir already." Kai lifted the teapot lid to glance inside as etiquette demanded before pouring for both of them, a maneuver so familiar he could have done it blind with sleep—and had more than once or twice, during a campaign. "Perhaps he will only demand a bride-price, or an easing of the trade concessions."

"I doubt it." The Emperor's brow was thunderous indeed with doubt and deep thought. Of course the great wains of negotiated tribute from their northern neighbor had not arrived even while the Crown Princess was alive, and that was a possible coincidence both strange and disturbing. "Khir received an envoy not long ago."

From where? "An envoy?" Kai kept his attention upon pouring, a job that must be done neatly in a mirror-lit, luxurious room. Not like in an army tent, where you drank from whatever you could find—boot, bottle, or puddle, as the saying went.

"From *them*." Tamuron's lip curled briefly, smoothed. His top-knot was greying; yet another mark of malady-driven decay, like a house left uninhabited fell quickly into ruin. "Tabrak."

Ah. Several implications reshuffled themselves and assumed a far different configuration inside Kai's skull. "And there may be a messenger from the Pale Horde moving toward us even now, I warrant." *That* news was chilling enough, no matter how grateful he was to be unsurprised by its advent. The Horde were a cyclic menace, but they could be dammed or turned aside and did not stay to hold what they had conquered, much like the metuahghi falling upon crops in their multi-year cycles. "I see."

"I would not have us fight Khir and Tabrak at once." Tamuron merely picked at his food, appearing to eat without consuming much. Another change; his appetite had ever been hearty. "Even if the former is bled dry."

And yet. Kai followed the line of thought to its natural conclusion, and mulled over the consequences, both possible and probable. "An invasion? Risky."

The Emperor's mouth pulled down; he took a mouthful of tea far back against his palate, swallowing hastily. He was drinking everything thus nowadays, as if the very act pained him. "Zlorih has a son left."

"Newly legitimized." There was precious little gossip about that particular byblow, and Kai had not found a way to broach the subject with Yala yet. "You are thinking of the Second Princess?" A Zhaon princess sent to a Khir prince—not the ideal solution, but perhaps the negotiations could be drawn out.

Gamnae was young, yet. If she was sent into Khir before Kai could obtain imperial permission for the wearer of a hurai to marry, would Yala go with her? The prospect was unpleasant to contemplate.

"Perhaps." Tamuron lifted his cup again. His strong copper wrist was losing its muscle-pad from daily saber practice; a thin line of boiling rash disappeared up the underside into his crimson-and-gold sleeve. "Khir only take one wife; Zlorih will not waste his last son upon us if he has a choice. Therefore, should we intend to send a princess, we must give him no leeway."

"What are his other options? A Tabrak dog-bride? A minor princess from beyond the northern wastes?" Faraway giant Ch'han, always eager to point the Khir's dagger at Zhaon's heart and extort tribute, might see that sacrifice as worth the return. Their coffers were ever hungry, and they held themselves to be the center of the world. *Even Heaven flows from Ch'han*, they said, *so the gold must be pushed uphill.*

Every country naturally considered itself central; Kai was, however, a son of Zhaon, and thought his own land best suited to the title. Where else had Heaven made such bountiful fields, such perfect heat in summer and such icy beauty in winter?

"It would help if we had a criminal to hang." Tamuron eyed him, taking a single sip of siao. The smoke in its liquid might bring his humors closer to balance. "Zan Fein and Mrong Banh can find no trace of the assassin, even with Takshin's help."

"So I am told." Kai weighed his most unsettling thoughts upon the matter and decided he could hardly avoid voicing them. "Does the sudden quiet strike you as ominous, my lord?"

"You like these, do you not? Take some." Tamuron subtly indicated the sliced pearlfruit with his eating-sticks before selecting a hefty slice and laying it within Kai's bowl. Protocol demanded Kai leap to his feet and bow at the sign of imperial approval—unless he wore a hurai. The Emperor had noticed more than one gaze bent in their direction, and was underscoring Kai's position once more. "And yes, it does. So many attempts upon my son's life, then... nothing."

Almost as if he was not the target at all. Kai did not wish to say as much, but Tamuron's coal hot glance spoke of understanding. "Who stands to gain?" the head general murmured, taking up his pair of silver-chased eating-sticks and tapping them once upon the side of the whisper-thin blue ceramic bowl for luck, another soldier's habit. "Is that not always the question?"

"I find it difficult to believe Khir *gains* from this, unless it is less onerous trade-duties. We dealt fairly enough with them." But Tamuron's brow wrinkled, two familiar vertical lines rising between his eyebrows. It was the particular look he wore when an enemy was not behaving as expected. Such impertinence from an opponent meant even the most basic of assumptions about relative goals and strengths must be rethought, an intensive labor indeed.

Kai suspected the Khir nobles would take issue with his lord's estimation of *fairness*. Still, the cold calculation required to send your daughter to her new home, then dispatch assassins... if Ashani Zlorih was responsible for this, he was a vastly different foe than the one Kai had fought to a blood-drenched standstill.

Which meant there was another player upon the board. Perhaps the king of Khir could not move as he willed in this matter, and his ministers—not to mention whatever nobles were left—had taken note of the fact.

Perhaps it had been this shrouded new prince, Ashani Daoyan? A fine, traditional name, but there was absolutely nothing about the man in any gossip, no matter how minor. If *he* had sent those of the Shadowed Path after his half-sister, he was a foe worth expending some silver upon learning about. Which meant questioning Yala upon her home—a pleasant enough duty, but one others at court might also be thinking of undertaking, and they would not treat a foreign lady kindly.

Kai gazed at his bowl, the shapes of food inside turning into a battle-map. Most of the assassins had borne some Northern stamp or another, but that could have been a clever feint if someone wished to inconvenience the Crown Prince by robbing him of potential heirs instead of moving against him directly.

"Eat," Tamuron continued, his tone brooking no disobedience. "My Second Concubine will be disappointed if I do not feed you well."

Kai decided it was time for this visit to move to business instead of chewing the old leather of stale news. "You plan to send me north." He nodded as if it had just occurred to him and set about denuding his bowl, his eating-sticks flashing. "To merely menace, or do you truly mean to invade Khir?"

Tamuron's own eating-sticks were carved of greenstone, that sacred, precious rock bringing good luck and proof against poison, their hand-ends sheathed in hammered silver. He preferred the square-cut, holding that it took greater delicacy to wield a blunt instrument with the requisite care. "Eventually. How soon can you leave?"

"I have some personal matters to set in order, that is all." How much was acceptable to delay? Certainly waiting for a letter to wend its weary way to Khir and its reply to arrive was too long, and yet.

"What personal matters?" Tamuron eyed him closely, and a disbelieving grin spread over his face. For a few moments he looked rather young again, an echo of the fit, broad-shouldered warlord who had taken young Kai from the ashes, forging him anew. "Well, well. Have you been lucky in a softer campaign this year, my son?"

"Not quite lucky." Kai almost winced. Nobody was close enough to overhear but the kaburei close-servant hovering to attend the ailing body of Zhaon himself. Still, even that creature could whine in an unfriendly ear if given leave—or enough inducement. "I have not been defeated yet, that is all."

It would not be quite wise to inform Tamuron of his intentions toward a certain Khir lady-in-waiting at this particular moment. What the Emperor did not see he could not prevent, and any mention of Komor Yala was likely to irritate him. The affair with the false eunuch—and Third Prince Takshin's reaction—was still fresh in the court's memory, though the rumor-mongers of the palace did not quite go so far as to intimate Takshin had designs upon a foreign woman either.

Did he? So far as Kai could tell, the Third Prince treated Yala much as he treated anyone useful or kind to Takyeo who had not yet managed to earn Takshin's own ire by some imagined slight or inadvisable expression of pity. The Third Prince's rude, mocking tone did not seem to upset or incommode Yala in the slightest, but then again, the lady could probably smooth the worst temper in the palace handily, did it become necessary.

Or perhaps it was only Kai's affection which made him think her capable of such victories.

"Well, do not take more than one wife, Kai. Women are trouble." Tamuron frowned, selecting sliced pearlfruit and musky aiju. It was difficult to tell what would deepen his malady, or cause it to retreat. Every morsel passing his lips would be reported to Kihon Jiao for analysis, in case a pattern to the malady's attacks could be discerned. "Leave when it suits you, but not too late. I merely wish your presence north of Zhaon-An to be remarked. Do not go too far."

In other words, he was to be a bolster to the Crown Prince *and* a menace to Zhaon's enemies at once. Maybe he would split in half,

like the old sage Hurong Daewon. "Partly why I chose Kutau for
the infantry." The fields there were rich, and the farmers would
be glad of extra help during the dry season's repairs and weeding
even as they bemoaned the extra mouths to feed. Cavalry, salted
about in smaller detachments, were a similar burden, but even the
elite among Zhaon's armies lent a hand with harvests and the like
in times of peace. "Headquarters at Tienzu Keep, I think—a few
days' easy ride from here, or a single courier upon a hard-used horse
may do better."

The Emperor considered, his eyes half-closed as a terrain map
unfolded inside his head-meat. It was a look Kai knew well, and so
was the faint air of dissatisfaction that followed. A multiplicity of
bad choices meant selecting the best available was no comfort. "It is
the best arrangement, yes. You never disappoint, Kai."

"I shall remind you of those words next time I lose at chess." Kai
toasted him with the teacup, and smiled at Tamuron's gruff bark-
laugh. It was almost as painful to see the shadow of the old warlord
as it was to mark the difference between the remembered man and
the actual.

"No shame in defeat, Kai. Only in incompetence." The Emperor
nibbled upon aiju, his frown deepening, and his other hand made a
short arrested motion, as if he wished to scratch and suppressed the
movement just in time. "Begin your preparations, then, but do not
hurry until—"

"—the situation clarifies itself." Kai nodded. "*If it were easy…*"

"*…all would be victorious.* Niao Zheu. You have been studying, too."

"You require it of me." *Along with much else.* But then, a man
owed everything to his parents, and this was the only father Kai
would ever have. He watched the thoughts moving within Tamuron's dark gaze; the breeze from the garden, tiptoeing into the room,
stirred the cauldron of food-smell, the various scents of minister,
courtier, and eunuch, and the sharpfuzz spoiled-hairfruit reek of
illness and medicinal tinctures into a close fug that threatened to
rob him of appetite.

Finally, Garan Tamuron arrived at what he most wished to ask. "Does Takyeo truly mean to retreat to the countryside?"

So that is what bothers you now. Kai's heart twisted once, a pang like a stabbing blade. He had taken the dropped hurai back to Takyeo, but the damage was accomplished, and it was deep. "I know only that he is making preparations." In other words, it might be a mere stratagem—but none who knew Takyeo well thought it likely.

It was not that Tamuron was a bad father, though certainly Heaven itself would blast Kai where he stood for such an unfilial thought if it ever accomplished itself inside his head-meat. It was that Garan Takyeo had borne so much, so patiently, for so long, that the final feather upon the pile had crushed any hope of swift reconciliation as thoroughly as the Hell of the Many Weights crushed a patricide.

"He must not, Kai." Tamuron laid his eating-sticks aside and regarded his general earnestly. "It will cause much uncertainty."

What could Kai say? These were not his silk-folds to smooth, and besides, Takyeo was not in the wrong. How could he let his father-Emperor, the warlord who had given Kai's own life meaning, understand as much? He was no courtier, with smooth words and soft pressure. Nor was he Yala, with her gift for providing a measure of comfort by mere presence. "He is grieving, my lord."

"It was only a wife, Kai. A foreigner, at that." The Emperor's free hand curled into a fist, the hurai upon the first finger glittering in its own sheath of royal silver. "Surely he must understand Zhaon needs him more than mourning."

"His mourning is sharp." What could he say? There were proverbs about intruding between a man and his son for a reason. Kai could not enter the battle in any meaningful measure, nor did he quite think he should. "He was very fond of the Crown Princess." Or more than fond; perhaps Takyeo had even loved her, though such a thing always ended in tragedy where princes were concerned.

It must have been strangely appealing for Takyeo to protect a creature placed in even closer confinement than his own royal self.

Tamuron's eyebrows met, his face congesting briefly as he weighed both said and unsaid messages. "You think me cruel."

You keep a shrine for your first wife, my lord, where the candles are ever-lit and the incense is continual. Mentioning as much was not very sensible, yet Tamuron deserved truth, and Kai was perhaps the only person who could serve that bitter dish.

Still, for the sake of Tamuron's peace of mind, he sought to season the plate with as much tact as possible. "I think purely political considerations in this matter are slightly unwise, my lord."

"I have little time for niceties." The Emperor stared at his plate, at dewy, innocent, sliced globes of pearlfruit with their mild sheen. "Tabrak will not halt for all Takyeo's grieving, nor will Khir."

"You are not your son's enemy, my lord. You are his father." *Should you not act as such?* Adding such a sting to *that* tail would not earn him any thanks, though, so Kai stopped short.

"Then I must be twice as harsh, to prepare him for his duties." Tamuron all but glowered, a relief from his recent, abstract air of pained discipline. "Come, Kai. Surely you can see as much."

"Would you have me lie to you, Garan Tamuron?" Kai set his own eating-sticks down, resting their tips upon a small fish-shaped dish as manners demanded instead of sticking them upright, banners for a stomach's war, in his bowl. This was a conversation apt to turn even a soldier's liver sideways. "It has never been my way, and I do not wish to start."

For a moment he was certain he had miscalculated, for his almost-father's expression hardened and a dull, ugly flush crept to the Emperor's thinning cheeks. But then, Tamuron's shoulders softened, and he exhaled sharply.

"No," he said, softly. "I do not wish for that. Time is slipping through my fingers, Kai, and I wish Takyeo to be safe when I am...gone."

"A father's kindest wish, indeed." Kai did not bother to assure the Emperor of continued heartiness. What was the point? If he were to serve his lord truth, it was best a constant dish or none at all. "I will speak to him, my lord. More I cannot promise."

"Good." Tamuron's mouth eased, He reclaimed and tapped his own eating-sticks, selecting another strip of aiju. "Enough politics, then. Tell me, what have you read recently?"

Kai would have vastly preferred politics to reciting his lessons, but he acceded and the conversation turned to Zhe Har. Kai had been reading the Archer much of late, but would only admit to the treatises upon strategy, not the story of the Moon Maiden and her warrior.

Still, the gleam in Tamuron's gaze told Kai his reticence had been noticed. Now the Emperor might exert himself to find out what court lady had caught the general's attention.

At least Kai could elude direct questioning upon that matter for some short while, especially if he left the palace and Zhaon-An for a post slightly north. There was no help, and much harm, in speaking to Tamuron upon such irritants as a lady-in-waiting he already disliked—and one who, despite all law and custom, perhaps still carried a hidden greenmetal blade inside the Palace walls.

Just wait a little longer, Kai told himself. Yala had not even brushed her letter yet, in all likelihood. *Patience brings a man what he needs.*

Later, he thought he should not have been so forbearing.

MUCH LESS
UNLUCKY

Across the hall from a sealed door in the Jonwa, a small set of rooms held dark furniture and some few restrained decorations. Yet the spareness, even under bright glowing mirrorlight, did not seem plain at all. The quality of each item, and the taste with which it was placed, spoke more loudly than a leather-lunged square leader berating his soldiers. It was strange how just a few wooden boxes and hangings could express an occupant's station so clearly.

Or so Anh thought, when she had enough time to consider such matters. "My lady?" The kaburei bowed, her braids swaying over her shoulders, as she halted just inside the partition. "The ladies Su and Hansei are here."

Anh's Khir lady looked up from the empty page. Her brush, poised over the inkstone, had hovered there for some while to judge by the fat black drop trembling at its end. Ink splashed free as Lady Yala gazed at the doorway, her wide grey eyes blank and haunted. "Oh?" For a moment, she looked as if she did not recognize her own servant, and Anh's chest suffered a strange twisting sensation.

"Lady Su and Lady Hansei," Anh repeated. "Shall I bring tea?" She shouldn't presume, but her lady's blank stare was almost terrifying. From the very beginning, her lady had been crisp and direct, never unkind but also never overly familiar—in all things, a true noblewoman.

"Yes, tea," Yala said, distractedly, and rinsed her brush before placing it, with infinite care, upon the rack meant for such cargo.

Anh bowed the two young noblewomen into her lady's quarters. Dreamy Lady Hansei was for once *not* carrying a bound book with her thumb marking the page; she wore her very best dress, too, bright yellow cotton with thick viridian silk edging. Lady Su was in a very prettily reworked pale-peach cotton with threadbare, faded orange silk edging, probably the closest she had to mourning. To show their sadness, neither wore hairpins in their nested red-black braids, and both had wide belts of unbleached linen to mark grief for a Crown Princess they had barely begun to know.

Anh's lady wore silk like a princess, though. In Khir, some highborn families shared that royal fabric instead of merely using it to edge their brightest and best garb. It was one more reason to take pride in her service, Anh thought, and sometimes she held her chin high in the Jonwa halls as she bustled about upon her lady's business, her chest full of smugness and her liver no doubt swelling dangerously. A prideful servant was a bad one, but there was a certain amount of justifiable pleasure to be had when one was not yoked to an embarrassing beast.

Even the proverbs said so.

Weighed down by a lacquered wooden tea tray, Anh made her steps as quiet as possible upon her return, and strained her ears.

"—to her aunt," Lady Su said, steadily. "She will ask to accompany us; I am not certain Lady Gonwa will give leave."

"The good Lady Gonwa no doubt has a more useful place for her niece." Lady Yala sounded far more like herself now, cultured, accented Zhaon crisp even through its softness. "And you, Junha?"

"I stay with you," the young lady said, firmly. "Liyue and I have discussed the matter."

"We are both determined." Hansei Liyue's tone was much sharper than usual; she was a soft-voiced one. "We requested permission of the Crown Prince, and he has granted it. I hear his estate near Nuah-An is very fine. Perhaps that is where we are bound."

Well, that was good news. Anh had been half afraid the Crown Prince would send Lady Yala swiftly back to cold, barbarous Khir, all alone and grieving. Of course Anh would go with her lady, she had decided as much—but it was a relief to keep her inside slippers on, as the proverb went. Travel was a barbarity, Khir was by all accounts a harsh land even if her lady was somewhat mild, and to be given to another household in the Palace was not a fate to be desired, much less when you already belonged to a kind mistress.

Kind, but also firm. A servant's disdain was cringing when it came to a cruel master, and sneaking when it came to an easily bullied or hoodwinked one. The middle ground, as Zhaon was balanced between the greatness of Heaven and the punishments of the many hells, was to be cherished.

"He intends for me to stay, then. At least for the moment." Lady Yala had moved to her usual thin but well-embroidered cushion at a low ebonwood table, where she often took tea in the afternoons. The noble girls, a pair of temple statues, barely turned their heads as Anh hurried in to arrange the tea-tray; Lady Hansei, as the youngest, arranged the cups with swift movements and began to pour without ado. "I had wondered."

"The Jonwa is brighter for your presence, he says. And travel is so dangerous without a proper retinue." Su Junha did not deign to glance at Anh, who settled upon her knees just inside the door, ready for more errands. "I'm glad you're staying. Lady Kue is too; she was there when we came from the Crown Prince's study."

"She frightens me," Lady Hansei murmured, and finished pouring. "This is Lady Gonwa's heaven tea, my lady. She sent more, though she kept Eulin to herself."

"Kind of her. I shall write a note of thanks." Yala lifted her cup and inhaled the steam, which meant the other ladies could drink—but she set it down immediately afterward, untasted.

A few strands of blue-black hair had escaped Yala's braids, and Anh longed to take the comb to them. It was unlike her lady to be even slightly disheveled, and doubly unlike her to halt, looking between her guests as if she could not remember what came next. If the Crown Princess were here, Lady Yala would be occupied in smoothing *her* way, and very prettily, too.

Well, the Crown Princess was decidedly *not* here. Her poor body had been crushed, Anh heard, and it was a shame. She had been so beautiful, and with the Prince, a real pair of love-birds in a gilded osier cage. They had all, from kaburei to housekeeper, expected a haughty foreign tyrant instead of a docile, kind noble girl sent all the way from the cold North with merely a single lady-in-waiting.

Su Junha took over the burden of conversation. "Of course you shall stay with us." She blew across her tea to cool it; fragrant amber liquid trembled inside simple but expensively thin blue-glazed ware. "After all, if the Crown Prince remarries—"

Lady Hansei made a small warning noise in the back of her throat, shook her head. "It is far too soon." The motion was strange with no hairpin dangling its cargo of bright decoration. "Even the Emperor must know as much."

"But with Khir—" Su Junha caught herself, lifting the back of her left fingers to her mouth to trap the remainder of an unwary sentence. "I am sorry, my lady."

"In Khir, ladies do not speak of politics." There was no reproof in Lady Yala's tone, she was simply remarking upon a difference. Her Zhaon had improved quite steadily, but the song of another language with much harsher consonants still wore through its rhythm. "Here, though, everything is strange."

"Well, what else is there to talk about?" Lady Hansei set her cup down and fussed with her sleeves, settling them properly. The three ladies looked very much like a wall-hanging, and Anh lost herself in admiration of their clear smooth cheeks, their bright and prettily sewn dresses, their soft hands. "They are saying General Zakkar will be sent north, and Third Prince Takshin will go to Shan."

"Now *he* gives me the shivers." Lady Su shuddered delicately to prove it, her sleeves rustling a fraction as she turned her cup a quarter, to help the tea absorb both luck and the pleasure of conversation. "Do you think he will go?"

Anh watched her lady's hands retreat into her own sleeves. There was no change in Yala's expression, but Anh though it very unlikely indeed that the Third Prince would return to the pierced towers and barbarous bandit-hunting of Shan. The First Princess had been sent to that land to marry King Suon Kiron, and though Suon and the Third Prince were battle-brothers, there was very little affection between the Third Prince of Zhaon and First Princess Sabwone.

There was gossip about the First Princess's raging when she was told of the match, too, though that great lady had—thankfully—behaved impeccably during the attendant ceremonies, with their great pomp, expense, and hurrying of every servant's feet down to the bone. Perhaps the First Concubine had finally taken the sudo to her daughter; high time, too, though it was not Anh's place to think such things.

The Third Prince and his scars were held to be unlucky at best and actively harmful at worst, but he had brought Anh's lady home the terrible day of Princess Mahara's pyre, fixing Anh with a cold stare and ordering the lady attended to while she wept as if her liver had broken into pieces.

And as if that was not enough, it had been Third Prince Takshin who stepped before the whip for Lady Yala upon a hot spring morning, and for *that* Anh was willing to believe him much less unlucky than gossip insisted.

"*I* wouldn't go. I hear they put lard in their siao." Lady Hansei did not quite shiver, but it looked a near thing. The two junior ladies had taken to dressing their hair very much like Yala's, and their close-servants treated Anh with due reverence, in the case of Lady Junha's kaburei, and distant but marked politeness in the case of Lady Hansei's common close-girl. "Will you sew with us after tea, Lady Komor? I could read aloud."

"You would." Su Junha laughed, a soft, merry sound. "But yes, please, Lady Komor. Come sew with us after tea."

"Perhaps." Anh's lady touched her blue teacup with a fingertip. "I am afraid I am not quite conversational today, but if you do not mind my quiet, I shall be glad to."

Anh's relief threatened to make her sway upon her knees. If her lady was attempting to sew, she was not sitting in these lovely but somehow suffocating rooms and staring at blank paper, or— worse—gazing intently at nothing, her pale Khir eyes blank and her mouth turned slightly down, her graceful hands cradling a strange sharp greenmetal blade with no proper hilt, just cross-hatching upon the long, bare tang.

That strange Khir blade had saved the Crown Prince and Princess, and brought Lady Yala to the whipping-post. Now the well-healed scratches upon a noblewoman's thighs and upper arms made sense, and Anh burned with deep satisfaction at her lady's exotic skill.

You, girl, the Third Prince had said the day of the pyre. *Make certain she does not use that upon herself, or I will have you flogged to death.*

No, she did not think the Third Prince would return to Shan. Anh's chin lifted a little as she sensed the visit coming to an end, the younger ladies having achieved their purpose of drawing Yala out. There would be the tea things to clean and rearrange, her lady's sleeping-robe to put on the smaller stand over a coil of healthful incense carefully chosen for the weather conditions and her lady's bath additives, the sewing-basket to fetch, the dinner tray to be planned or a dinner-robe to be chosen and placed upon the larger stand, a fresh jar of nia oil to protect soft skin—a kaburei's work, from before dawn to after the long summer twilight. It was pleasant to have as much to look forward to, but far more pleasant to know that Lady Komor Yala, and by extension Anh herself, were going to stay in the center of civilization.

Or, at worst, retire to what had once been the heart of lost Wurei.

"Anh?" Her lady turned her finely modeled head. "Bring more tea to the receiving-room, and my sewing basket."

"Yes." Anh bowed upon her knees to show she had heard, and her heart leapt for joy.

A Question of How

What she longed for was perhaps a single slice of peppery walanir, enough tea to drown her liver, and her own bed. What Komor Yala received instead was word that the Crown Prince of Zhaon invited her to attend his dinner, and that left her seeking to decide what to wear. She could hardly appear in mourning if he did not, but if he did, she could certainly *not* appear in normal attire. Lady Kue the housekeeper was busy with other affairs, and of course Su Junha and Hansei Liyue did not think to speak upon the Crown Prince's planned attire, even should they be apprised of it.

It was Anh who saved her as Yala stood before her clothespress looking at bright silk, carefully folded under-robes, and thin linen modesty-shifts. "My lady?" the kaburei whispered from the door. "Your dinner dress is upon the larger stand."

Yala half-turned, and of course, there it was, floating like a ghost. So, apparently the Crown Prince was still in mourning, for the dress was pale undyed silk, cuffs and collar unembroidered but stitched with great care.

It was an unexpected relief, and Yala told her knees, sternly, that they would not turn to pounded rai. Across the hall from her ante-chamber, the Crown Princess's door was sealed with royal crimson wax; it was only imagination to think a cold draft exhaled from it at odd intervals. "Ah, yes. I see. Thank you." Zhaon fit easily in her mouth now, and she hated the very sound of it. "I suppose I should ready myself."

Anh clasped her hands, a worried crease nesting between her eyebrows. "Shall I tell the Honorable Steward you prefer to—"

Yala shook her head. They did not wear hairpins while grieving here, but an unmarried Khir noblewoman would not go without that appurtenance, however simple, unless a parent had lately gone to the Great Fields. Still, there was no decoration hanging from her hairpin's head, and the lack of its sway was a constant reminder. "No, Anh. That will not be necessary."

If the Crown Prince required her company, the least Yala could do was attempt to ameliorate his grief. She owed her princess's husband a debt of gratitude, and a certain amount of obedience as well.

A half-candlemark later, dressed appropriately, she tucked her hands into her sleeves and glided into the now-familiar hall. As usual, she paused at the door opposite her own, barred with red ribbons and sealed with a large circle of crimson wax, the Crown Prince's personal device pressed sharply before it hardened. If she was accompanying Mahara to dinner . . . but she was not, and it was best not to think upon such things.

Yala's jaw set, an ache growing in her neck to match the lump in her throat.

The Crown Prince's private quarters were familiar now too, and the table in the receiving room was laid for three. Takyeo was at the sliding door to the porch, looking out upon a small gemlike water-garden, his hands clasped behind his back and his topknot uncaged. Yala paused at the doorway, performed her usual bow, and tried not to look at the closed sliding door to the bedroom.

"Ah, Lady Yala." He turned from the view and inclined his top half a fraction, accepting her bow. His bandaged leg bore his weight with stoicism if not grace, and the silver-headed cane stood ready, leaning against the partition. "I invited Takshin, too, but he is late."

"Am I?" She knew very well she was not, since not a single dish had been brought, or even the beginning tea.

"No, and in any case, to wait for a lady is a nobleman's joy." His mouth twitched, and she could not help smiling in return.

He had been kind to his foreign wife, kinder than Yala had thought a Zhaon capable of. To ease him, therefore, she could attempt a sally or two. "Is it so in Zhaon? There is no waiting for a slow woman in Khir."

"It must be why you are so punctual." He indicated the table. "Please, sit, unless it pleases you to view the garden while we wait for Takshin or tea." He switched the order of the last three words, a very deft pun upon "late," "tea," and a possible second character of the Third Prince's name.

In Khir, she would have had a pun in reply. In Zhaon, however, she was not so adept—but she was not helpless, either. "Or both," Yala replied, equably. "He tends to arrive just as one is pouring." The proverb was slightly different in Khir, meant to describe a guest eager for his host's table, but she could still play upon it well enough and rob it of any impolite connotations by reversing the position of the two verbs.

Takyeo's laugh cut itself to shreds in the middle. He cast a half-guilty glance into the garden—and how strange, that she understood that shame. To speak wittily, or to laugh, while wearing mourning—it could hardly be avoided, and yet it invoked a certain amount of guilt. "He has ever been so." Sober now, and with his Zhaon stripped of levity, the Crown Prince took up his cane and joined her at the table as a bustle in the hall announced that her presence had been remarked and dinner could now commence. "Tell me, how is…how is my wife's house? Is all in order?"

He could not visit until his own mourning was finished; the Zhaon customs were so different. "Very much so." She halted behind the chair he indicated, her hands clutching each other inside her sleeves. Hopefully, no twitch of fabric betrayed the sudden movement. "There is nothing left undone, Crown Prince Takyeo. You may rest assured."

"Good, good." His mouth tightened, and his left hand tightened also upon the cane's silver-sheathed head, bright with royal metal. "I am glad you came."

As if she could refuse? Yala gazed at the table. Three settings, the small bowls of black raiku ware; the triangular plates for bones or other uneaten matter; the tiny bright-yellow stands to keep the tips of the eating-sticks from touching cloth or table; a lidded, sweating, unglazed pitcher of crushed fruit; the fan-shaped bowls that would hold crushflower-scented water for dipping one's fingers between courses bone-dry and empty. If she stared hard enough, she could pretend the third place was Mahara's and that she had been sent ahead to bear a message or prepare some small item for her princess's advent. She could not find a suitable reply, and yet he seemed to expect one. "Yes, Crown Prince."

A shadow filled the doorway. "Ah, she is so formal." Third Prince Takshin, in his usual Shan-black long tunic—in Zhaon's southron neighbor noblemen disdained any bright fabric, leaving it for merchants or women, and its severity suited him—stepped into the room. The pale slash of a mourning-band upon his left arm glowed, but his expression was much the same as usual—sardonic and closed, admitting no observer purchase upon his cliff. "*Crown Prince* this and *Third Prince* that. We should have her teach proper address to the young eunuchs."

"Takshin." Another half-shamed smile lit the Crown Prince's triangular face, peering through his mustache and smallbeard. At least his younger brother's manner eased him, in its own strange way. "We were discussing how late you tend to arrive."

"How else shall I make you miss me?" The Third Prince bowed, a mocking fillip at the end of the movement including Yala in its communication, though such politesse was unnecessary from a prince to a mere lady-in-waiting. "The tea is hard upon my heels; you shall pour for us both, Lady Spyling."

Abruptly, Yala's hands relaxed. Takshin was very much like Komori Baiyan; her brother had the same rough, sarcastic way of showing affection. There was nothing to fear from his direction, at least, and he would hold the Crown Prince in conversation if he was not in one of his deep, silent scowl-moods.

"Must you name her thus?" The Crown Prince exhaled harshly, adding a *tch-tch* at the end, tongue clicking against teeth like a disapproving auntie. "I apologize for my brother, Lady Yala."

Takshin actually grinned, and the expression did wonders for his lean, scarred face. "No doubt she has some choice names for me as well, Eldest Brother. And if you were not kept busy apologizing for me, what would you do with your day? Now, come to table. The lady is pale, she may collapse."

"I most certainly will not." It was somewhat cheering to bristle at him, much as Yala would carefully wait until nobody was looking and make a face at Bai. Yala's liver settled easily into its accustomed place, and the relief was too deep to bear close examination. "Your concern is better directed at the Crown Prince. Have you forgotten he is wounded?"

"Recovering, Lady Yala." Takyeo held up a single finger, making a babu water-clock's *tha-thunk* with its sideways motion as a warning. "Do not tempt Taktak, he might throw me into the garden pond instead of coming to my aid."

"Only if you steal my dumplings." Takshin's smile faded; he watched his eldest brother tap-step for the table. Once the Crown Prince seated himself, Yala paused, and the Third Prince motioned irritably for her to sit. "Do not wait upon me, little lure. My temper is uncertain, I will pace before dinner."

Still she hesitated, so he dragged his chair free and dropped into it with a mutinous glare. Yala sank into her own with satisfaction she did not let show, arranging her hands decorously in her lap. The tea arrived, soft-slippered servants moving with quiet alacrity, and Yala poured with her pale sleeve held aside, losing herself for a few moments in that most ordinary of acts. *If worth doing, it must be done well*, the maiden aunts of Hai Komori had cautioned her, over and over again. Even the very smallest task should be accomplished neatly and thoroughly; a noblewoman's breeding showed not in the large gestures but their opposite.

Their silence warned her; when Yala finally filled her own cup and set the teapot down she decided that while rude, it might be permissible to approach the most pressing matter before a bite had been taken. It would save the Crown Prince any unease while preparing to digest. "Has it has been decided, then?" She busied herself arranging her sleeve, picking up her cup, and studying the tea. "What to do with me?"

"Forgive me for asking, Lady Yala, but do you wish to return to Khir?" The Crown Prince gave his cup a quarter-turn before picking it up, for luck. "It is an ill-mannered question, I know, but events are moving quickly."

"So I have heard." Yala let her eyelids lower halfway as if she was lost in the liquid's bright, fine aroma. There was much she might have liked about Zhaon, had it not been so hot or so cruel, and if Mahara were still here to enjoy it with her. "Is it possible for a lone noblewoman to cross the border? There are bound to be many…difficulties."

"Not so many." Takshin lifted his cup, took a token sniff, and set it back down. His scars were pale, but the kyeogra in his ear gleamed, a circle of rich mellow gold. Perhaps its loop, trapping the voices of ancestors calling a descendant who had walked too close to their shadowed country, was also keeping some of his sharp illtemper at bay. "I will take you myself, should there be need."

"I doubt her countrymen would look kindly upon such a visit, Taktak." The Crown Prince glanced at the door, motioning in a fresh batch of servants. The dishes and tureens were arranged efficiently, and the room cleared again. "Would your father send an escort to the border for you, Lady Yala?"

"I must write to him." She stared unseeing at the white of polished rai. Strange, that the staple of life should bear the mourningcolor. Other words trembled upon her tongue.

I would not say no, Zakkar Kai.

"There may not be time. And…" The Crown Prince bent his gaze upon his brother. "There is something else."

What else could there possibly be? Yala watched the tea tremble inside its clay prison. "Am I to be imprisoned again?"

"Of course not," Takshin snapped, stretching his legs under the table with perfect disregard of civility, though he gathered them back soon enough when she glanced at him. "What my Eldest Brother is attempting not to mention directly is the assassins. They have halted their attempts to dance."

"Yes." Yala raised her head slightly. *Of course they have.* She felt nothing but an agonized, guilty relief that such was the case. "There is little chance of an heir now."

"I do not think that is quite the reason." Takyeo bent a worried gaze upon his brother, but it was she whom he addressed. "Lady Yala, when the kidnapping was attempted, you were to be taken to the man who hired it done. Did they mention anything about their employer, anything at all?"

"They simply called him *the Big Man.*" It was almost a relief to think upon that event, for it was over now and her princess had been alive, then. Placing herself in that dark, smoky, remembered cellar and hearing the men who thought they had kidnapped a princess discuss her fate was preferable to much that had happened since, though she had not thought it possible anything could be worse at that particular moment. "Perhaps my knowledge of Zhaon was not sufficient; I *think* that is the term they used."

No, that was untrue, for even then she had suspected worse and been groping with bound hands for her *yue* in case the kidnappers decided to attempt...dishonor.

Had they done so, and Yala opened her own throat to avoid such a fate, would her princess have lived longer, or not? It was a chilling question, one she suspected would return late at night as she lay abed in the smothering heat.

"Nothing else?" Takyeo persisted, his tone very gentle indeed. No nobleman who deserved the name would enjoy forcing a lady to remember such events.

"I will think more upon it, Crown Prince. But no, nothing else." Now she raised her head a little more, the meat inside her skull returning to some version of its usual agility and order. Just what was he thinking, or implying?

The two might not necessarily be the same.

"Eat," Takshin said, and picked up his bowl. The thick green-stone ring marking princely status upon his first left finger glinted sharply, no less than his dark eyes. "And you too, Elder Brother. You are both walking shadows."

"*Eat, eat, you grow thin.* You sound like a maiden-auntie," Takyeo muttered, but began his meal.

Yala stared at the rai. Suddenly, the thought of chewing and swallowing nauseated her. Certainly some assassins' attentions had ceased because an objective had been achieved. That did not mean there would not be more, for Takyeo's station would certainly draw them, but a not-quite-new thought stole into Yala's head, like a dull-glowing lightstick used to kindle lanterns and the wicks of flame-flowers.

Somewhere in Zhaon, most likely in the Palace itself, Mahara's killer—and whoever had paid for the deed—was well satisfied with their work.

Anger was a warp to the weft of grief. Such a cloth was ugly and quite unfeminine according to the Khir, but she was helpless to halt work upon its weaving.

"Does nothing tempt you?" Takyeo's tone was gentle, and his expression—damp eyes, tight mouth, stiffness in the neck bespeaking a heavy invisible yoke—was a sharp fresh pain, because she suspected her own was similar. To be mannerly, she was required to place a portion in her bowl and attempt to consume it with her stomach closed into a knot and her eyes smarting.

"It is an awful subject to contemplate at dinner, I know," the Crown Prince continued, somewhat anxiously. It was a mark of great generosity to trouble himself so over a lowly foreign lady-in-waiting, a now-useless woman in his house. In Khir, there would be little but sharp words for such a creature. "Forgive us, Lady Yala. But I would see you placed safely, and so would Takshin."

He was truly kind, yet it was not a stone she could put weight upon—he was a prince, after all, and she merely a foreign woman at a somewhat hostile court. None of her father's letters, usually prompt in response to her own, had arrived for several weeks. She could have perhaps hinted to Mahara of her worries in that direction, but her princess was dead.

And Yala found she had decided, quietly but thoroughly, that as long as she was trapped in Zhaon she would seek some means of finding out just who had paid for the killing deed. Against her thigh the warm metal of her *yue* rested, sharp and slim, and if the heavens were kind and justice offered a chance, Komor Yala would take it.

"Eat, Lady Spyling." The Third Prince all but jabbed his eating-sticks at her, a rudeness not quite startling—for such was his manner—but curiously comforting. He was the same as he had ever been, and at least *that* was a rock that would not turn underfoot. She was lonely here, yes, but not entirely without allies. Even Zakkar Kai could be counted among them. "Or you truly will collapse, and I shall be forced to sit at your bedside again."

"A hideous fate, having Takshin glare at you while attempting to recover," Takyeo agreed mildly, but a small amused gleam had entered his dark gaze. "I should know."

Yala forced her lips to curve in an approximation of a smile. Merriment was out of the question, but at least none of them were weeping openly. "Has he nursed you before, Crown Prince? He does not seem quite fit for it."

Takshin snorted a brief, jagged laugh, and Takyeo's startled smile erased some of the fresh lines graven upon his face. Yala bent herself toward the conversation and found her appetite had returned somewhat.

Decisions were difficult. But once made, it became only a question of *how.*

And Komori Dasho's only daughter was well accustomed to solving problems.

Poor Beast

Many leagues from Zhaon-An, near the southron border with barbarous pierce-towered Shan, a procession accompanied by bright fluttering pennants step-clopped its weary way up a slight rise and down into a broad valley starred with the mirrors of rai-patches looking up to Heaven. Heat shimmered over the road's ribbon; corvée labor in this province was performed punctually and thoroughly. Summer filled every meadow with flowers, every hedgerow with fresh juicy green, every dress-fold with sweat, and painted uneasy moisture upon every nape, especially under armor or a noblewoman's heavy braids.

She had refused the palanquin, and Garan Daebo Sabwone, First Princess of Zhaon, kneed the black Shan mare into a canter. The horse was a wedding gift, deep-chested and long-legged, with a fine, intelligent gaze and a sweet disposition.

Nevertheless, Sabwone took perverse pleasure in reining the beast savagely at the top of the hill. None of her riding boots had spurs, which saved the mare's sides; behind her, confusion spread in ripples as servants, guards, and ladies-in-waiting, not to mention the Shan delegation sent to ferry her to her new husband, realized their captive had broken the cage and fluttered past its gilded confines.

The restive mare, annoyed at rough handling, arched her neck and pranced. Sabwone let her, then touched her heels to the beast's sides. More than willing, the mare shot down the long hill-curve. The breeze, likewise startled, sought to comb hair trapped in tight braids and stabbed with pins holding jeweled decorations, and Sabwone's veil, stripped away by impertinent, invisible fingers, tore with a sound like freedom.

For a few moments, as the horse's brazen shoes chimed and the gallop-thunder echoed through her body, she prayed something would happen like in all the novels. If she was one of Lady Funai's heroines, the horse would be a faithful steed swift as the Five Winds, bearing her away from this degradation. If she was in one of Lady Surimaki's novels, there would be a prince disguised as a poor fisherman or a wandering bandit to rescue her. Even Lady Kunhawae's historical warrior-women, closing around her with a hedge of bright Heaven-blessed spears, would be most welcome.

They thought her a spoiled child; some of them even said as much openly, for what girl would *not* wish to be a queen? But Sabwone was a *First Princess*, of Zhaon no less, and the jumped-up merchants from Anwei who held Shan's young throne—only a bare hundred-and-half-again years of dynasty, after all—were unworthy of a girl in whose veins flowed the ancient blood of Daebo. Her mother was only a concubine, true, but their clan had ruled Daebo and slices of neighboring provinces during the Blood Years. And while her father had only just reunified Zhaon, his was the house of Garan, old enough to be included in Murong Har's *List of the Kingdom*.

Besides, Father had the blessing of Heaven. How else could he have won all those battles? And how could a girl of such parentage allow herself to be sold to . . . to *merchants*?

"*Princess!*" someone called. Sabwone bent over the mare's neck, urging her on. How many of them would gallop after their prisoner?

For a few moments it was as if she had truly escaped, as if the black mare could outpace guards upon swift chargers and the group of Shan noblemen with their crude laughter and dark clothing. Shan noblemen held bright colors only fit for women and the merchants they sought to separate themselves from, and no doubt this Kiron would be like her brother Takshin—mocking, cruel-mouthed, and impervious to pinches, teasing, or any of her other strategies.

He had probably _taught_ Takshin to be so idiotic. Of course, when Taktak was a boy he had been easy to direct. _Don't cry, Sabi. Who hurt you? I'll make them sorry._

Except when he came home from Shan the second time he was silent, and now he was scarred and singularly unhelpful. He didn't even _listen_ when she tried to tell him how much she hated the very idea of this marriage. No, he'd been busy going out and drinking with those dark-clothed barbarians, and—

The mare stumbled, slowed. Sabwone clung to the reins, but no amount of applying her riding boots to the beast's sides would make it do more than a bone-jarring trot, favoring its left hind leg. Such a stupid, silly animal, just like the rest of them.

Just like Sabwone herself.

There was silk in her sewing basket, all she required was a beam strong enough to bear her weight. And wouldn't her mother be sorry then? There was the paring-knife for hard rinds, and the latest wedding gift—they were brought out punctually as certain towns were passed and the distance from Zhaon-An grew—was a light, gorgeously inlaid bow of the type Shan rabbit-hunters used along with a quiver of beautifully fletched arrows. Any of their well-crafted heads would be sharp enough to slice a wrist. She even knew the proper way to do so, since she had filched _The Story of Anwone_ from the First Queen's library and read it late at night with a single candle burning, ready to thrust the book below the covers if a servant alerted her mother to the stripe of fitful light under Sabwone's door.

Why had she not taken the edge to her wrists, yet? Surely it could not hurt _that_ badly.

The mare halted, spraddle-legged, and dropped her head. Even pulling at the reins would not make her move. The beast was lucky—if Sabwone tried such a strategy, the ladies-in-waiting her mother had sent would bundle her like laundry, and Lady Nijera, a poor Daebo cousin who relished such things, would coldly direct that the princess be placed in the palanquin since she did not wish to ride.

Yet another insult. A provincial cousin as her chief lady-in-waiting, since Sabwone had refused to choose any of her usual attendants—or her mother's—to witness her shame.

Still, Shan had already been ruled by a queen in living memory. No matter that she was held to be *mad*, they often called a woman that when she did not do as she was told. Sold into a dishonorable marriage, a princess had certain methods of recourse, did she not?

After all, she was Garan Tamuron's daughter. She would not be Suon Garan-a Sabwone; she would sign her name with the same characters she always had.

Hooves thundered and the advance guard surrounded her, spear-tips hung with crimson tassels gleaming under thick Zhaon summer sunshine. Sabwone sat, straight-backed, as the mare shuddered. Stupid horse, unable to even bear her rider from this trap.

"*There* you are." Lady Nijera, upon a much uglier chestnut mare, drew rein and pushed aside her own veil. Her nose twitched, rather like a long-eared soup-rat's, and her sober silk-edged gown, also ugly as befitted a maiden-auntie dependent upon charity, was in some disarray. "You've run your horse almost to death, wicked girl!"

Sabwone lifted her chin. *That is quite enough.* "She is *lame*, Auntie Nijera." It was very little work to copy the First Queen's icy, lisping address; Sabwone rather liked First Queen Gamwone. At least nobody would pack *that* lady off to Shan against her will. She ruled the Kaeje just as Sabwone's own mother ruled the Iejo, first among almost-equals. "What a horrid gift, after all."

"What?" Lady Nijera's color was high, and her round face dewed with salt drops. "Surely you do not mean to insult—"

I am not five summers high, madam. "Fetch me a proper horse," Sabwone snapped at the milling advance-guard. One of them—a squat fellow with a sly smirk and one eye larger than the other—spat sideways, a gob of dry phlegm splattering into dusty-leaved bushes. He muttered something she could not quite hear over the stamping of hooves and creaking of leather half-armor, and Sabwone's irritation mounted another frustrated notch.

"Poor thing." Another guard, a lean dark-skinned man with a provincial accent, dismounted with a creak and a jolt. For a moment Sabwone thought he would offer his back for her to dismount, like a Second Dynasty kaburei. Instead, the man reached for the mare's bridle and clicked his tongue, soothingly. "Look what she's done to you."

Sabwone's jaw threatened to hang unprettily ajar. It was only a horse. Nobody cared what had happened to Sabwone herself, of course. But the *horse*, oh, that was a *tragedy*.

Aunt Nijera glanced at the man, then at Sabwone, but she did not take the guard to task. Instead, she eyed the First Princess warily, and her back, soft though it was, could not be straighter. "Such a delicate creature," she murmured diplomatically, but Sabwone wasn't fooled.

"Are you hard-of-hearing, Elder Aunt? Get me another horse." Sabwone could not stamp her foot, nor could she yank at the mare's reins with the guard holding the bridle. "A proper *Zhaon* one that will not collapse after a single gallop."

Nijera studied her for a moment, then freed one foot from the stirrup. Another guard hurriedly dismounted and offered his aid; the maiden-auntie landed with more grace than her wide hips and square shoulders should have allowed. "Of course, First Princess," she said, kindly enough. "Please, take mine."

Well, that was mollifying, but nobody moved to help Sabwone. She sat there, riding boots still fast in the stirrup; none of the advance-guard would quite meet her gaze. "Well?" she finally said, in the First Queen's bored, sweet, lisping manner. "Have you all forgotten your manners?"

"Not nearly enough," the spitting guard said, low but very clear. A rustle went through the men, and Sabwone realized, abruptly, that she was all but alone with them. There was Nijera, of course...but still.

"Thank you," the maiden-auntie simpered to the guard who had helped her. "Please, aid our princess."

White-lipped, Sabwone accepted the fellow's grudging service in dismounting, and in short order was upon the chestnut mare. A commotion halfway up the hill was the delegation of Shan lords riding up the column to witness the disorder, and incidentally to find the prisoner being dragged step by recalcitrant step to the border.

And, to make matters worse, Elder Aunt Nijera's little helper held the chestnut's reins, trapping Sabwone all the more effectively.

"My lady," the provincial guard at the head of the black mare said, "please, take my mount. I shall follow with this lovely girl."

Yes, the horse received all their care, and Sabwone not a thought. In the palace, none of them would have dared disregard her.

"You are too kind, Honorable Tua." Nijera inclined her top half—not quite a bow, since her status was so far above his, but still kindly acknowledging a subordinate's merit. How, under Heaven, did she know the man's name? Sabwone coughed, delicately, reached for her reins—and was denied their use, leather twitched free of her gloved grasp.

It was infuriating. The Shan lords appeared, Nijera remarking to their leader that perhaps their progress could be delayed some few moments while the princess was cared for after her adventure. The black mare was blamed, of course, and though Nijera protested, one of the Shan delegation took the story of a runaway horse with ill grace and demanded the beast be taught the price of folly.

Sabwone was drawn away, still without the use of her reins, and Elder Aunt Nijera followed upon one of the ridiculously large Guard greys. A halt was called, a wide meadow found for the business of feeding the nobles, watering the horses, and closing the princess in a hedge of restrictive etiquette once again, and as the borrowed chestnut mare was led toward the campsite's seething bustle a high, wild equine scream pierced the air.

Elder Aunt Nijera turned sallow, almost pale as polished rai, and

Sabwone twisted in her saddle to glance back. A hedge-screen hid the event, though, and the guards around the women said nothing.

It is only proper, Sabwone reminded herself. *And only a horse, after all.*

But her gloved hands were cold despite Zhaon's summer heat, her head ached abominably after the rattling gallop, and she could not help but think that the mild, pretty mare was not to blame after all. It was an uncomfortable idea, and one she set herself to forgetting as soon as possible.

SNAG IN SILK

The Old Tower, its sides sheathed with sky-colored tiles, held no shortage of scroll-racks and bookcases for the study of history and other arts as well as strange appurtenances for decoding the motion of the stars. The tower's occupant was held, consequently, to be somewhat of an expert upon the vagaries of the human liver—that seat of courage and instinct—as well as that most recalcitrant of organs, the human heart.

One visited a physician for the physical or subtle body, a fortune-teller for the avoidance of ill luck, an exorcist or monk of the Awakened One's persuasion for most spiritual remedies. But for the great ship of state or the largest life matters Heaven's blessing was sought, and who better to discover the celestial will than those who spent the nights uncouched and gazing upward?

"Strange, isn't it?" The First Astrologer to the court of Garan Tamuron laid his eating-sticks down, pushed his quarter-full bowl away to indicate surfeit, and leaned back, lacing his fingers over his small but respectable potbelly. He belched comfortably, no doubt tasting pungent qur sauce again, and stretched his legs under the table, pointing his slipper-clad toes. "You would think I'd had enough tavern food to fill me to the back teeth, and yet in certain moods, eggfowl with qur and redleaf is the only meal I long for."

"Is it tavern food if it's prepared in a palace?" Zakkar Kai wiped at his mouth with the back of his hand—at Mrong Banh's table, manners were somewhat relaxed, and he did not need to wear armor of any kind here. A small splash of qur lingered at the corner of his lips.

"Kitchens, whether large or small, are perhaps the same in every corner under Heaven." Banh, his topknot no more askew than usual, gave a smile of complete, sleepy contentment, allowing a glimpse of the soft-eyed young man he had once been. "You are wearing a decoration, by the way."

"It is a compliment to the cook." Zakkar Kai scrubbed at his mouth again, and the fragment of qur vanished. "Impossible to eat such a dish neatly. One must swallow it whole, pay the bill, and flee before the stomach decides to begin speaking from both ends." Redleaf was a particularly active cabbage; physicians even made a digestion tonic from its leaves soaked in a solution of water, charcoal salt, and slivers of noxious duruhan fruit.

"Ah, between friends, even a stomach's speech is music." Banh intoned this in his teacher-voice, his eyebrows wagging and one finger lifting from his midriff to provide an accent. "I am somewhat surprised you are eating with me, though. You must be busy."

"I leave in four days. Anlon is hurrying about, his feet worn down like a kaburei maid's." Kai settled back in his own comfortable chair, its wicker seat curved by patient application of familiar buttocks over many years. His steward was visibly relieved to return to the familiarity of an army camp instead of the luxurious danger of Zhaon-An.

The assassination attempts, whether upon his master or the Crown Prince, had not helped Anlon's nerves either. He was an old soldier, and of the opinion that the best way to solve an intractable problem was to administer a flogging—or run it through. Kai's more indirect methods, involving the application of copper slivers and much listening to gossip in order to locate an evanescent enemy, were somewhat unfulfilling in the steward's opinion.

If treachery had been afoot within the army, Kai more than likely would have been informed as soon as the impulse was voiced, let alone put into motion. Within the palace his servants had little recourse beyond wearying, constant vigilance, and Kanbina's were not set to any task more challenging than keeping their own lady safe from intrigues.

Had he been granted a hurai years instead of mere moon-cycles ago, Zakkar Kai would have a network of clients and informers throughout the city and in varying parts of provincial Zhaon itself, ready to set their busy ears and fingers to the matter. It took time to build such a thing, and his patronage, while indispensable for any who wished an officer's career, had not been thought to offer much in the way of *political* surety. The current rush of those who saw some advantage in testing his purse and his patience could not be sifted with any great speed.

"No doubt he is pleased to be so." Banh spared a chuckle for Anlon's current worries. "*Food, fire, peace.*"

"The soldier's three wants, Huar Guin's *Book of Tactics*." Kai grimaced, scratching at the side of his neck with blunt callused fingertips. Even Takyeo's network of clients and informers were bringing nothing to light, and Takshin was not likely to search with any subtlety. If Kai had more time, he could plumb Makar's feelings upon the matter, always assuming the Fourth Prince would lower himself to plebeian speculation instead of keeping whatever knowledge he had locked securely in his head-meat. "Don't quote at me, I have quite enough of that elsewhere."

Banh's laugh shook his belly, and the rest of him besides. "You cannot say your life has not been enriched by study of the classics, Kai."

It was a pity the redleaf had not yet begun its work; Kai could have lifted a hip and made his true feelings upon the subjects of scroll-work and study loudly known. "As a field is enriched by night soil." He eyed the teapot, weighing the wisdom of another cup. Harsh tavern-grade tea, while wonderful for cutting the richness of qur, also moved the innards to much activity.

"What wondrous creatures humans are," Banh murmured, his eyelids falling halfway. An onlooker might think him ready to nap, but this was when his faculties were most active. Some men thought better hungry, but the astrologer had no use for such creatures or their asceticism. "Everything poured into them turns into fertilizer."

"Except for women." Kai's own slippers were worn and comfortable, held in a rack by the front door and dusted punctiliously by Banh when the general was gone upon the business of winning battles. "Then it becomes new humans."

"Wondrous indeed." Banh's dark eyes glittered under scanty dark lashes. His cheeks bore the pockmarks of a childhood fever, and bright mirrorlight picked out each crater's edge. "Is this your signal that you are ready for marriage, General?"

"Banh, you are my very dear friend, but I must refuse your offer." Kai could not afford to give so shrewd an opponent as the astrologer any information at all. Of course Banh would keep the matter under his robe, but no secret was safe once unleashed, no matter how trusty its receptacle. "I do not think we would suit."

The astrologer made a rude noise, and their shared laughter ruffled threadbare hangings, the scroll-racks, models of fantastical machines or the constellations made of sticks and paper hanging from the high, cool ceiling. Said ceiling was broken by white-painted apertures for caught mirrorlight to pour through, and looked very much like the pierced towers of Shan might to an imaginative youth lying upon his back and staring upward, listening to an astrologer's instructive nattering.

Of all the hours Kai had spent in his life, those were some of the most enjoyable.

"Of course," Kai said, when their merriment had subsided into hiccups, "I am of age and eligible, should you wish to negotiate an alliance. Yet that is not what I am here to discuss."

"Hm. I suspected a snag in the silk when you arrived bearing lunch." Banh settled his shoulders, scratching luxuriously against his chair-back. His face turned into a thoughtful peasant's, age settling upon his strong bones and stripping away youth's fidgeting. "Is this a problem which requires my feet upon the ground?"

"No, merely your liver and head-meat in functioning order."

"Very well." The astrologer shifted, and after a short rearrangement his slippered feet rested where his dishes had. He leaned back, balancing upon his chair's hind legs like a road-dog preparing to beg. "I am ready, General Zakkar. Proceed."

Kai, alas, could not relax quite so thoroughly. Instead, he drew the tiny, silk-wrapped thing from an inner pocket and laid it upon the table. The wrapping was crimson, the color of wealth, luck—and protection. He untied a small knot, and revealed a ring made of a curious material somewhat between metal and stone, with a quiet, evil gleam.

It was a strange adornment modeled upon a flying serpent, the wings cruelly curved. It was heavier than it should be—and colder, as well. He reached across the table to lay it near Banh's feet.

But not too near, lest it carry any ill-luck.

Mrong Banh looked to the left of his slippers, studying the gleam upon its crimson bed for a long few moments. His dark gaze was keen, sharpened by nights spent gazing upward, and the color drained from his rough brown cheeks under his wispy but well-trimmed beard. "Where did you find this?"

"Upon a fellow who meant me harm." Kai took his fingers away from the thing with a certain relief. The assassin in the dry-garden, so soon after Takyeo's wedding, was still causing a great deal of unease, and this was a fine place to begin solving some aspects of the mystery. "What can you tell me of it?"

"That such things are better left alone. It is an assassin's mark... *Oh.*" Mrong Banh exhaled sharply. "I seem to remember a certain corpse, not too long ago—"

It is much safer for you not to finish such remembrance aloud, my friend. "What *kind* of assassin, Banh, and from whence exactly?" Kai settled in his own chair, but instead of resting his feet upon the table he simply stretched them beneath, flexing his toes before forcing himself to stillness. "And please, do not take an overly roundabout way of explaining."

"*Shinkesai*," Banh murmured. The sibilants rasped each other, sending a shiver up Kai's spine. "At least, that's how I think you pronounce it. They have stories of them up North, coming from the wastes to pursue cattle in lean years. Venomous, and glides instead of... yes, look, the wings are short and not meant for more. I never thought to see one of these." He did not move to put his chair-legs down, however, merely eyed the ring warily. "The ring is made of a stone held to be hungry for misfortune. The stories about *that* all caution that one must be rid of it before it begins to consume good luck as well."

"Mh." Kai merely made a noise to show he attended closely; now that Banh was engaging upon his answer in earnest more would arrive if the stick did not beat the carpet, so to speak.

"The Khir fear assassins who wear these; they are most dire ill-luck." Banh's left hand made a short *avert* motion, brushing aside misfortune. "They are said not to sleep or eat from the moment they see their target to until they achieve his death, and their services are most expensive."

Kai's own eyelids fell halfway as he unfocused, watching the small metallic gleam. Yala's reaction to the thing made sense now. No wonder she did not wish to speak deeply upon the matter; Kai would not have even asked her, had he known the depth of the thing's ill-luck.

"Passing strange," Mrong Banh murmured. "Northern assassins, or assassins using Northern items. Unless the buyer was a very crafty—and very rich—Zhaon, the only other likelihood is..."

"Yes." A single syllable of agreement, held in the back of the mouth and exhaled through rounded lips. A Khir, definitely rich, more than likely noble and perhaps even royal, had sent those of one Shadowed Path or another to rob the Zhaon of a princess-prize.

Was *that* why only a single noble lady-in-waiting had been sent with Princess Mahara? Had Ashani Zlorih thought Yala would keep his daughter alive even as Khir nobles intrigued for the mud and murder of another war? But why, by Heaven itself, would *any* Khir, no matter the stain on their so-noble pride, wish for as much?

If Zhaon had borne defeat, would Kai himself clamor for fresh battles?

Banh was silent for a short while, but Kai could *feel* the thoughts moving in the other man's busy, nimble liver. Head-meat was all very well, but it was useless without the emperor of organs providing fuel and impetus.

When the astrologer spoke again, it was in the soft, reflective tone of a man relating a puzzling dream. "They cannot wish for war again."

"It makes no sense," Kai agreed, glad Banh's thoughts had traveled in the same cart-track ruts as his own. "And yet." It would have eased him immensely, had Banh arrived at a different estimation than his own.

But Zakkar Kai had not thought it likely.

"I won't ask why you chose to dispose of the body in that particular fashion..." The words faded, the astrologer clearly wishing to ask the question very badly.

Kai did not reply. What he did not explain, Banh could very well say was only a suspicion, not actual knowledge. It was best not to place his oldest friend in a position where he might have to lie.

For all his depth, Banh was startlingly bad at untruths. Finally, the older man closed his eyes, fingers still laced over his widening stomach. He very pointedly did not glance at the ring again. "They may not wish for war." Very softly. "But should war occur, they are well placed to deny Zhaon requests for aid, and to take a bit more than borderlands and bridges while a new Emperor is distracted."

"Yes," Kai said, heavily. "That is what I thought you would say."

"'Tis only a feeling. But with the Pale Horde sending emissaries..." Again, Banh let the sentence stay unfinished, but there was no question in its lilt, just the weariness of a peasant eyeing the approach of bad weather.

Kai closed his own eyes. It was no use. He could still see that hurtful, hateful gleam upon its pad of red silk, and even the remaining, often-remembered tingle of Yala's closeness in his arms and the exact space upon his chest where her cheek had rested more than once but not nearly often enough did not soothe his unease.

A Gift, Mustn't We

Deep in the Kaeje, a small round room was girdled twice with tapestries despite summer's crushing heat. Inside, mirrorlight softened through falls of sheer material, and the greatest lady in Zhaon was settled upon a cushioned bench before a low, exquisitely carved wooden table draped with bright peach cotton, its surface holding serried ranks of bottles, jars, implements, and other means to turn whatever skin, hair, eyes, and teeth Heaven had given a woman into fashionable equivalents.

"You're lucky to have no children, Yona." First Queen Gamwone's face was set as she stared into a highly polished brazen mirror, its back carved with characters to denote good luck; its metal was held to beam only the most healthful of reflections toward its user. "They bring you grief."

Her chief maidservant Eun Yona—for the First Queen only rarely allowed ladies-in-waiting to attend her dressing, confining their attempts to gain her patronage to social hours, luncheons, and the odd ceremony or festival—made a soft, noncommittal noise that could be taken for agreement or a request for further wisdom. It was a skill she had learned early in palace service and it stood her in good stead, just as the ability to keep her face a blank, river-washed rock did.

Yona's stomach ached ceaselessly, no matter how many ounces

of medicine from the Artisan's Home she swallowed. The pain had been very bad lately, but it did not affect her duties.

Nothing would. She kept to her work, her dry cool fingers busily stroking, twisting, separating, braiding. Her royal mistress did not abide idleness at any moment. It was better to *seem* busy at all times, and woe to the maidservant who did not grasp as much. Even the First Queen's eunuch steward, bland attenuated Zan Guin, took pains to achieve a state of steady motion when her gaze seemed likely to fall upon him.

"They are all ungrateful," Gamwone continued, after a short pause. Her round, beautiful face had not changed much in all the years of Yona's service, save for some fine thin lines at the corners of the eyes and mouth massaged with nia oil every morning and evening. "Just like men. You're lucky not to have a husband, either."

Yona made another servile noise. As if she could ever think of marrying, especially now. Her youth was past, pressed out of her and leaving only an urn of dry powder where her womb had once sat; even the thriftiest of care had not accumulated a dowry that might have induced some minor merchant or Golden officer to accept a wife with the skills and useful connections gained in palace service. She chose bone and metal implements with care, using each without tugging long black strands, knowing exactly how Gamwone hated having her scalp irritated on hot, dusty days like today. Next would come the question of hairpins—a difficult matter, but at least the queen didn't seem in a mood to find fault.

Not at the moment.

"Well," Gamwone continued, still studying the mirror. "I suppose they aren't *all* bad. If given proper training while young. Is there anything of interest today, Yona?"

"The Second Concubine visited the Emperor," Yona said promptly, her inflection suitably deferential and each word low but clear so her mistress could not accuse her of mumbling. A faint iron taste against her palate was the morning's medicine, tossed quickly down into her guts before dawn when she rose to harry slothful junior maidservants into activity. "Yesterday morn."

Gamwone's servants were to be ever vigilant as they went about their duties, and Yona was who they reported to. Oh, she knew what they called her—the dry stick for beating carpets, the woman all the juice had been pressed from, the pimple upon a queen's backside. Sometimes it rankled, but on other days, she felt only a peasant's mutinous joy at surviving.

In such a place as the great palace of Zhaon, survival was a victory. Yona longed to see a soldier or two, or even a vaunted prince, last a single day of woman's work.

"Suffering little mouse," Gamwone hissed. "No doubt she was going to beg more favors for that dog-general."

Yona did not think it likely, unless it was to request an imperial blessing upon the general before his departure to the North three days hence, but she held her peace. The next batch of braids was going to be tricky; some of Gamwone's hair was resisting the combined, constant pressure of comb, hairpin, and age.

Perhaps on some future day Yona could introduce padding to make certain her mistress was not embarrassed by thinning hair. Such an innovation would have to be deployed carefully, and she did not relish the thought of its advent.

"I don't deny he's useful," Gamwone continued, in a meditative tone. "But he does not know his *place*."

Yona made another sound of assent. This was a familiar song, one she could almost whistle, if such a thing were not bad luck. "He visits the Crown Prince regularly," she offered, knowing it would not even begin to satisfy the queen's appetite.

What would? Perhaps a long, slow, tortuous death meted out to one of her particular unfavorites. Zhaon's First Queen read accounts of convicted criminals expiring upon the machines of the civil peace service with great avidity. Occasionally she would repeat a phrase or two aloud for the edification of her servants.

Those were bad days.

"The trash clots together in a canal," Gamwone said softly. "What else is there today, Yona?"

"The bath-girl." Yona kept braiding, steadily. If she arranged the strands just so, they would cover the thinning portion admirably. "One of our under-servants has heard her family in Suyon now has a new cow."

"Whore a daughter, receive an ox," Gamwone muttered.

Yona thought it was quite likely the bath-girl the Emperor was so enamored with didn't have time to ask for her family's preferment, being run ragged by her jealous fellows in that part of the palace. Gamwone was unlikely to take Yona's next piece of news calmly, but keeping it in reserve was unwise. So she took care to keep her tone and inflection even more honorific than usual. "The Second Prince has requested her thrice as an attendant, and gave her a scentwood comb just two days ago. The entire bath quarter was talking about it."

"Is that so." Much to Yona's surprise, the queen smiled and stretched, catlike, yet kept her head still as a noblewoman learned to while hair was being dressed. Her son's cultivation of the girl the Emperor was currently showering attention upon must be a planned maneuver, then. *"Don't* pull my hair. You are inattentive today, Yona."

"Yes, Your Majesty." She had not tugged a single strand, but of course, protesting would gain nothing but ill-luck. "My apologies." Yona hurried to add more news, scraped from the lazy, chattering children pressed into palace service. The rest of the complex, from the Kaeje to the eunuchs' quarters, called Queen Gamwone's girls uncomplimentary things, and also noted that they did not grow sleek and polished in service, but thin and fretful instead.

It was no great loss, Yona thought. Their place was to serve, not to sit about on their fat hindquarters belittling their patroness. "There have been many letters from First Princess Sabwone," she continued, anxious to change the subject. "The Second Queen did not read the last two, instead leaving them upon her study-desk. There are rumors that the Emperor is considering a marriage for the Second Princess, too, since the First's was...advantageous."

"Selling off my daughter too." Gamwone tilted the mirror afresh, studying the curve of her plump cheek. Her hair was still very black and shining, lovingly combed and doused with scented oils every night before the queen retired to her well-padded bed, to dream whatever dreams a royal wife entertained when her lord husband no longer visited. "Well, anything less than a king won't do for Gamnae. But not Khir. After all, they lost the war."

Yona longed to ask if the queen thought Far Ch'han would take the Second Princess for their own august Emperor. *That* would be a bright hairpin for the First Queen to flaunt, a larger and more important country—though far more distant—swallowing another of Garan Tamuron's daughters.

On the other hand, maybe the Emperor *would* send his remaining daughter to Khir. A girlchild for a girlchild—how that would irritate the First Queen, her precious bovine-tempered Gamnae sent to replace a horselord's brat. Gossip about the foreign Crown Princess painted her as stupid but pretty; it was her lady-in-waiting with the catlike face and those same strange Khir ghost-eyes, so different than honest dark Zhaon gazes, who was held to be the greater danger. Especially once it was revealed that said lady wasn't a noblewoman at all but an evil feline spirit with a long greenstone claw.

Or so the stories said. Carrying an undeclared weapon in the palace was supposed to be death, but the First Queen's second son, the one who was supposed to have brought Shan to his mother like a naming-day present, had stepped between the foreign princess's guardian spirit and a whip.

It was a pretty tale, but not one which would soothe the First Queen's temper.

Yona looped the second braid, used a bentpin to secure it, and turned to the third as the pain in her middle subsided to a low grumble. Third Prince Takshin also spent his days in the Crown Prince's burrow, currying favor with the son of the Emperor's first, sainted, long-dead wife. It was difficult to tell what about the situation galled Gamwone most.

But Yona's mistress was no longer interested in palace gossip, or perhaps the queen knew nothing more of interest would be reported. She turned to the next item of business, usually far more pleasant and mollifying. "Who sent gifts today?"

"Lady Aouan Mau, for Gamnae. Lady Gonwa, for Gamnae too. The Second Queen sent ink and a length of silk for your naming-day. The Emperor sent a small package; it has been left upon your night-table as you commanded."

"Well, send someone to fetch it. My lord husband's gifts must not wait." But Gamwone's mouth pulled down bitterly. Her husband would not give her anything she wanted.

Of course, if he could divine what this woman longed for, he would probably strike off her head like the old tale of the King of Wurei and the faithless, scheming, but quite beautiful courtesan Ging Mau. High position was perilous, especially for a woman gifted with beauty, ambition, or any intelligence at all.

Sometimes Yona wished she had less head-meat or liver-strength; being dismissed from palace service was a stain upon one's prospects but might have been far more pleasant. At least begging in alleyways one *expected* to starve, instead of seeing luxury daily and being scolded or struck should one openly desire a fingerful.

Yona finished the third braid and bowed deeply before rising, hurrying to the partition on soft feet. Everything must be muffled for Gamwone's delicate sensibilities; it was a shock that the noble lady was sometimes so crude. Of course, the Yulehi were rumored to have bought some claim to nobility, instead of acquiring it honestly by sword or Heaven's will. That particular gossip—that her family genealogy was traced upon goatskin instead of upon stone stele—was not reported to Gamwone, but who dared to pass it along was.

There had been many such comments of late. More than usual, and that was a troubling sign.

When Yona returned, her mistress had laid the mirror face-down. "Yona," she said, very kindly, "there is something to be done."

"Yes, Your Highness?" The chief servant's hands turned even colder despite the simmer of Zhaon's summer in this round, padded room. She gathered the braids and began to twist them in becoming fashion, taking even more care not to pull, tug, or otherwise irritate a tender royal scalp.

"That fellow, so-called Honorable Tian." Gamwone touched a small crimson pot of anwa paste, hau bark ground fine and mixed with certain other essences to treat skin discoloration and slight pains. Her resin-dipped fingernails, too long for a woman who lifted anything heavier than a scroll or a brush, made a small reptilian clicking against painted ceramic. "The physician. He hasn't attended us in quite some time. We must send him a gift, mustn't we."

Oh, thank Heaven. As usual, Yona felt a great burst of swimming relief that it wasn't *her* neck upon the block. Tian Ha was the First Queen's personal physician—or had been for a very long while, and had been consequently very high in the estimation of the court. He had even, once or twice, deigned to palpate Yona's abdomen with a wooden pointer and tell her the pain was simply an imbalance of female humors, and nothing a common draught would not cure. Still, the First Queen had turned a cold cheek in his direction since the affair of the mangled corpse upon her front steps, so it wasn't quite a surprise that he had withdrawn to his estate outside the palace walls, probably sweating and trying vainly to remember his every word in order to find what had disturbed his patroness.

Yona could have told that august personage it was no use; the First Queen had decided her pet physician was either far too comfortable in her continued graces or worse, a danger to her own padded position. Once Garan Yulehi-a Gamwone decided such a thing, not even Heaven itself could move her to pity or mercy.

After all, Tian Ha knew certain secrets, just as Yona did. And Yona was increasingly nervous that soon, the First Queen would look into a mirror and murmur *we must give Yona a gift, mustn't we.*

"If Your Highness says so, it must be so," she said, and selected the hairpin most likely to please her mistress; it had a long fall of glittering gold beaten so thin it was like fluttering bebao leaves before an autumn storm. "His estate is upon the Street of Bright

Pearlfruit, I am told." *See how useful I am*, her fawning tone intimated, and how she hated the taste of it.

But those who smiled through a mouthful of noble shit survived, and there might even be undigested rai in such a dish.

"We must know someone in his household." Gamwone's tone was soft and pleasant; in that moment she was very beautiful indeed, round-faced, polished, black-eyed, and plump like the illustrations of the goddess of rai or the queen-wife of the Moon Himself. "Someone lowly, but...suitable."

"Certainly, Great Queen." The honorific, an ancient and somewhat ornate term for the only wife of Zhaon's Emperor, was the right move; Yona blessed her past self for some prudence in anticipating something of this sort. Only last week she had given one of the girls—a thin, lanky provincial creature with more presence of mind than most of her ilk—the duty of befriending someone suitable in Tian Ha's household. "I think one of our maids knows one of the kitchen-scrubbers there." Her throat dried too. Perhaps her humors were disarranged; whose would *not* be, in such a position as hers?

But she had chosen correctly, for her mistress relaxed, soft paws touching small things upon her beauty-bench. "Is that so?" Gamwone's smile stretched, languid and beautiful, her face a full moon. Next would come the lacquering of her braids to keep them in place, then the application of zhu powder upon cheeks, forehead, and nose; after that the slight touch of color to her lips, and by then, Yona's hands would have stopped wanting to shake as she attended to the largest and certainly cruelest goddess of the Kaeje. Then it would be time to whisk away the thin cotton capelet that kept zhu from dusting linen and under-robe before settling the day's dress over her mistress's shoulders, with two hurrying, silent undermaids in attendance to help tighten, tie, lace, and arrange. "Well. I am certain I have something small to send to the esteemed physician. Not this afternoon, but soon. Not too tight, Yona."

"Yes, Your Highness."

Gamwone picked up the mirror again. She studied the hairpin's bright glitter in its brazen depths. "Oh, no," she said, in mock surprise. "That hairpin won't do at all if I am to wear ear-drops today, Yona. Something a little less showy."

Yona swallowed bitterness from her rancid stomach. "Yes, of course," she repeated. "Your Highness."

A Comfort

It was best to ration anything pleasant, but Garan Takshin found he did not wish to. Being balked in every direction while attempting to find the assassin responsible for a princess's death was bad enough; the added gossip surrounding a lady under his personal protection was a maddening fillip. He did not care what they said of *him*, but keeping their chattering mouths from a certain Khir girl was all but impossible even if he did glower at any so stupid as to spend their breath so in his presence.

Consequently, he did not bother to scratch at the lintel as was his custom when entering the Jonwa's smallest sitting-room. Most days it pleased him to herald his arrival with a cat's claw-sound, but today his object was surprise. He found exactly what he suspected he would, in most regards.

Slatted wooden blinds cunningly designed as a partition angled half-open; beyond them a shaded portico looked upon a dry-garden of spiny succulents and stepping-stones in a river of smooth multicolored pebbles. This early in the afternoon the light had not taken on the customary, heavy oppression just before a summer downpour, but the air was electric with expectation and humidity in equal measure nonetheless.

Caught while leaning close to speak in Komor Yala's ear, Su Junha straightened, her primrose sleeve lifted to her mouth to hide a smile. Yala also smiled gently, abstractly, but Takshin could tell she was not listening to the girl, merely performing an appropriate expression. A ghostly Khir gaze, charcoal-fringed with thick lashes, came to rest upon him with some startlement.

His usual sullen fury retreated almost immediately, backing into its cage within his liver, and he found he could breathe again. So he essayed a small, tight smile of his own, and set himself to fret Yala into looking a little less wounded.

"There she is," he said, perhaps a trifle too loudly, and chose a square of bare flooring somewhat in front of her to sink down upon. Not directly before, as if he were a retainer seeking a favor or a merchant longing to show his wares to a noble, but slightly diagonally, so she did not have to look upon his scars.

But not *too* diagonal, because looking at his ugliness did not seem to upset her. The hoop in his left ear, gleaming gold, was tangible proof. Touching its satiny weight was always a surprise; he expected it to be gone each time, like anything else pleasant in his life.

"Third Prince Garan Takshin." Yala's expression did not change, and she simply murmured the formal greeting. "How pleasant to see you."

"Lie not to me, Komor Yala." Takshin folded himself down, waving aside Hansei Liyue's hurried attempt to find a cushion for royal buttocks. He chose to disdain such a comfort each time he visited this room, to drive home that he was *not* a guest and could leave at any moment. The refrain of a romantic, tragedy-soaked song currently famous in the Theater District lingered upon his tongue, but he did not attempt to sing, merely half-chanted it in the laziest, most bored, most formal Zhaon he could manage. "*Unless you wish to crush my throat and send me to my pyre.*"

The Hansei girl all but gasped, her own sleeve—yellow as sunshine crushflowers—rising to her mouth. Yala glanced at her, slim fingers toying with a scrap of roseate silk pinned next to a sunset-colored swatch of cotton. Her sewing basket sat obediently next to her knees, half-open and showing gradations of neatly wrapped thread as well as the gleam of metal implements used for gentle embroidery.

It was ill-bred of him to mention pyres while Komor Yala was still in pale mourning; still, his aim was to irritate her out of sadness. Unfortunately, the sally failed; his cavalry found no trace of the enemy, and Yala simply gazed at him silently, as if she had forgotten what politeness came next.

So. A change of tactics was called for. "You should thank me for not singing," he said, making plans to punish himself for a misstep later. "And greet me with less cursed formality, too."

A spark of interest brightened in her pale gaze. "Perhaps some tea for our guest?" She made a soft, restrained gesture and Lady Liyue bowed like a supple flower-stem, rising in the peculiar, fluid manner of a well-bred Zhaon girl.

"I am not a *guest*," Takshin said haughtily. "I live here. But yes, tea, and my thanks for your hospitality. What are you about, Lady Spyling?"

"Sewing, Third Prince." She acknowledged the thoroughly visible nature of her reply with a shadow of a wry smile, indicating the basket with a second graceful motion. "Or attempting to. I am out of sorts in this heat, it appears. Perhaps you are as well?"

"I am in exactly the temper I choose to be, little lure." His favorite name for her, with the stress laid upon the second-to-last syllable to turn the word into its feminine self just as slim and lightfoot as her. "Remember that. Are you wishing for a new dress, then?" As if he was a courtesan's patron, asking her which gift she would prefer.

Now it was Su Junha who almost gasped, but she was of sterner stuff than the Hansei girl and glared daggers at Takshin before dropping her gaze, perhaps remembering his reputation. Still, she was protective of Yala, and that warmed him clear through. Both young ladies wore wide, pale mourning sashes, too, well past the time they could have decently left such appurtenances in a ceduan box.

For that, he was willing to forgive much.

The lady herself did not rise to his impoliteness. "*I have many, yet wear only one.*"

"Khao Cao." Oh, it was quite a scholarly reference, though the

man who brushed it had been a general known for his cruelty—
and for mourning the death of another man's wife with such flagrant verse as to spark a duel near a barn full of nesting split-tail
brightbirds. Only Khao's death had saved him from indecency, and
now some few of his quotations were considered fit for the education of young minds—once they were suitably neutered, of course,
as eunuchs were largely considered safe despite much evidence to
the contrary in history *and* literature. "You are in a terrible mood,
to be quoting *him*."

"You find him objectionable? But he is of the Hundreds, my
lord prince." Clever girl, uttering the honorific with a slight twist
in its accent to turn a prince into a lucky, full-tailed cat. "And the
Hundreds are most proper and upright, just what a young lady
should read and take to heart."

"Only if she wishes to be bored past measure." He doubted she
had read Khao's collected works, for all her scholarship. The library
of Shan's palace had held a dusty copy tucked far back in a cob-
webbed corner; both he and Kiron had perused it at length for the
annotations and small drawings a former student of great boredom
and a little artistic skill had made in the margins. "Where is your
third chick today, my lady eggfowl?"

"Gonwa Eulin has been called to her aunt's for tea this afternoon." The lady folded her work, an operation that did not need
thought if a woman practiced her proper occupation often enough.
She did not halt halfway through and look into the distance this
time; there was no glimmer of salt water burgeoning in those
ghostly eyes, and the shadows under them had eased somewhat.
Komor Yala's chin set in its accustomed fashion, and she regarded
him levelly. "Am I to take it you are inquiring after her, then?"

"Careful." The sly intimation of matchmaking was intended to
irritate him in turn, and much of Takshin's black mood fled outright, vanishing from its liver-cage. "You sound a jealous auntie."

"I must make certain the ladies in my care are properly chaperoned."
Now her gaze outright gleamed, and her movements quickened. "And
you, Third Prince, have an ill reputation."

"Entirely deserved," he assured her. "But no, I have no interest in Lady Gonwa's niece; imagine, having such a court gossip married into your affairs."

"So it is Lady Gonwa you are after instead?" his Khir minx inquired, sweetly. "I shall be certain to compliment you to her, to smooth your way."

Su Junha lifted her sleeve again, this time to catch a laugh she could not quite swallow in time. Yala's mouth twitched, and Takshin mock-glowered at both of them, beetling his brows and finishing the glare with a monster's face as if they were children still in the nursery, eager for a story and a scare.

"Careful," Su Junha burst out, "or it will freeze that way." She darted a glance at Yala, gauging the reaction, and their lady smiled fully this time.

The last vestige of his usual, damnable bleakness fled Garan Takshin, and he arranged his expression into one quite proper and more soothing. "It might be an improvement," he said, lightly. "Do you think so, Lady Junha?"

"It certainly cannot get any *worse*." She glanced again at Yala, whose mouth did not turn down at the corners.

No, their lady's eyes all but sparkled, albeit briefly, and it appeared Komor Yala was hard-put not to grin.

They thought they could play with him, and he was more than willing if it eased a certain pale-eyed girl. "I like this one," he said abruptly, indicating the Su girl with a brief motion, hand cupped to avoid the impoliteness of a finger-spear. "She speaks truth almost as bravely as you do."

"An indirect compliment indeed." Yala inclined her head. A single, very plain hairpin of dark wood nested in her carefully wrapped braids; apparently the Khir did not strip themselves of that small adornment while grieving. "You grow quite skillful with their use, Third Prince."

"It must be your influence." Sometimes a man could allow truth, suitably disguised in a jest. "Run along, Lady Junha, and bring something sweet with tea."

The noble girl could have bridled, for she was no kaburei or servant to be ordered about, but Lady Yala nodded acquiescence and Su Junha rose with a flutter of primrose cotton and green edging. She flowed to the door, perhaps relieved to be saved the trouble of making conversation with the worst and least polite of Garan Tamuron's many sons.

Takshin wondered if his lord father regretted the profligate luck in siring such a brood. It was generally held to be a sign of Heaven's favor, but if childhood misadventure or disease did not take half your descendants, they might make up for it by jostling violently in adulthood, no matter how moralists *tch-tch*'d their tongues at such impropriety.

"And now we are alone," he said, softly, "or as close to it as possible. Tell me truly, how do you fare?"

"Well enough." If Yala disliked the intimation of their solitude bringing familiarity, she did not show it. "But surely you could have asked openly."

"And have you gracefully deflect me? No."

One eyebrow arched, and her almost-surprised air was charming in its own way. "Gracefully?"

"Grace is in your nature, as dissatisfaction is in mine." Along with a certain amount of sheer stubbornness, and Garan Suon-ei Takshin had reason to be glad of both. They had, after all, kept him alive.

Yala did not search for a witticism, simply regarded him with mild interest. Mirrorlight was kind to her face, too sharp and thin for beauty but still arresting the gaze. "Are you so certain?"

Of which, little lure? "Passing sure, indeed." Bare, uncushioned floor was uncomfortable, but he liked the sensation, as well as the phantom coolness of plain wood. In Shan the summer wind would be fluting through pierced towers before afternoon's hush fell and a great heel of heat crushed field, town, city, and palace alike. "Now, answer me."

"I have; I am well enough." Steady, and unruffled. Was she bearing that sharp claw-toy of hers, hidden in her skirts? "Is it cooler in the countryside, then? I am quite ready to begin a journey tomorrow, should it be so."

How could he tell her Takyeo would never manage retreat? His eldest brother could not leave a limb behind in the stone trap of Zhaon-An as a lizard might, to save himself.

It was not in him, as surrender was not in Takshin and cruelty was not in Yala. They were all trapped as surely by what they were as by what they were *not*. Such was life, that execrable burden he could have done well without.

Except if he had not been born, he would not have met *her*, or been able to step between her and a whip. So Takshin shrugged. "You prefer the countryside, then?"

"There is much here that reminds me..." She halted, composed herself, and fool that he was, he'd provoked sadness instead of ire.

"Of your princess." Takshin rested his hands upon his thighs. It pleased him, though he would not settle directly before her as a retainer, to sit as one. "Yes." *Tell me what you wish for, and be quick about it so I may grant the desire.* He could not say as much, though.

Or, he *could*, but he found he was not inclined to. Not if it caused her pain.

"You are a comfort," Komor Yala said, folding her hands decorously in her lap. "Anyone else would avoid the subject."

"Speak upon what eases you, then. Heaven knows I do often enough." He could admit to his failings with equanimity, at least. The world was cruel; wearing your flaws as armor served to divert both poison and claw. If he struck himself first, others were reduced to throwing flowers.

Komor Yala leaned forward slightly, which meant he was helpless to avoid doing the same, a dayflower following the Sun's great lamp. "There is a matter I would ask your aid upon," she began, and Takshin suppressed a flare of sharp, hot satisfaction.

Finally, she had asked. "Name it, then."

At least she did not hesitate. "I wish to—"

"Lady Komor?" Su Junha hurried from the door, her skirts

swaying, and Takshin's right hand itched for his sword. "There is a letter for you."

"Ah." Yala accepted a triangle of heavy pressed-paper in both hands, nodding her thanks. The seal was bare, a curious blob of indeterminate dun wax, and the outer layer held merely Komor Yala's name in fine angular characters both like and unlike Zhaon. "How curious." She examined it with an air of puzzlement. "It is in Khir, but is not my father's hand." What color she had regained now drained from her cheeks, and Takshin bit back a curse. Of course a filial daughter would fear that such a missive contained news of a parent's ill health—or worse, censure.

"Go read it, and come back for tea." He settled back over his heels, and had to remind himself not to glower at the Su girl for the interruption. "Or I shall be forced to frighten your chicks, eggbird."

"Such a thing would be below your princely dignity, Takshin." Perhaps she used his name because she was distracted; her Khir accent softened the first vowel while cutting the last short, not to mention the very fetching sharp sibilance she gave the *shi*. She rose, bowed hurriedly but with that exquisite grace, retreated to a small desk set partly behind a screen painted with a snow-pard upon a cliff watching peasants at harvest in a deep valley, and broke the seal, scanning the letter with a faint frown.

Tea arrived, and normally Takshin would be in no mood to linger. But Komor Yala had been about to ask him for aid, and he found he did not mind waiting.

He did not even mind attempting polite conversation with Ladies Su and Hansei, for her sake. Third Prince Takshin sat, sipped at an afternoon cup of smoke-heavy siao, stole a cake of pounded rai stuffed with crushflower-flavored mungh paste, and tried not to glance too often or too longingly in his Khir lady's direction.

It was not, he decided, an unpleasant way to spend an afternoon.

A Prince and a
Wolf

The mystery was somewhat solved when she broke the seal—
and deepened as well. It was not that she did not recognize
the hand immediately; the sender would have to brush with his left
to deceive her, and quite possibly in reverse as well as the sage Kao
Luan was said to have done.

No, the riddle lay in why Ashani Daoyan would send her such a
curious letter.

On the surface, of course, it was a matter of little import—a
Khir merchant politely begging the favor of a noblewoman's
patronage, inviting her to send for a sample of his wares or, were she
sufficiently intrigued, to visit his humble shop. She could certainly
choose to take no notice, since it arrived while she was in mourning. And yet, she *knew* that writing, and the form of address, while
plausibly supplicatory, held a few odd character choices that could
be mistaken for imperfect literacy if they did not allude to certain
childhood events.

He might have thought her witless from grief to need such
explicit clues, or he wished to be very cautious indeed. Had her
father sent Dao to collect her? Impossible, of course; he would have
had to leave Khir well before Mahara's...

Her death.

Yala tucked the refolded letter into a sleeve-pocket and stared at
the desk's glossy, well-waxed surface of fine lyong heartwood, more
suitable for bows than holding paper and brushes. Here in Zhaon,
luxury had come to seem somewhat normal, and therefore ignored.
Such fine wood, wasted upon a *table*.

The simplest solution to the puzzle was that Dao had trusted
a merchant with some other more direct message, one Yala must
collect discreetly, and this was a means given to said messenger to
catch her attention as a lure caught a hawk's gaze. Perhaps it was
even a warning, arriving far too late—but why would a plot against
Mahara be discovered in Khir?

It was the first moment since the dreadful afternoon of her
princess's last ride that Yala felt entirely *awake*. Her liver settled
in its proper place with a thump so loud she was mildly surprised
nobody else in the room noticed, and her head was not mazed with
dreadful, devouring weight lingering behind eyelids and filling her
throat at odd moments. Her gaze fell upon the Third Prince as he
accepted Su Junha's trembling pour of siao into his drained cup
with a very proper nod. He was even taking pains to put the two
ladies at their ease, and Hansei Liyue was carrying the burden of
conversation as adroitly as her own caution of his temper would
allow.

Perhaps if Yala appealed to his sense of justice... or of mischief?
He was very much indeed like her Baiyan, who would enter the
fray for some matter of pride, or, more often, for the sheer fun of it.
If Bai was here, Yala's *yue* could have remained safely in its sheath.

But her beloved damoi was smoke upon the wind, riding the
Great Plains like her princess. There was no use in wondering what
he would say of these events, or of a certain Zhaon general who
was proving to be a steady ally she could ask for a measure of aid in
discovering who had paid for a royal death.

Her thoughts had turned to Kai again, rebelling against all propriety. It pained Yala to consider herself possibly merely a treacherous, weak-willed sister in a low novel. How could she even consider
marriage, much less to...

...an honorable man? There seemed to be a few of them in Zhaon despite the country's sneered-at softness. Even the Crown Prince was kind and forthright, and had treated Mahara well.

Which led her, circling like embroidery thread tied in a strong knot, to scarred, mocking Garan Takshin, who bore yet another scar across his back for Yala's sake; the weight of that strike—a whip against a nobleman's flesh, distasteful and not to be borne—was a heavy debt accounted against her.

Of course he had done it because the shame of a whipping would reflect upon the Crown Princess, and thus upon his beloved eldest brother. Yala had been prepared to bite through her own tongue as the whip descended, hoping to bleed to death with some measure of honor left.

Yala almost shuddered, quelled the motion just in time. The young women would cluster her with solicitude, and she would have to wait to approach the Third Prince.

The urge to ask his aid was sudden, but not entirely unreasonable. He could, after all, ask questions she could not, if she could secure his more-than-mocking aid. He seemed almost well-disposed toward her, as a miser might prefer a pet bird in a cage to his human kin.

It was easier to receive a kindness from a stranger who could not, after all, harm you.

Yala settled her sleeves, rose, and glided across the sitting room. Hansei Liyue greeted her with quiet but unconcealed relief, and Su Junha hurried to pour the tea, smoky and overpowering to cut the summer drought-dust creeping into every corner and force the body's humors to cool in reaction. Yala would have chosen something else for tea with Mahara; siao was much stronger than her princess preferred in the early afternoon.

For once, the Third Prince behaved admirably, inquiring with much interest into what Lady Hansei was reading. That turned the conversation into a woodland stream instead of a halting wax-drip from a guttering candle; nothing pleased dreamy Liyue better than speaking of imaginary figures caught in paper and characters.

The prince listened to her statements upon Zhe Har's *Lament of the Water-Clock* with much patience, and his own comments were brief and to the point but not dismissive, or even surprised that a young lady would be attempting such an intricate verse-work.

Yala was left free to exchange pleasantries and sewing plans with Su Junha. The primrose cotton and silk Lady Junha wore was a reworking from one of the deep ceduan chests in the attic, and Mahara had chosen it herself due to the quality of its cloth and the generosity of its cut, which could be easily altered to fit.

Junha did not smile when first presented with it, well-aired and neatly folded. Instead, her chin had trembled for a moment, and even Gonwa Eulin had studied her own embroidered cuff for a few breaths, allowing her fellow lady-in-waiting time to compose her features.

There had not been much to finish, even with Yala's needle wandering griefstruck. Mahara and Liyue had already done most of the work.

After tea, the girls settled to put their sewing to rights, Hansei Liyue sneaking longing glances at the corner of a flatbook peering over the edge of her basket. Yala retreated through the partition-blinds to the porch, though air above the dry-garden's stones rippled with heat. As she'd hoped, Garan Takshin followed, studying the vista with his chin slightly down and the suggestion of a scowl returning to his face like an old friend.

"Well?" he inquired, before she had even reached the railing. "Is it what you feared?"

It was almost what Bai would have asked, except he would have reached for a fan instead of simply crossing his arms upon his chest and directing a glare at some quite innocuous, thorn-spiked succulents.

"It is from a Khir merchant seeking patronage." A ridiculous urge to offer the letter for inspection made her palms slightly damp. There was no more certain way to make him suspect something amiss, and while she wished for his aid, she did *not* think it prudent to draw attention to a message that might, after all, simply be one of Dao's infrequent, subtle pranks, sent before he could have any idea what had transpired. "I worried for nothing."

"Still. You are in pale cloth." The scar along his cheek vanished into his hair, a grass-snake seeking escape, and the twist of his lip showed what he thought of such an impertinence from a mere merchant. "You thought it from your father. Do you wish to return home, and must politely decline when Takyeo asks as much?"

His directness was the relief of a tepid bath in this terrible heat. "I cannot imagine how such a journey could be attempted, in the present circumstances," Yala admitted. Misting sweat, gathering along her neck and in the hollows under her arms and behind her knees, would bring no relaxation. "Which leaves me in a somewhat delicate position."

"*Dangerous* is the word, little lure, but have no fear." His profile was startling; even with ill temper drawing his eyebrows in and turning his mouth down there was an intimation of handsomeness. Shan's severe dark tunics suited him, but she wondered what he might look like in more princely garb.

Have no fear, he counseled. Easy enough for a prince to say, but there seemed nothing in Zhaon but suffocating sweat and creeping dread. "I have already been sent to a prison cell once, Third Prince." And, her tone suggested, she had no desire to repeat the experience.

Unless it would somehow uncover who had paid for a princess's death. Was it cowardice to hope such a move would not be necessary? She was marshaling her forces for a different war than men performed; if she was still at court when the end of her mourning came she could begin to sift gossip and carefully, subtly set Junha and Liyue to gathering more—very delicately, of course, as delicately as if she were performing some foiling of intrigue in Khir's Great Keep, shielding Mahara from ill-luck and envy.

Takshin's scowl deepened a fraction, and his fingers tensed upon his upper arms. The greenstone ring, its characters sharp-carved, gleamed wetly. "And were you harmed by such a visit?"

"No." All in all, for visiting the palace dungeons, she had

returned remarkably unscathed. Yala decided to address him much as she might Baiyan, and chose unembroidered truth. "You suffered for it, though."

Garan Takshin continued studying the garden. It was upon those very stepping-stones she had used her *yue* in earnest for the first time upon a hot spring night, holding a murderous man at bay.

Zakkar Kai had killed that first assassin. This place had sought to murder both Yala and her princess from the very beginning.

"My princess rides the Great Fields," she continued. The obstruction had returned to her throat, a hot rock to match polished stones reflecting the sun's terrible, all-seeing eye. "I would know who sent her thither, Third Prince Garan Takshin. I would know who paid for the deed, too."

He did not move, not even to eye her sidelong. Was he offended by the mere request? "And what would you do with such knowledge?"

What I must. "I know I have little right to ask, Third Prince. I owe you much for your—"

"No." *Now* he moved, a single restless step with his head just barely restrained from tossing, a wary, restive horse longing for the gallop as a nobleman might long for the hunt. "I told you there is no debt, Yala. Do not provoke me."

She decided that were he truly provoked she might well pray to Heaven for protection, for all the good it would do. Still, he had not denied her outright. "Will you be happy if I ask for your help instead?"

"Exquisitely." But he turned his head slightly and his mouth drew down upon both sides, his scarred lip twitching once. "Ask away." When she hesitated, he glanced at her, but not sharply. "Well, what will you have of me?"

"What I have already asked." It had seemed much simpler when the idea of this conversation entered her head a few moments ago. She had expected him to require some manner of circumlocution, giving her more time to hint and prepare. "I wish to learn who paid for the deed, and who performed it." They honored their ancestors in his adoptive Shan as well as here and in Khir; perhaps that consideration would move him. "I must, Third Prince. For her shade." *And my own honor.*

"Do you think we have not been looking?" Now he half-turned upon one leather-slippered heel, not watching the garden but facing her, and a girl who had not grown up with Komori Baiyan's rough affection might have quailed under that dark glare. "Do you think *I* would let such an event pass unremarked?" *Especially*, his tone said clearly, *when my own brother was the likely target?*

The Crown Prince had leaned upon his cane at Mahara's pyre, his round face set and terrible—and resembling, very much, the portraits of his father Yala had seen far more often than Zhaon's living Emperor. There was deep strength in Garan Takyeo, for all his kindness.

"I may ask questions or hear news you may not. And you, likewise." Yala folded her sweating hands inside her sleeves. How did they *breathe*, here? She longed for a bath; perhaps she would stay in the water until she grew fins, as in one of Murong Cao's delightful but terrifying little fables. "I would not be kept ignorant of news *you* come across."

"Ah." He nodded as if she had said something profound. His scars were not flushed; he did not seem to notice the oven-breath from the garden. "You drive a hard bargain, little lure."

"I am no merchant," she bristled in return, and his smile was unexpectedly soft.

"There she is," he murmured, and his arms relaxed. He dropped his hands to his sides. "There is my Lady Spyling."

Were the heat less enervating, she might almost think him attempting to fret her, another echo of Bai. She almost envied Takshin's sisters; a damoi was a poking, prodding burden but also intercession and a measure of protection for any noble girl. "I am no spy, Third Prince."

"Do you trust me?" Now Takshin regarded her intently, and his tone lacked all levity or mocking. He sounded younger, without the weary cynic's drawl and faint echo of Shan's dialect.

Did she? The crack of a whip, a bloody furrow sliced through skin, and her *yue* wrapped solicitously in silk, laid in her palms again. Yala's throat had dried like the powdery sands of the Third Rainless Hell in some of Hanjei the Monk's more fevered visions, but she was able to produce a single syllable. "Yes."

He nodded gravely, and did he look like this more often, fewer of the court ladies might consider him terrifying. He might, in fact, find himself outright pursued. "How far?"

"As far as you will let me, Takshin." Did he mean he might solicit her for intrigue in order to uncover the culprit? A woman must not meddle with high politics in Khir; it was not seemly. Here, though, they spoke freely of such things while sewing and sipping tea, and Yala was beginning to think it was the only way to achieve any progress. "You hate to be complimented; I should think you despise trust as well."

"When it is a trap, yes." He leaned forward slightly without shifting his feet, a swordsman's readiness, and examined her face as if deciphering cramped characters on shoddy paper in an ill-lit corner. No doubt an onlooker would think them merely discussing some household matter, or perhaps the Crown Prince's health. "In Shan, a wolf must be wary. But he must also care for his own."

If it was an allusion, she had not read its source, but the meaning was clear. He meant to find those who had attacked the brother he, despite all his prickliness, cared deeply for, and in that, his aim and Yala's were two arrows for the same target. "You sound almost as if you miss it."

"Someday I'll take you, if you like." Another slight toss of his head, shaking aside the jest and returning to the matter at hand. "They will pay, Yala. I will bring you their heads to make the ball for that horse-racing game of yours."

Now she was beginning to doubt her senses; had he been studying the history of kaibok?

He did not give her time to wonder. "And I shall tell you all I learn along the hunt, if it will make you content." He offered his arm, a carelessly polite gesture that could be retracted if she refused. "Come. You are wilting."

She did not need his aid to retrace their few steps, but she laid her fingers in the crook of his elbow. His heat was of a different order than the day's relentless steaming. Would the rain break the back of the dry drought-snake, or simply turn it into a cloudveil bath? "Do you promise?"

"Wolves don't promise." Garan Taksin halted, gazing down at her. "They simply bite."

"You are a prince, Garan Takshin." Yala took care to keep her pace slow, decorous. Was he warning her, or seeking to reassure in that sharp, oblique way of his? Either was likely, and once more, missing her brother was a sharp ache in her heart. "Not a wolf."

"Most scholarly lady, you are innocent indeed if you think one is very different from the other. And my answer is *yes*. Since you ask it of me, I promise I will bring you their heads."

That is not what I asked. "And tell me whatever you learn." It was, she discovered, *exactly* like wheedling a favor from Baiyan, only this was not a light mischief or a book with certain strange illustrations filched from her father's library.

No, this was a different game. He was a mercurial ally indeed, and Zakkar Kai a steady one—but Kai would be gone soon, with Zhaon's Northern Army. If war came again, the general would do his duty, and many a Khir would die.

It was a sobering thought, especially to a lone, trapped, foreign woman.

"No merchant, and yet you press me for a bargain?" Takshin's levity, edged afresh, was indistinguishable from a warning. "I said I would, Yala. That is enough."

It was not, but Yala's stomach settled and trembling certainty bloomed all through her, ink wrung from a brush in clear water. "I shall hold you to it," she murmured, and Garan Takshin, surprising everyone in the sitting room—including Yala herself—threw back his head and laughed without any bitterness.

Su Junha frankly stared, but Hansei Liyue, her thumb caught holding her place in a bound-book, beamed like a scroll illustration, softly, myopically, upon hearing that joy.

A CLEAR POND

A few restless, splattering drops fell upon thirst-groaning earth as Mrong Banh hurried along a long colonnaded walk, his scholar's robe brushed clean and the ink upon his fingers likewise scrubbed but retaining its vigor. His topknot was redone, pulled high and tight, and he winced as he raised a hand, perhaps intending to loosen it and visibly realizing mid-motion such an operation would make him late. He dropped his free hand, hugging the scrollcase to his chest like a noble boy hurrying to a tutor's studio, and a flash of saffron across a garden merely earned a distracted glance.

The orange-yellow was Second Princess Gamnae's dress, and she was accompanied by lithe, usually smiling Sixth Prince Jin, their heads close together as they conferred. It was almost enough to make Banh feel young again, seeing children he had welcomed into the world and done his best to instruct.

He had been so busy there was no prospect of children of his own unless he married with haste. A wife would disrupt his well-ordered existence; an astrologer, humble or exalted, was married to the chariots fording the riverbanks of the night sky, dancing to express the will of Heaven.

Garan Tamuron's descendants would perhaps be the only ones to offer at his tomb, and sometimes Mrong Banh thought hard upon that prospect. The hours of darkness lent themselves to much consideration of one's previous life, he found, and though others might laugh at his dishevelment and the wildness of the machines he created from thin sticks and cunningly twisted or treated rai- or pressed-paper, theoretical constructs satisfying in their wild fancy and sober attention to detail, he was not ill-content.

After all, he had been born a peasant, sold to a tavern-master during a lean apprenticeship year, and been swept up in a warlord's reunification of the Land of Five Winds. His was a lucky lot, though he sometimes, as any man so blessed, lost sight of as much.

Why, even the court eunuchs in their sober dark colors and high clicking jatajata sandals separated to allow him ingress to the Kaeje's great chambers of state, passing through the vermilion-pillared Great Hall where many were at low tables, administering stamps and seals to well-brushed scrolls meant to be sent to other ministries. *The Emperor commands, the Emperor disposes, the Emperor requests.* The machinery of rule, varied and intricate, was of a different order than an army's direct, simple rules.

The apartments of Zhaon's ruler, spare but comfortable, folded around Mrong Banh like a well-worn robe. Courtiers both noble and ministerial bustled and more eunuchs hurried, all with varying airs of distraction or nose-high disdain, but none challenged him or gave him more than a passing, indulgent glance. He was part of the very machinery, and sometimes Banh thought of a great millwheel, splashing and spinning, and himself a simple slat meant to catch the current and pass its message of power to the miller deciding what to grind.

Garan Tamuron was no longer the tall warlord, firm in the saddle with laughing dark eyes. Now he was a wizened man with a great prow of a nose and thinning hair, held fast in a bed's soft embrace like an ox trapped in a mudhole, and his gaze was a caged tiger's—dark, hot, and promising vengeance.

That gaze was very much like his third son's, or his fourth's. Or even Zakkar Kai's direct, weighing look, in fact. Banh performed his bow, clutching his scrollcase, and took stock of the royal temper.

It appeared much the same as ever. Some said a man changed

when power arrived at his doorstep, but Banh was of the opinion *that* particular millstone merely polished away courtesies and uncovered the man beneath. None were so polite as the weak, and none so merciful as the truly strong.

"Ah." The Emperor attempted a smile. His teeth were still as fine as ever; the malady had not attempted to take that fortress yet. "There he is, my tavern companion. Come, Banh. Draw up a chair, and let us hear what the heavens hold."

"This is a strange tavern, my lord." Much relieved by the heartiness of the greeting, Banh did as he was ordered. "No sohju jug, and not a dish of qur sauce to be found."

"Well, we shall do the best we can, and drink what we find." The old joke must have pleased Tamuron, for he smiled as broadly as his wasted cheeks would allow.

Banh's own grin in return felt only slightly strange. "Except the puddles, my lord; I'd rather drink falling rain than gathered. I would ask how you fare, but..." He sobered, and settled upon a plain three-legged stool at the bedside.

"You know I shall tell you, so why bother?" Tamuron's smile turned wry instead of pained, but it faded by at least half. Still, he visibly appreciated his astrologer's directness. "My eldest son refuses to see me, my second son is his mother's creature, my third will not return to Shan—there is much refusal, Banh."

"Sons grow into men, my lord." Banh settled himself more firmly upon the stool. The discomfort of balancing upon such a seat would keep him sharp. "Takyeo is grieving, it is only natural; Takshin has ever been difficult. Kurin...well, he is filial in form to you and in deed to his mother. What son could not be?" Trapped between his father's iron dish and his mother's steady trickle of dissatisfaction, Kurin no doubt did his best.

Or so Mrong Banh wished to think.

"At least Makar troubles me little. Sensheo, though—he is in the sinks of the Theater District nightly, I am told." Tamuron's tone suggested the latter, while not unprincely in moderation, was not a thing to be regularly indulged, but then again, he had more often found his joy in battle instead of in theater-flower beds. "And Jin will not stay in his mother's house but leaps the walls to search for dice-games and displays of strange weaponry."

"Makar is a scholar, Sensheo has ever been a sybarite, Jin is still young, and a longtail to boot." Banh could have recited each son's name in his sleep, as well as their qualities, princely or not. "You have an embarrassment of good luck, my lord, with heirs to guide Zhaon and provide each other strength."

"Ah, is that what it is?" The Emperor for once did not have kombin to hand, but his fingers moved, counting off invisible beads. "Sabwone is still sending those letters. She imagines herself a heroine."

Well, Sabwone had ever been a dramatic sort, prone to reading light novelists instead of more appropriate but less exciting works. "Marriage will calm her headstrong nature."

"It did not calm..." But the lord of Zhaon glanced at the portico, crowded with courtiers fanning themselves and eunuchs conferring. "Enough of that. Come, spread out your star-maps, and tell me what Heaven wills."

Banh almost winced. "The stars are uneasy, my lord." Pressed-paper did not crackle as its thinner rai-pounded counterpart, and he had drawn his charts with care. He could not sweeten the cake, though for once he longed to. "Disorder lurks in every house, and the northern horizon is making room for a newcomer." In another time, such motions would be welcome, and Banh would have attributed them to new life swelling within a princess to provide one more link in the chain of Garan.

He wished he were doing so now.

"Ah." Tamuron's glance said he guessed as much. "Come closer. Closer."

Brought to his lord's very side, Banh could smell the malady ravaging Tamuron's frame. Sweetish and faintly sharp, sweat full of acridity instead of a healthy man's faint sour edge of oil and muscle. "I know what you wish to ask," he murmured. "I cannot tell, my lord. I wish I could."

For a long moment Tamuron was silent, and Banh almost feared the peevishness of ill health and the habit of command would push him to another hasty judgment. The affair of Lady Komor's blade, not to mention the attack upon the Crown Prince ending in the murder of his foreign wife, had not merely shaken the court. It had cost Tamuron some of his beloved first son's affection—a disaster brewing for years, only seen as inevitable in retrospect.

The stars had not spoken of such a small thing; it was beneath their notice. Yet Banh sometimes wondered if they *had*, and he had not seen the warning because the ever-modest, ever-patient Crown Prince simply seemed too tame to bolt.

A dog could not rule, and while it was a blessing Takyeo was finally showing his teeth, it might be too late to avoid…certain things, certain inevitable disorders when the Emperor's malady finally took his inner posts.

Banh had known all his life that all men are mortal, but somehow, it did not seem to apply to the warlord who plucked him from tavern servitude and went on to unify the most ancient of lands, the great bountiful bowl of Zhaon. Even during numerous battles, while an astrologer listened to the chaos in the distance, trumpets and gongs passing commands along the army's lines, he had not thought Garan Tamuron would fall.

Even now it was difficult to compass a world without him.

"Is it so uncertain, then?" Tamuron settled against his square pillows and rectangular bolsters. "I have ever done as Heaven wills, why torment me in my last days?"

"Perhaps it is not a torment," Banh hurried to remark, though it was more a wistful hope than an accomplished fact. "Uncertainty does not mean defeat, my lord. The stars have always blessed you; this is perhaps only another battle."

"I hope you are right." His lord's eyelids lowered a fraction. "The northern horizon, you say?"

For a moment, Banh's throat closed and he could not say what he suspected. A newcomer among the stars, yes—and who, among all of Zhaon, had burned brightest? Who would be judged worthy to mount to Heaven itself if not Garan Tamuron? "There is great uncertainty," he hedged. "I have compared the map of the night sky to a fragment from thirty winters ago, my lord, and to other maps from fifty and seventy." He meant to add *since Heaven treads in cycles*, but then he would continue as a pedant. Instead, he contented himself with the barest of necessities. "I have found…much to provoke concern."

"So. It is not a question of *if*, it is a question of *when*." The edges of Tamuron's gaze, like those of his voice and temper, were sharpened with fever now. His body might be failing, but he would ride it to exhaustion and beyond. He did not even need a spur; what beast could be recalcitrant with such a masterful rider? Pure will kept him a-saddle and swinging his plain, heavy, priceless-ancient sword. *It looks like a poor fellow*, he had remarked upon that blade, *but so do I, sometimes.*

Banh had ever taken it as a sign that his lord knew quality, even when it came wearing a less-than-pretty face. "Tabrak will ride, my lord. But I do not think you will meet them." It was as painful a truth as he had ever uttered.

"Then I must leave Zhaon in a condition to face such a danger." Another tight, pained smile, as if Tamuron intended to put his astrologer at ease. His cheeks were mottled, both with the paleness of discomfort and the spreading of the malady. Non-infectious, the physicians agreed, for no courtier or servant had taken ill yet; the physicians also agreed it was not poison, and yet it consumed the great strength of its victim in ever-larger mouthfuls. "How shall we do so, Banh?"

"The Crown Prince has my aid." The astrologer could not help another serving of plain truth, like unpolished rai. "And he always will."

Their gazes locked; Banh hoped his lord could decipher the message. He sought to be a clear pond, one Garan Tamuron could see the bottom of.

"That is good," the Emperor murmured. "I have no fear of you, Banh. But remember to take refuge, should it become necessary."

It warmed him, that his lord would worry for the safety of a humble servant. Perhaps it was only the tightness of his topknot that made his eyes prickle, and he sought refuge in memory as old men were wont to do. "When arrows fall, who can be *careful?*"

"Wandering like a cloudfur, oblivious to the counterattack." Amazingly, Tamuron laughed, a wispy, reedy sound shaking his thinning chest and bobbing the pad in his throat meant to keep a full-grown man from choking upon life. "Had Kai not pulled you into shelter, Banh, I would be missing you now."

"I was missed *then*." Banh's own smile was unforced, and for a moment they were merely friends upon a sunny hillside, discussing politics, stars, classics, women, and whatever else a warlord would have use for or satisfaction in. "And glad of it, too."

Afterward, Banh would wonder if he did well or rightly, keeping Kai's suspicions upon the northern origins of an assassination plot to himself. The general had enjoined him to silence, to keep the field of battle clear. Suspicion was all very well, but more proof was required—and Banh had the idea that Zakkar Kai would seek to insulate his lord from what they suspected by bringing the matter first to Takyeo.

Who would be the next Emperor. And, Mrong Banh thought, *that* event would be sooner rather than later.

For Garan Tamuron had the look of an old man not quite resigned to Death, but entertaining the guest as politely as possible in the meantime.

GROWING UP

The gardens were always lovely in summer, but her breath was short. "He threw a sauce-dish. And a plate. Broke them both." Gamnae pulled at Jin's arm, sweat prickling under her dress as they passed into shade. "Do not *hurry* so, Jin. My feet hurt."

"You are such a baby." But at least her youngest brother slowed so she was not run to death like one of Lady Surimaki's enchanted villains. Garan Jin, lean in his practice half-armor and usually smiling, was sober and thoughtful now; he scratched delicately at the scalp near his leather topknot-cage with its gilded wooden pin. "What did your mother do?"

"I don't know." She was more than content to have it so, but still, perhaps she should have tried to find out from the servants. "Kurin told me to leave; I left."

"And?" Jin's eyebrows raised. He halted, looking over a railing at the throbbing green of a water-garden under bright midmorning sunshine thick enough to be honey; light darted cruelly from the fountain's play.

Those glitters threatened to poke right through her head. "He wants me to be friendly." It had taken some doing to nerve herself up to this—it wasn't like telling a *secret*, Gamnae had decided. It was more in the nature of seeking counsel from a minister or an exorcist. Father was unapproachable, Takyeo had more pressing concerns, Takshin would be uninterested, Makar would tell her she was being silly, Sensheo would be cruel, and Mrong Banh was not in his tower that morn. She had nowhere else to turn. "To Lady Komor."

Jin swung from his study of the fountain and examined her for a few breaths. When he sobered and looked down his nose like that he slightly resembled Sabwone, which was disconcerting, and very *much* resembled Father, which was downright frightening. "What does he want with Lady Komor?"

"*I* don't know." She was glad he'd stopped walking, too. Her jata-jatas produced lovely sounds and were prettily lacquered, but they made her calves and her back ache. The shade was just as welcome; her dress, a pretty light babu green, was appropriate for summer but was a little too heavy for exercise. A noblewoman shouldn't caper about, in any case; Mother was very clear upon that point. Gamnae's heart would not cease cantering, not quite a full gallop but refusing to return to a steady trot. "He wants me to visit her and be friendly."

Their gazes met, her youngest brother's expression matched her own, and Gamnae felt a certain relief. Jin didn't suggest that per-haps Kurin was just being kind, as Makar or Sensheo might if they could be induced to listen at all to their baby sister's reports.

But Jin, nearer her age and the recipient of Kurin's brotherly ire more than once, knew better. And that was why Gamnae had put herself upon his way to the drillyard this morning, interrupting his second weapons-practice of the day with the duty to take a turn in the gardens with his youngest sister.

"I like Lady Komor," Jin finally said, slowly, resting his hands upon the carved stone railing. His hurai was a green gleam upon his left first finger, its characters familiar as her own name, and his knuckles bore a slight scrape, well on its way to healing. "She is brave. And kind."

Well, the Khir lady had been kind enough to Gamnae, but that was hardly the point. When Kurin took an interest in someone of lesser rank it was because he had his own plans, and those were not likely to be comfortable for his target—or for any tool he used in the meantime. "So do I. But, Jin..."

"You can be a good friend to her, Gamnae." Jin nodded sharply, as if he had just made up his mind. "And protect her from Kurin."

"Protect her?" Gamnae all but squeaked. Who would protect *Gamnae*, if she went against Kurin? Certainly none of her brothers except perhaps Takyeo, and he had much larger matters to worry over. A hot breeze fluttered her skirt, touched her sweating nape. "I thought you would help me find a reason not to visit, Jin."

"He'll send someone else," Jin pointed out. He even rubbed thoughtfully at his chin, in imitation of Mrong Banh's more serious moments. A faint shadow of prickling showed upon his upper lip. "Better if he thinks you're stupid, right? Because you're not."

It was nice to have someone think so, Gamnae decided. She knew she was not a scholar like Makar, or even middling at her studies like Sabwone, who still managed to terrify her tutors into complimenting her efforts. Sabwone also filched novels she shouldn't be reading, and sometimes gave Gamnae hair-raising little details about what they contained, but there would be no more of that now. "I don't know," she hedged. "Between him and Mother... perhaps they will forget all about me if they are busy with each other."

"Those two always have time to give someone else misery," he muttered, then caught himself. "Sorry, Gamnae."

Of course she should take offense at such an estimation of her mother and eldest brother. And yet, she could not. "It's true," she said heavily. "Should I go to Takshin?" She devoutly hoped he would speak against the idea, but it had to be broached. "He is in the Jonwa too."

Jin considered the notion. He was very fine at his studies when they interested him. Weapons and martial play were better, he said; brushes, to Garan Jin, were the most boring thing imaginable. "Maybe we should go to him together? He will want to know."

Since he was not being impossible, she decided to risk a little more truth. She wished she'd brought a sunbell; the walk back to the Kaeje would be very warm. "He frightens me now."

"He's our *brother*. And if Kurin plans mischief, Taktak is best for foiling him." Jin's eyebrows drew together like two ferocious caterpillars, an expression he was much given to when thinking deeply. "Takyeo's busy, Kai is too, Banh can't do anything. At least Sabwone's gone, so she won't make it *worse*."

If she was a bad sister for not defending Kurin, he was a bad brother for saying such a thing about Sabi. All the same, he wasn't *wrong*, and Gamnae's head hurt a little, untangling the implications. Perhaps both of them were bad, but not overly so. "Kurin wants something," she said, slowly. "I do not know what yet."

"You do not *have* to do what Kurin wants." Jin said it as if it were easy to contemplate doing otherwise.

She didn't like stating the obvious, but in this case it was perhaps permissible. "He will make me pay if I don't." Gamnae stared unseeing at the garden. It was pretty, but also familiar, and the beauty meant to soothe and uncomplicate troubled minds was not working as intended this morning.

"Who will pay if you do?" Jin asked, softly, as if to himself. "Lady Komor?"

It was on the tip of her tongue to say *she's only a lady-in-waiting, and a foreigner too*. But Lady Komor had been kind to her as well. Not only that, but her princess—round pretty Mahara, not a barbarian at *all* despite Mother's disdain—was dead. How awful was it to travel so far and be so alone, losing the only claim one had to a place in the palace? In a novel, Lady Komor would either pine away or meet some less fetching end.

But this was not a novel. Whatever Kurin wanted from the Khir lady could not be pleasant.

And it wasn't *fair*. Gamnae would have liked to visit Lady Komor anyway. At least in Takyeo's house nobody called her a dolt, and the oppressive, stifling tension in Mother's part of the Kaeje didn't close its bony fingers around her liver and turn her into a clumsy, stumbling fool. "Yes," she said, decisively, and her hand tightened upon Jin's arm as a distant babu water-clock *thik-thock*ed, its heartbeat brought to them on the back of a fitful summer breeze redolent of perfumed dust and green, growing things. "Of course. You're right."

"Am I?" Jin blinked, visibly startled out of his own musings. At least he gave her time to think, instead of prodding like an impatient tutor. "I think that's the first time you've ever said so."

She longed to pinch him. "Well, you *are* an idiot, otherwise. But you're right now."

He gave her a gentle poke in the ribs, and that was new, too. Before, he wouldn't have been nearly so careful. "*Ai*, Naenae, I should pull your hair. What will you do?"

"I will write to Lady Komor asking when she will receive me," Gamnae decided. The shade over them, full of leaf-flutter, was like warm liquid. "And you, will you speak to Takshin for me?"

"You're really scared of him?" Jin sounded half as if he did not credit the notion, and half as if he understood.

"I suppose not. Not really." Anyone who wasn't a true fool, Gamnae thought, would hold Taktak in some caution. Kurin was mean, but Takshin was *unpredictable*. Still, he did not taunt or torment; she remembered very little of him before he'd been sent to Shan and come back scarred and full of that tense quiet that filled Gamnae's head with painful scraping, but what she could remember of her third-eldest brother wasn't cruelty. "You'll see him before I will, that's all. If you're going to the drillyard."

"Mh. Good point." Jin nodded thoughtfully, another surprise. His shoulders had broadened lately, and some of his favorite tunics were a little short in the sleeves. This one exposed more of his wrists than was quite proper, but the wear upon its nap said it was well-loved, just the thing for cushioning the drill-armor that creaked as he shifted his weight slightly. Not as if he was eager to be gone, for once; he was proving much more patient than she had dared hope when she set out from the Kaeje.

"Are we growing up?" Gamnae looked across the garden's shimmer, and a strange thing had happened to her voice. It didn't seem to work quite in its usual manner. "I don't think I like it, if we are."

"Well, soon you'll have a husband and be out of the Kaeje." Jin said it lightly, but a frown still creased his brow. "Maybe you'll go to Khir and Lady Komor will go with you."

"Maybe." Gamnae wasn't certain she liked the idea of marriage, but on the other hand, what else did grown-up princesses *do*? And the prospect of leaving the Kaeje was terrifying and compelling in equal measure. Imagining a morning without Mother's moods or Kurin's edged mockery was almost beyond Gamnae's power. "Maybe I'll make Father send you too."

"What, to marry a Khir princess? They don't have any more, the Crown Princess was the only one." His frown deepened and his fingers moved once, a habitual tapping motion as if he felt a hilt under them. It was strangely reminiscent of Zakkar Kai, whom he had spent more than one summer attempting to imitate. "I'm glad I'm the youngest. Nobody cares enough to try to assassinate me."

"Or me," she agreed, loyally. Her hands were sweating freely now, tucked properly in her sleeves, and she longed for crushed fruit or tepid tea. "Have I made you late, Jin?"

He shook his head, but his thoughtful scowl didn't disappear. All in all, Garan Jin was unwonted serious this morning. "Nobody would dare assassinate you anyway. I'd kill anyone who tried."

Now *that* was new, and though comforting, also somewhat frightening. "You would?"

"I'm your brother, Gamnae." He moved as if to poke her again but halted, another new thing. He had never been so restrained before. "Of course I would. Now, go write to Lady Komor, and have some tea. You look pale."

He was bossy, but she went on tiptoe to kiss his cheek anyway. "My favorite brother."

He had just begun shaving though he did not really need it, and his skin had lost some of its child-softness. "That's something else you've never said before."

"Because you've been a terrible longtail." She accepted his arm, shaking out her other sleeve to make it fall properly. "Come, walk me to the garden entrance."

"I'll be even *later*." But he did not take his arm away. "Gamnae?"

Her chin dropped slightly, her jatajatas making their grown-up sound, slow taps marking off smaller moments than a water-clock's. "Hm?"

"I'm glad you told me." His profile smoothed, and he guided her around a small depression in the paving. "Be careful, and once you find out what Kurin wants, tell me."

It was an unexpected relief. At least she was not alone in this small matter. "So we can decide what to do?"

"Yes." His frown returned, and now he looked very much like Father indeed. "Kai says it's all tactics, in life. Everything."

Well, of course Kai was a general, he would see war everywhere. "He's being sent North. At least, that's the gossip."

"I know." Jin sounded dismayed at the prospect. "I don't like him being sent away."

"Neither do I." Especially with Takyeo so grieving. Her skirts made a soft subtle music, and she was glad she wasn't a boy. Being sent away to fight sounded unappetizing at best. "Do you think Ah-Yeo will retreat to the countryside?"

"I think he'd like to." Jin gave her a sidelong glance, but without his usual mischief. Sober and thoughtful, he looked much older now, and instead of Father or Sabi, he resembled his mother. The First Concubine had never been ill-tempered with Gamnae, but her languid reserve—and the First Queen's disdain—precluded any closeness. Not like Second Concubine Kanbina, who always had time for a visiting child. "But no, Gamnae. I don't think he'll manage it. He always does what Father wants."

"Is Father going to die?" she whispered, surprised at her own daring.

"I..." He glanced at her again, probably meaning to give her a brusque, polite *of course not*, and his shoulders stiffened. His own reply was equally soft. "Mother thinks so."

Gamnae's own mother thought so too, and her barely concealed satisfaction at the prospect turned Gamnae's middle into a mass of snakes. Her liver was perhaps too small, Gamnae reflected. Courage was a man's game, and she had none of it. "I hate growing up."

"Me too, Naenae." He patted her hand, and they had reached the garden's trellised entrance. "At least we're doing it together?"

"At least that," she agreed. It should not have made her feel quite so relieved, but it did, and she sent him to the drillyard with yet another kiss upon his shaven cheek before turning her steps reluctantly for the Kaeje to write a letter or two.

SOME LITTLE
BLOODSHED

The man was not quite a caged beast trapped in Zhaon's largest city, but it was close. This tavern in the foreigners' quarter was reasonably clean, and any post came promptly, for the owner—a round-bellied mud-eyed Khir commoner whose gaze bespoke some quasi-noble ancestor—was punctilious and proper in paying the accepted bribes to city officials, including those responsible for the circulation of paper through the country's veins.

The merchant he was impersonating had two rooms—an antechamber and a sleeping-closet, though he used them but infrequently in order to confuse his trail—and it was the first time in his life he was largely at his own pleasure. He was finding he rather liked it. Even the prospect of earning his silver by a display of bladesmanship or in other, darker ways had much to recommend it, accompanied as it was by a sense of complete and utter freedom. It was perhaps how a hawk felt when the jesses fell free and a never truly tame creature bolted for the wide blue sky.

Four days after he had brushed his careful, tempting missive the reply had finally come upon respectable pressed-paper with a subtle scent caught in its weave. Ceduan and jaelo, tiptoeing into a sensitive noble nose as he held it close and inhaled. Even breaking the seal felt like an intimacy, after so long.

Her reply was courteous but not overly so. The lady, being of delicate nerves, was unable to leave her home. She did, however, feel her responsibility to fellow countrymen keenly, and consequently invited the merchant to appear with a small sample of his wares. The date and time were delineated carefully, the location something called the Artisan's Home inside the palace complex of Zhaon-An. Enclosed was a pass for a merchant, two servants, and a bundle of goods to enter the palace complex; the seal was large, crimson, and quite official-looking, the snow-pard device of the Crown Prince. Of course, she would still be part of that household. When mourning was done, perhaps some other accommodation would be made for a lone foreign lady-in-waiting.

Or perhaps he could work a trick like a wandering exorcist making paper flowers vanish, singing a chant to chase away ill fortune—and spiriting away a lady upon horseback, vanishing into the night.

Would she be grateful for such an event? Would she be pleased to see him?

He scanned the letter again. It was cautious, giving nothing away—did she think him still trapped in Khir, put to plow like a plodding ox? He had been as explicit as he dared. No doubt she would be prepared to meet a merchant with icy formality, to receive a sealed communication from a childhood friend, and perhaps to entrust a letter in return.

Perhaps she would even attempt a plea for rescue, if he was lucky.

Imagining her face when she recognized him was a thorny pleasure. He reread the letter, looked over the pass again, and smiled, lifting the paper to his nose once more. Outside, the streets of Zhaon-An heaved and muttered under a pall of golden summer dust.

Ceduan. Jaelo. Though it was unlikely, he thought he detected a faint thread of *her*, too—in the close confines of a theater box, with her brother present and watchful, at least he could still inhale the scent of a black-haired girl with wide pale eyes and a fluttering fan, a slight smile playing about her lips as a farce rollicked across the stage between acts of a suitably impressive or tragic play.

Her letters, at least the ones arriving before he left their shared homeland, had been careful too, and he could glimpse between beautiful brushwork strokes a vivid restless bird trapped in a cage of honor, duty, obligation. How many missives were accumulating since she could not know he had left Khir as well? It was like a song, letters flying wide while their intended recipient was close enough to touch.

To see that hunter take wing, to possibly lure her to his wrist, was more than Ashani Daoyan ever thought he would achieve. Perhaps it was his honorless mother's passion burning in his veins, or perhaps it was simply that she had never treated him as a bastard *or* a prince, simply as a nobleman's son.

The world was wider than either of them had ever expected. He did not think, after enduring this vile place, she would demur at leaving. And of course, if she accepted his help...

It was too sweet a prospect to be contemplated for more than a few moments. More pressing was the need to make sure he did not bring other admirers to his lady's door, for he suspected he was being hunted.

It was no change. He had been hunted all his life.

Ashani Daoyan smiled for the first time in days, and rested his boots upon the table. Servants would not be hard to find, and a bundle of small tempting trinkets either. Money was of little consequence at the moment, and in the future, well. He could write, he had a sword; many a fortune was built upon much less.

The world was wide and Yala would come with him. She *had* to. The world was not as they told close-confined noble girls, and he could see why—who wanted an unchaste wife? And after all, who did she have to rely upon here in Zhaon? He even had a silver signet ring she would recognize, and her father's semi-blessing. What Khir nobleman would not want an acknowledged son of the Great Rider for his daughter? Daoyan could very easily lead her to believe whatever was necessary, a small matter they would laugh about later as they used to poke restrained fun at a particularly sentimental play.

By the time Yala thought to protest, she would already be his. His intentions were honorable indeed; the old way of taking a war-bride upon your saddle was still a legal marriage and she had been raised to be a dutiful, honorable wife. He would not repeat his royal father's mistake.

What Ashani Daoyan took, he would *keep*.

Smiling, the letter held just under his sharp nose, the once-bastard son of an honorless noblewoman, now the legitimized Crown Prince of Khir, lowered his eyelids and contemplated his eventual freedom as well as the one piece to make it complete. Yes, everything was going well.

And all it had cost was some little bloodshed.

DISPOSED OF

The Emperor has spoken." Kai clasped his hands behind his back, looking out onto a Jonwa dry-garden. It was early yet; the sun had not lifted above the Palace's eastron walls. He was not in leather armor nor in a prince's house-robe; instead, he wore the padded tunic and trousers that would sit under the half-armor and provide their own faint protection from edges and bolts. His feet were under-wrapped for polite cleanliness instead of slippered; they would be thrust into boots when he left the Jonwa. "There is some urgency; I cannot delay another day."

Yala's hands clasped each other tightly as well, inside her wide, pale sleeves. She had rather thought he would accompany her to the table for tea, but instead he stood at the partition to deliver ill news. Perhaps he thought she would be in an ill temper, hearing of his departure.

"Of course," she murmured, glad to be on her own slippered feet to face such tidings and doubly glad she had arisen early, unwilling to lie abed and sweat. "There are rumors everywhere." Some of them even had the stamp of truth, but untangling which was a task she must lay aside at the moment.

"The bridges over the two rivers have been taken, the ford at Khua-An is watched, and Khir patrols ride the borderlands. There have been a few clashes already. No crossing of the border may be expected in the near future, I am sure." He gazed steadily at the succulents, deep-set eyes glittering. "I cannot tell what you would wish to know, Yala, so I often refrain from saying much at all. I think it unlikely you will be sent home."

"Yes." It was hardly a surprise...and yet, her heart was uneasy within its cage of ribs. She studied his profile, her tight-clenched fingers aching. "When exactly do you leave?"

"Between now and midday. I shall be within a few days' courier-ride of Zhaon-An; letters will reach me swiftly."

"I shall write." Her throat was dry, her fingers numb. After tossing and turning upon her maiden's bed across the hall from her princess's sealed, empty room, sweating the night through, she was even more exhausted than when she had dismissed Anh and laid herself under a sheet. Some among the Zhaon slept naked, but no Khir girl would ever dream of such a thing, no matter the heat.

Still, Yala had thought somewhat longingly upon the prospect, and more than once.

"I depend upon you to do so." His knuckles were white, and his shoulders swelled as if he pulled against himself, an ox straining at the yoke. "Perhaps I should go to the Emperor now, Yala? You have not heard from your father, of course, but...do you think him likely to deny you some safety?"

What safety can there be, for me? It was an unpleasant thought indeed. "I am under the Crown Prince's protection." It was a diplomatic answer, even if her throat bore an obstruction while giving it. "I will be safe as a folded robe in a cabinet, and you will not be forced to worry for me while you perform your duties."

"I would ask your feelings, to carry something with me." His chin dropped as he glared at the garden, and for once, Zakkar Kai wore a frown instead of the usual set expression of faint amusement that was its own armor. "You must think of yourself, too, Yala. I am not so bad, am I?"

"You may carry my assurance like a feather upon your helm, Zakkar Kai. Were I free to choose, you would already have my entirely plain assent." There, it was said. Perhaps too boldly; she had not meant to sound so sharp. "I regret I cannot give more at this moment."

What Khir noblewoman could say more when her father had not spoken? And yet she longed to tell him more. *You are honorable, you are kind, and I long to rest against you*—perhaps a novel's bold heroine could say such a thing, but she could not.

He half-turned from the dry-garden and regarded her, and his expression now held such patent shock Yala almost lifted her sleeve to hide a smile. It was not meet to be grinning in mourning, especially before her daily visit to the white tombs.

Anh alone would accompany her upon that duty now.

"Well?" she added. "I rather think you should say *something* to that, at least."

"I am afraid to." He leaned toward her, his toes planted but the rest of him like a babu stem under heavy wind. "For then you will tell me I am mistaken or have misheard, and I will be embarrassed as well as caught out."

It did not seem possible that he would fear such a thing. A small, still easing crept into Yala's chest, loosening her liver and her pounding heart at once. "Caught out?"

"I have tried not to appear overly enamored of you, Lady Komor." His admission, paired with a shadow of a wry smile and a slightly tilted head, interfered even more with her treacherous heart's rhythm.

"And I of you. And we have succeeded roundly; I thought us natural enemies, besides." A Khir woman and Zhaon's Head General; and now she worried what her father would say. Would he understand necessity, or think her a traitor? The question of just how to delicately hint at the news that she had been offered for and would accept if given permission was one she had rarely thought upon. "My last letters have received no answer," she remarked, turning her gaze again to the garden so she was not tempted to gawk at a man who had grown almost-beautiful. "Perhaps the border will reopen, since events are moving so quickly."

"Some merchants are still crossing." Zakkar Kai stayed as he was, though the floor creaked slightly as his weight shifted a fraction. "I will do all I can."

She suspected he would, indeed. Small comfort that Khir had been defeated by a man who, were he born in her country's stony embrace, would make any father proud—even her own. Komori Dasho would indeed have liked him, Yala thought.

Thinking of Kai meeting her father was amusing, and it distracted her from other, darker imaginings. Her father was not *elderly*, of course, but he was older, and had no son to rely upon or daughter to fuss over his comforts now. It would not occur to him to take his ease or shift some of the burden of being clan-head onto a junior branch, and his reply to her gentle remonstrances or hints to take another wife had ever been silence. Spring had been coming but winter had not relaxed its grasp completely when Yala left home, and the shifting of seasons brought illness and upset to every household.

She smoothed the insides of her sleeves, pale raw silk nubby against her fingertips. And now her wrists had relaxed, and her shoulders were not quite so tense. "I am grateful for your aid, Head General of Zhaon."

"Will you address me by title when we are married?" Amusement colored his tone, and she suspected his dark eyes were dancing.

"If you like." Her cheeks were rather warm, but there was a breath of moving air from the garden. Dawn meant the bellows of the sky were readying for their work, and the inhale was almost pleasant compared to what she knew afternoon would bring. "But I thought to ask you something else and I must soon, since you are not accompanying me this morning."

"I can." He shifted again, regarding the garden as she did. Perhaps it was easier to speak if they were not staring at each other's faces. "If it would please you, my lady."

"To be asked, or to accompany me?" Oh, it was soothing to speak to one you knew would take your words in the best possible way, and doubly soothing to feel as if she was not quite so...

Well, not quite so *alone*.

"Both, as it pleases you."

She could not halt her smile. The heat of him at her side, at a distance not quite formal, was much different than the day's breathless gasping as well. Much softer, and yet unsteady, as if it would shift within her and cut with little warning. "You are quite accommodating today."

"It must be your influence." What would it be like, to hear this warmth in a man's voice daily and to know it belonged to you alone?

"Zakkar Kai." Yala turned her back to the garden, her skirt swaying, and took the decisive step closer to him. Once they had stood like this, not so long ago, each facing a different direction. Then, she had been watching a garden pond and he the path, as if he expected reinforcements. "I would know who killed my princess."

He did not move. "If I knew, you would as well. If the assassin has any sense at all, he has collected his ingots and left for a more congenial climate."

Her shoulder, in silk, brushed his, in plain padded cotton. "I would also know who paid for the deed." Yala, committed to her course, plunged ahead. "That is the standard practice, is it not? Someone pays, and someone in the palace dies."

Kai was silent for a long moment. When he spoke, it was lightly but quietly, a man only half in jest. "Or someone pays, and someone in the palace is briefly inconvenienced."

Yala's hands pulled against each other again. Her finger-bones were likely to snap if she kept squeezing so, and the prospect filled her not with alarm but with a dry, unsteady feeling. She felt, indeed, like the strange powder flame-flowers were made of, that volatile grain that blossomed with fire. "Please do not mock me."

"When I know—and have addressed the matter—you will know as well." No trace of levity marred Zakkar Kai's tone, now. "You may put the entire affair from your mind, Yala."

If it were possible to do so, would she? The suggestion might almost be insulting, if she did not know he meant merely to ease her. "I may need allies, in order to uncover the truth." Yala decided to press a little further. "When I rejoin court life, I may make quiet inquiries, and therefore—"

"No."

Yala studied the small sitting room. There was the table she had been at, tea cooling and mirrorlight bright, when the news arrived of Mahara's...misfortune. It was a lovely, restrained, noble room; all the same, she longed to see it aflame, or perhaps merely broken. A man could take up his sword in an excess of sudden grief and do what he wished; she had only her *yue*, hidden until extremity.

"Do not, please. Do not even *think* upon asking such questions. It is too dangerous," Kai said. "I would have you kept safe."

Safe? Or trammeled in a hutch, like fattened long-ears? She had been kept close-confined all her life, like any noble Khir girl. Perhaps she was infected with a Zhaon woman's forward ways, for now the tight wrapping rankled. "Very well," she murmured.

His own sharp exhale was not quite a word, and she suspected it might contain a phrase too pungent for a noblewoman's ears, pulled back at the last moment to die in his throat. "It is not that I doubt your ability," he said, finally. "It is that I fear for you, left here without friends. You may rely upon Takyeo, of course, and I have spoken to Takshin."

Oh, thank Heaven he did not doubt her *ability*. It was, at least, some small comfort. "Have you, now?" She was being disposed of, much as her father and Bai would have discussed possible alliances. It might even have soothed her, if she had not...

If she had not changed. The difference had crept upon her unawares, like a well-wrapped thief slipping through an unsecured window while a household slept.

"He agrees you must be kept from trouble, of course; his methods of doing so might cause more than they soothe. He is not subtle, our Taktak." The hilt of Zakkar Kai's sword, its dragon-mouth open and snarling, regarded her sidelong. The creature did not look so fearsome now; instead, it seemed to yawn with sleepy goodwill.

"I had rather thought to ask you to moderate him, since he will not listen to me."

He has already agreed to help me. It would not be advisable to say as much, though, and no matter how like her beloved brother Garan Takshin seemed, he was not truly her damoi. Action and misdirection were called for, as in any hunt—or during those times she moved to save Mahara from inconvenience, or to achieve some mischief with Bai's indirect aid.

In any case, Zakkar Kai could not yet quite forbid her to do aught, for she had not been dressed in crimson and carried in a palanquin to his door.

Yet it irked her somewhat. *The men have discussed*, Kai's tone said, *and it is decided.* Had she heard her father or Bai use such a tone, Yala might well have bowed her head under the weight of custom, childhood training, and a certain measure of relief.

Yet she was leagues from Hai Komori's dark walls and high hall, leagues from the high mountains and the ancestral strictures held in common by every person around her. She had traveled into the heart of Zhaon, and her *yue* had tasted blood defending her princess—and she had failed. The stain of said failure blemished her *and* her greenmetal blade, passed from mother to daughter since the First Dynasty.

I am Komor. This is my pride.

Despite any promise, the Third Prince might or might not tell her the result of any investigation as he saw fit. And Zakkar Kai, while he might offer for a foreign, friendless lady-in-waiting even after her princess was dead, was still Zhaon, and a man.

Neither would give her beloved princess the justice her shade would crave. Yala had appointed herself Mahara's protector, and that was not a promise to be laid aside when faced with mere difficulty.

It was not a duty to be laid aside at *all*.

She did not speak, so he continued. "My adoptive-mother will take you into her household should Takyeo be forced to relinquish you for any reason. You may trust her, and Mrong Banh."

Kai's padded left shoulder held a fine tassel to be drawn through the leather cup of half-armor as a security, moving softly upon the warming breeze. Even the breath of dawn was a kiln-blast, here. "You are not without some safety, but please, Yala, do *not* take yourself into any danger."

"I will do my best," she said, again quiet and soft. It was the exact tone to be used when propitiating uncaring, unbending authority, and she stole a glance to see if her feint had been noticed.

"That does not help." He did not look at her, studying the garden as if looking for an enemy to outwit upon its map. "Now you are the only Khir in the Palace. No embassy has come, though one was promised once the Crown Princess's bride-seclusion was done."

That was news, and upon a point she had wondered some little about. A Khir nobleman in the palace could be appealed to, perhaps, if she was very careful. It would likely be a hidebound elder, though, and Yala forced to accommodate him as well as everyone else.

No, she was a solitary piece of grit within the shell of Zhaon. She had hoped, with Mahara, to be two small pearls lost in a glittering backwater.

But even a single grain of sand could turn underfoot; even the sages said as much. Perhaps all her small pranks and indiscretions at home had merely been training for this, as practicing with a blunted, weighted piece of wood prepared one for the *yue*'s sharp kisses.

"More than that, though..." Kai shifted uneasily, a restless hawk mantling upon a perch. "There are certain suspicions, ones I would not burden you with until I have more than an uneasy feeling. Will you trust me enough to make no move for the present?"

All trace of male command had fled. Instead, he eyed her sidelong, and his tone was one soldier to another, frank and somewhat rough. Or at least, so Yala might imagine words between soldiers, having little experience outside some no doubt sanitized passages in the Hundreds and other classics.

"Certainly." When he spoke thus, she could understand why

other men might follow him. And, truth be told, if he had put the matter to her in such a way to begin with, she might have agreed with good grace and that small, sneaking relief. "For the present," she added, lest there be doubt or recrimination later.

"Good." He nodded sharply, and the gongs for the dawn watch began their brassy, ringing clamor upon the palace walls. All intimation of coolness had fled the breeze; Zhaon's day had begun once more. "Now I would ask you something, Komor Yala."

Was he about to exact a price for his offer, or for her inaction? It did not seem like him, but Yala braced herself nonetheless. "Then ask."

"What is customary, in Khir, when a woman sends a soldier into battle?"

"Customary?" *And do you expect battle?* Her skin roughened and her knees softened. It was the same strange, atavistic feeling when Bai bid her goodbye before Three Rivers, his helm under his arm and his clear grey gaze locked with hers.

I must go, Yala. Keep your yue *close and think of me often.*

And oh, but her heart now hurt. The dowager aunties of her childhood had succumbed to illness and old age, and she had heard of misadventure claiming lives among other noble families, attended pyres when necessary to show Hai Komori's respect. But Bai, and now Mahara...that was different, and the prospect of Zakkar Kai torn from the world, leaving only a frayed hole in the cloth of daily life, called forth a strange panicked feeling well behind her liver.

If this continued, all her internal organs might well change places.

He still did not look at her, but a high flush had risen along his cheekbones. "A sweetheart may send a Zhaon soldier away with a kiss, but Khir is no doubt different."

Oh. "Very." Yala's cheeks were afire as well, a scorch to match the rising sun. "A hairpin is...traditional. I may send Anh for—"

"No, stay." He freed his hands, shaking them loose, but did not touch her. They fell to his sides, empty but tense, and strangely, the refusal to reach for her was more telling than if he had. "Please. We have little enough time left."

"In that case…" Her fingertips found what they sought, and she drew forth the plain, heavy fan from her left sleeve. "I carried this from Khir."

"A well-traveled fellow; I shall show him the sights." He accepted the gift with cupped palms and a bow.

"Zhe Har." It was strange, to smile and yet feel a piercing high inside her left ribs. "You rather favor the Archer, my lord general."

"A fine compliment." He held the fan somewhat awkwardly, and if he thought its plainness less than his due, he did not show it.

Keep him here, Yala. They did indeed have little time left. "Do you expect battle, Zakkar Kai?"

"A general must." He acknowledged the obvious with a slight shrug. "You have your *yue*?" His Zhaon accent turned the word into a half-swallowed syllable instead of the crisp sound of cloven air.

"My honor is safe." What would it be like, to have a man—*this* man—keep it? Once married, with her own household…it was the summit of a noble girl's desires, to make a good match. To not shame her family, despite the accident of birth that left her less than a son.

"Good." His face changed slightly, distance like cruelty settling in his expression. It was armor, just as the stiffened leather he would soon be buckled into. "Takyeo would counsel you to tell people you have laid it aside. He might even command you to do so in fact. But, Yala…keep it sharp, keep it close, and do *not* hesitate."

"Of course." At least now he was encouraging her to do something she would in any case. The Crown Prince was kind and deserved much obedience as well as aid, but she had no intention of laying her honor aside.

Not in that particular way, at least. The temptation to perhaps…

There was a susurration in the hall. Anh appeared with a bow, and waited just out of earshot. Their interview was at an end, and Yala suppressed a quite uncharacteristic flare of irritation.

He did not turn, but Kai must have sensed it. "You will write?"

"Daily."

"Weekly." He ducked his head slightly, eyebrows drawing together again as if the garden displeased him—or as if leaving her did. "I do not wish to be known as the man who does not reply."

"Weekly, then, unless something of great import happens." Yala half-turned to face his shoulder and strove for a light tone, to put him at what ease she could. "Gossip, weather, a torn glove. Emergencies of that nature."

His tight, pained smile did not change. Now he moved, facing and regarding her somberly, leaning forward by increments. His nose approached hers; he studied her eyes, her forehead, her mouth. "I do not wish to leave you, Yala."

"I do not wish you to go, Kai." Anyone who passed the sitting-room door would see them in deep conversation. Only the most obtuse would not guess at Kai's intentions.

Perhaps her own were likewise visible. Silence returned, a fragile rai-paper lantern-shade holding them in its heart. Yala ached to move. Perhaps he did too, but there were voices in the hallway; Anh's avid gaze and the paleness of Yala's own mourning-dress kept her nailed in place, a longing statue.

"If you have need, send for me." His pained smile didn't ease. "I will answer, no matter what." Then, he leaned swiftly the rest of the way and planted his lips upon her forehead.

Yala froze. The warmth pouring through her held no relation to Zhaon's choking summer. Instead, it was a fire upon a spring day after a hard winter, when one's cloak or quilted jacket could be laid aside without shivering and one's fingers ceased their cold-aching.

Zakkar Kai stepped away, and he did not look back. Anh had to hop hurriedly aside as he passed through the door like a scorch-heavy wind during the season of mountain fires, smoke creeping from timber-clothed mountainsides. Yala stood rooted, her cheeks burning no less than her brow.

Of course a Khir noblewoman did not give tokens, even to a betrothed. A hairpin was a sister's gift.

In the Hundreds, and in the books that were definitely *not* suitable for young noblewomen, lovers exchanged fans. And she had given him Baiyan's.

Perhaps she was no true daughter of Komor. And yet, she did not feel she had done anything... incorrect.

Far from, in fact. Very far from.

"My lady," Anh whispered, hurrying across the sitting room. Her braids bounced, and her eyes gleamed, dancing with restrained merriment. "My lady, you are blushing."

Indeed I am. Yala stood, stiff and unbending, for as long as she could, careful lest the whirling inside her break free.

She did not wish to lose the feeling. It was the second time Zakkar Kai had kissed her as a brother might, and she wondered why this time she felt it all through her, top to toe.

SMALL PLEASURES

Daebo Nijera had not endured years of neglect after failed wedding negotiations without learning a few lessons. Chief among them was the ability to remain cheerful, pleasant, and so pounded-rai bland even the most fiery temper could not gain purchase upon her slopes. "We will reach the Shan border by noon," she repeated. "You are most fortunate; your husband has come to greet you."

The tent was supposed to be as luxurious as any room in Zhaon's palace, but its fabric walls moved under a strong, steady breeze pouring from rich, fertile bowl-lands shimmering beneath the haze of beginning summer. Shan had its own fields and farms, and was affluent with trade from Anwei besides, but Nijera had not yet seen either southron land. A glimmer of river in the distance was the border, approaching in tiny steps like a staggering foot-wrapped Ch'han princess.

This far south, small pierced towers began to rise in every village and town, some gleaming-white with strange chalky alkaline wash and others a hard glitter of polished stone. Some even had crimson caps, usually where one of Garan Tamuron's battles had been won or an attested miracle of heavenly intercession had occurred.

Nijera had her doubts about the latter, but the south of Zhaon was also the belt of great monasteries raised to Heaven's nobles or the Awakened One, where shaven-headed monks chanted their prophylactic syllables in robes of saffron, dun, or blue; of course a Heaven invoked more frequently might well be moved to more activity, like a bubbling yeast-sponge.

It was enough to make even a poor relative break off an alloy sliver or two to toss into a begging bowl, accumulating merit through generosity. Nijera made certain the poor were fed at each stop, the largesse expected from a princess dispensed in amounts carefully calculated to overwhelm the local notables with imperial generosity. Once over the border, the Shan delegation would take over that duty, and she was heartily glad of the impending relief.

First, however, the princess must be made ready, and only a fool would think Garan Sabwone likely to cooperate without a bright bauble hung before her, like Ghu Haijung's ox.

The princess in her peach silk morning-robe, her round, beautiful, sharp-featured face set in a most disagreeable scowl, stared at her breakfast as if there were insects breeding in the polished rai. "So," she said, softly. "There really is no escape."

Nijera's teeth ached, and her jaw. The ache spread down her neck most days; surely it was unladylike for her to clench her chewing-bones so tightly. She simply could not seem to stop lately, even to eat properly, and her dresses were looser than they had been at home. "Do you fear marriage so much, then? It is natural for a maiden to feel some trepidation, but—"

"I do not need your empty little platitudes." The princess's hair was dressed high, two ivory hairpins thrust into its morning nest; her mother was a celebrated beauty.

It will be unpleasant, Garan Daebo-a Luswone had told Nijera, staring at a point somewhat over her poor cousin's bent head. *My daughter is willful, and has already been troublesome.*

The Second Concubine to Garan Tamuron, Emperor of Zhaon, had, Nijera suspected, politely understated matters. The child was a thoroughgoing brat.

"If you cannot tell the difference between empty platitudes and a sincere desire to ease your burdens, your married life will be difficult indeed." Nijera kept her tone steady, pouring a single amber stream of haru-ah into an exquisite Shan bonefire cup. The cup did not appear to be a wedding gift, but there was some pleasure in the girl's grimaces every time she drank from it. Apparently the princess hated everything from Shan, either because one of her own brothers had been sent as an adoptive hostage or because her intended hailed from that land.

For a moment the dark-eyed girl stared at her, as if she could not believe someone had dared to make such a mild observation. Behind screens of stretched, painted material, the scurrying of servants and bustling of ladies-in-waiting quieted, but that only meant everyone else was about their breakfast. The heat and the ceremony meant a busy day, and they were content to leave Sabwone to Nijera's attentions.

Heaven knew nobody else wished the task.

"What do you know of married life?" Sabwone made a small spitting sound of irritation. Perhaps it was considered charming in the palace, but Nijera would have been roundly slapped as a child should she have dared perform half the aggravating feats this girl achieved on a daily basis. "I know all about *you*, poor cousin. They couldn't even get a merchant to take you."

It only hurts if it is untrue. Nijera carefully set the square teapot painted with yeoyan blossoms aside. "What an ill-bred thing to say," she answered, pleasantly. "A queen will not win her husband's affection in that manner, nor the affection of the court." Let alone the common people, but that mass was fickle, and best awed into submission instead of courted.

Sabwone's mouth opened slightly, closed with a snap as her temper kindled afresh and her eyes narrowed catlike. "I am *First Princess of Zhaon*," she hissed, "and I do not need some *horsefucker*'s affection."

Where had she learned that term? Nijera could not imagine First Concubine Luswone ever speaking in such a manner. "You may think so now, indeed." She found her own breakfast appetizing for once, and was sure no poison-taster had spat into sauce, rai, or greens. Even her broth was likely to be unadulterated, though she could not swear to the princess's. She lifted the lid on said broth, took a cautious sniff. Very good, the cook had strained it twice as she'd requested.

Some few kaburei or servants were ever ungrateful, prepared to cheat their masters in protest against their Heaven-decreed position. The rest, however, were most amenable to a long-suffering lady who interceded with authority or took the brunt of a high-ranking brat's displeasure. Not in *every* instance, of course—even servants disliked those who showed no mettle.

But a kindness performed was most often an ally, or so she had always found.

The princess studied Nijera closely, those feline eyes narrowed and her robe slipping from one shoulder, showing an unacceptable slice of linen under-robe. Since she slapped away the hands of the ladies who dressed her, they did not tighten laces or seat the buttons as they should, and the heavy crushflower-patterned peach silk morning dress had developed some very unflattering wrinkles. Her hair was not dressed quite to accepted standard either, since she had snarled at the quavering kaburei who could not avoid the task of braving her presence to comb and braid.

"I don't like this." Sabwone indicated her breakfast tray with a jabbing finger, another ill-bred movement. "There is no walanir."

"Is that your favorite?" Nijera already knew as much, for the First Concubine's housekeeper had given her a list of the daughter's preferences, such as they were. "I shall see if we may acquire some in Shan." It was an easy enough task. Maybe it would even ameliorate the brat's howling.

"I don't want to go to Shan."

Who would? And yet that was where they were bound, and dragging one's feet only meant one would be bundled along in a palanquin. *That* was a lesson this girl had yet to learn, and Nijera was heartily tired of awaiting the moment when it would sink in. "What do you wish for, then? To return to Zhaon-An?"

"Yes." Sabwone's chin settled in a manner she perhaps thought was decided, but was, when viewed from outside, rather sulky.

"Ah." Nijera nodded as if she had said something profound. "Then you wish to be a flower in a brothel, or perhaps an acrobat?" Her tone was brisk but wondering, much like a village matchmaker's when faced with a family that held an undeservedly high opinion of its own worth. "Should you return, do you think your father will open his gates and let you in?"

"Of course he would. He's my father." But a slowly dawning horror had replaced Sabwone's ill temper. Far too late, in Nijera's opinion; but then again, she did not seem very *bright*, this girl.

"Well, then." Nijera took a long sip. Still hot, and spiced correctly, it was her favorite breakfast. If she was to be a maiden-auntie, she would take her small pleasures where they were to be found. "Then you have nothing to worry over, even if there is war."

Sabwone pulled at her sleeve, visibly irritated with her robe's looseness. "War?"

"Well, you are promised to the king of Shan." Nijera did not add *you ungrateful idiot*, though she was sorely tempted. "If you return to your father, after all the gifts and ceremonies... but why worry over that? You are very certain your father will welcome you, instead of casting you into the slums and sending your younger sister to Shan."

"Gamnae? But why would he..." Sabwone trailed off, viewing Nijera with unease instead of superciliousness now.

Her broth was the perfect temperature at last, so Nijera drank long and deep, the filigree sheath over her smallest left fingernail—a gift from First Concubine Luswone, in thanks for what the woman must have realized would be a truly, deeply unpleasant task—digging slightly into her right wrist. All things must be done neatly and thoroughly if one wished to escape more trouble than Heaven had already decreed before one's birth, and once the Zhaon escort turned back Sabwone would be at the mercy of the Shan.

The princess had already made that nest as foul as a ratbird's, but Nijera did not think her likely to alter her behavior much. Nijera finished and exhaled softly. "Very nice," she said. "Are you certain you are finished with breakfast, First Princess?"

"There is no walanir." But the girl's bottom lip trembled. Sometimes she seemed merely fearful instead of truly petulant, but both roads ended at the same city, as the proverb ran. "And the rai is sticky."

"Yes, travel is difficult." Somber agreement was called for, so Nijera set her empty bowl aside and contemplated her lacquered tray. There would be fruit later, and she had eaten her share of gluey rai in life. "One must keep one's strength. You will need it if you intend to steal a horse and return to Zhaon-An. Of course they will not flog you if caught, you *are* still a princess—"

"Why are you being useless?" Sabwone cried, her knee striking the table's underside with a padded thump as she made a restless movement. "The least you might do is help!"

Ah, so the girl wished to rebel, but would not do it without a servant or two. How utterly typical. "I can hardly saddle a horse for you and fight off a band of Shan lords." Nijera decided upon her greens next, and her own rai was not sticky at all. They must have scraped the princess's from the bottom of the pot. "I could perhaps change robes with you, but that will not do much good. The lords know your face."

Sabwone waved a soft hand, a short, chopping motion. She had no filigree sheath yet, and her nails were not dipped with resin as was fashionable in the palace or some very rich provinces. "You're useless, then."

"Very well." Lady Nijera applied herself to her rai, the tart-smoky sauce upon greens providing just enough savor. "If the First Princess says, it must be so."

Sabwone fumed, staring at Nijera as the older woman ate enough to blunt the edge of hunger but not to stuff. A poor cousin did well to cease chewing while she still felt a pang. When she laid aside her bowl and poured another cup of tea, the girl's temper boiled over again.

"Stop padding your nose. Get out. Go tell them I want to ride before we leave Zhaon."

Nijera set the teacup aside immediately. "I am not certain the lords will—"

"*Go!*" Sabwone shrieked, and Nijera was hard put not to smile as she left her tray and rose, performing her bows correctly as she left the princess's presence.

Just outside the cloth divider, the proud-nosed Shan nobleman Lord Suron stood, his hand raised as if to tap the flimsy lintel-post for admittance. Nijera glanced at him somewhat curiously, and he had the grace to flush.

It was even more difficult to contain a smile. "Lord Suron. I am sorry, the princess is finishing her breakfast, and is not dressed to receive visitors." It was a patent lie, and she managed an expression of pained modesty, the exact look of a lady-in-waiting caught within a dilemma.

It must have worked, for the tall, sleep-eyed Shan fellow swept her a bow much deeper than her station required. "Lady Daebo Nijera." His tone was confidential. "I shall wait for her readiness then, and make my apologies."

"Whatever can you have to apologize for, my lord?" Nijera did not affect surprise, only patient weariness. "You have treated us with every consideration."

"Ah. It is difficult to do less, for such ladies." He wore not the usual black but a very deep blue that was nonetheless too plain for a Zhaon man, and his topknot was caged in sober but highly carved scentwood. For all that, the slightly curved sword riding his back was of high quality and possibly noble lineage as well, though its scabbard was worn and its hilt wrapped with leather to veil the glimmer of metal. Such things marked a man whose ancestry was carved upon stone stele instead of painted upon goatskin, and a poor cousin must be adept at determining the difference. "But there will be no horses available to the princess before we cross the border. I shall make it clear this is my failing, Lady Daebo."

So he had heard Sabwone's ill-tempered command through the fabric, and was already moving to forestall it. How interesting.

"My lord..." Now was the moment for a frightened glance over her shoulder, so Nijera deployed it. "I could not possibly—"

"Come." He offered his arm, the very picture of quasi-barbarian solicitude. The Shan ate rai and drank tea just as the Zhaon did; it was perhaps impolite to think them completely uncivilized. Nothing could match Zhaon, but perhaps some lands could attempt to rival the oldest and first of Heaven's blessed reflections. "I shall wait outside; let me accompany you that far at least."

She could not refuse, so she assented, and each step was a small victory.

Barbarian or not, Shan was far better than home.

CREATURE NEEDS
TAMING

The site for the princess's afternoon rest had been chosen with care, not least so a high hill opposite the river with a white piercetower spire at its summit could frown a warning at Shan's luxurious, sometimes warlike northern neighbor and also look down upon the tents and picketed mounts. Zhaon's offering had crossed the great bridge over the broad glittering back of the Golyeon exactly at noon, the most auspicious time for such a passage according to custom and the resident astrologer of the closest noble house possessing such a retainer. The Zhaon honor-guard was a smudge of dust in the northern distance, probably glad to be returning to the center of their country.

The princess was fully in Shan hands now. Whether she was relieved or apprehensive remained to be seen.

A lean man upon a fine black charger drew rein halfway up the hill, surveying the riverbank camp below. The brush had been trimmed to admit such a vantage point, and ranged on either side of him were similarly fine-mounted riders, all in the dark half-armor of Shan noblemen.

Long-nosed, his hair cut into a high crest and pulled into a princely topknot caged with blackened silver, the rider stripped his gloves and rubbed between his fingers, grimacing slightly. He also shifted in the saddle, settling with the ease of one long accustomed to such a seat, and though his dark eyes were direct their fire was veiled.

He had learned long ago not to let any stray thought cross his lips, his face, or the wells of his gaze.

The tents were fabric growths along the riverbank's sward, and the largest pavilion held the rider's attention longest. Finally, he slapped his gloves against his thigh to free them of dust, or merely as a punctuation to his inner dialogue. "Well?" He did not turn his head, since—presumably—some of the present bloodriders could answer the question he was about to voice. "What's she like?"

A susurration went through the nobles. Most had accompanied their lord north from the capital at a punishing pace, and wore the dust to prove it. The others were half the delegation sent to bring his foreign bride home, and their relief at crossing the border was matched only by another unease, one he could sense.

He had been surrounded by anxiety all his life. It was nothing new.

"Spoiled." Lord Suron, his nose not any smaller for the exercise of travel but his cheeks somewhat more roughened by sun-kisses, sounded rather sour. "Though pretty enough, as Zhaon goes." The proverb held many layers of meaning, and no doubt Suron had thought long and hard before employing it.

All who remembered the Mad Queen's reign were accustomed to weighing their words carefully, and Suron had not only survived but also been the closest thing to a counselor that lady would permit. Even in her rages, she would often smile in his direction, a gem-hard gleam in her very fine dark eyes. *There is a man who knows his worth*, she oft remarked, a phrase of insult or compliment depending upon what happened afterward.

Suon Kiron nodded. He would have been more pleased to see his battle-brother, but at least he had sent those few nobles Takshin seemed to like best, with orders to drag the man back if he pined for Shan or seemed in any danger. "What does our Shin say?"

Round, oft-smiling Ku Wuoru laughed, a short bark like a red brushtail's. "He says you are a fool to marry her, and to beware her bite." Ku's merry mien had misled more than one opponent into thinking him a fool—or worse, inattentive—but he had survived Mother as well, and that spoke of either luck or a great deal of canniness.

"Ah, a creature who needs taming." Kiron's disappointment at his battle-brother's absence was somewhat eclipsed by having the other half of his wolf-pack back and ready to ride. "Excellent."

"We may arrange a glimpse of her, if you like." Lord Buwon, ever ready to placate, still did not sound as if he cherished the notion.

The girl seemed to have found not a single kind word among the bloodriders, a remarkable achievement in so short a time. "I've waited this long, I may wait a little more." A female form exited the largest tent, halting briefly to exchange words with one of the guards. The man's bow was brief but correct and respectful, though the woman was a short, plump thing in bright blue with her hair dressed high and stuffed with glittering ornament. "Who's that?"

"Daebo Nijera." Suron handled the strangeness of the Zhaon name with much facility. Kiron's mother had oft called upon him to recite poetry or scatological songs in different languages, and been amused more often than not by his inventiveness. "Head lady-in-waiting, and a more patient woman among the southerners cannot be found."

"Really." Kiron glanced sideways, noting that none of the others laughed or took the opportunity for a jest. Passing strange, indeed. The deep shade of this copse was a balm in this weather, and leaf-liquid shadows played over them all. "Is that a *compliment* for a woman, Suron? You are not usually so kind."

"Not so strange." Obju Sunjosi, lean as Kiron but significantly less easy-tempered, took up the thread—perhaps to save his fellow bloodrider some discomfort. He was a quiet man, with little use for those not of his clan or in the pack, but Takshin liked him well enough. *There is a man who will let no one insult him*, Shin had remarked more than once. "She keeps those beneath her from feeling the lash."

"Ah." Kiron nodded, his gaze sharpening. Every man present knew exactly how difficult a task that could be; the Mad Queen's displeasure fell even more randomly than rain.

He studied the distant figure of the lady-in-waiting as she paused near a group of bright-robed Zhaon ladies. They greeted her with soft enthusiasm, no few leaning into her presence as she bent over one engaged upon a bit of embroidery under the lacy shade of yeo-yan trees. A ripple of soft laughter threaded uphill, barely discernible from the breeze. The cloth pavilion housing his royal bride stood closed and secretive. "Did she send her ladies outside?" The bank's edges were shaded, but still, it was not like Zhaon women to sit upon grass when there was an enclosure to be had.

They were like cloudfur, happiest when fenced.

"They prefer it to attending her, I suppose." Suron watched the group as well, almost hungrily. "The Great Awakened knows I would."

"It is as well you do not wish to attend my wife." Kiron's laugh held an edge similar to his mother's, and a movement passed through his closest lords, those who dined at his table and rode in his hunt. "Well, she stepped over the border at the sun's height, and now she's ours." If the girl showed any sign of becoming like his mother, the wolves would have found it and taken appropriate steps while still upon Zhaon's back.

Besides, Takshin would have warned him.

"In any case, it is impossible. I could not wear a hairpin," Suron muttered, and the sally drew a growl of amusement from more than one of the pack.

It would be good, Kiron thought, to have his eldest companion settled with a wife of his own, and why else send so many ladies if Zhaon did not wish Shan husbands for them? New faces at court to tempt his men, released at last from his mother's strictness. "Did Takshin say aught else?"

"Not unless we were at dice." Wuoru, his reins fastened to the pommel, rubbed his hands together much as Kiron had, forcing blood and humors alike back into stiffened fingers. "Just that he will return when he can, and an apology for his lack of letters."

How it must have irritated Takshin to send any apology at all, and yet he had. "So. He intends to stay." At least until the so-powerful Emperor had been irritated enough for his son's pleasure. Well, Shin had warned Kiron of as much. *Do not send for me unless it is dire, brother. I have matters which need attending.* "And of his father's health?"

"Nothing unless it is uncertain, and the Crown Prince's marriage is upon steady footing." Suron did not bother to add a wish for his lord's own to follow suit, knowing it would be an unwelcome jest indeed. "The Khir girl is a beauty, and seems docile."

"Maybe I should have asked for her instead." Kiron shook his head, wishing once more that Takshin had seen fit to return, or better, not to leave at all. Some were no doubt glad that the Zhaon prince had not returned to his battle-brother's side; Shin was singularly unmoved by petty considerations and thus, a dangerous influence upon a just-crowned king. "Go, and I shall meet her in good time, then."

The half of the wolf-pack who had *not* brought the princess from Zhaon replaced their gloves and helms, wheeled their horses about, and fell into a quick jogtrot down the hill to take their brothers' places, helm-plumes floating with the motion. Summer promised to be long this year, enough time for ripening. Even this far north, the noblemen moved in formation, outriders to alert the main body should bandits appear and the rest staggered for greater flexibility of engagement.

"The *nomhya* envoy will wish to give his congratulations," Lord Suron murmured, sensing the king's thoughts had turned in that direction. Those who had brought the bride home were now relieved of the responsibility, and Kiron would have the benefit of whatever news they had been able to gather, diplomatic or otherwise. "I take it he is still in the capital."

Tabrak was the matter upon everyone's lips now. The stinking, dough-skinned barbarian menace from the west—bandits writ large, but without any of a bandit's rough charm—was assuming larger and larger proportions in fever-dreams of peril his robed ministers spent their hours sharing aloud, and Kiron did not think those dreams overwrought for once.

His mother had often spoken of the Pale Horde and its practices with great savor.

They have the right idea, my love. When they come, not even a blade of grass is left standing. She only spoke thus when in a very good mood, and usually with her fingers in child-Kiron's hair, pulled tight while he froze and tried not to grimace. Attracting her notice was just as dangerous as enduring her neglect.

He set the memory aside, an interior motion performed so constantly nowadays it had become reflexive. The Tabrak envoy kept pressing for a reply, as if he thought Kiron too stupid to know any alliance with their Horde was provisional at best. "Indeed he is, waiting for the wedding celebration. We will have to give an answer." The king of Shan attended to his own gauntlets, slowly. "And it will not be one they like to hear."

"I take it you have kept him occupied." Suron paused, and even though he had been absent, very little would escape the grasp of his head-meat. And, though cautious, the strength of his liver was unquestioned. "Is it wise to immediately deny them?"

I have had my fill of waiting. "It has been anything but *immediate*, Yonjak has been stewing the pale creature in the fleshpots nightly." The queen's demise had loosened more than one girdle, and the brothels had barely waited for the pyre to grow cold before reopening, ostensibly to celebrate their new ruler. That bothered him little; the noises made by the Pale Horde's envoy disturbed him far more. What manner of king would he be if he sent earth and water to the Tabrak, hoping they would skirt his land to fall upon his neighbors? And yet a small gesture now might give Shan time to prepare for the inevitable blow, for sometimes even submission did not stop the Horde from riding through when it suited them. "And whatever wisdom there is in refusal is greater than that of accepting. Come, I would ride before I see the creature which needs taming." The word—expressing a dangerous or well-bred animal known to have a temper—delighted him afresh, especially since Takshin would have caught the joke the first time it was produced. His battle-brother had a sharp, if well-hidden, sense of humor, much akin to Kiron's own.

Fortunately, Suron saw the humor now, and laughed. It had been a long while since Kiron heard that particular sound, and he relished it as the charger turned with alacrity, just as eager for a romp as his rider.

It was good to celebrate where you could.

WORLD, ORDERED

Hot darkness full of insect-singing enclosed the palace complex, a night upon the edge of summer's deep dry well. The crimson-tiled roofs, sharply pitched in most places, creaked and muttered as day-heat leached into air still just as scorching despite dusk's advent, and there was no sleep to be had for one bred and born in the northern mountains.

There was also nobody to witness her, so Yala, fretful and sweating, loosened the laces of her sleeping-shift. Anh was deeply asleep, sprawled upon a mat before her lady's bedroom door, and had not even moved when Yala stepped over her, a slow careful movement akin to sliding past a snoring maiden-auntie's guard in the halls of Hai Komori, silent as a tiny bronzefish in a garden cistern. Her bare feet spread, toes gripping slick wooden flooring, she edged through the Jonwa's spare, ink-dark halls, avoiding the guarded passages.

It was not so difficult, when one was accustomed to patience.

A dusty, neglected staircase rose into a little-used slice of the attic, the partition at its foot closed without a click. Slow, careful movement, the wood giving no betraying creak or moan as she moved with infinite care—just as much practice as the stretching before every *yue* session and the moments of silence after, heart thundering and ribs heaving as a cold blade rested against the frantic pulse high in her throat.

She moved silently between lumps of shrouded furniture, loosening her laces even further. The thought of stripping material free and practicing naked as in a bath-house was wonderful, liberating, and impossible.

Still, she was tempted.

There was a wide rectangle solicitously swept clear of dust; Yala had attended to that duty herself many weeks ago and regularly since, so her princess would not put her face in the grit of ages during stretching.

We must find you a husband, too, Yala. Light and laughing.

What would Mahara think of *this*? Would she call Yala honorless, or foolish, for even granting the general some hope? She had liked Zakkar Kai well enough, considering; he had proven a good friend to both princess and lady-in-waiting. It was Kai whom Mahara had thanked for Yala's safe return after the matter in the Great Market, and very prettily too.

Thank you for returning my Yala to me.

And Kai, bowing, his reply formulaic but uttered with such genuine warmth. *It is my duty, Crown Princess.*

Tonight Yala did not wish to stretch, but she did anyway. The split tree, the jewelwing's hips, the inclined plank, flowing upright and beginning the standing poses, small teeth nipping and snarling as they hid in her muscles. One courted injury without proper stretching, but Yala drew the *yue* from its sheath after only perfunctory bending and exhales.

A slim greenmetal blade, its unwrapped hilt merely a longer cross-hatched tang, the *yue* clove air with a silken whisper as she began the warming exercises. Even those did not satisfy her.

Her memory was well-trained. She stood, eyes closed, and lifted the blade, thinking of the Jonwa's great receiving hall and her princess seated next to the Crown Prince, both of them determined to do their own duty. A false eunuch had sprung from the crowd crying *For Zhaon*, his fan-case weighted and springing a sharp blade from its length. The jolt of parry, the cut in return, bending aside as a dancer, and next would come the attack from Hawk

Stance—except it had been interrupted, that battle, by a palace guard who had vanished afterward.

Those guards, in their bright armor, were supposed to be unimpeachable, and personally, wholly loyal to the Emperor himself.

Yet another golden-armored palace guard had been suborned earlier than the attack in the hall; their plan had been to kidnap Mahara in the Great Market. Yala had saved her princess from that particular indignity, and performed her duty later in the receiving hall too. That she had been taken to a prison cell afterward, leaving her princess unguarded, gave her cause for much thought.

For Zhaon, the man had cried.

Here, with dust stinging her nose and the *yue* whispering, she could think clearly—and uninterrupted as well, as she hardly ever was during the day.

The false eunuch had not expected Yala to be armed and ready. Had the guard who stabbed him from behind been part of the plot, simply retreating to try again another day? She had heard the arrowheads from the attempt upon both the Crown Prince and Mahara while riding were large, barbed, and Northern.

Ihenhua. Horse-killers.

Then there was the dreadful gleam of a shinkesai, its glitter lingering between stone and wet metal, clasped about the finger of an assassin in a Jonwa dry-garden just after the wedding. Zakkar Kai had stabbed *that* fellow while Yala was busy fending him off; the honor of the kill belonged to the general. She seemed to be a front-lure or a feint, drawing out the prey while the hunters rode it down.

An honorable position, indeed. The more danger, the greater the esteem. And it occurred to her now, as the maiden's blade whispered and her body sang with effort, that there had been so many attempts, of such different manner and nature…

Was it possible they had flowed, like some rivers, from more than one source?

She slowed. The *yue* did not forgive inattention, and there were thread-thin scars upon her thighs and upper arms to prove it. Not many—she was a good, careful student, and some of the marks upon her forearms were hawk-kisses instead, with ink rubbed into their stinging to prove she was of noble blood.

A series of flurries, her toes tapping at each impact, pulling back instead of committing to each blow. Dancing to bleed an attacker dry.

It would be so easy, after all. A moment's miscalculation, a bright jet of blood, and she could atone for her failure in the old way. It was frowned upon nowadays, of course; these were modern times. Robbing the clan of your service by honorable suicide was even, in some quarters, seen as selfish and detrimental.

Only in some, though. Not in Hai Komori's dark, ancient halls. Was that what the shades of her clan would demand of her?

The *yue* spoke, a thin thread of fire over her left knee, stinging. She would worry about the slice in her sleeping shift later. Yala bent aside and began to work in earnest, holding each pose—Mountain, Hill, Hawk, River—for a bare moment, blurring between them lightning-quick, short exhales when the blade met imaginary flesh, letting imaginary blood and other vital humors free.

The blood she had washed from Mahara's broken body was *not* imaginary. She could still feel the clots and the silken tepid water, still feel the aching in her throat as she keened, singing to speed her princess's passage and to ward off hungry spirits who would cluster a shade as it left, seeking to seduce it into thirsty and malignant lingering.

Not Mahara, though. Yala's princess would ride swift and true, free at last and braver than many a warrior.

It was blasphemous to think so, of course. They were only women, and not of much account. Still, the sacrifice in marriage had halted Zhaon's demands for more concessions from the conquered, and now, the revocation was a spark upon dry tinder. In what manner had the news reached Khir, and how much of it? *The princess was killed*, of course. *By the Zhaon*, some would add.

They expected little good of the South, especially in the borderlands.

Now Yala wished she had spent more time listening to politics,

though a woman did not intrude into male business. The men
rode to war, the women to hunt, and between them, the world was
ordered.

The world, however, did *not* seem particularly ordered now.

Well, little sister. Bai's voice, a thorny comfort. *Shall I give you
the answer?*

Her memory of him would provide nothing new. The dead did
not speak to the living, unless it was to an exorcist or to some few
exalted by the Awakened One's favor. Yala was neither nun nor
shade-cleanser.

Moving more quickly now, feinting with her left hand clasped
over the thumb-side of her right to brace the stab, twisting the
blade free of muscle-suction as she retreated, ducking the inevitable thrust or swing in reply—now she knew why *yue* practice was
constructed in its particular manner, each heavily accented point
in training only achieving its proper proportion once a battle had
been won through.

Or merely suffered.

Yala whirled upon the ball of her left foot, the *yue* a whisper-
scream through hot southron stifling. Sweat greased her limbs,
gathered in her hollows, and the nightdress was a sodden irritant.

Faster, Yala. Spinning again, fending off two-at-once, the *yue* a
needle and she the thread drawn behind its singing point.

The shadows did not bleed. They were everywhere at once,
crowding her, and a scream rose in Yala's throat, a hawk-cry as if
she rode at kaibok or to hunt.

Yala. Mahara's soft voice now, the most hurtful of all. *Stop.*

The floor gave a small, sepulchral groan; her hair swung, the
heavy braid done by Anh's quick clever fingers whipping as she
spun, the *yue* swiping at the terrible, jostling specters. Then, stillness, and the finishing of every practice, the flat of the blade against
her own throat.

It would take so little to turn it, to drag the edge through her
own flesh. She would join her princess, perhaps—not riding, for
she had not died in the battle of childbed or defending her honor.

No, she would trudge the plains, listening to the horns and hoofbeats and cries of the hunt, barred from the joy and glory, and *still* she would be left behind.

There was another matter, too.

You may not open your throat with that claw-toy of yours. Takshin at her bedside, after carrying her from Mahara's pyre. She had intended to mount its wooden hill, and stand amid the flames.

The fire could hardly pain her more than the loss of her sister, her princess, her... friend. Her *best* of friends.

Cessation of frantic motion brought a manner of clarity. Zakkar Kai had not borne her from the flames, and he had not stepped between her and a whip. It was uncharitable of Yala to think that the Third Prince would not help her exactly as he had promised, despite his sharp, prickling disdain.

Zakkar Kai wished her to be safe. But she had not married him yet, Yala decided. And her obedience—that central quality of any Khir noblewoman, that greatest of womanly virtues—was not owed directly to a prospective husband, or even—another blasphemous thought—to her father, safe leagues upon leagues away in Hai Komori.

She was dependent upon her own wits here in the palace of Zhaon, and furthermore, her obedience was wholly owed to the shade of a moon-faced, pretty girl who had sat next to Yala through endless cups of tea, hip to hip, sharing warmth. To the princess who had, with chin high and mien serene, done her duty to homeland and Great Rider, offering herself as sacrifice.

The immolation was accepted by Heaven, a princess cut free of mortal life. Was she now insubstantial but present, watching her lady-in-waiting as she often had viewed Yala's *yue* practices, with bright eyes and clasped hands?

Yala? You are my friend. My best friend.

Yala's lips parted. She almost spoke her princess's name—an act to be avoided even though the end of mourning approached. There was a letter from Garan Gamnae waiting upon Yala's bedroom table below, with pretty sentiments upon loss and an invitation, once Yala's time in unbleached silk was done, for her to accompany the second of the Emperor's daughters to the theater. Here in Zhaon princesses could do the unthinkable, and watch such things with the common crowd instead of sending their ladies to report upon staging and acting.

Mahara had never visited the theater. Now, riding with the great goddess, she never would.

Yala had, and as she squeezed her eyes shut, seeing a reflection of flame-flowers across the inside of her lids, flat metal warming as her pulse pounded against it, she decided Garan Gamnae could perhaps be half an ally. Or, if necessary, a well to be plumbed. Perhaps her mother, that hateful First Queen, wished to use Yala in some fashion.

It did not matter. Yala's wits were sharp enough to sting even a queen who sought some mischief. After all . . .

You are Komor, the dowager aunties who had trained Yala in the *yue* chorused, as they did at the end of every practice. *This is your duty.*

"I am Komor," she replied softly, and denied the urge to turn her wrist, loose her own blood and humors, and gratefully slip from confinement as she would slip from this sleeping-shift were she not Khir. "This is my pride."

For pride, then. And for Mahara.

Yala lowered her *yue*, exhaled sharply, and retraced her steps from the attic with a tranquil heart.

CAUTIOUS
MANEUVERS

The Noble District, hugging the walls of the palace complex like a child at motherskirts, also held a princely home for each of Garan Tamuron's sons. Kurin's was among the smallest, but it was exquisite and upon the most desirable, well-swept avenue sprinkled daily to damp the dust. His mother's padded, draped palace, every edge cushioned and every wall smothered to keep any chill from touching her round softness, contrasted with the more restrained preferences of her eldest son. Instead of gardens there was a central courtyard, saplings and shrubs in pots moved when the season changed, only the central stone cistern with its heavy bronzefish moving lazily in still depths staying in place. Yeoyan had been much in garden-fashion this past spring, but the saplings were gone to be planted in orchards at one of the Second Prince's country estates; tall rustling babu and lyong had taken its place, the courtyard's stones reflecting heat upward and masses of carefully tended flowers in stone boxes or between turf strips watered from the cistern each morn and evening.

The tall ruddy-robed owner of this effort barely glanced at it, indicating a small table and two lyrate chairs near a carved-stone railing on the second level mezzanine, all three of superb craftsmanship like the chessboard upon the table's wide marble surface. "I had thought you would return an excuse again, Makar."

"We all have our duties, and Father required me last week." The Fourth Prince, in his sober dark scholar's garb of much higher quality than a poor scribe could dream of, glanced at the board. Long-nosed, with winged eyebrows, he was held to be the most serious of the princes, and indeed saw little use for levity in one of his position. "A new game?"

The Second Prince dared his younger brother to object with a familiar expression, half amused, half watchful. "The old one was boring."

In other words, Kurin thought there was a chance he might not win. Makar denied a faint smile, freeing one hand from his sleeves to stroke at his chin. He could grow no beard and rather liked the lack, but was still punctiliously shaved each morning by a servant chosen for steady hands. "It took us three years to arrive at its particular configuration."

"And neither of us would move so much as a soldier afterward; this is much better." Kurin made an elegant motion, indicating the guest's chair. "Should you prefer, though, we may return the board to its former state."

"No," Makar said, thoughtfully. "You are correct. There is no turning back, not after some things."

The Second Prince still waited for his brother to be seated, a host's politeness if not quite royal protocol. "Is that conscience I hear troubling you, or old age?" The babu in the courtyard rustled its secretive song; some sages said there was wisdom to be had from attention to that noble plant's quiet play. It was like no other green thing, indeed—not a grass, not quite a tree, definitely not a shrub, and some strains of its clan grew so quickly in certain places one could almost hear the stretching of its wooden tubes on warm, still nights. It uses were many, its secrets sublime and useful at once.

In fact, it was so useful it was often taken for granted. Makar's smile, now allowed to bloom, was rather gentle. "I defer to my elder upon that question, of course."

"*Ai*, but I have not your scholarship, elder though I am." Kurin, his fulvous house-robe balanced decorously with a simple topknot-cage of carved horn, touched the chessboard with a fingertip. A hurrying in other passages was the bustle of a well-regulated household stirred into motion to provide for a noble guest; somewhere on the first level a sathron sounded, repeating certain passages as if the player was at her lessons. Perhaps a mistress, or a pet artisan—Kurin had exactly as many of either as suited his position, and availed himself with moderation.

Or so the rumors went. Makar suspected his second-eldest brother played at mistress or artisan much as he played at anything else, with consummate skill but very little real interest. Were they ten years younger, Makar could perhaps have named what Kurin was *truly* interested in. Nowadays, though...well, children were simple; princes could not afford to be.

Especially if they wished to survive.

Tea was brought by silent, slipper-soled servants, along with small cakes of pounded rai with various fillings. Makar wished it was Zakkar Kai he was playing against; the Head General's cook was superior to the Second Prince's. He dutifully complimented the cakes, though, and Kurin's favorite chu-an tea was a trifle too sweet but otherwise strong enough and served scorching to make the sweat rise and cool its drinker.

They inquired after each other's health, bemoaned the amount of losses real or fictional at the races in the Great Bowl, exchanged compliments. One could never hurry Kurin; the Second Prince always wished to lead the dance and Makar was content to let him.

For now.

Finally, Kurin set his hand to one of his chariots, and eyed Makar speculatively. "I suppose we have been polite enough."

"I suppose." Makar poured a fresh cup for his elder brother and set the fine Gurai slipware pot aside. "Is that your first move? Untraditional, and interesting."

"I have not moved yet." Kurin's tone was gentle, all things considered, and he wore the sleepy expression of a man in command of his situation, whatever it might be. "Nor have you."

Ah. So that is what we are discussing. "Of course not, I always play the West." It put him at a disadvantage in the beginning, or so his opponents thought.

"Why East and West, I wonder?" Kurin's fingernail caressed the chariot's side, precious ivory harvested so as to leave its great toothed mountain of a beast-bearer still alive. It was said those who performed the task also guarded the great quadrupeds, and that their warriors knew a secret art allowing them to strike an opponent with as much force as their sad and intelligent charges. "Why not North and South?"

"Tradition, I suppose." Makar considered the series of moves that would flow from Kurin opening the game in this manner. It was so *easy*, but he had long ago discovered not many of his fellow men possessed the ability to do so. At first he had suspected the capacity was innate in all, and only laziness or the crushing burden of daily work kept most people from developing it.

Now, however, he was not so certain.

"We are modern princes." Kurin, for once, remembered that another of Garan Tamuron's sons was a prince just as surely as he. Of course, with the First Queen whispering in his ear his entire life, he could be forgiven for thinking himself utterly unique. "Tradition should not hold us."

"It has an iron grip." Makar adopted a thoughtful tone, his gaze upon the board. It would not be difficult to win if Kurin insisted on moving his chariot first. Idly, he wondered at the chances his elder brother would do so. Calculating such things was a sure way to stave off boredom, keeping the mind sharp and engaged. "Sometimes I wonder whether it keeps much worse at bay, like a roof in winter."

"You are philosophical today." Kurin chose a soldier, and the first move of the game was, despite his play at the chariot, utterly orthodox. "It must be the weather."

"The afternoon storms have come." Makar considered the board afresh. Kurin either intended to say nothing new, or wished to lull his brother into a false sense of security. Makar's own move was orthodox as well, a cannon moving slyly forward. "Expected, and yet an inconvenience."

"So many expected things are." Kurin paused. Now would come the entire point of his invitation, the matter he truly wished to discuss—or its handmaiden, preceding a mistress into a hallway, smoothing the way and announcing one of great import. "The physicians are in agreement. Father's health is failing."

"Ill news indeed." All at once Makar was weary of double or triple meanings, of subtle games, of careful, cautious maneuvers. It was a feeling akin to impatience, and a man could lose much with a single inadvisable movement or word. Still, there was some utility in a direct approach. "What do you think will happen," he continued, keeping his fingertips upon the cannon in case a better move presented itself at the last moment, "when he ascends to Heaven?"

"Is that where you think he'll fly?" Kurin's smile didn't change, a faint curve of his balm-rubbed lips. He took the usual care with his appearance, no more, no less. Servants did not respect a shabby master, or an overly kind one. "And is that your move? I only ask because your hand seems to have forgotten its duty."

Makar would not be hurried, in this or any other game. "Do not all Emperors ascend to the Celestial Halls, especially the just? You must agree he has unified Zhaon."

"The god with the Five Winds in his keeping would agree, of course." The garden-breeze touched Kurin's hair, mouthed the board. The babu continued its observations in its own sibilant tongue, a constant rubbing counterpoint to the sathron's meandering. Practice was over and the player was amusing herself, snatches of melody shifting from one song to another. "Otherwise, why would he be so blessed? An empire—and a multiplicity of heirs."

Indeed. Makar was largely uninterested in gods beyond the lip service that must be paid to keep the uneducated from rising to trouble their betters. He was, however, curious as to Kurin's purpose in addressing the fact of Father's approaching demise, that child's nightmare. "Do you think Heaven blind to Father's faults?"

"Ah, you say the Emperor has faults?" Kurin's grin was that

of a fox with a mouse under its paw, and the gleam in his sleepy gaze sharpened. "Quickly, fetch Zan Fein, someone has uttered treason."

A jest in very bad taste, elder brother. Makar arched an eyebrow. "We cannot speak wisely to each other?" He would not say *openly*, since one rudeness did not balance another.

Not at the moment, at least.

"Of course we may, Makar, but perhaps only by accident." No doubt the Second Prince thought it a stinging reproof. "If it is wisdom you are seeking, perhaps your old tutors are still available."

It would be quite satisfying to tip his general over, let the tiny carved thing hit the board, rise, and leave without a further word. Quite theatrical, and also stupid. Kurin, like many a cat and some sawtooth fish, tended only to pursue prey that struggled or bled.

Instead, Makar made a *tch-tch* sound, like an old maiden-auntie remonstrating with a spoiled child. "You are in a terrible mood."

"No, merely thoughtful, and I did not think you so delicate as to take offense." Satisfied that he had perhaps unsettled his conversational partner, Kurin pressed a fraction further. "Is that truly your move?"

"Do not hurry me, Second Prince." Makar allowed his tone to sharpen, but only slightly.

"Ah." Kurin made a mock-repentant face, still possessed of a childlike facility for mimicry though he rarely exercised it. "Now I've truly hurt your feelings."

Unlikely, Elder Brother. But I will let you think so. "Assuming I have any." Or assuming Makar was foolish enough to allow whatever feelings he did have to become dependent upon anything his brother said.

"Just think, when Father was your age, he had already won his first battle." Finally, Kurin was moving onto the floor. It took two to dance or spar, and Makar was a willing partner—at least for a few babu-clicks of music.

"And when he was *your* age, he had lost the next two and married our First Mother." The most archaic term used by a child addressing the first wife in a household was polite, but hardly common; nowadays, a significantly shorter honorific was employed.

Kurin's smile was, for once, unfeigned. "How she would rage to hear herself referred to so."

"Would she?" First Queen Gamwone, Makar reflected, would rage no matter what. She seemed rather fond of her explosions, given the regularity with which gossip whispered she'd had a new one. "I thought she liked me."

"Only because she considers you unthreatening." It could be compliment or insult; Kurin's tone was excessively neutral. He rubbed his hurai with his thumb, a thoughtful, habitual polishing.

"And happy to be so." *You cannot know how happy, brother mine.* "I have a pleasant life; ruling Zhaon would disturb my brush practice."

Kurin sobered. He was finally ready to arrive at the point. "You think disinterest will save you?"

Makar took his fingers away, let the cannon stand. His attention sharpened and the thrill of a game finally joined in earnest ran down his back, suppressed before it could become even close to visible. "I think my brothers are too wise to consider me a threat."

"Or not wise enough, if they think you do not have plans for your own survival." Kurin adopted an attitude of profound thought, watching the board as if he suspected its dimensions would change of their own accord.

Perhaps he found it easier to speak directly if he did not meet his opponent's gaze.

"Every man wishes to survive." Each choice upon the board limited the range of possibilities, and paradoxically widened several individual probabilities within certain narrow confines. The world hung in balance between those two motions, breathing in and out, the cold and warm humors that made the physical and subtle bodies as well as everything around them. It was a great, complicated machine, and the Fourth Prince of Zhaon wondered that others could not see the interlocking parts as clearly as he seemed to. "There is no shame in such a desire."

"Exactly." Kurin exhaled heavily. "He is weak, Makar. You know as much."

Not weak as you think, nor in the way you obviously wish him to be. This particular conversation was an old acquaintance, and Makar usually turned the observation aside with a witticism or a refusal to engage. Today, however, his forehead wrinkled as he stared at the board. There was no servant within hearing; nothing but the wind and the board to witness this. "Perhaps he will step aside."

Would Kurin pretend agreement? Abdication was a dream, like Hanjei the Monk's seven veiled women before the Awakened One descended upon the sage, either driving him mad or granting him absolute clarity according to which interpreter you believed.

Many things were permitted to a prince, but neither escape nor surrender were among their number.

Kurin touched one of his own cannons, then a junior general safely behind the front lines. His nails were buffed, and very clean. "And if he does? What then? Legitimacy is fragile ice upon a winter puddle, and any noble family not satisfied with their place may apply to Takyeo for relief or raise their banners as our lord father did. Instead of one Emperor, there will be several, all jostling over Zhaon like dogs at a dead curltail. No, there is no way but the most traditional, Makar. I am surprised you do not see as much."

"Takyeo is too kind." The kindness had been obvious all his eldest brother's life, and would not change for wishing it otherwise. "But he is far from *weak*, Kurin, and he has aid. Takshin, Kai—"

"Oh, *those* two." Kurin's hurai glinted as he waved aside both the God of War's beloved general and his own mother's second son. "My brat of a little brother and a lowborn granted a prince's ring. Staunch allies, I am sure. When Takshin's pride is touched over some trifle and he returns to Shan, and Zakkar Kai is fighting Zhaon's war in the North or elsewhere, how will Takyeo rule? Even Banh is more fit for it, and *he* a tavern-boy turned astrologer."

"Mrong Banh is very learned," Makar murmured. He had suspected Kurin could be induced to speak more plainly than usual today, and the dull dissatisfaction of being proved right in such a matter threatened to bind his temples with a headache. "You are quite harsh, Kurin. Takyeo may prove ruthless with Zhaon's enemies and mild with its friends. Is not such a ruler to be desired?"

"With the Pale Horde sending envoys and Khir's princess dead within months of marrying our brother?" At least Kurin did not snort in derision, though it sounded perilously close; the question of what exactly he had to do with the latter event he listed—if anything—was not even close to answered to Makar's satisfaction. "I do not wish for a may-prove, Makar. I wish for a certainty."

And you think you are that certainty? "So do we all wish." It was depressingly obvious, Kurin was nerving himself to take the step from complaint to action, or perhaps already had. Valuable information, certainly, but not unexpected or unplanned-for. The Fourth Prince kept his gaze upon the board, almost wishing his brother had not sunk to expectation. Still, it was better than a nasty surprise when a piece upon the board rose above the anticipated. "Is there such a thing as certainty under Heaven's halls?"

"Do not philosophize further, Maki. *Listen* to me." Kurin leaned forward slightly, his fingertip tapping the board before his front lines—a god striking before an army, an omen for the small pieces if they chose to interpret it. "If Takyeo were strong enough to cause me sleepless nights, I might almost welcome the inevitable when Father dies. Instead, I sleep like a child dosed with nightwort, unless I think upon the scrolls and flatbooks written thirty winters ago after the Horde came riding, smashed the Three Small Zhaons before our father was granted a miracle by Heaven to turn them back, and vanished with their spoil. Have you ever considered that perhaps our father is not strong, it is simply his opponents who were weak? *Have* you?" Kurin scowled at inert, voiceless pieces arranged and moved at the pleasure of larger beings. "I know you have. So answer me, younger brother. When Father dies, what will you choose?"

It was almost an insult that his brother thought Makar stupid enough to make any declaration at this particular point. At the same moment, he understood the Second Prince's dilemma, perhaps better than Kurin himself did. "I have not yet considered the possibilities, since Father is still alive." It was almost a lie—he had considered much, but found it profitless to move without a few more prospects ripening. Makar leaned back in his chair. "Takshin was adopted by Shan; he may not take the throne. I am uninterested, so is Kai, Sensheo is too stupid, Jin—ah, he is beloved, but he is a child still."

"Are you so certain Kai is uninterested, my brother?" Kurin settled against his own chair-back, stroking at his well-trimmed smallbeard. His hurai gleamed again, and an observer could be forgiven for thinking he habitually arranged himself in such a way as to let it show. "Our father was a warlord, and Kai has the favor of the peasants despite the misery war brings them. They think him the God of War."

Makar could have argued that they thought him *blessed* by said god, but that was unhelpful and besides, not quite accurate. The blessing and the celestial being merged in peasant-simple minds. "You have ever disliked him." *And more so because he does not seem to care.*

Kurin's eyes narrowed; he looked rather like Sabwone when they did. "Not as much as Sensheo."

"That is true." The Fifth Prince's antipathy to Zakkar Kai was a tree rooted in childhood and nourished assiduously, near-daily, by Sensheo himself. Makar's worries lately centered upon that fact, and he wished the noxious plant could be uprooted and burned, if only to ease some of his mother's concerns. The Second Queen deserved a tranquil old age, and it was her eldest son's task to provide as much. "But, Kurin, Takyeo is young and fit. Father expects this of him, and he is ever Father's faithful servant."

"Not so faithful lately." It seemed the event pleased the Second Prince immensely. Any discord between the Crown Prince and the Emperor would be nectar to his mother, too. "Do you think he will truly retire to the countryside?"

That is the wrong question, my brother. Makar was beginning to wish he had never accepted the invitation to play a game and pass an afternoon. So far, this conversation was depressingly as foreseen. "I think he wishes to, and may even prepare his household for the eventuality."

"Do you think he will *actually* escape?" Kurin persisted.

They both knew the answer, but apparently his elder brother wished to hear it said by someone other than himself. Makar saw no reason not to oblige, mostly because he felt a certain heaviness when he contemplated the prospect of the Crown Prince's proposed retreat. "No."

"Of course not." Satisfied, Kurin tapped his cheek with his forefinger. He looked over the railing into the regimented green well of his courtyard, and whether he saw the clipped bushes and ruthlessly trimmed babu or something else entirely was an open question. "And why? Because he is too weak, Makar. We both know it."

It would do no good to let his elder brother know Makar considered him mistaken upon one or two critical points. It would change nothing, and if two roads ended at the same city, the traveler's choice between them was often more aesthetic than practical. "I know that it is my move, and you are chatting to distract me."

"Yes." Kurin, still gazing aside, picked up his teacup. "It *is* your move."

In more ways than one. Makar allowed himself a mouthful of tea as well. When he set the cup down, he had decided. "Let us say, for the sake of argument, that some accident befalls our Eldest Brother—may Heaven keep such a thing from happening," he added, a formulaic plea. "What is to keep Sensheo, Jin, and myself from fearing *you* as you now fear Takyeo?"

He had never stated the problem so baldly, but Kurin would not cease until he had gained something from this game, and it might as well be something Makar did not mind giving.

"I do not fear him," Kurin said, turning to face him again. His gaze was direct as his brother had ever seen it, direct as it had been once or twice in childhood when the second-eldest of Garan Tamuron's sons had proved to be telling an absolute truth. "That is the problem."

Indeed. For now, Kurin was restrained by Father, by custom, by the very fact that the board was not set and the players had not seated themselves.

Not all of them. Not yet.

"I fear *for* him," Makar said, slowly. "But I think it is beyond reason to expect none of us to take... certain precautions. In case he proves to be a snow-pard in truth, and not a cloudfur in a horse's skin." The cats who eked out a living in the higher mountains were canny, but they were often mistaken for dogs until a hunter threw a rock in their direction. A dog would flee, but the pard would ascertain whence the missile issued from; they possessed long memories to add to their cunning.

Not to mention claws.

"Whether we will it or not, Makar, it is victory or death once Father ascends to whatever awaits him."

"Shall we no longer be friends then, Second Prince?" Makar held his brother's gaze. "It would sadden me immensely."

"We shall be friendly to exactly the extent I do not fear your knife between my ribs." Kurin's sigh was deep, the exhalation of a man expecting a heavy burden to descend at some indefinite future moment, and, for once, he looked away first, if only to gaze across the balustrade and into the courtyard's murmuring green well again. "We are brothers, after all."

"And princes," Makar reminded him. "At least there is the comfort of honesty, between us." *If I plan a knife for between your ribs, my elder brother, you will not suspect it. Not unless you are much more intelligent than I have ever found you.*

There was no turning back, indeed. For either of them.

"Yes," Kurin murmured. "At least that. Now, will you move, or shall we admit no more play today and call a sathron-player? Or perhaps tell each other riddles?"

Makar selected another chariot, set it down upon the best intersection available. "It is your move, Kurin."

They played in deep, thoughtful silence through intensifying heat and rustling from the courtyard until the light through the open courtyard took on a heavy yellow-green storm-cast, bringing polite visiting hours to a close. Makar made his perfunctory good-byes and called for his horse. He even returned to his own quiet home before the rain began, but that was no comfort. He found himself worried, after all.

It was not like Kurin to be so... direct.

CHOICES

The Jonwa was a hive of well-regulated activity, like a good racehorse needing only the lightest of touches, heel or whip, to direct its gallop. The hand responsible for giving those flicks and teases was the housekeeper's, and Takyeo flattered himself often that he had found one of the best in all of Zhaon, never mind that she hailed from somewhat farther south.

"My lord." Lady Kue bowed in the Shan fashion as she entered the study, her dark cotton trousers whispering and her small, sober wooden hairpin glinting under mirrorlight. Her round, placid face was just as set as ever, and a few more lines had been graven at eye- and lip-corners since she had taken the responsibility for a prince's domestic comfort many winters ago. "You sent for me?"

"Lady Kue." Takyeo glanced up from the cluttered desktop. He had no more time to contemplate the *Green Book* or similar texts; the business of caring for those under his protection had waited as long as it could. Paper, brush, and inkstone crowded the wide wooden estate before him—each advance in bookkeeping was supposed to ease the flood of pressed rai fibers or heavier pounded rag-paper, but the amount seemed constant no matter what inventiveness was applied to the problem. "How long?"

"Ten days, my lord. Unless you wish to hurry, in which case five." She clearly wished to add more, but instead clasped her hands and gazed at some indeterminate point upon the desk.

He longed to be gone *today*, but that was not possible. So, as he always did, he merely turned to the next problem requiring a solution. "And Steward Keh?"

"Quite formal since you spoke to him, my lord."

"If he continues so, good." It was almost laughable, how clumsily Keh had attempted to lay his suit before the lady. Takyeo could have told him he would meet with little success, but a prince did not mock his servants *or* interfere with their heart-strings unless invited—or unless said strings looked fair to trip the entire household. "Though it would ease me to see you settled with a fine husband, Lady Kue."

"It would ease me too, my lord. But the Steward, though a man with much to recommend him, would never suit." Now there was the hint of a grave smile lingering on her finely modeled lips. She was not prone to merriment, his housekeeper; she was even quieter than Lady Yala. "I am a solitary cat, as they say in Shan."

"Very well." Perhaps in Shan some chose not to marry the manumit, either. He should ask Takshin. Keh's restrained and quite unrequited passion for his master's housekeeper could simply have been a function of what the man thought was fitting in two servants of such an august personage; the steward had some rather strange ideas in that regard. "Though if you change your mind, I should like to know. Seven days, then. Is it possible?"

"Very." She hesitated, her gleaming hair braided in loops over her ears, a nest of similarly rope-twisted braids dressed much lower than a Zhaon woman's, held at the base of the neck. "My lord..."

"If this is another plea to remain in this palace, Lady Kue, I might believe you acquiring a taste for luxury." His own smile felt like a mask. Of course a good and faithful servant spoke to save their august master from a deep mistake; such speech was not to be penalized even if said master had equally good but unspoken reasons for committing what might be judged an error. "Nuah-An is now a small town, it's true, but there are several estates nearby. We will not become provincial."

"Yes, my lord." She bowed again, warned that she was reaching the edge of her master's patience. "Steward Keh is engaging porters and dray animals; we shall be ready. I must ask after Lady Su, Lady Gonwa Eulin, Lady Hansei—"

The noble girls would do better to scatter like dropped rai, but Takyeo could not say as much. "Lady Yala will know."

Lady Kue's expression brightened somewhat, an entirely welcome event. "Will she be accompanying us?"

"Unless she chooses a different household." Takyeo glanced at the list of figures upon the paper before him and the book underneath. Moving was expensive, especially when you didn't wish to leave a single scrap of rai-paper for enemies to gloat over. "I will not leave even a single kaburei behind, lady housekeeper."

"Yes, my lord." Her approval, while quite unnecessary, was still pleasant. "Lady Komor should arrive soon; I spoke to her of your summons."

"Invitation, Lady Kue." One did not *summon* a silk-wearing woman, after all, even if she was foreign. "Thank you. Ah, one last thing. The matter of my wife's clothing."

"Yes?"

"Distribute the dresses among her ladies, save the wedding robe and headdress. Those will go into the household shrine."

"Yes, my lord." At least she did not call him *Crown Prince*. He was beginning to hate those syllables with an intensity quite unnatural to his usual even temper.

She took her leave, and he bent to his work again. A nobleman had to spend well, but profligacy was discouraged. Finding the way between while every gaze in Zhaon rested and every tongue loosened its hinges upon you as well was nerve-wracking.

Sometimes he wondered if his father felt that weight, but it was ridiculous. Even now Garan Tamuron was the unquestioned master of all he surveyed, and no doubt counted the burden of gaze and gossip light—if he acknowledged it at all.

Takyeo would be measured and found wanting, of course. That he had managed to stave off the inevitable for so long was perhaps deserving of a little applause...but not much. Achieving the bare minimum was not enough.

A soft tap at the door interrupted that unpleasant meditation. "Enter," Takyeo barked, and rose to ease his wounded leg when his visitor stepped through with a soft sweet sound of dark-blue skirts.

The dress was of Khir cut, high-necked and long-sleeved. It hung a trifle loosely upon Komor Yala's frame, perhaps because grief had robbed her of any pretty roundness she might have once possessed. Her blue-black hair was dressed in its usual fashion, and the pin—a strange, imprecious stone wrapped with red silk thread and dangling a single crystalline bead—was a familiar one. The only change from the grave, agreeable woman who had traveled from Khir was the mourning-band around her left arm, a wide, thick strip of pale linen that could have done duty as a bandage, if there were any wounds about to need one.

And her clear grey eyes were very like Mahara's.

He all but winced. He had made up his mind not to think of his wife until evening. Docile while she was alive, her shade was proving otherwise.

"Crown Prince Takyeo." She bowed, much less deeply than Lady Kue. Of course, she had her pride. Though bled white by years of semi- and open warfare, Khir was nothing *but* pride; even his tractable warrior-wife had a certain tilt to her chin.

That morning his close-servant had placed a sober brown robe upon the larger clothing-stand for him, too. He wondered if Yala felt as uneasy as he did in proper garb. Mourning had its time, yes...but his heart was not yet finished with the task, and he resented pretending otherwise.

"Good morning, Lady Yala." He hoped his genuine pleasure at seeing her would show just clearly enough. "I see our servants have decided the end of mourning is upon us."

"They appear to have, yes." She folded her hands inside her sleeves, despite the morning's heat. "*But we may wear it upon our arms as long as we please.*"

"Siao Kuen." He nodded in appreciation. The rest of that passage was a retelling of a Ch'han emperor's search for an exorcist who could raise the shade of his beloved empress in order to discern if her death was truly an accident, or a minister's poison. Neat, precise, and yet oblique—he had come to expect such behavior from her. "I will not put away my armband soon."

"Nor shall I." With her hands tucked into her sleeves she was the picture of demure waiting, but he was not fooled. It was exotic, a woman carrying that slim sharp blade and yet so soft and retiring in every other way. Such a greenmetal claw was not spoken of in the treatises he had read upon Khir, and he wondered at the lack. "Lady Kue told me you wished to speak to me; I ascertain you have decided where to place me."

"You are not a hairpin, my lady. I thought to ask you which of several choices you prefer."

Her smile, somber as his housekeeper's, was nevertheless a balm. "It is not often a noblewoman has *choices*, my lord. I look forward to them."

He might have remarked that in that they were akin, but alluding to his own lack of freedom before someone even more closely confined by tradition and rectitude would be impolite at best. "Come, sit. Will you have tea?"

In short order they were both settled, Takyeo's leg itching furiously. He ignored it; the bone had been badly bruised and Kihon Jiao said the itch meant healing. "In seven days this household departs for my estate near Nuah-An to the northwest. From there, arrangements may be made to bring you to the border, though crossing may prove difficult. There are those in the Palace who would offer you shelter too; the Second Concubine has sent me a letter asking if I may do without you. It is a graceful solution, should you wish to stay here."

"Did she?" Yala lifted a cup of strong tea, inhaled the scent with a noblewoman's appreciation. Her fingertips lacked resin, and no filigree glittered upon her smallest nails, but then again, she was young and unmarried. "This is very kind of her. Forgive me, but... will it cause you less trouble to take along a foreign lady-in-waiting, or to give one such as me to the Second Concubine?"

"Trouble?" He did not have to feign perplexity. She could hardly be unaware that trouble was, as Xan Geong said, the price of living. And she could hardly have missed that a prince would suffer a larger share of unpleasantness to accompany the luxury due his station. "It would be best to return you to your father, but I cannot see *mine* taking the time to negotiate such a small matter right now. I have sent letters to the border posts and am awaiting replies; it may be that we can reach some agreement. If so, I would certainly not begrudge you a small party of servants and chaperones, and as many guards as can be found. Once you are in Khir, though...I am told women do not travel unaccompanied there, and any men I send with you may meet with a hard reception indeed."

"You are kind to take such efforts upon my account." Her eyelids lowered thoughtfully. Mahara had sat as she did, her back very straight and her gaze masked. "I must confess I feel somewhat superfluous here. I have no duties save the care of my princess's tomb; and while honorable, those are hardly onerous."

"I would dislike to lose your influence in my household. You are a scholar, Lady Komor, and have proven yourself loyal and adept." There was also the matter of that greenmetal blade. However useful such an item might be, it was still wielded by a woman, and it was unprincely to expect her to use it upon his behalf.

How best to broach that particular subject? Was there a way?

Yala inclined her head slightly, her hairpin's dangling bead accenting the motion with a graceful curving swing. "You do me much honor, Crown Prince."

"Retreating to the provinces might expose you to gossip. Staying in the Second Concubine's household might do so as well, but in a different fashion." And now, he came to the most difficult question of all. "Of course, if you have received any—"

He was interrupted by another knock at the lintel. Takshin did not wait but strode into his eldest brother's study dressed in his usual Shan black, his topknot-cage bearing some gold filigree to match the hoop in his left ear. He had not laid aside a pale mourning armband either, though, and that oblique mark of respect for his eldest brother's grieving was a comfort and irritant in equal measure. "Good morning, brother. And you, Lady Spyling."

"Takshin." Takyeo suppressed a burst of annoyance. "Good morning. I was discussing some matters with Lady Komor—"

Takshin had a dangerous glint in his dark eyes. "I must be rude; there is a matter I must bring you, Crown Prince." He glanced at Yala. "You may return in a half-mark or so, my lady. By then we shall have set the world to rights."

Yala set her teacup down and prepared to rise. Takyeo's irritation crested. "Takshin—"

"Or you may let her stay, Takyeo. It is as you like." His most maddening brother crossed to a loaded bookshelf and regarded the spines and scroll-caps with feigned interest. He was quite fond of that maneuver, employing it more and more lately.

"In any case, I must think upon the question," Komor Yala said, softly. It was a quiet, polite way of smoothing any trouble from the interruption, as was her habit. "Grant me some small time to do so, Crown Prince. I thank you for your kindness to one such as me."

That brought Takshin around, his slippered heel digging in sharply as he swung and regarded her. "What question is that?"

"Little brother," Takyeo hissed. "Have you no manners?"

"None at all," Takshin said with a smile, but his eyes had narrowed. It was an expression that usually meant trouble upon the horizon, Taktak ready to fling himself into a battle that could be avoided with a fractional turning-aside. Of course, such a turning had never been in his nature. "Has my Eldest Brother asked you a question, Lady Yala?"

"Once or twice," was her equable reply. "I have even answered a few in conversation, as one is wont to do. Crown Prince." She bowed in Takyeo's direction as etiquette demanded and was gone in an instant, the sound of her skirts merging with the morning-hurry in the hall.

Takyeo's jaw loosened, but he composed himself as Takshin watched the doorway as if she might suddenly reappear, a line between his eyebrows.

It was extremely pleasant to see someone else get the last word on Taktak. Heaven knew few others had managed the feat.

"Well." His younger brother swung back to face him, and Takyeo was glad not to be found grinning like a fool. "What question have you asked her?"

"The Second Concubine has offered to take Lady Komor into her household." The Crown Prince could not tell if he hoped the lady would accept that invitation or his own. "Though I suspect the lady in question might wish to retreat to the provinces if a graceful way can be found to avoid gossip."

"Then I arrived in time." Takshin drew himself up and clasped his hands behind his back. "Look no further for a solution, Ah-Yeo. I'm going to marry her."

GRANDFATHER

In Zhaon-An's Great Market, the wealth of the world gathered for display and sale. Spices, wines, pets and small livestock—larger was held outside the city in the Blood Pens—as well as fabric, medicines, fireflowers and sparksticks for celebration, ornaments, vegetables, flowers, rai both polished and unpolished, other produce, various weapons and implements, crushed fruit, cooking oils, and body oils in great clay jars; all these and more sat ready and waiting in small booths or larger shops, the wide paved trapezoid broken into a thousand crazy-twisting alleys jammed with fabric awnings and clamoring sell-chants. Smoke, perfume, dung, hot metal, the finishing of fabrics, sweat, stalls selling snacks for those exhausted by the business of selling or buying, tiny temporary tea-houses clinking cups and shouting orders to kettlemasters—commerce was a mad, smelly effort, Zhaon's digestion busily turning effort and raw materials into luxury or sheer survival.

For all its glitter and throb, the Yaol turned its head from certain profitable items. For those, one must visit the Yuin, the Left Market—just as crowded, just as noisy, but with an edge to the bustle.

There were apothecaries and weapon dealers in the Great Market, but those in the Yuin specialized in different, darker applications of the medical, medicinal, or martial arts. It was also the place for cloth acquired cheaply by whatever means necessary, embargoed items, certain varieties of fallen flowers—both male and female—plying their wares, and impresarios. Not the theatrical type; those stayed in the Theater District with their fellows and clients. The word, with its associated character of a baton striking a curve that could be head, back, or buttocks depending upon the brushstroke, also meant one who was conversant with the walkers of the Shadowed Path, capable of arranging all manner of disaster while keeping a patron's hands clean. Thieves of every kind also gathered in the Yuin, even those who subtracted life from the well-guarded or otherwise inconvenient.

However, the man in the rich dark robe and high, shadowy hood despite the morning heat was not here to engage one of those masters of the possible death. His quarry was different and his step was wary; the sword in his left hand was expensive though an attempt had been made to wrap its rich hilt with leather. More, the soft authority of his step spoke of weapons training, and so he moved unaccosted though the gangs of child pickpockets kept careful watch upon such a plump bird step-hopping into the Yuin's crooked, changeful alleys.

The pickpockets, however, scattered as soon as the rich man passed beneath a hanging sign that simply read *Ton Ren Tan Guh*, each character carved in the simplest manner possible. Below, the smaller characters denoting an apothecary's place of business were likewise stripped of all ornamentation.

A quiet, fragrant dimness enfolded the visitor, who did not politely push his hood back or remove his gloves.

A wizened, nut-brown figure perched upon a high stool behind a long, glossy wooden counter. Behind him, a wall of small shelves and drawers, some with faded paper slips bearing characters that might or might not have a bearing upon the contents, loomed high and threatening, ready to crash over the fellow.

"Good fortune greet you," the fellow chirped. "A guest, so early in the morning! It is good of you to visit, young man. What may Grandfather do for you?"

The visitor took his time, peering from the hood's shadow.

Finally, he pushed the hood's border back a fraction. Mirrorlight fell softly upon the shelves and drawers; not a speck of dust was to be seen.

Of course, the Old One of the Yuin would have no shortage of apprentices to fetch, carry, and scrub, but none of them were in evidence at the moment. Baskets and hutches crowded the shop, stuffed to the brim with the effluvia of an apothecary's trade—khonsu root and various other plant material; puff puen; dried snake tails; horns, hooves, and livers of strange beasts from hedgerow or foreign plain, dried, smoked, or powdered; strong fragrant tea-leaves mixed with healthful essences; oils and unguents; zhu powder mixed with various substances for the care of the skin; and much more.

"Greetings, grandfather." The visitor's tone was respectful enough, but a slight stress on one or two of the sharper syllables shouted his quality. "I have come for what I left."

"Ah. Yes." The elder did not move, but his eyelids lowered slightly. Beneath them, filmy grey orbs moved with no relation to each other or to his attention. "My memory is not what it used to be, but your scent is familiar, yes?"

The visitor said nothing, his attention focusing upon a certain shadowy patch near the end of the counter.

"That is merely my grandson," the elder said hastily. "Get up, you waste! Show some respect."

Even though the visitor was watching, he still did not see the transition from shadow to man. One moment there was nothing but a tenebrous corner, the next a young man in close-fitting dark trousers and an indifferently hemmed Shan longshirt was there, examining his fingernails in the uncertain light. "My apologies, Grandfather." His voice, not yet broken despite his size, was clear and sweet. "I was asleep."

"Lying little waste," the old man said, affectionately. "Go fetch breakfast from Madame Yulema, and be quick about it."

The barefoot young man, his toes misshapen with callus and hard, horn-colored nails, bowed his way past the august visitor and plunged into the river of the Yuin outside.

"*Ai*, children. A joy and a burden at once." The Old One did not shift upon his high three-legged stool. "I am forgetful, oh gracious patron. What was it you left here?"

"A dray bar." An archaic term for a bent metal rod used to lever or pry, with its first syllable pronounced in the old way. "An old item, but very effective."

"Indeed, indeed. Hm. Well. Difficult, very difficult...I have no memory..."

The nobleman's gloved hand flicked, and a small bag landed heavily upon the well-waxed, painfully clean counter.

The Old One exhaled, a short sound of polite wonder. "Ah, now I remember. Unfortunately, I lent it to a neighbor. But perhaps the noble lord will return in three days? By then it will be ready."

"Certainly." A gloved finger twitched, an indicator of irritation or merely an itch. "If you cannot find it, another of similar size and shape will do."

"Of course, of course!" The Grandfather nodded, a passable impression of a doddering sage. "Does the noble lord have any other...preferences?"

"Only that it must be well made. And...artistic."

"Yes, have no fear." Grandfather did not take offense at the intimation that his shop might sell something of low quality. Or if he did, it did not show. "Of course, it is difficult to tell one dray bar from another."

"That is the point of such an item." Deep in shadow, the nobleman's nose twitched. "I wish a completely anonymous effect."

"Then you shall have one." Such an item was not to be had cheaply, of course. Grandfather's fingers, stained by tincture, paste, resin, plant-juice, and other items, rested neatly upon the countertop. "Bring another such bag next time, my lord."

The nobleman could not protest at additional expense, and in any case probably did not wish to. "If the item performs, you shall have a third bag as well."

"Grandfather is not greedy."

"Consider it a gift from a loving grandson." The nobleman did not bow, but he did incline his head slightly, a mark of high honor for such a plebeian merchant though possibly wasted upon one whose eyes had been blasted by illness or Heaven's ire. He wrapped his cloak more securely, and left the same way he had entered.

For a long while afterward the old man sat upon his stool. Other customers, not quite so august but all heavily muffled, visited, and each time they requested a small item no apothecary would have in stock. Others, bareheaded but nervous, asked for actual medicines, and one of the Old One's many apprentices would appear to grind, mix, weigh, and take payment.

Much later, as the weary, heatstruck morning trudged into a breathless, oppressive afternoon, the barefoot young man in the Shan longshirt returned, somewhat rumpled and bearing a package of waxed rai-paper. A toothsome smell rose from its cargo, and the apprentice slipped behind the counter to fold himself at the stool's feet, opening the hawker's lunch—small chunks of anonymous vegetables, even more anonymous meat, and leftover fried rai—with a small, happy sound.

"Well?" the Old One inquired, prepared to be indulgent after a morning of good business.

"Went to the Palace," the apprentice said, as his dexterous fingers plunged and lifted to his lips. He did not, however, speak with his mouth full.

Grandfather held that to be a sign of poor taste and even worse intelligence.

"Well, yes. But which one of that brood is coming to our door, Yu?" Grandfather's patience was not eternal, and one of his own feet, bare as his little birds', tapped the young man's slim shoulder.

"Couldn't keep up. But it ent the Crown Prince, and ent the General, and ent that Shan longtail."

"Useless," Grandfather muttered. "Go fetch *me* something to nibble, idiot. All morning I work while you play."

The apprentice, used to this and grateful the Old One was not very irritated, scrambled to obey. Of course he had caught a glimpse of the prince's face, but telling the younger ones apart was difficult, especially from below. *Palace* meant *trouble*, and even though the Yuin was largely left to its own devices the heavy hand of the Emperor could descend to crush the flies at any moment.

It was only a momentary disruption to profit, but still, every insect knew enough to dodge a horse's tail, as the proverb went.

So it was best to keep his mouth tightly closed, the apprentice decided. Of course Grandfather would know more than *him* who was visiting, and as long as an apprentice pleaded ignorance, he would have a happier—not to mention much much longer—life.

A Blameless Life

I t is very simple," Takshin repeated, settling his hurai upon his first left finger as if he suspected it would slip free. "Father will not agree; he already dislikes her and will deny me simply to do so. So I will have it in your hand now, to make certain."

"Cunning of you, Taktak." Takyeo exhaled sharply. "If Father refuses, you have me; if *I* refuse—"

"Why would you refuse me?" Takshin cocked his dark head, his gaze settling somewhere over Takyeo's head. "You wish her safely placed; can you think of a better cabinet to guard a doll within?"

Takyeo could not help but admire his little brother's certainty, having precious little of it himself. At least Takshin was never indecisive. Still, there were one or two points to the plan his brother might not have considered yet. "And what if *she* refuses?"

"How can she?" Takshin waved aside any possible impediment from that quarter with an airy gesture. "Consider: She is alone in a foreign land; if war comes, it may be years before she returns—if she does indeed wish to flee northward. I do not think such a thing likely now that she has seen Zhaon, do you?" His smile was of a variety Takyeo had not seen upon his brother since childhood. It was Takshin's particular expression when he held what he considered a winning, quite unanswerable argument.

Takyeo considered the notion, glancing at his cluttered desk and all the business waiting patiently for his return. Of course Lady

Yala seemed to...moderate...some of Takshin's sharper moods. She was noble, too, though foreign; there could be no insulting intimation that Taktak had married lowly. And certainly few courtiers would dare involve her in much intrigue if the scarred, reticent, but generally feared Third Prince was her husband.

Yet Takshin was not gentle, and Yala, for all her short, sharp blade and likewise wit, seemed nothing but. How would the First Queen take the news of this match? Such a mother-in-law might not be to Lady Yala's liking at all, especially since she would no doubt take her daughterly duties as seriously as all others.

And what of Khir's response to the news that another Zhaon prince had married another Khir lady, so soon after her princess was shot like a roundbird?

Takyeo never wanted to think of that morning ride again, the leaf-shadows, the hoofbeats, his wife's laughter...then, the shattering, crunching, world-ending pain. Yet the world kept thrusting the event at him like a jabbing opponent on the drillyard. He was failing dismally at keeping Mahara from his head-meat's halls.

Perhaps her shade *did* linger despite all care taken to avoid it. It was unwise to wish for such a haunting, and yet Takyeo could not help it. Foreign though she was and wed to a stranger besides, his wife had been a relief—at least one creature who had seemed to like him as he was, instead of wishing him of a different mettle.

The problem before him, however, was not a shade but a brother and a court lady. "Have you gained her consent?" The Crown Prince did not offer his rude brother tea, but then again it seemed Takshin did not want it. He was in a mood that only sohju would answer, if Takyeo was any judge. How long ago had this solution to Lady Yala's predicament arrived at Takshin's liver? Was it a passing idea, held fast only because Taktak suspected resistance and liked to swim against a current, or something more?

"Do you think her likely to refuse me?" Two ruddy crushflowers had bloomed upon the Third Prince's cheeks, that was all. "Because I am ugly, or because I am Zhaon?"

"Neither, Taktak." Smoothing his brother's temper was a

dismally familiar chore. *And why would you care? You call yourself ugly with the regularity of a water-clock.* "I simply wish to know. Have you declared yourself to the lady? Will she wish to write to her father for agreement? Such things are important."

"That is the beauty of it," Takshin said, turning and stalking for the desk like a cat intent upon a sunny basking-spot. "With the border so uncertain, how would a missive ever reach him in time? And she knows I will not..." For once, he halted, seeming to reconsider, but habit won out and Takshin plunged ahead. "She knows she is safe with me. Is that not enough?"

Safe with you? A curious statement, indeed. "It is not merely a matter of safety," Takyeo said, heavily. His leg itched, and now he was having difficulty sitting still. "Lady Yala has endured enough."

"And I am to be *endured*, I know." For once, no bitterness was evident in Takshin's tone, merely strict fact. "At least none will dare harm her if I am at her hem."

"That is a consideration." And a heavy one, indeed. Then again, Takshin's method of answering any insult nowadays was likely to be of the manner that would widow anyone he married before long.

The Third Prince glared at him. "Why are you not writing the endorsement, Eldest Brother?"

"I would love to help you, Taktak. You are best-of-brothers." The itching reached a crescendo, so Takyeo spent some few moments arranging his leg, picking up and resettling his cane. "But I am retreating to the provinces. I plan to renounce the throne." Which would make said brushed marriage endorsement worse than useless.

"Oh, certainly, but will it renounce you?" The crushflowers in Takshin's cheeks were fading fast. He considered the chair Lady Yala had so recently perched upon, visibly decided against sitting at the moment, and fixed Takyeo with a steady stare. "And you cannot possibly think Kurin will leave you unmolested even if you step aside."

I am not stupid, Takshin. Saying as much would not help or convince. Besides, this was a course his enemies—and his father—had never expected, and Garan Takyeo found he liked the feeling of having performed such a trick.

Of course Kurin would not want to leave him unmolested, but public opinion—that strange, unwieldy beast—would paint the Second Prince in bleak colors if he pursued a forbearing foe. "He would have no need, if I have publicly renounced—"

"I did not think you such a fool, Eldest Brother." Chillingly formal, and Takshin would never know just how much he looked like his mother in that moment, gazing down his nose with a pursed mouth.

It was undoubtedly for the best. If the current discussion was designed to put Takshin in a fine fettle, mentioning the First Queen would drive him into mute or active intransigence, and it would take much time and coaxing to bring him forth from *that* cave. Takyeo took a firm grasp upon his temper, an operation performed so often it was reflexive. "Not a fool."

"Then what is this? Grief?" Takshin now cast himself into the chair Yala had vacated, settled back, and laced his fingers over his midriff. He did not put his feet upon the desk, though, and thankfully he was properly in house-slippers rather than stomping about booted as if they were in an army tent. "There is no quarter given to princes, Ah-Yeo, even retired. You should know as much by now."

"I do not expect quarter." Takyeo stared at his desktop. "I wish only for peace, and that will not be found while I live." Now that he said it aloud, his course was painfully clear.

He had not thought of it in such stark terms before. Giving the idea breath was to give it life, as the sages said. Like the beast he had taken for his device, when brought to bay he would fight—but upon his own terms, in his own time.

And with every claw he possessed, visible or otherwise.

"Ah." His brother once more surprised him by becoming quiet, dark eyes fixed upon Takyeo's face and the last trace of ruddiness leaving him. The gold hoop in his left ear gleamed against red-black hair. "You have plans, I suppose."

Nothing so elegant as plans. But maybe he should. The rest of his life had been one test after another, from the merely annoying to the actively murderous. Why should the end be any different than the beginning *or* the middle? "I shall retire to the countryside and live a blameless life."

"And?" One of Takshin's eyebrows lifted fractionally. Now he looked like the Emperor instead of the First Queen, but telling him as much would simply garner a disrespectful snort in response.

So Takyeo did not. "And wait for whatever transpires." It was pleasant to choose his own course, after so long following a marked path.

Even if it led to the same place, like the two roads in the old proverb.

A short, pained silence bloomed between them. No bird sang in the garden beyond the study's blinds, and the air was breathless-still as usual before every summer afternoon downpour.

Finally, Takshin spoke. "You mean wait to be slaughtered like a fat curltail."

Put that way, there was not even the romance of filial piety to adorn the truth, and it would be difficult to keep his equanimity if Takyeo responded in kind. "If that is Heaven's decree, nothing I do will change it."

"If Heaven wishes to kill us, it should bring an army." His spike-tempered younger brother's steady gaze changed not a whit. He obviously considered that an argument in and of itself. "Do you think she will be waiting for you, your foreign wife? How will she welcome you if you allow Kurin to win?"

And of course, Takshin would see it so. Takyeo wondered if Father ever felt this weary, faced with those who saw the world as a simple toy or a mere test of brute strength. "It is not a matter of winning or losing." None of them understood that everything was already lost.

Even he had not understood as much before this conversation, either. At least Taktak was bringing the matter into absolute clarity.

"It is *precisely* a matter of winning alone." Now the Third Prince was an impatient tutor with a slow student, each word sharp-accented and precise. "No other outcome is acceptable."

"You sound like Father." If Takyeo could irritate him past bearing, Takshin might temporarily leave him in peace—or at least, so he now hoped.

"No." His little brother—and his favorite, if in a different way than Jin or Kai—fixed his gaze upon the blinds behind Takyeo, and his tone was much softer than usual, almost kind. "I sound like a man who was sent to die and somehow fought his way out."

"Takshin..." There would never be a better time to ask, and Takyeo had wondered for a long while now. He brushed a pile of paper aside, folding his hands in the clear space upon his desktop. It was a day for uncomfortable questions and perhaps even more uncomfortable truths. "What precisely happened in Shan? You never seemed disposed to speak upon it, before."

"I died, Eldest Brother." Takyeo tilted his head slightly, presenting the scar that vanished under his hair. His lip did not curl, but the scar was still there, glowing in the mirrorlight. The one upon his throat did not glare either, but it was more disturbing. "Can you not tell?"

What was there to say? *Forgive me*, perhaps, but what could Takyeo have done? Ridden to Shan with his brother, refusing to let a younger sibling suffer alone?

Perhaps he should have. "You seem very spry for a dead man."

"That you may attribute to a certain Khir lady." Takshin put his chin down, stared at his eldest brother. The soft commotion in the hall crested another notch. Lunch would be brought soon; the tea upon the tray at the margin of the desk would be whisked away, and the stacked paper demand attention once more. "*Now* will you give me what I want, Takyeo?"

I wish I could, Takshin, but what is it you truly desire? Once a man had what he was chasing, he turned to another pursuit. One need only look at their own father to see the truth of *that* maxim. "Have you courted the lady? Made yourself known?"

"I took a lash for her." Takshin shook his head like a horse scenting fire, his topknot-cage gleaming. "What else is required?"

"Women like different things, younger brother." Was he actually giving Takshin courting advice? The world had grown exceedingly strange of late.

"There speaks a voice of experience." Now, scenting worn-down resistance, Takshin tensed in the chair and leaned forward a fraction. The moment to pursue, to ask for details, had passed, and the business of living—such as it was—hemmed them both in.

There was no harm in offering Lady Yala another choice, to add to the very few a noblewoman could consider. "Very well. Win her consent, and I shall give my blessing *and* write you not only imperial permission but a marriage contract."

"Her consent?" Takshin looked puzzled and his tone plainly asked, *What on earth would I do with such a thing?*

Takyeo had to hide a smile. His lips threatened to twitch, and his leg had temporarily stopped itching. "Unless you mean to carry her off like a Tabrak barbarian with a curltail upon his pommel."

"Do you think she would like it?" Takshin rubbed at his chin, a soft, reflexive movement. "Khir do love riding."

"No, Takshin." Takyeo lost the battle on both fronts, and his mouth curled into an unwilling smile. He did not *think* Takshin was serious, but it was always best to be clear nonetheless. "I do not think she would like that at all."

It should have felt like a defeat, but Takshin's immediate brightening—and his difficult little brother's attempt to stay in the study and aid in the travel arrangements, now that he had achieved his purpose—made it seem otherwise.

Maybe by the time any of this would make any difference Takshin would change his mind anyway. Or Yala would perform another of her small miracles, and soothe a difficult prince into smoothness.

What You Came
Here For

All manner of folk could hide in the skirts of a great city, despite the attempts of the Watch to control, corral, contain, and stamp seals upon passes and manifests. Of greater efficacy was the periodic cleansing of the streets, especially at the fringes of the great markets, both Yaol and Yuin.

The close northerners—Khir, instead of those from the far fringes of Ch'han, with their smooth faces and their disdain for all younger civilizations—preferred a slice of tangled streets just north of the Yuin, where women walked with lowered eyes a few steps behind their men, spices foreign to Zhaon noses filled the cooking odors, and horses were generally accorded more spacious accommodation, not to mention better fodder, than the men who could afford their keep.

A slightly larger room was available for those with the metal to pay for it, and the Khir waiting patiently in one of those comparatively luxurious apartments watched the strange yellow-green light of Zhaon's close, oppressive summer days drain between slatted wooden blinds. Everything in the rented space was clean and neat, no distinguishing luggage left under the bed, in the wardrobe, or in the lath-fragile cabinet nailed to the wall.

For a burrow, it was a strange one. Then again, his prey had ever been cautious.

He waited through the long slow afternoon, breathing through a mouth left slightly open in order to keep some fraction of the ambient stench from his nose. Longing for a strong wind to clear this place of filth from the back of the earth was only natural, he told himself for the hundredth time, and once more he thought of home.

His victorious return would not quite be celebrated, Narikhi Baiyeo thought—one did not reward a dung-sweeper for perform-ing his function—but it would be remarked by his elders. And, more importantly, his clan's honor would finally be free of a living, breathing stain.

Yellowing stormlight and a wet, hot wind had risen by the time the door to the hall rattled and a man stepped through, his very fine boots whisper-light. The new arrival was mimicking a mer-chant's status, a long dun robe and a plain leather topknot-cage, but those with some little knowledge would note the value of his footwear as well as the quick decisiveness of his movements and know he was of a quality.

Or at least he had been raised to believe himself so, and trained in warlike arts his betters had perfected.

Baiyeo made himself a stone in the deep shadow of the corner, the place most likely to grant him both escape through the close-by window and a certain measure of surprise should his quarry be inattentive. He was a hawk upon a fist, hooded and impatient, awaiting the slip of the jesses in order to strike.

Then he could wing swift and sure for home.

His prey closed the door. There was no gleam of weapon-metal or visible shape under the dun robe, but that was no indication. The quarry did not pause, but strode for the small table set in another corner of the room, holding only some sheets of expensive paper and an ink-and-brush set of Khir make, robust but not terri-bly attractive. Perhaps he merely did the accounts of the merchant he was impersonating in this fetid little room, tainting whatever noble blood managed to speak through the shame of his birth with counting-beads and profit-dreams.

The man's back was to him. Baiyeo's palms did not sweat. He had rehearsed this moment over and over, yet it was somewhat of a disappointment, like finding a famed courtesan was merely a creation of powder and cloth instead of true beauty or seeing an otherwise handsome horse stumble before it was bought.

His position wasn't quite right for a strike yet, so he took a single soundless step. The blackened knife, drawn free of its sheath before the victim's entry to keep the whisper of blade leaving its home from alerting the intended target, raised slightly as he stepped forward.

"Put that away," Ashani Daoyan said, somewhat irritably. "You should have kept your boots on, Bah, and come through the window."

The single, dismissive syllable of his childhood nickname filled Baiyeo with an unsteady colorless feeling, like too much sohju igniting in a man's head all at once. He froze, and the honorless *bastard* actually laughed, a short disdainful chuckle.

His quarry turned. His eyes—as clear and noble as Baiyeo's own, a grey gaze that should have veiled itself before his betters— glowed in the uncertain illumination from the slats; the heap of Zhaon-An under an oppressive storm-hooded sky held a strange dim furnace-glow giving a fitful gleam to metal, damp, or polished things. "I wondered when I'd see you," his prey continued, as if politely greeting a distant, impecunious relative.

Baiyeo's throat was dry. How did this bastard say such things, with such an air of noble disdain? Had he *no* shame?

Of course not. Narikh Arasoe, an accursed honorless shoot of the clan's great tree, had spread her thighs for a man not her husband, and this was the result. "Fitting." Baiyeo managed not to clear his throat *or* spit. "To find you in this dungheap, *Dah*." One childhood nickname for another, and Bah remembered, with great satisfaction, holding this fellow's head in a trough when both of them were eight winters high.

He had been punished for it, of course. But it had been so *satisfying*. And the punishment, while showy, had not really hurt, especially when his own father had patted him on the shoulder and smiled with quiet approval afterward in private.

"No more a midden than the halls of Narikh. Did you ride a gelding all this way, Bah? It would suit you." His bastard cousin tilted his head, raising a languid hand to scratch at his stubble-roughened cheek.

To hear this foulness compare the great dim, cool hall of his clan's home to a refuse heap was the larger insult, but the smaller jab stung more. He was like that, this bastard, quick with a reply or worse, irritatingly lordly silence.

"Don't answer that," Daoyan continued, almost kindly. It rankled that he was accorded the honor of the Great Rider's clan-name, but a Khir, especially a Narikhi, was only called upon to clear the insult to his own family. "You never have anything interesting to say. Did you come to beg me to return, or to attempt murder? I hardly think it the former."

To be anticipated stung also. Bah took two more sliding steps forward, gauging his victim's readiness. No weapon was apparent, and the bastard did not flinch.

He never flinched. He hadn't since the beginning. If he had just *once* acted as if he knew the depths of his own humiliation, Baiyeo would not be here.

"Murder, then," the Great Rider's bastard son continued, thoughtfully. "And with a knife. How very droll."

"You miscalculated," Bah hissed. "Leaving your *father's* protection. Did you think to present yourself to the princess, and make yourself a lord? Or did you—"

"My affairs are none of your concern, cousin." Light and dismissive, the tone of an elder to an erring child. And *still* the man did not move. "And never have been."

"You are a stain upon the honor of Narikh."

It should have made him crumple, but the bastard merely lifted one shoulder a fraction, dropped it. "So I've been told."

"You will never rule Khir." It was the final insult, flung like a round clay bulb packed with the black powder that made Ch'han flame-flowers and bearing a sparking fuse, ready to send sharp shards in every direction. "No noble rider will follow an honorless bitch's whelp."

"My very dear cousin," his victim said, rather gently, "you are a fool, your clan is a collection of buggering longtails, and the Great Rider of Khir may kiss my fundament."

Bah was on him almost before the words had died, the knife sweeping in; there was a great red burst of pain in his neck and the world turned over. The room rotated upon a hidden axis; it happened so swiftly Narikhi Baiyeo was not quite aware of his own knife, taken from his hand and buried in his throat.

"I'd ask you what is happening at home," the other man said softly, "but you would have nothing of interest to tell me. Just die, Bah. It's what you came here for."

There was a strange gurgling sound and the pain swallowed him whole before a sharp blow hit his solar plexus. Shocked heart and lungs struggled to function, the liver blindly attempting to pour courage into its carrying-case. Dah's hand struck again, flickering at two places where the invisible subtle body touched the physical, and all Bah felt was a dozing, faraway concern.

He had never guessed his bastard cousin was so *good* at unarmed combat. But then, Ashani Daoyan had survived more than one attempt upon his bastard life even as a child. The Great Rider of Khir could spread seed where he willed; it was a man's prerogative.

But a clan had to punish a woman's transgression. Such was the way of the ordered world, and Baiyeo was Heaven's hand righting a wrong. Or so he had thought, listening to his father tell the other clan heads *that bastard brat has gone missing.*

It had not been difficult to follow; he had known this man from childhood. And yet, he was still surprised.

When the body upon the floor finished its kicking and choking, the intended victim straightened, shaking out his fingers. He hadn't needed the sword under his dun robe, or the brace of knives similarly hidden. He hadn't even needed the thin, almost flexible blade in his boot. Bah had a very pretty seat upon one of the Narikh's blooded mares, and was very showy when it came to saber practice. But the art of striking without mercy or warning was not his.

He, like plenty of others who sought to assassinate the Great Rider's indiscretion, was not overly *bright*.

Still, if he had found his cousin, more would follow. A water-seller was chanting in the street below, hoping to dispose of the last half of his tank before retiring to tend his rain-jars; the cry overlapped with an early bone collector, the two tunes harmonizing in pleasing fashion for a few moments before a scuffle broke out.

The once-bastard, now legitimized Crown Prince of Khir considered the body, then glanced at the window as the stink reached his nose. It was just like Baiyeo to fill his trousers like a common soldier when death arrived.

It didn't matter. Ashani Daoyan had disposed of more than one assassin's body. They had, after all, started arriving when he was eight winters high and looked likely to survive into adolescence, if not maturity.

He would shake the dust and filth of this place from his person soon enough, but he would not be rushed. Not until he had accomplished everything he had set himself to.

And *certainly* not before he had seen Komor Yala at least once more.

UNREMARKED FOR
LONG

The sky deepened to the color of an old, yellowing bruise, and the air was thick enough to cut with a blunt rai-scoop. Nevertheless, she was glad she had worn this particular dress; it reminded her of Khir, and even if it was too warm for southron summer, she would gladly suffer for the privilege of comfortable armor.

"You are very kind." Yala folded her hands in her lap. This had become her other daily visit; in the morning her princess's tomb required care, in the afternoons the Second Concubine's tiny gem-like quarters closed around her with a soap-bubble's iridescent, fragile peace. "The Crown Prince spoke to me today."

"Does he still intend to leave the Palace?" Kanbina, her loosely dressed hair piled high atop her pale face, lay quietly against square and rectangular pillows stuffed with fragrant herbs, cloudfur, and spent, washed feathers. "Poor boy."

"There seems some uncertainty as to his true plans," Yala admitted. "And our chat was interrupted; he had not time to speak fully. But as far as I know, he is determined. I begin to think he may even accomplish it." Not only that, but she devoutly hoped he might find some peace in the change of scene.

Of all the princes she had met in Zhaon-An, she was beginning to think she admired her princess's husband the most.

"Perhaps he may." Kanbina's eyelids, thinning almost to transparency like the rest of her, lowered a fraction. "Men are not like us; they may leave where they are placed."

"It is not the leaving that requires thought." Yala looked across the bedroom to an exquisite illustration scroll of bronzefish in winter, swimming slowly before they sank into mud to hibernate. Many of the Second Concubine's hangings were similarly retiring and peaceful. "It is surviving where you arrive."

"Well said." The Second Concubine now moved fretfully, sighing, her feet two tiny hillocks under a pair of loose-weave cotton summerblankets with silken trim. Evidently she was cold even in this terrible oppressive weather. "I wish I could play, but the sathron disdains my weakness."

The sathron's voice was one of the few true pleasures Kanbina had, as far as Yala could tell. "And my own playing is terrible; it would only grate upon your nerves." She paused, to give the other woman the chance to speak if music would soothe her, then continued when the hesitation brought no answer. "Perhaps I could read you some poetry? Or we could simply be silent with each other."

"I like that best of all, but it is a poor hostess who requires such a thing from a guest." Kanbina smiled. Each evening her close-servant—the girl with the scar—rubbed nia oil into her face with careful, gentle fingertips; Kanbina's papery skin swallowed the oil and left no trace of its passage. "Have you heard from Kai?"

He has but barely left. But Yala understood the longing. An adoptive son was far better than none at all, especially when he performed his filial duties. She could not imagine Kai doing otherwise. "No letters yet. I am awaiting the chance to fold my own to send with yours. If holding a brush tires you, Lady Kanbina, I am more than willing to take dictation."

"Now *there* is an idea. I miss his visits." The elder woman stirred herself to reach for the bedside, but Yala was swifter, finding the tiny brass bell and giving a small, decisive shake.

In short order, the servants brought paper, inkstone, brushes, and a small, cunningly designed wooden lap-desk inlaid with glowing Anwei shellwork. "A gift from my adoptive son," Kanbina said proudly. "If you prop me up, I may brush my own characters. You may serve if I falter."

"With good grace, my lady Second Concubine." Yala set herself to arranging covers, blankets, desk, and supplies. It was very like caring for one of Hai Komori's ailing dowager or maiden aunts, but this Zhaon lady was far less querulous or demanding. "I shall occupy myself with watching the garden. This light is very strange." She almost said *unhealthy*, but that might be taken as a comment upon her hostess.

"Stormglow-in-summer," Kanbina murmured. "An old word; they say it has its roots in Khir."

"I cannot recall seeing this light in the North." There was no chair by the sliding partition to the water-garden with its pleasant, white-painted gazebo, but two embroidered cushions served very well and Yala sank upon them, arranging her skirts with habitual movements. "The storms in the mountains above the Great Keep and its city are dry at this time of year, though there is rain in the lowlands for the rai and other crops."

"Hm. Perhaps the term fell into disuse after the First Dynasty."

"Very possible." Yala stilled as a babu water-clock thump-chucked in the garden. A faint haze hung over glimmering water and rustling babu. A handful of rai planted at the Knee-High Festival was also thriving, tall and green, ready for its buds to swell with life-giving seeds. The serenity on display almost managed to overcome the hushed breathlessness and gathering irritation of the approaching storm, Heaven and Zhaon holding themselves in readiness for a shattering assault.

It was restful to sit and gaze, her hands folded and her wits at leisure. A lady's life was held to be indolent by both southron and northern neighbors, but her duties were immense. Needle and thread, brush and paper, sathron and poetry, comb and earring, ceremony and intrigue—the list was endless. And after she married, the overall management of the household—steward and housekeeper, kaburei and servant—rested within her hands as well. Not to mention pleasing her husband, and producing heirs.

And, if one married a prince, perhaps fending off assassins as well? If Mahara had kept her *yue*...

But that was useless. She had not, and Yala had not been with her when it mattered. The *yue* could not defend against a horse-killer while riding, either.

Had Yala been riding upon her princess's other side, though...

A sigh caught her unawares, and she lifted the back of her left sleeve to her mouth as if to trap a yawn or some other inattention. The risk of being seen, judged, or found unfeminine was a constant. *Even if you are alone, Heaven's eyes are upon you*, the maiden-aunties of Hai Komori intoned, *and it is the duty of a Khir noblewoman not to be found wanting under that gaze.*

What was her father doing right now? It was the day of the month reserved for Hai Komori's high table, heads of the junior and extended clans or their approved representatives required to dine in the high, draughty main hall with Hai Komori Dasho upon the low dais available to judge matters both large and small between his kin. Far too early in the day for the feast, of course; housekeeper, steward, and cook would be hurrying to and fro while their master attended to preliminary business in the study, including matters which could not be spoken of openly but still needed addressing between the clan's spreading limbs.

Was he worried for her? Had news of Mahara's death reached him yet, or news of her own shameful survival? And how could she tell him of Kai's offer?

Would it be better if he considered her dead? Bai was gone, and unless her father remarried and produced another heir, leadership of Komor would pass to a junior house. It was not quite an idea too terrible to contemplate...but it was close.

Then there was the matter of Dao's letter, and her own response. She would meet this merchant, see what Dao had sent from Khir, and judge whether a reply was necessary. If it were a prank or gift she could hold either close, a moment of relief among all these jostling cares and competing intrigues.

And yet it could be news of an altogether different sort. There had been attempts upon Daoyan's life before, and it was only recently that she truly comprehended what her childhood friend must have suffered. Before she left Khir, such matters had been left to older, male heads far above hers. It seemed knowledge of them had merely lain in wait to spring upon her once she had the means and experience to compass the implications.

Yala, quite rudely, almost wished the Second Concubine would hurry through her letter. Leisure sounded enticing, but it gave her entirely too much time to brood.

"Lady Yala?" Kanbina's voice was a thin reedy whisper. "Perhaps I will need to impose upon your patience after all. My fingers are somewhat shaky."

"Of course." Yala took another long look at the water garden and unfolded, somewhat glad to be pressed into service. She arranged her skirts and halted, glancing at the Second Concubine.

Kanbina's paleness was no longer fetching or indolent but startling. The fine lines graven at the corners of her mouth and eyes had deepened alarmingly. Even her lips were bloodless, her body withdrawing its vital humors to deep caves. Glimpsed without the screen of habit painting her in better health, she looked not just ill but deathly.

Dowager Aunt Tala had looked so, before the great goddess of horse and hunt claimed that lady's redoubtable self.

It will not be long, Yala realized, and could not make the *avert* gesture to ward off ill-luck with her kind hostess watching. So she essayed a bright smile and sank again upon the chair at Kanbina's bedside, settling the lap-desk over her own knees. "There," she said, carefully twirling the brush upon the inkstone and covering the beginning of the letter with a blank, folded sheet to protect the Second Concubine's privacy. "Proceed, Second Concubine Garan Kanbina."

"Do not write just yet." Kanbina folded her hands upon the

summerblankets. "Tell me, child, will it do you good to join my household? It would certainly do *me* good to have another lady present."

"You are kind to offer, and even kinder to ask." Yala had given much thought to the matter since the Crown Prince had broached it, and was relieved to have an answer ready. "If I may be of use and the Crown Prince has no need of me, I would be honored. There is the small matter of one or two other ladies, of course—"

"The Su girl, and the Hansei? I shall be glad of their company, should you wish to bring them. Not the Gonwa niece, she goes straight to her aunt." Kanbina's lips pursed briefly. "I would not have Lady Gonwa watching my household. She is very close to the Second Queen."

"Is that so?" Yala kept the brush poised over the inkstone instead of the page, to avoid splotching. "I had thought Lady Gonwa would be sending her niece to a household with better marital prospects."

"Perhaps." Kanbina's expression said there was more to that observation than she would speak upon, which naturally was a matter for curiosity. "Then it is decided, especially if the Crown Prince wishes to take a holiday in the countryside. You shall alleviate my loneliness, and I shall alleviate the vexing question of where to place a Khir noblewoman in the current conditions."

"You are wise as well as kind," Yala murmured. "I did not know quite where I would be placed, and it appears I may not return home just yet."

"I do not think my son would let you." A dim sparkle of amusement lit Kanbina's dark, very fine eyes. How beautiful she must have been, when young. "Has he asked you yet, my dear?"

Oh. "Before he left, yes." There was no reason to dissemble, but Yala's cheeks warmed. It well became a maiden to blush when the subject was broached; at least she need not attempt to hide that response.

"Good." Kanbina's chin dipped, the impression of a brisk nod. "Then I shall leave him in your care."

Yala again could not make the *avert* gesture, and unease curled behind her wide, low, silken sash. "Lady Kanbina—"

"Hush. Write this... *The garden is doing well, and the rai from the Knee-High is full of small beads. Lady Komor is writing now, since my hand shakes; I no longer play the sathron but am making arrangements for a visitor or two in order to hear the strings again.*"

Yala bent her head and wrote. Her cheeks were afire, and she was glad of the task to focus upon. Kai's... affections... were no longer a secret, if they ever had been.

Her own could not hope to remain unremarked for long.

REWORKING

The crossing of Shan's border was anticlimactic at best since she was locked in a palanquin and dragged at a shuffle over an antique stone curve, the Enshuan River that the Shan named *Golyeon* instead receding grudgingly from its spring rush but still muscular enough to carry away weakroot trees, chunks of bank, or those unwary enough to attempt ford instead of bridge.

Sabwone shut her eyes. Hooves moved clip-clop at a walk; pipes and drums and gongs drowned out the river's retreating, purling chuckles. The moment the palanquin had tilted slightly downhill she was technically in Shan, and a bubble of hot sourness rose in her throat as she remembered that lurching decline. Even halting upon the riverbank afterward was hideous, the consciousness of being outside her native country acute and prickling like an old woman's night-sweats.

If she had expected any difference in the method of journeying, she was roundly disabused. They would not give her another horse, so she was closed in this shoe-casket for hours every morning and every long, hot, unendurable afternoon.

She could not even open her palanquin's slatted windows; chastity and custom demanded she sit inside the ridiculous overpainted box and sweat until the next stop. Her dress was not folded correctly, the ties and buttons were crooked, and she was ravenous. Her hair was inexpertly coiled, too, and the pin was sliding. Her ear-drops jangled unpleasantly, and she had read every novel sur-reptitiously stuffed into her baggage as insurance against boredom.

In fact, she had read them twice, like a junior eunuch at lessons.

There was the fruit-basket, and the horn-handled paring knife. The short, curved blade was sharp enough, and she had already rolled up her sleeve.

Her wrist bore a slight, dark ring settled in parallel creases since she hated bathing at inns. She longed for the palace baths, for her own comfortable bed, for walanir with her breakfast and proper, not-sticky rai. And Lady Gonwa's heaven tea, a mark of high respect from that old biddy.

The knifetip pricked against a blue vein-line. Really, veins should glitter like rivers; it was unpardonable that they were so drab.

Come now, princess. A little sting, and it is all over.

A ruby drop welled. It really didn't hurt that much at all. Less than a child's scraped knee, or the cramping, hot-stone pain of her red time. At least travel was held to disarrange the humors badly enough to alter *that* steady cycle.

It was almost like slitting a seam on a dress needing reworking. Was this what fabric felt when paired blades or a razor sliced with a satisfying dry sound?

Sabwone loved that small noise, and was disappointed when her own skin did not behave so appropriately. *Now* there was pain, but it would be embarrassing to only perform halfway.

The welling became a streamlet, running to either side of her wrist. Sabwone hissed out a long breath, looked at the palanquin's roof, and applied more force to draw the paring knife up.

The difficulty would come, she realized, when she had to make her right arm match. But she was a princess of Zhaon, and she would see this done.

She only regretted she'd taken this long to set herself the task.

REALIZE
CONSEQUENCES

A haze hung to the South, and for once it was warm enough even for the beautifully plump, lacquer-haired woman in viridian silk who smiled benignly, indicating a small round table with two straight Shan-style chairs. It was unlike the First Queen of Zhaon to take any sort of nourishment, whether liquid or otherwise, in a room with an open partition. Her gardens, though she did not often go sauntering about them, were highly regimented, not even a jaelo vine daring to stretch a curler in a stray direction.

"I was somewhat surprised by your kind invitation," Second Queen Haesara said coolly. If it irked her to perform the slight incline of her upper body due her slightly-more-than-equal coeval, it did not show; the lady of Hanweo was correct in all her movements, including the polite hesitation to allow her hostess to sink upon the chair instead of the cushions she preferred.

"We are queens." First Queen Gamwone visibly admired her guest's hairpin, letting her gaze linger upon that decoration, but she did not move to compliment it. Her gown was quite amply cut, with wide sleeves and a longish hem, but the color did not suit her at all. Instead, it brought a certain sallowness to her complexion, but what else could you expect of such a woman? "That should make us true friends."

"Friends." Second Queen Haesara repeated the word softly, without the lilt of a question. She took to the proffered chair and studied the cuff of her left sleeve, tiny exquisite crimson stitches upon flattering deep peach silk double-threaded in some cases to make a relief of the *han-we-ohi* characters of her birth clan. Her uncle Hailung Jedao would no doubt caution her not to be overt or hasty. *Our fortunes rest upon you*, he had told her those many years ago, and since then she had borne the weight—of a warlord husband, of children, of her clan's survival—without a single word of remonstrance.

"Oh, I know we have been at odds once or twice." Gamwone's smile did not alter. If it pained her to bend her tongue to conciliatory speech, she made no sign. She even poured for her guest, a mark of high respect from one who had every right to expect all other wives and concubines to busy themselves with such a task.

Haesara found herself thinking of her eldest son's eleventh autumn, the clashing of metal and the bright alloy taste of fear. The assassin—a man with blackened, decayed teeth and two new-moon swords—had reached the inner quarters of the house surrounded by citron trees in Hanweo-An, and the smell of those fruits was ever afterward associated with the deadly fear that her child, her precious firstborn boy, would take the woundrot or worse from one of those curved blades.

Makar had killed the assassin, of course. Even at that age he knew what was expected and had performed without question, qualm, or incorrectness. *I am not frightened, Mother.*

But he had been so very, very pale, and her heart, not to mention her liver, had known true terror that night.

Haesara had known exactly who was responsible. Oh, it could not be *proven*, of course. Just as the true cause of the Second Concubine's ill health, or the affair of the burning gloves in First Princess Sabwone's fifth summer, could not be. Allusions to any of those matters—or quite a few more—were deemed imprudent at best; investigation met blank walls, and Gamwone's petty insults and unbearable smirking had, after all, been borne.

Year after year, the millstones had pressed upon the second wife of a rising warlord, and when she was acclaimed Second Queen of Zhaon she had allowed herself to be thought pleased. She had done her duty, given Garan Tamuron two sons, and defended both those sons and her clan from an emperor's neglect and this swelling, gloss-painted poison-toad without a single murmur crossing her lips even at night in the curtained recess of her bed. What she did not let escape her lips could not be turned against her.

But it curdled. Yes, that was precisely the word. It clotted and soured within her.

"Indeed we have." Haesara barely touched her lips to the rim of her cup. It was not quite rude; she was known to have an aversion to sweet tea before noon. Certainly nobody could fault her politeness, trotting out into the heat when the Emperor's first wife sent a careless little invitation.

It was best to find out what the lacquer-haired bitch wanted sooner rather than later.

"But now, with things as they are..." Gamwone patted delicately at her lips with a bit of folded, roseate rai-paper. "We are both mothers, after all. And mothers wish the best for their children."

Even in Zhaon's summer, the Second Queen could imagine a block of ice encasing her entire body, an armor no less durable for being entirely imaginary. "Certainly." Haesara had a certain reputation for calm—not like First Concubine Luswone's masklike, aesthetic languor, but the true restraint of a Zhaon noblewoman. Decades of prudence and brooding served her well now, presenting a bland, sheer cliff Gamwone would find no purchase upon.

Gamwone studied her narrowly. "Must you be obtuse? We will both find ourselves childless when our glorious husband ascends to Heaven."

Will we, indeed. "In the old days, we would be placed within his tomb." Haesara set her tea down after the simulacrum of drinking, letting her sleeve fall gracefully. "It is comforting to live in modern times." There was, she reflected, a certain amount of satisfaction to be had from watching the First Queen realize the consequences of her constant intrigues and petty jealousies.

"Hanweo Haesara." Gamwone's pretty, plump hands lay in her lap, but her fingers had tensed the tiniest fraction. The sheath over her smallest nail on the left hand sent back hard darts of light, pure silver filigree pressed into service upon a common paw. Did it feel the sting of insult? Metal was held to be above such feelings. "I shall be very plain, since you seem rather uncaring. When our husband ascends to Heaven, that common-whelped brat from his spear-wife—"

"You are referring to the Crown Prince," Haesara murmured. You could never be too certain, especially in her rival's part of the Kaeje. And of course the First Queen would address the Second by her clan-name, as if she were a court lady instead of a fellow wife.

Still, she enjoyed seeing ruddy crushflowers bloom in Gamwone's round, zhu-powdered cheeks. They faded quickly; the woman had much experience in strangling her own humors as well as those around her.

"And when he orders your precious Makar to open his veins after some manufactured intrigue, will you still be so polite?" Gamwone did not bother to murmur, though any true noblewoman might well blush at her bluntness. "What of your youngest, too?"

"Our husband has ordered the line of succession; ministers and eunuchs have received Red Letters." Haesara turned her gaze to an atrocious though no doubt very expensive illustration scroll hanging upon the opposite wall. It was a violently untalented treatment of Niao Zhou's famous fording of the Enshuan, the brushstrokes clotted and the sage-general's face somewhat blotchy. Even the garden here was overdone; a certain amount of aesthetic untidiness was to be expected in living, growing green. "When he ascends his sons will behave as men; that will please Heaven and grant us all merit."

Gamwone's jaw worked for a moment. Haesara felt a completely reprehensible, not very noble burst of hot satisfaction, and made certain her face showed none of it.

All along she had known this day would come, and mused at length upon how to face it. Garan Tamuron's first queen was of a rich family, yes—but she was a *merchant's* brat, ersatz antiquity purchased and scribbled upon goatskin rolls. Yulehi was an old name, to be sure, but their true descendants had died out in the Second Dynasty, waiting for a grasping tradesman to resurrect the form but not the substance.

Not like Hanweo, with their genealogy carved into stone stele for the entire world to see. Haesara had been sold to a warlord, certainly—but even that warlord's ancestors were noble. The Garan had the blessing of Heaven, besides—how else to explain her husband's success?

"Do you truly believe that?" Gamwone, clearly, hardly credited the notion of *merit*.

"It is our duty to see that they do so," Haesara answered smoothly. "Do you think your eldest will act…unbecomingly? Or perhaps it is the Third Prince you fear for? He was sent to Shan so very young."

Oh, it was not *polite* of her, certainly. But this tradesman's daughter had been placed far above her natural station and no doubt thought she would never be toppled from such a heap. Heaven, sooner or later, had a remedy for all such creatures, and Haesara wished to live long enough to see it applied.

"I know *my* sons." Gamwone's eyes had narrowed slightly. "I thought to help you, Hanweo Haesara, because your scholarly Makar fools nobody. He slinks about like an impresario, and that younger brother of his is even worse."

Even for *her* this was insulting behavior. Haesara's smile, gentle and remote, creaked with the strain of holding her own feelings in abeyance. Still, it was worrisome—*had* Makar been tempted into an intrigue? He was normally wiser, her first and most winning child. Or was he continuing to tidy Sensheo's messiness again, without telling his anxious mother? It was so like him to insulate her; he was a filial child.

Impresario was a troubling term, too. Was the First Queen

attempting to insinuate Makar had bought the last round of assassins troubling the court?

The First Queen was waiting for Haesara's reaction. The Second Queen of Zhaon let her brittle smile stretch a fraction. "Your nerves seem somewhat disarranged, First Queen. Perhaps you should engage a better physician." Of course, her last chief physician was rumored to be in some poor health now; Tian Ha, called the Grinning Skull by some wags, had lost his patroness's protection. It could be a coincidence, certainly ... but nobody within the palace complex thought so. She gathered her skirts, rising fluidly. The fall of glittering crystals from her hairpins, with their subtle pink sheen, echoed her gown's rosiness. "I could recommend one, but I hardly think you will listen to me."

Gamwone's mouth fell open slightly. This was visibly *not* how she expected this interview to go. "Are you leaving so soon?"

"I have no desire to endure more of your shameful displays," Haesara said, very softly. A noblewoman should never *shout*. "You have thought yourself strong, Garan Yulehi-a Gamwone, all this time. Others have too."

"I am strong," Zhaon's First Queen hissed in return. "I have had to endure rival after rival, and I am still First Queen."

"No, Yulehi-*pau*." The extra syllable denoted a shoddy, tradeworn substitute instead of a quality item, and Haesara rather liked the implication. It was a bitter pleasure to say out loud what she had thought for so long. "You are not. It is merely that all this time, those you thought enemies have disdained you. Friends would have served a First Queen better."

The effect of her retreat from Gamwone's over-padded, stifling burrow was somewhat marred by her rival's deadly silence and the scurrying in the hall when she opened the partition; she had hoped to actively catch the servants listening. Still, the satisfaction of seeing them scatter like rai chaff at the far end was wonderful, and so was the sense that Garan Hanweo-a Haesara had—finally, blessedly—left Garan Tamuron's first wife quite bereft of words.

SAY THE WORD

Z haon's great palace complex held an artisans' warren, where those with patent or patron could tempt the hive of royalty, nobility, minister, and eunuch with bauble, necessity, or luxury. Those Zhaon merchants who could claim a small closet to display their wares had the right to display a small crimson and yellow banner at their shop outside the palace complex, a sign of quality— or of possible influence. The prettiest youths and most winning wares were dispatched to the Home, of course, and if a nobleman took notice of the former more than the latter, well, good luck and merit flowed from those closer to Heaven, as the proverb ran.

At a discreet hour—junior court ladies secluded for daily lessons and pondering the serious, vexing question of what to wear for the afternoon social calls, young noblemen instructed by private tutors, ministers attending Council and eunuchs presumably busy upon scribal duties—the most respectable of the elder court ladies often visited the Artisan's Home, its name so archaic it was sometimes simply called *the Home*, with a pleasant intonation to make it a proper address.

The light had not yet turned to the deep unhealthy bruise-color of summer storming, so the lady in dark blue carried a cerulean sunbell; her kaburei, following at the proper distance, held an oiled cloak in readiness should the weather decide like a peasant farmer that earlier rain was better. Lady Komor Yala was hardly remarked upon, though one or two brightly clad Zhaon court matrons slowed their pace or quickened just enough to keep her in sight but not nearly close enough to politely greet. One could not ostracize a silk-wearing woman, but it was far safer to wait and see where she would land like a forlorn falling leaf—and at least the foreign woman was well-bred enough not to press her company upon any who avoided her.

It took a short while for Yala to find the proper room in the confusing passages of the Buneju-bird House, that largest wooden structure of the Home divided over and over until it had become a maze of lease, sublease, sub-sublease, arrangement, percentage, and licensing. These were the rooms for merchants who had managed to wheedle a moment of notice or been summoned with civil but complete imperiousness, given a pass for the day and enduring much waiting and many cupped hands to cross with an alloy sliver or two to ensure proper treatment.

One such room was pleasant enough, narrow but long, with bright mirrorlight and an air of brisk use—they were not allowed to stand empty much, these tiny vesicles of commerce. It had the proper character upon its door, and as Yala entered, she almost froze in shock.

A man in a dark but very fine merchant's robe bowed deeply, welcoming her in fluent but accented Zhaon, and his leanness was surprising. Most merchants softened early; this fellow showed shoulders which rivaled a Golden Guard's but a complete lack of middle-padding. He also looked much older now, and instead of a dark, secretive Zhaon gaze, his eyes were as grey as Yala's own, and dancing with familiar merriment besides.

It was Ashani Daoyan.

Recognition burned through her, a jolt like kaibok stick meeting ball, and Yala might have stumbled except she was already lowering herself into a small, intricately carved, backless chair set next to a similarly restrained table with a carved apron edging its polished top. Anh hovered solicitously, her arms full of sunbell and oiled cloak; Yala glanced at her, hoping the girl could not see her mistress's sudden discomfiture.

"Do not crowd so, Anh." Yala's tone was kind enough but very firm, though her throat was dry and her hands shook inside her sleeves. "I wish to examine the wares without being breathed upon."

The girl colored, bowed, and retreated to the door, where she settled upon the mat placed for just such personages. The merchant motioned to his own pair of assistants, and they began fussing among what was presumably a stack of wares behind a painted screen, for no noblewoman would wish to gaze upon crates. The presentation was just as important as the item itself when dealing with the rich, and a successful merchant was one who understood that fact.

Among others.

Yala's mouth barely moved, but her Khir was as soft and crisp as ever. "How is it you are here?" It was a relief to speak in her own tongue again, and a double relief to see a familiar face. He had lost some little weight as she had, and there was no pale armband upon his sleeve. Of course, a mere merchant could not mark a foreign princess's death, here in Zhaon.

Dao's gaze was somber, though his mouth curved in an obsequious smile. It was the same expression he had used once or twice upon some noble Khir he disdained but had to endure, and could be mistaken for cheerful placidity. "I had to come see what they were doing with my sister, and my Yala."

So he had hied himself forth into the center of Zhaon? It beggared belief, yet he was here before her. How long had he been in the city? The urge to touch his arm, perhaps even to pinch and make certain he was real, made her fingers tingle. "How..." She sought for appropriate words, found almost none. "It is *dangerous* here, Dao." How long had he been waiting to slip her a message? She could not ask, and the shock threatened to maze her wits completely.

"Every place below Heaven is dangerous." Her childhood friend spread his hands a little, mimicking even a merchant's expressive gestures. Perhaps it was a grand game to him, akin to accomplishing mischief at a feast among imperious Khir nobles who could not openly disdain him but made their feelings plain in many little ways. "Already scolding me, and I came all this way."

So you did. "How did you come here?" She could not decide what to ask first. "What news of my father? When did you leave Khir?"

"One moment." His bright, oily merchant's smile faded slightly; he clapped his hands before bellowing in Zhaon. "Tea, and kou bah for the noble lady! Hurry!"

Two large needles pressed inward from Yala's temples; she realized it was because her jaw was clenched so tightly. "Dao." She could not address him in more than a whisper. What was this, some manner of fever-dream?

"Here." He laid something small and round upon a pad of blue velvet spread upon the table to show small sparkling wares to advantage. His smile was now exactly that of the shy boy Bai had brought to meet her when Yala was merely five summers high. *This is my friend*, Bai had said, with the particular tilt to his chin that warned her even at that young age not to disagree.

It was only later she had found out exactly who the boy was, and why her father did not acknowledge his presence with more than a nod. It was all very well for Bai to graciously notice a noble youth his own age, and some might have thought it was Komori's ancient fidelity to Ashani covering even an illegitimate sprig of that clan, but her father could not publicly countenance it—and Yala could never meet Daoyan without her brother's presence.

Until Bai was gone at Three Rivers, and Dao had been dragged from the field in a rage to keep the Great Rider's clan alive.

Yala dropped her gaze to the silver gleam, and the sensation of being trapped in a dream just about to slide into nightmare folded over her like a hawk's wings beating to disorient small prey.

Even worse, for a moment she was reminded of a ring in another man's palm as well, but this circle of silver bore no resemblance to the evil, stone-metal *shinkesai*.

She had never asked what Kai had done with the assassin's ring.

No, this was the great seal of Hai Komori, from her father's own hand. She touched warm metal with a trembling fingertip. There was the small chip on the edge of the flat face, one she had run her thumb over every time she was allowed to hold her father's hand. The komor flower and the setting sun, carved with brief, spare strokes meant to be pressed into wax, stared at her. "Is he..."

Daoyan did not let her linger in uncertainty. "He was alive when I left him. There is also a letter."

Relief burst inside her, and she was surprised she did not sway upon the chair. "When *did* you leave?"

But the tea had arrived with alacrity, and they must pretend to be merchant and lady, him spreading small glittering things upon a roll of blue velvet, she deigning to glance at intervals. The tea was even good, though one could not drink it while boiling here in the lowlands. Small, exquisitely flaky kou bah sat, shiny with honey and starred with salt, upon a fine Gurai slipware plate.

She could no more taste the delicacies than she could swallow stones; her stomach had closed to a pinhole.

"I could not wait," Dao said, his own lips barely moving. They were both well practiced in this method of communication, engaged in at the theater or during a festival-feast. "I left two full moons ago, and I still arrived too late."

"An assassin lay in wait with ihenhua." She tried not to shudder. "Even before that, there were so many of them. I did all I could, Dao." Was she pleading with him, or with her father? "I tried to protect her."

"I know." Dao's genial smile faltered for a mere moment but his clear grey gaze did not, and the forgiveness there was enough to ease the sharpness inside her. At least he would judge her kindly; he always had. "We do not have long, especially with your chaperone at the door."

"A kaburei," Yala murmured, but he was right. His finely honed sense of what was permissible to one in his position had not dulled in the least. "We must arrange some other way to meet."

"Tell me, and I shall do what is required." As always, he did not bother to clothe the offer with any pretty, meaningless words. Ever direct, her Daoyan—and now it was not merely her brother Third Prince Takshin reminded her of, but also him. "My blood burns at the thought of what you have endured, Yala."

You wrote as much, several times. "It is nothing." Before, the letters had made her uneasy. Now, they were a comfort. "Only...my princess." Her eyes stung, and she had to look away at anonymous, glittering things laid next to the seal. The plain, heavy ring outshone them all in value, though anyone else might not know as much.

"Do you know who ordered the foul deed yet?" Dao's tension was as familiar as her own, now, the constant readiness of a boy who knew the precariousness of his own continued survival.

"No, but..." Of course that failure could not be judged kindly, and she dared not glance at his face. Dao was Mahara's elder brother, after all, though the Great Rider had kept the son born of an honorless mother away from his daughter lest the taint spread. "I already work to discover it, though. As I am trapped here, there is little else to do." It felt good to say it aloud.

None of the Zhaon would understand her duty to a princess's shade. Not even Zakkar Kai, as affectionate as he was.

"You are no longer trapped." The small, definitive line between Dao's eyebrows—an old friend, and a mark of his stubbornness— had returned. "Say the word, and I shall take you from this place."

I cannot see how such a miracle may be attempted, let alone brought to pass. "And return to Khir?" What would her father say, were she to return unchaperoned with the Great Rider's only remaining son? Even were her honor unstained, the implications dizzied her and would force Komori Dasho to complete severity with an erring girlchild.

"If you like." He turned aside as one of his helpers scurried to the table with another armful of implements—hairpins, eardrops with bright ribbons, and a thin roll of silk holding a fine chain necklace of Ch'han silver. "Ah, the very thing. Here, my lady. The seal is too large for your small fingers."

"You are too kind," she murmured in Zhaon, a warning.

He used Zhaon as well, and his tone was all bluff heartiness. "Who can be cruel to a lady such as yourself? Consider it a gift, Komor Yala, and my thanks for your patronage." And, cheekily, he *winked* at her.

Yala had to swallow a small laugh. He was ever the same, Ashani Narikh'a Daoyan, and her liver turned within her, settling easily. Her heart followed suit.

Now she was not friendless in this place. But it was so dangerous for him—and what madness, to leave Khir and his duty to his father.

She would have to convince him to return swiftly.

The chain was wrapped in short order, a linen packet tied with heavy waxed crimson thread in the Khir fashion, and her father's seal was safe inside her sleeve-pocket, deftly flicked into her hand as Dao had been wont to pass her small notes or polished pebbles during theater-visits. Dao insisted she take a few ili of heavy golden Khir tea as well, and a triangular-folded missive with her father's familiar seal was slipped into its wrapping with admirable dexterity. "I rather like playing merchant," he said in Khir, softly, as he laid the tea upon the small table with a bow. "But I will be glad to leave it behind me, when you are ready to quit this place."

It was a gift of another type, one Yala accepted even as she rose, restraining herself from giving the deep bow due a son of the Great Rider. Dao did not stint on his own obeisance, of course, and smiled as she swept for the door, Anh leaping to her feet and hurrying forward to take any packages.

Now, apparently Heaven-sent, Yala had a way to leave Zhaon, if she dared take it and could find some way to keep her honor unstained during the journey. She could leave a softly brushed letter for Zakkar Kai, and silently bear the pain of duty with her head held high.

Yet part of her knew—oh, quietly indeed, but with the iron voice of the deepest truths—it was dishonorable indeed to flee for safety before she had discovered just who was to blame for Mahara's death.

THE WUREI BOY

L etters first." Anlon shuffled into view, his greying head bent as he rummaged in the leather dispatch bag. "Always letters first...ah, there is a dispatch from Kou Banh's detachment, my lord."

"That first, then." Kai grimaced as the young soldier serving him as armor-son today worked the gilded helm free of his top-knot. The ceremonial drills in honor of his arrival required bright armor, soldiers longing to see the man who would send them into battle looking reasonably personable. "And some soldier's tea, I am famished."

"I have already sent for it, and your lunch. Head Cook is threatening to burn the kitchen hall down to clean it of hangers-on, but your quarters will be ready for the banquet tonight."

The banquet to mark his return—and, not so incidentally, to announce any changes in the army's upper echelons—sounded as comfortable as passing a piss-stone, even with sohju to ease its fall. "A treasure, Anlon. That is what you are." Kai nodded at the young soldier, whose nimble fingers had stowed the helm upon its stand and were now working at the laces to his shoulders.

The steward, with the peculiar catlike half-smile he wore when well pleased, began sorting the dispatch bag onto the table. No Red Letter showed its royal face; Tamuron had sent no official orders yet. Kai was held in readiness, an arrow in the quiver if Khir found more resources to match their martial spirit. The Northern Army was now a skeleton, reduced to its bones of hardened career veterans—conscripts and others had melted away after Three Rivers, taking their last pay and a scrip for a certain minimum amount or more of arable land before returning to whatever corner of Zhaon they called home, or would *like* to call home. Still, a trickle of new recruits came, and the armor-son was one of them.

If the Khir crossed the bridges and took the border marches, the Northern Army would have to rise like an iuaheke, flesh ribboning over burned bones and hair standing straight up as it clawed for fresh blood. The northerners could not be that stupid or insulted, even though their princess was smoke from a costly, oil-drenched pyre.

Yet here he was, in readiness for just such a stupidity.

He did not glance at the desk, though his neck ached with the effort of refraining. Would she write after all? It was useless to wonder; he was two full days' hard courier-ride from the capital with fresh horses at every stage, not so far but far enough. It was small consolation that with the Crown Princess in her tomb nobody would be much bothered to rob a lady-in-waiting's small life.

That was not a comfort that would keep him calm, though. To draw its teeth, he turned his attention fully to the armor-son. "Where are you from, solider?"

"Wurei, my lord." A greasing of sweat glistened on the young man's brow. It was a hot morning, and armor-duty did not exclude one from drill.

"Ah." Sudden unease filled his belly, for no reason he could immediately discern. "My adoptive-mother is from Wurei. It is lovely country; she speaks of it fondly."

The young man muttered something no doubt polite in return. He appeared to be having difficulty with the laces, stiffened leather under bright burnished metal recalcitrant though warmed by both sunshine and a body's lesser radiant heat.

The tent's entrance filled with moving shadows. That was the only warning Kai received, but it was enough; he dropped, unable to roll because of the armor's rigidity; the shoulders, loosened but not lifted free or fully unlaced, would impede his arms. One leg straightened with a snap, catching the boy on the thigh as a bright curved knifeblade parted air where Kai's throat had been a moment before.

The young man blurted a curse and the tent's fabric walls moved strangely. Anlon bellowed, snatching his shortsword from its scabbard with a bright ringing noise; metal clashed outside. The peculiar *thrip* of heavy barbed arrows at short range melded with tearing cloth, and suddenly Anlon stood over his master, teeth bared as his blade drove the youth from Wurei back.

Kai was helpless as a stripped jewelwing upon its back, waving thread-thin multiple legs as a child prepared a pin to mount it on heavy pressed-rag paper.

Side-thrust, lunge—Anlon was slower than he had been years ago, but in any battle experience counted as much as youth or skill and the Wurei boy had only the short curved knife. Good for opening an unsuspecting victim's throat; not so useful when the quarry was alerted—or had even one loyal guard.

It was the tent Kai was worried most about as he rocked, arms and legs thrash-slipping the chain of conscious will. Anlon lunged again, almost spitting the Wurei boy, whose backward shuffle bespoke a great deal of natural talent and hard training.

A soldier was to be a son to his general, but this particular youngster was murderous. The penalty would be severe indeed if he did not die upon Anlon's blade.

Kai rolled to his side with a fish-jumping, gasping effort, curling like an armorbug to provide some manner of leverage. The tent sagged, light failing in its cloth confines as its vents distorted and the burnished mirrors bouncing sunshine through the interior moved in their rope cradles.

One of those great discs or rectangles could shear through skull or ribs if dropped from sufficient height.

Kai made it to hands and knees. He was trapped in syrup-stone like an ancient leaf, its impression cunningly jointed to resemble a living thing. His shoulder-armor had slipped sideways so he shrugged free, hearing laces snap, and surged upright just as Anlon's foot turned upon a wadded carpet and his steward was forced to recover by stagger-stepping aside.

The Wurei boy lunged, and the tip of the curved blade tore across Anlon's middle, scratching stiffened leather but without the force to truly bite.

A soft rushing added to the confusion, thin fingers of acrid smoke crawling along sagging fabric walls, and Kai understood the boy's fellows had set the tent afire. "*Keep him alive!*" Kai yelled, hoping it would not prove a feat beyond Anlon's means.

A dead assassin could not be questioned.

Anlon made no sign of hearing, driving the boy toward the tent's entrance. Cries, clashes, and running feet sounded over the rushing of heavy, painted, sun-dried cloth freeing flame from its warp and weft.

Kai surged to his feet, and his own sword sang from its sheath. At least he had not laid the blade aside; the boy would have done better to attend to *that* task first. How many confederates did the assassin have, and what was their entire aim?

Anlon lunged again, and this time Heaven or luck was with him, for the sword-tip pierced the boy's right shoulder at an angle, sliding into the valley between chestplate and stiffened leather shoulder. The young soldier cried out, a high, piercing, childlike note of pain, and his left hand drove forward, suddenly full of the wicked gleam of a fingerknife, its horizontal hilt held across the palm's pad and its blade poking between the large and third fingers.

Kai's steward made no sound, simply slid the blade deeper, the shortsword's broad tip twisting slightly, seeking the ball-joint of the shoulder to cripple the main blade-hand.

Smoke billowed. Kai found his footing—the flames would swallow the tent whole, soon. It was a decision—slay the assassin and possibly lose whatever he could be induced to say of the plot or let the blasted boy stab Anlon, the fingerknife possibly finding artery or punching leather, skin, fatty apron, and gut-channel. Once those channels were breached sepsis all but inevitably followed, and that was a death no soldier was stupid enough to wish for.

Tamuron would have chosen in a heartbeat. A general could not afford the luxury of friendship or favoritism, and sacrificing a tactical victory to gain a strategic one had brought him an empire.

The sword left Kai's hand, a bright bar of silver, and buried itself with a solid *thunk*, piercing armor and flesh both. Kai hurled himself after it, his hand closing upon the familiar dragon-snarling hilt, and with his weight behind it the thirsty steel drank deep of blood and other humors. The Wurei boy staggered back, mouth opening slack and his dark eyes full of wondering surprise; Kai's hip hit Anlon's to thrust the steward aside.

The tip of Kai's sword hit bone, chipping the spine's thick base. His wrist turned, a reflexive movement practiced just that morning, and the cutting edge sheared bowel, gut-muscle, and what little child-fat remained upon his opponent. A gush of foulness undercut the pouring smoke, and Kai slapped the fingerknife from the boy's hand, a contemptuous little strike.

Anlon made a soft, hurt noise, and Kai grabbed his elbow. *"Move!"* he yelled, and thrust the man for the tent-flap, where shouts and more clashing metal told him the battle was not yet done. It was short work to free his sword from what was not yet a dying body but would be in a matter of moments, and he had to shove Anlon again. Many a man wandered during a battle, his reins held by habit; the steward was heading, dazed like a horse near a burning barn, for the table where the dispatches lay scattered.

And all the while, Kai was curiously grateful. At least if assassins were after *him*, he could be relatively certain Komor Yala was safe.

Or so he hoped, and a man in battle needed any hope he could garner.

PRINCE YOU
PREFER

The palanquin's side opened and Yala peered into damp, purple Zhaon-An summer dusk. As always, her heart trembled slightly as she blinked—the stories of attacks upon palanquins made it clear that the opening was the most dangerous moment, and even a sharp-witted lady with a *yue* was at a disadvantage.

But it was only Takshin, who offered his hand with a grave, uncharacteristic half-smile. The greenstone seal-ring upon his left first finger glimmered, and the kyeogra in his ear did the same. Would he still regard her so kindly if he knew of Dao's presence? Impossible to tell.

Second Princess Gamnae stood just behind him, her hands tucked in her bright yellow sleeves and her hairpin dangling a string of golden crystals. Her dress was still entirely too flounced and ribboned for Yala's taste, but at least she had not rouged her cheeks or doubled her ear-drops. With only the lightest dusting of zhu powder her fair round face was much prettier, and she had taken to wearing only one hairpin instead of loading her braids with adornment.

Perhaps with the First Princess gone, she no longer felt as overlooked.

A lean shadow at Gamnae's back was Sixth Prince Jin in a sober scholar's robe and modest topknot-cage, giving orders for his sister's palanquin in a strong, light tenor. Many of the throng were simply pressing to enter the great stacked-roof theater, the largest of its kind in Zhaon-An, its eaves dripping character banners announcing the week's celebrity actors and a few of the more notable vignettes, their sinuous lengths flapping desultorily on a steam-freighted breeze. The peasant and merchant class loved their follies and did not even mind pressing through the low, mean doors meant for their ingress. Puddles reflected the dying sunset in rich, noble colors; the afternoon storm had been short but furious and now the sky was clean, stars poking their bright needles through indigo fabric.

Gamnae's jatajatas clicked as she stepped close. Takshin growled a few short orders at the palanquin bearers. It was a nobleman's honor to do so for a noblewoman, no matter that it fell to steward or kaburei when such a man was unavailable. In Khir, Bai would have been the one to perform that service for her, while Daoyan offered his arm and made light conversation. She would enter the massive, low-roofed Great Theater through the Rider's Entrance, through which it was death for peasant or merchant to pass, with Bai glowering behind her both to guard his sister's honor and to make certain House Komori's private box was not double-sold—at least, not upon that particular night.

Here in Zhaon, she stepped close to Gamnae. "*The sunset is a painted screen,*" she murmured, and smiled at the girl. Indeed, it was difficult not to.

"That's Zhe Har, isn't it? Right before the Moon Maiden appears." Gamnae's own smile was a gift upon her round, Moon-beautiful face. She would grow to be a coquette unless given some firmness now, Yala thought, but perhaps the example of a Khir noblewoman would correct her course somewhat. "I am no good at reading."

"Well, you know that reference." What was Kai doing at this moment, Yala wondered? Nothing so pleasant as attending the theater, to be sure. And yet, she hoped he would find her letters a relief. "How would you answer it, at court?"

"Probably by hiding my mouth and pretending not to understand." Gamnae raised her sleeve, but only to free a fan from its pockets. The gown was patterned with branching hart's horns and the stitching was very fine, though Yala would not have performed the bulk of it upon the back and skirt. Cuffs and hem, certainly— but more was too florid, and did Gamnae's ripening shape no justice. "They all know I am stupid."

"Do they? Then they are wrong." Yala's fingers found her own fan, lacquered black and a little smaller than she preferred for the theater.

The one she would have *liked* to carry was with Zakkar Kai. At least her hairpin held the pebble, so Bai would be present to watch this night's folly.

How he loved plays—the night out, the excitement, the dining in an inn, Yala behind a screen while Bai and often Dao chose small bits of meat for her and poured her a thimbleful or two of sohju. She, of course, poured their tea, careful not to lean too far forward and let the room see her face. Only a sleeve, a wrist, a graceful hand.

What would Daoyan think of Yala's promise to Zhaon's greatest enemy? *Were I free to choose*, she had said...and her father's seal was a reminder she was not. And her father's letter, giving her a blessing as if he suspected it would not be long before his health deteriorated.

"You look sad." Gamnae's fan began to work, lazily. "Is it...may I ask, does this remind you of your...of someone?"

"Somewhat, yes." Yala might have had a stinging reply if the question was unkind, or meant to allude to her grief, but she had warmed to this child. There was very little unkindness in Garan Gamnae, she thought, a miraculous thing given her parentage. "Khir's princesses do not leave the Great Keep, unless for a hunt or to be married."

The Zhaon girl's eyes widened considerably, but not in mockery. "Not to the theater?"

"No. Nor to the market, or even to the apothecary." Even a noblewoman did not venture far from her father's home—or her husband's. "It is very different here."

"Not at *all*?" Gamnae could hardly credit her ears. "But what do they do instead?"

"There is much for a princess inside the Great Keep," Yala answered, equally enough. "And if there is a lady-in-waiting with the gift for it, a report upon the plays in the Great Theater is brought back to the princess—who may decide to petition her father for the players to be brought to amuse the Great Rider."

"Oh." Gamnae's fan began to work harder, and she glanced nervously over Yala's shoulder. "Come, walk with me."

And leave our escorts behind? Yala decided upon a diplomatic answer. "Should we not wait for them?"

"We won't go very far." Gamnae's mouth turned down at the corners briefly, and she seemed uneasy. The hem of her skirt fluttered like Yala's, fingered by a breeze that held no evening coolness. "I dislike standing upon the steps, it is dreadful to be watched like a butcher's cart."

"I should think court is similar," Yala observed. At least the clinging water in the air had been temporarily washed free by a downpour.

"Very." Gamnae halted. She was slightly taller, and when she looked down her nose in that fashion she looked very much like her mother—though indeed, Yala had only seen the First Queen briefly. The princess drew close enough onlookers could suspect them friendly, if not friends. A faint breath of the incense used to perfume her gown reached Yala over the simmering smell of a Zhaon-An street, never mind that the theater employed an army of sweepers and sprinklers to keep its apron clear. "Lady Yala…"

"Yes, Second Princess?" Yala's fan arranged itself, hiding both of them as Gamnae leaned ever closer. It was a habitual movement, often employed when Mahara wished to share some confidence.

"I was going to invite you anyway," the girl said, hurriedly. "But my brother...Lady Yala, he asked me to be kind to you. Not Takshin. My eldest brother." She had gone pale under the zhu powder, and though she said *eldest* it was not the word appropriate for the Crown Prince.

It could only mean another of Garan Tamuron's sons.

"Should I thank him?" Yala's back ran with shiverflesh for a moment. Second Prince Kurin, sleepy-eyed and languid, did not please her. Oh, his behavior toward Mahara had been perfectly proper, except for his ill-bred remarks upon their first informal meeting.

Yala herself had met that moment more than adequately, but now she wondered at his purpose.

"*Shu*, no." Now Gamnae actually looked horrified, paling briefly. "That would be terrible. Lady—"

That was all they were allowed, for Jin appeared on Gamnae's other side. "It would be easier with horses," he announced. "Next time we will ride."

"I should say *not*." Gamnae snapped her fan closed and her right hand made a short motion, as if she longed to pinch her brother's ribs. "Not to the theater. You're a terrible escort."

"Oh, I could go home." The youngest prince had gained a few more fingerwidths of height since Yala had last seen him; he was of the age where such a change happened nearly overnight. He was brave, though—and he had struck down the traitorous guard in the Great Market on that terrible afternoon not so long ago. "And you could be stuck with Taktak for the rest of the night."

"*Stuck* with me indeed." Takshin, his steps cat-soft, was at Yala's side again, appearing like a theater-trick. "It will be just as warm inside, but with less dust. Let us proceed."

Yala, however, let Gamnae precede her. By all rights Takshin should have been escorting his sister, leaving younger Jin with a lady-in-waiting as the rules of etiquette demanded, but the Third Prince offered his arm and waited for Yala to lay her fingertips in the crook of his elbow before moving. "What are the doves whispering about?"

"The Khir theater, and its marvels." Yala gave him a smile. Why would the Second Prince wish his sister to cultivate a foreign lady in some fashion? With Mahara...gone, Yala was a dish that did not match any set. "I look forward to seeing if Zhaon can surpass them."

"Mh." Takshin glanced at the doors as they were ushered through the high narrow nobility's keyhole, paint-faced dolls on either side bowing low and repeating the traditional utterance, *schi-schi, come in, come in*. Their bright gowns, and the patterned tunics of the acrobats-in-training who welcomed the crowd to their elder siblings' performance, were a relief from the drab dust outside. "This is my first time in the Great Theater."

"Is it?" Yala had to move her hand as a passageway swallowed them, lit only by tremble-fading mirrorlight and floating hala lamps, those wonderful, ingenious things that snuffed themselves when overturned so as not to cause conflagration. "I would have thought..."

"The Mad Queen of Shan disliked the theaters. Players would come to perform, and if she was in a good mood she would load them with ingots and send them away. If not, well." He stared straight ahead, and suddenly closed his right hand over hers upon his left elbow. "I left Zhaon too young to visit this place. I think I did not miss much."

"Perhaps not." Yala's throat was dry. The little she had heard of Shan's former queen was unpleasant at best. Not only that, but his scars spoke of barbarity as well.

She threw me down a well, he had said, and Yala had offered the kyeogra during that conversation. Not from pity; at the moment, she could not name the impulse that had moved her.

She still had difficulty finding the proper word for it.

The Third Prince rested his free hand lightly upon his other forearm, index finger tapping to some private music. "And you, my lady Spyling? Are you here for diversion, or to keep Gamnae company?"

"I love the theater," Yala admitted. "I was sent to gather the plays for the Crown Princess." It felt strange to say Mahara's formal title, a position instead of a person, but it was for the best. The danger of her shade lingering was largely past with mourning's closure, but respect was due those who rode the Great Fields. "Sometimes her father brought the players to the Great Keep, but if not, I would gather them for her." There was no term for it in Zhaon, so she used the phrase for bringing one's superior a bouquet.

Takshin absorbed this with a faint air of puzzlement. "You would gather them for her?" He repeated the term, but with the lilt that told her she had not been incorrect, merely opaque of meaning.

"I would describe the stage, the costumes, the light, the puppets of *bunjo* and the actors of *tuijo*." Yala could not help but smile, though her chest ached. It was a sweet pain, but pain nonetheless. "I would declaim the parts for her, too." Largely from memory; it was good practice.

"We should send you nightly, then, to gather the play like crush-flowers in a market girl's basket." His scarred lip twitched once, but after that a smile relaxed his mouth. "And keep Gamnae at home."

"Princesses in Zhaon seem to have a great deal of freedom," she hazarded. Every Zhaon woman did, as a matter of fact. Now there were green-carpeted steps leading to the upper levels; Takshin preceded her. Before him, Gamnae's gown brushed the step below as she balanced upon her jatajatas, climbing steadily. Sixth Prince Jin appeared to be teasing his sister for her slowness, and one of Gamnae's replies was a short, scathing term much more suited to a laborer than a court maiden.

Takshin moved sideways, his back to the carved banister hammered to the wall, and Yala realized he was watching above *and* below them upon the staircase. Did he expect an attempt upon his sister's life, or his brother's? His own?

It was exhausting to think one could not even attend the theater in peace.

"Much freedom indeed," he said at the head of the stairs, his hand now cupping her elbow as if she had stumbled. "I worry for Gamnae, left alone with *that woman.*"

He said it with such venom it took her a moment to realize he meant his own mother, and Gamnae's as well. It was Yala's turn to glance about, to make certain there was nobody near enough to catch such an ill-advised statement.

Takshin caught the motion, and his smile broadened apprecia-bly. His scarred lip was a trifle crooked, but for all that, the expres-sion held true amusement. "You worry for me, then?"

"You seem as bold as your little sister."

His expression turned sardonic, but his eyes gleamed. "Do you prefer bold princes, my lady Yala, or retiring ones?"

"Princes are above my preferences." She reclaimed her own arm and set off after Jin and Gamnae, who had taken her youngest brother's with a surreptitious poke to his ribs—a maneuver Yala well remembered performing upon Bai once or twice.

Her damoi was an irritant sometimes, but he never pressed too far. And Yala could count upon him for intercession, or for succor as the need arose. Under her dress, the thin silver chain holding her father's signet was a warm reassurance.

But why had he sent it? His letter was troubling. *You are the last flower of Khir*, he had written, *and I wish for you to land softly.* He did not mention Dao, had not included instructions—it was not like him at all.

It was more a farewell than a letter, she decided, and that wor-ried her.

Takshin kept pace beside her, his footfalls soft though he was booted as a soldier. Shan must be a harsh land, to train him to such vigilance. "Indulge me."

It was her duty, so Yala did. "A bold prince may be a tyrant, a retiring one ineffective." Too late she realized what the allusion could be construed as, in light of the Crown Prince's travel plans. "Though a prince who retires at the proper moment is full of wis-dom." The two final syllables could be a play upon the words for *crown prince*, which made it a very neat duet, with its sting in the tail instead of between its wings.

"Yala." Garan Takshin caught at her elbow again, the leashed strength of his fingers sinking into her sleeve. Gamnae and Jin disappeared through a curtained recess, which left her in a theater-hall, witnessed only by the flowers and junior acrobats at intervals ready to guide a patron to a proper seat or send an order for crushed fruit or appetizers to a nearby restaurant.

"Takshin." She searched his face, familiar now, and cold threads touched the sweat at the hollow of her back. Her hairpin's dangling bead tapped her hair as she halted. "Have you discovered something?"

"Discovered? Oh, that." He shook his head, a short, fierce motion. The kyeogra gleamed at his ear, a secretive fire. "No. Or yes, but not in the way you mean. I would know the manner of prince you prefer."

"Prefer?" She did not mean to sound so blank. If it was a riddle or an allusion, she lacked the scholarship to answer.

"Surely you must have some slight wish, for a royal—"

"There you are." Jin hurried through the curtain and beckoned them. "Come, the first farce is beginning, and Gamnae wishes her companion."

Yala tugged free and swept away, which meant Takshin had to follow. For some reason, her cheeks were burning. She settled next to Gamnae upon a low padded bench, casting a practiced eye over the theater as the peasant-crowd in the bowl began to hoot and throw rinds and nutshells.

"So, is this like Khir?" Gamnae asked, high color standing in her own plump, pretty face. Excited to be free of the palace for a night, excited to be in the grown-up world, and doubly excited to be showing a foreigner such a jewel as the Great Theater of Zhaon-An, with its famous columns, its stage with its mechanisms for raising and lowering, its modern lighting and expensive, wonderful effects.

Yala could only shake her head and raise her fan. Its motion provided little coolness; Jin braved the corridor again to send for crushed fruit and other niceties, and Takshin settled in the most shadowed corner of the box.

Every time she glanced in his direction, his gaze was fixed upon her rather than the stage. And she was troubled by the persistent, quiet thought that perhaps he was not brotherly at all.

FINE STRATEGY

C h'han kujiu was not a complex game, but its very simplicity was deceptive. The crunch of a heavy leather-wrapped ball being deflected by the West Guard's ribs—the fellow could not get his hands down in time—was lost in a roar from the crowd, and the intensity of unofficial betting mounted another few notches.

This was not the Great Bowl reserved for chariot races but a smaller hollowed playing field just outside Zhaon-An's walls, and the jostling on temporary stone and timber half-circle seating slowly accreting into permanence was severe enough that the better pickpockets were probably having a fine day. Smoke rose from a nearby Ch'han temple, its stacked roof hiding in a haze.

They were offering sacrifices for the Emperor's health. A useless endeavor, as far as Garan Sensheo was concerned, but forms must be observed.

The Fifth Prince watched as the ball bounded away, the West Guard's naked chest gleaming with oil and a dust-mark upon his ribs. Both teams scurried after the prize, though the West and East Guards stayed in their places, tense and alert like hunting dogs. A few stray canines lingered at the edges of the crowd too, darting for dropped objects that might possibly be food despite the risk of being cuffed or kicked.

A dog's hunger was predictable and natural. A man's was... otherwise.

At Sensheo's shoulder, watching the game with every evidence of satisfaction and attention, Second Prince Kurin stood in a sunset-colored robe, his thumb moving lazily over the hurai on his left first finger. It matched the ring on Sensheo's left hand, too, but the Fifth Prince also wore a heavy, luxurious archer's thumb-ring of carved horn, often tapping it with his fingertips while deep in thought. Today both rings were collecting sweat under their smooth inner faces, though the afternoon storm was merely a dark smudge upon the horizon.

"You must cease," Kurin said finally, in Sensheo's ear. Though the temporary awning and a few frown-faced, sweating servants gave them a modicum of elbow room, this was not the Bowl with its luxurious—by comparison—amenities. "We need that fellow."

"*I* do not need him," Sensheo answered, smoothing his face as a scowl attempted to rise. Of course he could not deny his second-eldest brother the pleasure of accompanying him, but he did not have to be lectured while he watched what was, in his opinion, a very fine game despite its plebeian character. "They are rattling empty scabbards, Elder Brother. And consider: one death for them, one death for us. Think of it as a peace-gift, not a tribute."

"All gifts are tribute," Kurin muttered darkly, his dark gaze sweeping the crowd instead of the field. His expression stayed pleasant and open, though none of his brothers would miss the tension in his shoulders and the slight, cruel curl to the left corner of his mouth. "You are a fool, Sensheo."

Well, while Sensheo knew his elder brothers thought him of less wit than their own exalted selves, it was still a trifle ill-bred of them to *say* as much. It was becoming increasingly difficult to keep from scowling. "I am simply more courageous than those who sneer behind a fan while bowing to his hurai."

"It irks you that Father gave him a prince's seal." Kurin, for once, was irritated enough to state the obvious. "I did not think you so small-minded, brother."

"Say what you came to say, Kurin." *And be gone*, he might have added, but it would only make his elder linger, if only to torment.

"I enjoy this game, I do not wish to have you singing in my ear during the final act."

Kurin paused. He moved a half-step closer, as if conferring excitedly with his brother about the spectacle. "Did you get it?"

"Get what?" Sensheo's hands dove into his sleeves as he leaned forward, a tuneless whistle escaping him as the West team passed the ball with quick flickers of foot, knee, or head. Intricate and wonderful, parts moving together to achieve an end—it only *appeared* artless. It took a connoisseur to understand the various permutations of play, the fine strategy, the—

"Hand it over," Kurin all but shouted in his ear, less than a whisper in the swelling crowd-noise. "I weary of this, Tentin." The childhood nickname, born from young Gamnae's lack of proper pronunciation, was a poke upon a bruise.

Sensheo's fingers caressed the small bottle with its sliver of soakwood stopper, safe in his sleeve pocket. He enjoyed the sensation of withholding almost as much as he enjoyed the low sound a sudo made as it cut air, or the *thock* of an arrow into a straw-stuffed target. A bow was much finer than a sword; it required more finesse. "I don't have it," he lied. "Your apothecary pretended not to recognize the words."

"Sensheo." A promise of retaliation in Kurin's tone. His elder brother jostled him; if he were younger, Sensheo would brace himself for a poke to the ribs or worse. Sabwone liked scratching, but Kurin did not care to break the skin.

Only what was underneath.

Sensheo wondered what Sabi was doing, carried off to Shan. Anyone who married *her* was in for a surprise; she should have been the First Queen's daughter instead of silly, simple Gamnae.

"I told him, *I am here for what was promised.* He laughed at me." Sensheo set his chin and was finally able to scowl briefly. He was perhaps overplaying this part, but Kurin was too dim to notice.

"You dragged me out here to tell me this?"

"*You* wanted to go somewhere we would not be overheard." Sensheo tensed as the East team took the ball, a lanky kaburei with a leather-wrapped club at his nape moving with thoughtless speed

to subtract the prize from his opponents and run the length of the
yellowing grass field. The crowd began to bay, sensing consummation; Sensheo leaned forward. The barrier between the play area
and the spectators was flimsy, and often broke into splinters when
the crowd, maddened by heat, victory, or defeat, surged forward
to tear at invisible tormentors like a maddened animal. "Now be
quiet, this is…oh, *move*, you tortoise egg!" The cry slipped free
before he could halt it, as the West team clustered the lone East
player, caught unprotected without his mates.

Kurin shoved him, and for a few moments Sensheo and his elder
brother were hip to hip, straining against each other like massive
N'hon wrestlers sacred to their thunder-god. Kurin even sank his
knuckles into Sensheo's stomach, and the small scuffle was lost
in a roar as the crowd watched the East kaburei shake free of his
pursuers, running and kicking at the same time, rolling the ball
under his bare foot and turning, putting a hip into a West player's
midsection while the latter attempted to drag him down, throwing
off the fellow for a crucial moment while his leg flickered to send
the ball bouncing between and under other flying feet into range
of one of his teammates, a lanky man in a breechclout and a high
topknot caged with leather, his brawny arms shouting *blacksmith* as
loudly as the soot staining his spatulate fingers.

A collective cry of gratification rose from every throat surrounding the princes, and Kurin had found what he wanted—the small
bottle in Sensheo's sleeve. He subtracted it, shoved Sensheo aside,
and in a few moments was gone into the press of spectators beyond
the few servants attempting to keep the Fifth Prince from the grasp
of pickpockets or importunate bet-masters.

Sensheo coughed, wiped at his mouth, and returned his attention to the game. Oh, Kurin thought himself very brave indeed,
beating upon his brothers; Kurin thought himself very clever,
sending little Sensheo to collect such an article.

The game was not yet over. It wasn't even begun.

Sensheo's belly hurt, so did his knee, and his arm was probably
bruised, but he wore a very slight smile.

It was the expression of a fisherman whose nets were very full and home harbor near. He wiped at his mouth again with the backs of his fingers. *"Run!"* he yelled, the unprincely howl lost in the crowd's roar as the East team moved for the goal and the West Guard spread his arms, daring his opponents with a disdainful motion. *"Run, you idiots!"*

WITNESS

Six days after the end of formal mourning for a foreign princess the Palace lay under a bruising flood of white-hot sunlight, but in the Second Concubine's part of the Iejo there was relative coolness and a deep, expectant hush. Lamps burned, thin golden gleams adding to a pall of mirrorlight, and the thin blanket upon her chest was a heavy weight. There were soft voices, soft footsteps—even now, there was no privacy.

All she had ever asked was a small space to hide within, but the world pursued mice as well as tigers.

"My lady." A cool hand upon her brow; she was lifted, a goblet of crushed fruit put to her lips. She refused it with a murmur. "My lady, you must try. For your strength."

It was the servant girl with the scar upon her jaw. She was a quiet one, steady, with good hands. Best of all, she was not one of the First Queen's little spiders. Kanbina's adoptive-son had put an end to *that* spying and sneaking within the household, and the Second Concubine was grateful.

So Kanbina merely shook her head, her hair a heavy river. Her neck was a frail stem and the pain, a constant companion, had retreated under the tinctures Zakkar Kai's physician mixed for her. Now she floated, and as she did so, memory filled her in successive waves.

Her rotting childhood home, great holes in the roof and the

elderly, shuffling servants, her father's bony liver-spotted hand upon a knifehilt. *You must strike for Wurei*, he had said, pressing the weapon into her own maiden's hand. *If I fall in battle. In the very marriage-bed, if you must.*

Perhaps she might even have found the strength to do so if Father had not died in the Battle of Nashua-An and Garan Tamuron had not ridden to the door of the keep with blood still smoking upon his armor. He seemed a very spirit of battle and murder, a creature sent by Heaven to visit terrible vengeance upon the living. *I will keep you*, the warlord said, *but I cannot have another wife. What say you, lady of Wurei?*

Had he thought her silence pride, like his first queen's, or even aristocratic disdain, like his first concubine's? No, she had merely quailed before the armored warrior with his great horned helm as the elderly servant woman who performed both as chaperone and teacher moaned in fear and fat roundbirds called softly in the rafters of the keep that had once held Zhaon's rulers.

Wurei was a noble house, and she its last twig. Was that why Gamwone had done it?

Kanbina moved fretfully upon her bed. She did not wish to think upon that woman, not yet. Instead, she rallied her fading strength and opened her eyes.

A faint hot breeze came from the verandah, and upon a pillow near the open partition was the Khir lady-in-waiting, her head bent as she sewed. Her hairpin, dark and sober as her dress, was thrust through a nest of blue-black braids and she raised her head as if she sensed a gaze upon her, laying aside the silk—it looked like a sleeve of bright, cheerful blue cotton with plum silk edging.

She was quiet, this girl, and when she visited Kanbina's adoptive-son watched her closely. He tried to hide it, certainly, but Kanbina had so few visitors she had sharpened her observation upon them until it was capable of slicing a hair into quarters, as the saying went. She approved, and had written to Zakkar Kai to tell him so.

If she had birthed a son...oh, but that was useless. All she had birthed was a spreading stain upon bedding, clots of semi-liquid flesh passing in chunks while invisible blades ripped into her vitals. And Garan Tamuron's face, bloodless as if he already suspected...

Had he known from the beginning and simply left her here as the years accumulated? She had never asked for any preferment or prize, even when the red lanterns hung at her door to show the Emperor was with his concubine. At first she had been dazed, and those few nights of his passion had not quite hurt, but...oh, she had been so young.

So very, very young.

He could have left her alone, rotting in that manse. It would have made no difference to the conqueror of Zhaon. But he was nothing if not thorough, her husband, and no house that had once ruled was left with sons to rise against him or eldest daughters to bear other heirs.

It was the children who had come to her, by day or night. Little Takshin, with his hunger for plums and his fierce, prickly pride hiding the softest of hearts; sometimes plump little Gamnae fascinated by a recluse. Somber Takyeo, long-legged and biting at his thumbnail before remembering he was a prince and such creatures did not chew so; Sensheo visiting to see if she would give him small items his mother would not. Makar's visits had grown perfunctory, Kurin's slightly scornful, and Sabwone's simply frittered into nothingness as she found other pastimes.

But Zakkar Kai came again and again, listening to her play, performing small tasks, bringing her gifts.

Takyeo, too. *Father said I should*, the not-yet Crown Prince had informed her once, and much later, after drinking a cup of sohju and watching flame-flowers bloom to announce a Knee-High Festival's conclusion, he had glanced at his father's second concubine and smiled. *We are lonely together*, he had said, and Kanbina could have wept with the shame.

At least they had not accused her of ill-wishing other children since she could have none of her own—except Kai. His return from Three Rivers had brought peace in its wake, but now he was gone again, and she was too weak to even write.

The Khir girl was at the bedside now, and laid a soft damp cloth upon Kanbina's forehead. "You are flushed," she murmured in her accented Zhaon. She was a child too, despite her quiet reserve, but she would make a fine wife to the boy Kanbina had secretly pretended was hers all these years.

She was glad she had made the formal request to adopt him, even though her fingers had trembled when brushing the characters. The heavy, royal greenstone seal she hardly ever used, its characters of her adult name strange and sharp, had been pressed into service. It was a mark of the position she had never wanted, but she had used it and waited in an agony of half hope, half terror.

Did it matter that she had not heaved and groaned through birthing him? Would she have loved him more if she *had*?

It seemed impossible.

A hot breeze touched the garden, gaining at least the illusion of coolness as it moved over water and through a filter of rustling green babu. *Ka-thock*, the water-clock said, and a bird in the high, lush green replied. It sounded like a redthroat, that messenger of Heaven.

Is it time?

But her body, not yet at the end of its blind, selfish grasping, forced her eyes to reopen and her chest to rise again with a long, slow inhale. She stared at the strange-eyed girl hovering over her before realizing just who it was and moved fretfully, disturbing the cool, scented cloth upon her brow.

"Write," Kanbina managed, through dry lips. "Write...for me."

"Of course." The girl turned aside, spoke in a low firm tone, and servants began to scurry. Kanbina had never learned that trick; the elderly kaburei serving her father had bossed her relentlessly.

"And how fares my royal patient?" This voice was new but familiar. It was the physician Kihon Jiao, newly arrived in his shabby cotton robe, but with his topknot oiled and immaculate in a carved wooden holder.

"Asking for brush and paper, Honorable Physician." The Khir girl could not bow to one of his status, of course, but she inclined her head and smiled warmly enough. A true noblewoman treated underlings with distance, yes—but also with kindness.

"No harm in that." The round-cheeked physician bowed deeply in Kanbina's direction. "Lady Komor, I must attend to the Second Concubine; I do not like to ask, but may I have your chair?"

Be still, Kanbina thought. *I must concentrate.* It was coming, amid the constant pain in her vitals—sometimes better, sometimes worse, but never more than ameliorated. She *felt* it, a chill amid the heat of summer's beginning. The garden shimmered past the physician and the girl in deep indigo silk; she bent all her attention upon it and breathed through the heatless, cresting sensation.

"Stop," she said. It was no more than a cricket's whisper, but both physician and lady-in-waiting halted. Two gazes, one ghostly and the other proper dark Zhaon, fastened upon Kanbina's face. "I have little time."

The physician settled upon the chair, and his fingertips were dry and warm as he felt for the levels of her pulse. His face did not change, but Komor Yala, hovering behind him, tucked her hands into her sleeves as if she too felt a chill.

That one has seen an elder leave the house before. The thought was amusing, and Kanbina forced down a laugh. She did not wish to, but merriment, even diluted, brought the coughing spasms in its wake, and with it the metallic slickness of blood filling her throat.

Kihon Jiao glanced up, and she read the truth upon his features as well. Neither he nor the Khir girl bothered to lie, with voice or countenance.

It was an unexpected gift.

"I wish…" Kanbina's throat filled, and she thought for a

moment she would strangle on warm, slippery tea from the morning's attempt at breakfast. The coughing attacked like a sleek, well-fed cat shaking a toy or a pinchnose mouse; the physician slid an arm below her slight shoulders and lifted her. Yala hurried to bring a small covered metal bowl for the wad of bright crimson with its mixture of yellow bile. When the spasm had passed, the physician nestled her among pulled-high pillows and bolsters with a son's solicitous care.

Kanbina tried again. "I wish both of you to witness," she whispered, painfully. The corners were darkening despite mirrorlight, a tenebrous veil rising like a painted screen to keep a noble bride's modesty. "Witness...my words."

"I hear, Second Concubine." The physician's mien was grave. He did not dig in his bag of essentials or hurry to the small table for the mixing of tinctures. Instead, he kept his hand upon her wrist, following her pulse.

The Khir girl murmured something in her own language, her face rising over his shoulder like a moon. Kanbina beckoned, bringing her to the other side of the bed. She wished them both close. "Hold...my hand. Are you?"

"Yes, Garan Kanbina." Excruciatingly polite, the girl ducked her dark head, her hairpin's chained bead swinging.

"*Mother*," Kanbina insisted, the affectionate Zhaon term for a mother-in-law. Kihon Jiao did not so much as glance at Lady Komor, though he must have wondered.

"Yes, Mother." Komor Yala had paled. The poor girl, her princess gone so soon and now this. Kanbina had wanted to protect her, for Kai's sake at least. Where would she go now?

There was no protection under Heaven for the meek or the righteous. "Witness my words," she whispered, and her eyelids sought to fall. She denied it, her will once more mastering the tired, shuddering horse her body had become. At last, the habit of years stood her in good stead instead of forcing her to plowing endurance. "I wish for you *both*."

They did, the physician's dry fingers still upon her pulse and the girl...oh, the girl, older than Kanbina had been but still, still so young.

"My...son," she whispered. "Care for him."

"I will," Komor Yala said, and her strange eyes glimmered, full of warm salt.

"I...wish no ill...on anyone..." The wad of blood rose in Kanbina's throat again, and the idea that she would perhaps die with the most important half of the sentence left unspoken filled her with a great, heaving, pointless rage.

It was the first time in her life she had ever let herself feel such a thing, and its sharp temporary heat spurred her.

"No ill," she said, and her voice had become a brazen gong. "Unless it is upon Yulehi-a Gamwone, who poisoned me. I will take news of her treachery to Heaven itself—"

"My lady," the physician began. He had turned ashen under his wispy brown stubble. "My lady, save your strength."

"To Heaven itself," Kanbina insisted, and the susurration near the door told her the servants had gathered. Death often came with a retinue in great houses, and for once she welcomed the attention. She wished the tale of hers to be told through the palace; she wished it to pad with the servants and be whispered behind court ladies' fans, she wished for the eunuchs to discuss it in their enclave and the ministers to exchange significant looks as they hinted. "I will tell of poison in a gift of hrebao tea, and the Great Consort of Heaven Herself will hear me."

The pang arrived, a spike through her heart and her throat filling, her eyes bulging as she fought, for once. The last lady of lost Wurei had bent before the weight of expectation, suffering, and duty. Marrying the conqueror had halted any who might take up banners in Wurei's cause, and thus, the land devastated by war again and again could heal. She had not even minded so much.

Until children, the children she could have borne and loved, had been stolen from her.

Years of patient waiting bent under the burden of Gamwone's

hate and Garan Tamuron's negligence had turned to gall. And now, finally, she had the means to strike back.

She had thought the shades of children she could have had would cluster her bedside—perhaps a strong tall son with Garan Tamuron's eyes; she would have been endlessly content even with a daughter. Instead, it was a foreign woman and a stranger who held her hands as the shadows whispered her declaration, over and over again.

"*Do you hear me?*" she cried, and denied the coughing again. "Witness, Heaven and all the hells of evildoers—"

"My lady," Kihon Jiao began, again. Of course, it would be dangerous for him to hear this.

"Hush," Komor Yala snapped.

Oh, Kanbina liked the girl, and it was not fair to place her under this burden. But Kai would protect her, as he had protected his adoptive-mother.

"Witness," Garan Wurei-a Kanbina cried again, and the shadows gathered at the bedside. They were somber and solemn with large dark eyes; they were not children but her ancestors, stern tall men and round, long-sleeved women with their smallest fingers on each hand glittering under filigree sheaths. There was her father, too, his mouth drawn down in a disapproving curve.

Of course they found her unacceptable. She had not struck down the conqueror or borne descendants; their shrines would go untended and their spirits hungry.

"Wurei!" Kanbina called. "Wurei! *She is to blame! Yulehi-a Gamwone is to blame!*"

She lost consciousness soon afterward, her wasted body deflating as its inhabitant was drawn softly forth. No more did Garan Wurei-a Kanbina speak, her lips starred with bright blood and mucus, and she did not need to.

Her servants were loyal, true. But not even the stern gods of silence and rectitude could keep this event from being spoken of. Besides, she did not wish it to pass unremarked, and perhaps service to their lady—kind and retiring, shy and pleasant—loosened their tongues.

Her only revenge was to make certain all knew, and to pronounce the doom upon her deathbed. The last words of the dying held weight and consequence, and she would have both flung at the First Queen like javelins, like stones from a trebuchet, like Heaven's very own bolts.

She lingered until the afternoon storm nestled over Zhaon-An, lightning stabbing black clouds to make fertilizing rain, and when the clouds raced away to spill over Zhaon's fields and pastures, it carried a dying woman's curse with it, free at last.

Hrebao Tea

"Ridiculous." The First Queen of Zhaon settled against a rectangular bolster, her hair piled high and held in place by old-fashioned braids and two hairpins, one with Anwei shellwork upon its flared head and the other plain dark metal. She patted the nia oil with the third finger of each hand, delicately dabbing beneath her large, dark, very fine eyes.

"Nevertheless." Her eldest son was behind an expensive screen painted with bronzefish enjoying a summer night's feast of glow-flies, as was often his wont while she attended to these nighttime chores.

She had forgiven his former indiscretion at the breakfast table almost as soon as it was committed. What mother could not pardon such a son? He was, after all, high-spirited. Not inert, like Gamnae—girls were no good—and certainly not an ungrateful quillmonster like her *other* son.

No, her firstborn was her sole hope.

"Her servants are not known for gossip and I have done all I can," Kurin continued, relentlessly. He did not shift upon his cushion but his strength was evident even in his shadow, a prop for his mother's old age. "I suppose I should ask if there is any truth to the rumor."

"Rumor?" Gamwone scoffed again. What she did to keep her position unchallenged was, after all, for her children's benefit. Who else should or would she extend such effort for? "It is ill-bred to ask a lady about *rumors*, much less your own mother."

"How can I not?" Her beloved son's sigh was irritating, since it was very much like his father's. "Shall you be hiring another exorcist, Mother?"

Gamwone regarded herself in high-polished bronze. A ghost-woman met her gaze, her eyes unacceptably round for a few moments, and she firmed her mouth into its usual slight curve. There was no reason to look frightened or even particularly ashamed when one had done only what one must. "For what?"

"To cleanse your steps of ill-luck. There seems a surfeit of it lately."

"They would do well to gossip about that Khir bitch." Gamwone hoped someone *was* listening. Everyone knew Northerners were cold and secretive, untrustworthy. "Perhaps *she* slipped something into the little mouse's grain."

"Mother." Kurin's tone held a warning. That was new; he would never have dared to speak to her so, before. Novel events, from breakfast table to nightly discussion, were crowding upon the Kaeje fast and thick these days.

"I do not say anything I have not heard others mutter." Unmollified, she turned her attention to the next step in her routine, the crushflower attar. "No need to lay anything at *my* chamber partition."

"I would counsel you to keep quiet about this, Mother." Now Kurin sounded weary. His shadow did not move, however, so he could not be too upset at a rival's disappearance. Thank Heaven the little Wurei bitch had not spawned, there were enough problems as it was.

And was there a single word of thanks from her uncle or her son? Of course not. Gamwone did what they dared not; she shielded the entire *clan* and provided them with high honors and wealth, but they presumed and threw tantrums.

Just let them go a single day without her efforts, though. They would feel the lack.

"Oh, you would counsel me thus?" Gamwone studied her collection. Jars and lidded pots; unguents, oils, powders; brushes and pads for spreading or dabbing; creams and solid bars, perfume flasks and warm wooden or greenstone implements to smooth, chafe, shape, sculpt. Generals had soldiers and weapons, mothers had sons and decorative arts. "Don't worry. I have swallowed so many insults, what is one more?"

"This is no insult, Mother." Kurin still did not move. His shadow was a familiar shape, tall and broad-shouldered. The screen watched her, glowflies caught in daubs of yellow paint. Brief lives, ending in dark snapping maws—normally, it pleased her to contemplate its artistry. "It is quite a serious matter."

"She raves upon her deathbed, and I am supposed to quail?" Gamwone did not shake her head—he would not see the gesture, why bother? "I think not."

"It is well known she had no children."

"So she was barren. What of it?" And Gamwone had not lifted a finger. No, with her pet physician so eager to please, a hint sufficed. Thank goodness that fellow had recently eaten something indiscreet too; his belly had swollen and fellow physicians had been called to his bedside. The Honorable Tian Ha, once chief court physician with her powerful patronage magnifying him, now lay raving in agony, not expected to last long.

Yes, Gamwone had done nothing. If others felt moved to smooth away wrinkles in folded cloth, as the proverb ran, why should she bother deterring them? And she could easily find another physician to attend her household's needs. There was no shortage in Zhaon-An.

Kurin made a short, irritated noise, much as he had when a childhood toy had been broken beyond repair. "Can you not simply *pretend* to care?"

"Why should I?" It was time to turn her attention to Haesara, that nose-high Hanweo whore spurning a higher queen's offer of friendship. She would have to move carefully, there.

But it could be done. All manner of things were possible with the Palace in such a state.

"Because she mentioned hrebao." Each of Kurin's words held a crisp edge, not quite a remonstrance but very close.

Gamwone's fingers did not halt their dabbing. They merely cooled a bit, her resined nails held delicately free while the soft pads massaged. "She had a favorite tea?"

"If you do not cease being obtuse, Mother, I shall leave you to your fate."

She had just been thinking what a good child he was, too. Well, he could be allowed his little rebellions, since he was always so winning afterward. "And what fate is that, my son?"

"Poisoners suffer the Hell of the Blue Waters, or have you forgotten?"

"What are you saying?" Gamwone's legs were strangely numb, and her stomach took it upon itself to quiver just a fraction. What did he know of a mother's sacrifices, a mother's attempts to keep her children safe and her own position secure? "And to your own mother. First you throw dishes, now this."

"You *are* determined to be obtuse." Movement brushed behind the screen, cloth shifting. Her son's shadow swelled and changed shape, briefly monstrous against the screen.

"Kurin." Gamwone set aside the jar of attar. When she struck the small gong, her close-servants would creep in to finish the work of pampering and preparing a royal body for bed just as usual. Tonight, she could lie in the dark and think upon the death of a rival with no little satisfaction. Or at least, she could have before this conversation. "Exactly what are you implying?"

"Everyone knows." He sounded weary; her son paused at the edge of the screen as if he meant to peer around its edge, as he had often when a child. How soft and easy he had been, how attached to his dear mother. Why, he could not stand to be sent to Yulehi, even, to reside with her uncle for a week or two in summer, despite the healthfulness of retreating to the country when the season of dust descended. "Father will be forced to act."

"What, from his own deathbed?" She touched a comb, another small jar of crushflower attar with a slight stinging portion of jellied jau to cool small inflamed dots upon the skin. "He has little time to punish me, even if I did anything worth it."

Garan Tamuron had, after all, ignored her for years. Much trouble could have been avoided if he had treated her with some bare consideration, but he had not, and what she had been forced to was *his* fault.

"He might leave such a matter for Takyeo to attend to." Kurin shifted again, as if he was preparing to rise.

Oh, it would be just like him to let others do the foul work while he shuffles into Heaven. Gamwone exhaled sharply. "And will you defend your mother, if that brat decides to blame me for something unproven?"

Kurin was silent for a long moment. Gamwone quelled an uncharacteristic, unwelcome shiver.

More motion behind the screen. She glanced at the shadow-shape. Kurin was not merely stretching to ease an ache or pour a cup of sohju. Instead, her son had risen, and he turned from the screen, his darker self shrinking but no less misshapen by movement.

"I will not be providing a pyre-gift for you this time," he said, finally. "I counsel you to think deeply upon what to send. It should be something you value, to avert a shade's anger."

Gamwone's scoff burned her dry throat, but she did not move. She watched her son's shadow, her eyes narrowed, and had any servant been present they might well have found reason to cower or swiftly find work elsewhere in the halls. "Are you so superstitious?"

"They say she died as the storm moved over Wurei." Kurin's tone was colder than it had ever been. "There is much gossip, Mother, and it makes matters difficult for me."

Oh, so now he admitted he was used to her smoothing his way? The problem with sweet boys was that they became men, and those creatures were deeply ungrateful as a matter of course. "Do you think it is ever easy for *me*, Kurin? Do you?"

"All you must do is refrain from making it worse. I warn you, Mother—"

"Warn me?" Her hands were cold, her feet numb, and the idea of sweeping the jars and pots from the beauty bench with a single violent motion was satisfying in the extreme. If he could throw dishes, what stopped *her*? "A worthless brat, speaking to his mother so."

"It is because I value you that I bother to warn you." Kurin's shadow shrank still further. He had not asked her leave to depart, either—his rudeness was increasing. "A fine pyre-gift, Mother, and keep your tongue still. Or I will not be responsible."

He was gone before she could reply, the partition to her dressing-chamber sliding shut with an authoritative click. Gamwone stared at the painted glowflies upon the screen, her jaw working as her teeth—still good, since she cared more for meat than sweet things—ground together.

She was still plump, still pleasing, and her hair held no betraying pale strands. She did not look old enough to have such a son. Attempting to scold her, to *warn* her, what next?

Yes, she decided, taking a deep breath and staring unseeing at the beauty bench's crowded, cowering inhabitants. Now that her husband was moored in a deathbed, Tian Ha was attended to, and one of her rivals finally, irretrievably gone, she could turn her attention to other matters. Like the Hanweo bitch.

Or even a certain spear-wife's brat.

The Insulted
Maiden

M y lady," Daebo Nijera said, softly. "There is a visitor."
Sabwone rather liked this new side of the Daebo
maiden aunt. The elder woman crept quietly in, gave her news, and
fussed over her princess's silence. It was far more enjoyable than
being trapped in a palanquin all day. For one thing, the bed was
just as soft as her own despite being a Shan-style box with no short
compass-pillars at the corners; the rooms were the best for several
miles and the innkeeper's family was relegated to the stable while
their royal visitor recuperated. For another, several of the physicians could be bribed to send letters home.

"A visitor?" Sabwone took care to make her question tentative,
despairing. It was more than worth a few moments of pain and a
fraction of her humors splattering a palanquin for such a satisfying
turn of events. She should have done this before the border, maybe
she could have been sent home.

"Yes." Nijera hesitated. "There must be a screen."

So. The visitor was a man, maybe one of the Shan lords. That
would be entertaining. "Of course. What does this visitor wish
of me?"

"I am sure *I* cannot say. I have written to your mother."

"Have you?" Sabwone wriggled her toes luxuriously. The rai

was not sticky now, and when Nijera brought it she offered each bowl with both hands like a servant. There had even been walanir with breakfast, sharp and pungent so early in the season but very welcome in both greens and tiny red-rimmed slices. Imagining Mother reading shakily brushed characters and bursting into tears was satisfying, but highly unlikely. Still, she might have a pang or two of conscience at sending her daughter off in such a fashion. *My baby, bleeding in a palanquin*—just like in a novel, indeed.

"The dispatch rider carried little else; it will be swift." Nijera's skirts rustled as she moved. Travel did not agree with her, she was losing whatever pleasing plumpness she had found as a poor cousin eating another family's rai. "They will see to the screen now, First Princess."

In short order, servants had hauled the plain but serviceable item into the darkened bedroom, arranging its joints around the bed with Nijera supervising with a sharp word or two and plenty of tiny *tch-tch* sounds, like a peasant girl preparing for motherhood by play-wrapping a doll. With that done, the maiden aunt went to the door and spoke softly into the hall; a man's footsteps and the creaking of leather half-armor—a familiar, tame sound, reminding Sabwone of her brothers—intruded on the bedroom.

"First Princess Garan Sabwone." His Zhaon was quiet and cultured, but the burring of the Shan dialect would win him no prizes. "You brighten Shan with your presence."

"Many thanks for the compliment." She could afford to play the wilting reed now, and made every word soft and melting at its edges. "Whom do I have the honor of addressing, my lord?"

He was silent for a moment. "I bring news, and a question."

"Is the news your identity?" In a novel, he would be here to rescue her, a true prince instead of the descendant of merchants she had been sold to.

"Do you really not know?"

Put that way, the answer was clear. Sabwone's entire body, chafing at enforced rest, turned cold. She watched the blurred figure behind taut, waxed rai-paper—there hadn't even been an attempt to brighten the screen with drapery, or with paint-daubs. A number of things became clear, and she began to suffer the strange, altogether unsettling feeling that this interview would not end well. "You must forgive me for being unable to rise, Suon Kiron, King of Shan."

"Hm." A half-amused sound, cut short, was a trader's laugh. "You are not wise, but at least you are not stupid."

The insult was delivered in such a quiet, thoughtful tone it reminded her somewhat of Takshin. "You sound like my third-eldest brother."

"I would prefer to have *him* here, true." Faint creak of leather—had he chosen a chair? Or was he shifting in his boots, scuffing the ground like a boy called before his betters? He was speaking to a princess, but he did not sound as if he knew as much. "I will ask you one thing, Garan Sabwone, and after your answer, I shall know how to proceed."

Very high-handed of him. Well, they called him a king and all of Shan bowed despite his ancestors, so she supposed it would be up to her to teach him his place, should she deign to. "Very well, then. What would you ask of your betrothed?"

"Would you prefer me to marry your sister? Takshin told me plainly she is far more agreeable. If you prefer, I will allow the dispatch riders with news of your...display...over the border into Zhaon. Your father will be embarrassed, of course, but such is the love Shan bears Zhaon that I will take the younger daughter instead."

For a moment she was uncertain of having heard correctly. He wanted *Gamnae*? Who in their right mind would want that brainless, soppy little pudding? "How *dare* you—" she began, in a tight, colorless whisper.

"Do not play the insulted maiden, First Princess." The Zhaon title sat uneasily in his mouth; his handling of her native tongue was too accented for its proper deployment. "In Shan, the only reason for a woman to slit her wrists in the bridal palanquin is because she already has a lover, and desires not to be parted from him."

The insult was so huge she could barely grasp its tail. Sabwone fought the urge to surge upright. The screen was a thin barrier, but as long as she played at being too weak to move, they would not drag her farther from Zhaon. "My virtue is—"

"Oh, you've been very careful in this caravan, no doubt. But before, at your father's court, who knows?" There it was again, that faint creak of leather, the pressure of a booted foot upon a floorboard. What a *barbarian*, wearing army hooves in the presence of a sick lady. "There were no rumors my lords cared to listen to, but I'm sure some could be found."

A cool bath of dread slid down Sabwone's spine. Was this truly a Shan custom? She'd never heard of it. "There is no—"

"Spare me the protestations, *princess*." Stripped of its honorific inflection, the word was a chopped-middle, broken-backed nag. "I will have only yes or no, from your royal little lips. Do you wish me to take your younger sister instead? I will return you to Zhaon with all speed if you do."

"You cannot be serious." Was the man mad, as his mother was rumored to be? Surely Takshin would not have let her marry a madman—but then, the Third Prince might have caught some madness himself.

Certain types were held to be infectious, after all, slipping from body to body like a thief in a row of houses.

"I have no time for childish antics." Now Suon Kiron dared to speak as if to an inferior, his intonation brisk and curt. "My lords have watched you and found you wanting; you have shamed your father deeply."

How *dare* he speak of her father in that manner? "I am *First Princess of Zhaon*—"

"Of course, this will give me an excuse to have you beheaded later, should one be necessary." The indistinct shape behind the screen shook his head, shadow swelling and shrinking like an exorcist's opposing, only half-tangible monster. "Or immured in a tower, with the entrance bricked. That might suit you. Answer me now, Garan Sabwone. Would you prefer me to take your younger sister? They might even find a husband for you among Zhaon's nobles; one who does not mind the feast's leavings."

Sabwone lost the battle with her indignation and sat bolt-upright, the linen and light summerweave blanket pooling at her hips. "Are you finished insulting me?"

"Insulting you? You spilled your own blood in the bridal palanquin, and you say I have insulted *you*?" A bitter little bark of a laugh—that must be where Takshin learned it from. The Third Prince had come back scarred, abrupt, and mocking as this fellow; they were two of a kind, indeed. "You are lucky I do not give you to my bloodriders for amusement. Answer me, girl. Shall I take your virtuous sister?"

"You are the son of merchants," she hissed. "I am a princess of Daebo and Garan, and you are *nothing*."

"Very well. We shall send you back to the border."

"No!" Sabwone almost yelled. She could not start from the bed, but oh how she longed to. "You cannot!"

"Oh, I can, and I will." Now, to insult her further, his tone had the same steely timbre of her father's voice when Gamnae or Jin went crying to him over some little game. It was not Sabwone's fault that they could not take a joke or were too stupid to avoid a poke or pinching, but Father never took *her* side—not until she had learned to arrange things more deftly. "Should you make it necessary."

Sabwone groped for an appropriate insult to match his. "You rode all the way from the capital to—"

"To see my new wife, and what did I find but a spoiled, selfish little *ekanha*." There was a slap of leather—was he carrying a sudo? Did he mean to push the screen aside and strike a *princess*? "So you do not wish me to take your sister, very well."

Now she groped for the sheet, clutched it to her chest. It was a thin protection indeed. Her bandaged wrists—she had not managed to cut very deeply, after all—ached abominably. "I will make you pay for this."

"Will you?" Now he laughed outright, instead of barking. The note of true amusement was another deep insult, and she suspected he knew as much. "If I had anything you could take from me, Garan Sabwone, I might almost be worried."

"I will stab you on the wedding night—" she began.

"Why not now?" He waited, and Sabwone writhed within her own helplessness. "That is what I thought," he continued, finally. "If you do not wish me to send you back to your father as a stripped flower, then you must behave appropriately. My lords will be watching, and your servants too. It ill befits a queen of Shan to act as you have."

Another faint creaking noise, and his shadow changed shape once more. Perhaps he was a numiao or a humor-sucking hua-wone'gia, and had murdered the true prince before taking his place? He stood, and now she understood the slapping sound, empty gloves against a rein-callused palm. "You will begin for the capital once more tomorrow. I suggest resting, for you will not see the palanquin you dishonored until you enter the city. If you mis-behave again, my lords will send you from Shan without hairpins or robe, and your sister will receive the honor of a kingly husband."

Sabwone set her jaw. Tears swelled hot as a smoking summer downpour in her eyes, and she despised them. The hate was a dry rock in her throat. Oh, he had no *idea* who he was insulting.

"I shall take your silence as agreement. Goodbye, *ekanha*."

She did not know the word, but it could not be complimentary. "Merchant pretender," she said in Zhaon—but softly, and only once the door had closed.

Her wrists ached, *ached*. And tomorrow she would have to ride. It was insupportable.

"Nijera?" she called. "Auntie Nijera?"

There was no answer, of course. The bitch was probably bowing to that merchant prince right now, murmuring *Your Majesty*, and there was nothing Sabwone could do. Worst of all, she had not considered that her grand gesture could be... misinterpreted.

Soon, though. She would find soon a way to make them all pay.

Sabwone sobbed, rage and fear curdling in her chest along with the unhappy, bile-laced knowledge that she had miscalculated.

Badly.

Marrow from the Bones

Two pyres in less than two months. It should have been Zakkar Kai lighting this one, but he could not move from north of the capital in case Khir took it upon themselves to display more of their threadbare martial spirit. So it was Garan Takshin who held the torch.

Chief among the witnesses was the Crown Prince, though, his pale armband much wider and bearing two knots of the kind called Elder's Burden, their tails tucked like slinking dogs. Also in attendance was Komor Yala, pale under her copper coloring, her own mourning band single-knotted in the Khir fashion and her hair, for once, bare of any pin; the Khir mourned parents without adornment.

Even, it appeared, when the relationship was purely informal. It was an unexpected mark of respect, and one Takshin wished he could thank her for. A pall of heavy morning sunshine pressed upon Yala's slim shoulders, but she eschewed even a sunbell. Faint traces of dewy sweat glittered upon her cheeks and forehead.

She had come from one tomb to see another's occupant undergoing the change of flame, and several lengths before her, Mrong Banh, bareheaded in a pale mourning surplice, watched from upon his knees as the torch spat and crackled, borne by the Third Prince in his customary black.

The scarred son of Garan Tamuron did not admit of mourning except his own plain white armband, and he carried the torch to high-stacked wood drenched with costly oils to make the burning swift. The pyre-gifts were nestled in their appropriate places, and First Concubine Luswone, her hair dressed low and naked of pins instead of in the high asymmetrical fashion of Daebo, stood with her retinue, every single one in ghostly unbleached cloth. Second Queen Haesara abstained from attending, a move held to stem from her great tact and delicacy, but her pyre-gift was in its proper place, both her sons were in full mourning as befitted children suddenly bereft of even a junior mother.

Second Prince Kurin and Second Princess Gamnae were likewise in evidence, and both had brought their own pyre-gifts to nestle within the wooden structure. The princess's gift was a crimson-wrapped sathron box; only she and Takshin knew that inside it was cushioned not a new, untouched item but one of her own childhood instruments, one the lady of lost Wurei had patiently taught a plump, lip-biting girl to pluck. The princess had also laid a handful of red crushflower, feeder of bees and most royal among its brethren, carefully upon the lid. Her lips had moved silently as she did so, perhaps bidding a kindness goodbye.

Do you think she would mind if I . . . Gamnae had asked her second-eldest brother, haltingly, and Takshin had, for once, been gentle in his reply.

I think she will treasure it above all the sathrons in Heaven, Naenae.

Takshin paused before he lowered the flame, his head hanging, and in the stillness a redthroat bird called. His own gift was in an unmarked box, plainly wrapped in heavy crimson silk and full of bright false fruit made of painted paste, a surplus fit for feeding a shade royally in the land beyond life. How others would laugh or look down their noses at what it contained, but it was all he could think of to give the woman who had cooed over his scraped knees and pretended not to notice stolen plums from her garden-tree.

He hoped she would understand. Kanbina had never needed

stupid, weightless words in order to comprehend, to offer a gift—or to accept one.

The fire had to be quick in high summer, especially since the afternoon rains came with water-clock regularity. Still, he lingered before he lowered the torch.

Kanbina. He tried to think loudly, in case her shade was watching. *I will make certain she pays for this. I promise it to you.*

She would have gently chided him. *Do not say such things*, she had often murmured. *She is your mother, after all.*

If anyone could lay claim to that title, it was not Garan Gamwone who had birthed him and then cast him away like spoiled fruit, and it was not the Mad Queen of Shan. It was the woman who now lay, a tiny, inert husk wrapped in crimson from top to toe like a bride. Sometimes he had even fantasized that he was her child instead of Gamwone's.

Kai could not be here, he thought, addressing her again. *Watch over him when I cannot, Mother.*

For such would he call her, if only in the secret chambers his skull contained.

Takshin laid the torch in its proper place. The pyre coughed as he retreated, and flame spread hungrily.

The space where the First Queen's pyre-gift should have been was bare, an empty tooth-socket. Even now the First Queen of Zhaon disdained to notice a rival who had not, after all, done what was required and borne a child for her lord.

First Concubine Luswone's lips were thin, pressed together in a tight line. Second Prince Kurin stood in a proper attitude of quiet bereavement, and if it bothered him to have so many gazes rest speculatively upon him, he did not show it.

Takshin retreated, step by step, to Yala instead of to Kurin and Gamnae. Mrong Banh folded over his knees upon white stone, his forehead touching lightly. He did not have to—his task as chief court astrologer was to find the most auspicious time for the pyre and mark the space below the greatest palace bell with chalk; when the bell's shadow reached that mark, the ceremony could begin.

Yet he lingered as well, bent in the attitude of profound reverence; slowly, Komor Yala sank to her knees as well, light as a leaf. She placed her palms upon sun-hot stone and bowed until her forehead was three lengths above them, pausing to drive the honor home before rising gracefully as Takshin halted at her side.

Takyeo, leaning upon his cane, stepped forward. He bowed, too, deeply as a Crown Prince was not required to do before any but his royal father. A startled rustle went through the onlookers as those lower in rank hurried to follow suit.

The Third Prince did not care who saw, now. He took Komor Yala's hand, ignoring the surprised twitch as she sought to pull away—not very hard, though, aware of causing a scene at this most inappropriate moment. He laid her palm in the bend of his left elbow and locked his right hand over hers despite the heat. Sweat slid between their fingers, and Yala's swift, startled glance was a thorny pleasure.

You see, little lure? He hoped his expression was not as forbidding as his frozen face felt. *She is gone, but you are not alone.*

Yala's throat worked. The glitter in her eyes, salt drops welling, was an enemy he could not kill. So Takshin settled, his boots set in a swordsman's readiness though he had left his blade behind in deference to the lady's pyre, and made himself a pillar to lean upon.

Of course eunuchs and courtiers watched from the shaded galleries along the sides of the ceremonial ground. Even now, there was rumor walking among sober robes and high-crowned hats, whispering into ears whetted sharp by years of insinuation, gossip, backbiting, and occasionally even truth. Takshin imagined what they were saying, and it was a grim joke indeed.

The Emperor's illness, the chief astrologer's knee-bowing, the Crown Prince's honoring of a junior mother, the Third Prince's support given to an otherwise friendless foreign lady—all was juicy, but in the end, it was only scrapings from the bones of the largest roast, indeed.

He knew—taking care to know such things was a prince's duty and a wolf's instinctive habit—they were whispering of Garan

Yulehi-a Gamwone's beauty, her roundness, and her complaints of cold even during the hottest weather. They were whispering of her servant-girls: large-eyed, frail-fingered, scuttling, flinching things, and of the queen's own pet physician who had habitually grinned like a skull and was now being prepared for his own pyre after a sudden, fatal belly-gripe. They spoke behind their sleeves or fans of certain shops in the Yuin where all manner of substances could be purchased, and they exchanged meaningful glances after studying the blank spot where a first queen's pyre-gift to a concubine should have been.

Suspiciously absent from any of Wurei Kanbina's pyre-gifts was any manner of tea.

HEAVEN
UNASSISTED

I do not see why it should trouble us overmuch," the Second Prince said, languidly stroking his chin. Of late he had made long strides toward growing a larger beard like his imperial father, and it was said it suited him. His hurai was freshly polished after sealing some few letters, greenstone also sealing the vein in the first finger against ill-luck; he did not now arrange himself so that mark of royalty could be seen at every angle.

One who wished to curry his favor, or at least avoid his disdain, would say he did not need to.

"Your mother did not even send a pyre-gift." Binei Jinwon, head of the Yulehi clan and chief minister to the Emperor for this half of the year, did not bother to truly taste his tea, simply set the cup down with a grimace. Normally, this conversation would be had in the First Queen's part of the Kaeje, but the Second Prince had retired to his estate *outside* the Palace complex and wore a mourning armband as well.

Some might say it was grief for a junior mother. Those adept at watching the tides of influence swirl inside the high walls of Zhaon-An's liver and head-meat had noted that his own pyre-gift had lacked nothing in taste or costliness, and thought the message Garan Kurin displayed was discreet aversion to his queenly mother's behavior.

A good son could not openly make such a statement, of course, even a royal one. But his delicacy was being noted. "I *did* counsel her to." He did not touch his own tea, since his guest had not begun to sip. Kurin's topknot-cage, wood without any filigree, was sober to match mourning's dictates. "Perhaps she did not listen."

"I wonder that your sister did not think to..." Lord Yulehi hurried to amend the sentence when Kurin made no move, simply examining his uncle with that disconcertingly sleepy gaze.

"Gamnae has other tasks. Including readying herself for marriage." Kurin's fingers twitched, each tapping the tabletop once in turn, and he looked away, over a carved balustrade to a small, ruthlessly organized dry-garden full of river rock carved into fantastical shapes by years of flowing waters before being hauled by porters and groaning oxen to Zhaon-An, set in place by a gang of sweating laborers, and now contemplated by the man who had set the entire dragging, moaning mass in motion. The courtyard's change had been sudden, but princes were allowed their whims. "Father is thinking of it too, I'm sure."

"Your lord father has made no arrangements in that direction as of yet." Binei Jinwon shook his sleek dark head. His own topknot-cage, silk drawn tight over a wooden frame and stabbed with a lacquered pin, meant both wealth and consequence, not to mention a certain amount of ministerial restraint as well. "Well, may he continue to guide us for many more years." He touched his teacup with a finger, ostensibly gauging the temperature.

"I'm sure he will," Kurin murmured. It seemed he was not disposed to be helpful this morning. In fact, the putative head of Yulehi—though he had heretofore been too young to take on those responsibilities—appeared rather bored with his mother's uncle.

"Still..." Binei Jinwon did not shift anxiously upon his cushion, but he did eye his royal grand-nephew consideringly. He might well try the Third Prince's uncertain temper, if the elder son proved unsatisfactory.

It did not, after all, matter *which* Yulehi sat upon the Throne once the Emperor's illness reached its... natural conclusion. A good steward cared for his granaries, and Zhaon was the largest granary of all. There was nothing wrong with a clan benefiting as the rest of the country did from a strong, amenable man in its central seat.

Perhaps Garan Kurin knew which way his uncle's thoughts were wending, because his gaze settled unflinching upon the older man. "Are the riders ready?"

"Thieves and cutpurses," Lord Yulehi muttered. "But yes, they are in readiness. The dovecote servants are all beholden to us, our Golden are in position, and there are arrangements for the guards upon the main roads. It's only prudent, after all."

"I doubt Father would see it so." Now Kurin's lids lifted a few fractions, and Binei Jinwon began to feel a trifle uneasy. Nothing about the arrangements was illegal, of course. Except suborning the Golden, and they had merely been given a few gifts by the reigning minister—very quietly, of course, in thanks for their service to Zhaon's Emperor. But they knew from whence their good fortune flowed, indeed. "And they were paid as I instructed?"

"Of course." The chief minister's expression held some minor dissatisfaction. "Though I dislike giving a man ingots *before* his service has been rendered."

"I know what you dislike, Honorable Binei." Kurin's faint smile didn't alter, but he also did not reach for his fan, or touch his Gurai slipware teacup again. "I am *thoroughly* aware of everything you have expressed a preference upon for the last fifteen winters or so. Please do me the honor of not repeating the list from the beginning again."

Honorable, as if the clan head was no more than an artisan or scholar to be given lip service; until now, Kurin had always been deferential, if somewhat sarcastic at the same time. Binei Jinwon shook his head, *tch-tch*ing like an old dowager. "Your mother taught you to speak so, my nephew?"

"My mother remembers a time when you were merely an offshoot, *Uncle*." The title was robbed of its honor by Kurin's stress upon the first syllable instead of the last. "I take it you do not like our household tea?"

"It is still very hot, but I am certain it is of the highest quality," Lord Yulehi answered haughtily. There were also cakes of pounded rai and a sweating jar of crushed fruit, but until the first teacup was drained fruit could not be even alluded to. "Have you no sense, young one?"

"I think I have enough for the task before me." Kurin still studied his lord uncle, and his gaze was not like Gamwone's at all. It entirely lacked the glinting malice the First Queen's had hardened into, bit by bit, over the years.

If Binei Jinwon had been married to such a creature, he would have found some way to be rid of it long ago. He could not think Garan Tamuron above the task, or quailing at it. The Emperor must have kept his First Queen from the pyre for some reason, but Lord Yulehi could not, though he had thought upon it long and deeply, discern *what* that reason was.

Perhaps it was for the sake of this son. Kurin was certainly far more satisfactory than that whelp from the Emperor's spear-wife; Binei Jinwon had more than once subtly suggested as much—oh, very carefully indeed, and been ignored by the Emperor each time.

Yes, at the moment Garan Kurin looked very much like his lord father, and it was an echo as unwelcome as unexpected.

Perhaps that was why Binei Jinwon's palms were a trifle moist. Or perhaps it was the tea, very fragrant and sweet. Surely it was not a message.

Surely Kurin could not be so...overt.

"Of a certainty," Lord Yulehi said, quietly. He had bent before the inevitable once or twice in his life, and now he wondered if he was to do so again. "Should what we fear come to pass..."

"You *fear* it? Why?" Kurin might have been simulating surprise, for his eyes opened wide, showing all their whites like a frightened kaburei's. His mobile mouth moved through mock-startlement, then firmed as he sobered. "All you must do is your part, Uncle. If it goes awry, I am the one who will suffer."

"My most lordly nephew—"

"Of course, should something happen to the head, the rest of the clan follows." Kurin lifted his cup, which meant Lord Yulehi, as a good guest, had to as well. A cloying fragrance filled his nose, and even a wary, skilled physician might not be able to discern any admixture. "That is the way it is in the Hundreds and in tradition. Even in modern times, such a fate might be visited upon a clan under certain conditions. Don't you think so?"

"Of course." Binei Jinwon's lips were numb, but perhaps that was only the heat of the tea collecting against them, dislodging other humors. "It falls to a clan to arrange a hedge of spears about its head." The allusion, from Cao Luong's *Great Filial Book*, prefaced the tale of the great Garan clan in the Years of Blood, and extolled the sacrifice of the current Emperor's illustrious forebears. It could be taken as a warning or a statement of support, depending on Kurin's mood.

"It does, indeed." Kurin's smile turned slow and very sleepy, and his resemblance to his father faded slightly. "Now, my esteemed uncle, when you leave your servants shall bear a small, heavy chest. Keep it out of sight."

Summer heat was better than winter frost, but all the same Binei Jinwon's back was alive with chillflesh and slick, greasy sweat. "May I ask what—"

"Ingots, of course. And a few letters in a hand very much like one of my brothers'. Do *not* use either yet. Everything must be timed correctly, and the moment the Great Bell begins to ring we shall move. But not before, and while we're speaking upon this, Uncle, you are to ensure none of our clan—especially Mother—engages an impresario of any sort. I want nothing at all to touch my Elder Brother until *I* give the word. Is that clear?"

"Y-yes, my lord nephew."

"And when I say *of any sort*, I mean both the theater and the Shadowed Path. We are in mourning for Garan Wurei-a Kanbina, and there must be no merrymaking in any Yulehi house or courtyard. In fact, I want most of those ingots to go for hiring mourners, and we shall make offerings at her tomb as well."

Binei Jinwon almost choked. To do so would say very plainly

that Garan Kurin knew what was rumored, and had no part in the scheme. Of course, he had been a mere scrap not even past his fifth winter when the lady of lost Wurei miscarried her lord husband's son.

It was a blow to First Queen Gamwone's prestige, and not one she was likely to sit prettily upon. But Binei Jinwon dared make no remonstrance, for the small, heavy chest was undoubtedly already in the possession of his servants.

He could not refuse such a thing, nor make a scene in his royal nephew's house.

Kurin took a mouthful of tea despite all hospitality and protocol, and his uncle mechanically followed suit. Guest or not, you could not refrain when your host drank. The tea coated his throat and continued down, and knowing it was likely pure did not help his racing heart or the sweat now coating the hollows of his armpits, gathering behind his knees.

"When the Great Bell rings," Kurin continued, softly, "our mourning will continue, and those we have hired so carefully will swear they were hired by Sensheo's favorite bootlicker to do a certain prince a disservice. The bootlicker will say what he must, or his daughter will suffer."

Yes, *now* the head of Yulehi understood his nephew's plan. It was an elegant one, certainly, and it preserved the appearance of Heaven working unassisted. "And if the Great Bell does not ring before…"

"I have a plan for that too, Uncle, and you will be called upon." Kurin shook his head as if he were the elder and his uncle the rash youth. "It is all well in hand, and you may rest easy. It might almost be time to think of retirement; you have served the clan well."

"My lord nephew." And now it was time for him to set his cup down and grovel, a feat he had performed many a time in the last twenty winters. Ever since Garan Tamuron's star began to rise, in fact—a mere stripling with a gift for inspiring soldiers taking slices of the Garan neighbors' holdings, and keeping them.

"Oh, don't." Kurin's grin was now quite open and fetching, if you overlooked the gleam of sharp white teeth. He smoothed one fold of his muted, sober silken robe. "Drink your tea, Uncle. In a little bit we can be said to have had a decent visit, and then you'll be off to do what you must."

The boy had become a man. When had that happened?

It did not matter. What mattered now was keeping the brat's favor, at least for the present. So Binei Jinwon steeled himself to finish his cup.

For the fragrant, cloying tea was hrebao.

So Little

Sun lay thick upon golden dust, tents marching in rows, the glitter of helm and shoulders gilded or merely reinforced with metal edges. It poured over a temporary dais in the paved courtyard of the keep, where under a bright yellow canopy Zhaon's greatest general sat upon a backless chair in gleaming full armor, watching the floggings.

Even if Kai would have preferred not to mete out punishment this way, there was no choice. The traitorous shield-square—four men and a captain, including the armor-boy from Wurei—had fired a general's tent, almost assassinated him, and killed loyal brother-soldiers.

No mercy was allowed those who killed their own. There were exceptions, as when a shield-captain or square-commander was a certain type of martinet, but the skeleton of the Northern Army was not upon campaign and there were precious few chances to strike down the meritless during a melee. There was even a word for the erasing of a hated commander, its character akin to the sharp tool for pruning dead orchard branches.

The characters for treason were differently shaped.

The whip cracked again. Shield-captains and square-commanders stood in their allotted spaces, marshals and other officers in theirs, watching from under striped awnings. Some generals left the square when there was bekuya-in to mete out, but Zakkar Kai was not one. It was not meet for a man to close his eyes to what his orders wrought; Kai and Garan Tamuron had shared many a meandering conversation upon the topic and its implications.

So Zakkar Kai watched every stripe laid against the broken bodies tied to metal posts, the three whipmasters stripped to the waist and gleaming, bright blood spattering from the sorrowful snakes of braided leather, the bone-stripping flechettes flaying meat from the faithless.

There were no mutters among the spectators. A general was a father, soldiers his sons, and no mercy or intercession could be expected for attempted patricides—they would descend, skeletons with strips of meat hanging from cracked bone, to the Hell of the Many Weights. Besides, he was the hero of Three Rivers and the beloved of Heaven's own chief general who used thunderbolts to strike evildoers and malignant spirits; the thought of celestial displeasure if the boy from Wurei and his compatriots had managed to strike true was enough to make even the least religious—or even merely superstitious—soldier blanch.

"They were paid well." Anlon stood at Kai's right hand. The steward was not pale, nor did his shoulders slump, but the bandage around his midsection peered from under loosened half-armor. "Copper ingots found in their tents. They would not say who suborned whom."

I did not expect them to. Here, in camp, there were no eunuchs to practice the Art of the Tongue upon malefactors. Eunuchs did not belong among fighting men unless they were bearing orders from the Emperor, a few generals of the Second Dynasty notwithstanding. "No papers, I expect."

"Their braziers were lit." Anlon's hair perhaps held a touch or two more grey now. He would become a snow-pard before long, with mottled fur.

"Perhaps the rain chilled them." Kai's chin raised slightly as a commotion at the keep gate rose into stifling, dust-choked morning air. One of the traitors screamed before the whip descended again, and the high, piercing note was very like a woman's.

"My lord." Anlon did not approve of levity in this situation, but he would not dream of scolding his master publicly. "I searched every corner personally. Hurong Tai and Sehon Doah are searching again."

"Distribute half the ingots among the soldiers who put out the fire." Kai forced his gaze to lie quietly upon the three grieving pillars and their almost unrecognizable lumps of treachery.

"And the bodies?" Anlon knew what Kai wanted done, of course, but this was for the benefit of the third of his marshals, lean, far-sighted Hurong Baihan from the fringes of Daebo—no relation to round, smiling Tai, but the name was a common one indeed in Zhaon.

Sometimes Kai suspected Mrong Banh did not change his name because agreeing to a more common one would touch his pride. He gave the required answer crisply, as befit a military man. "Leave them upon poles for three days. Then give them a common pyre. The families…"

"Three of them had not been with us long enough to gain pension merit, my lord."

Kai almost winced. "Pension them anyway, at half."

"Just and kind." Baihan, at his left, did not move to resettle his helm under his arm, which meant he had more to add. "The other half of the ingots?"

"Into the treasury, Tall Hurong." There was no army so laden it did not seek to make room for fresh spoils. "We may need it if Khir decides they are not quite supine."

"Bastards." But Baihan said it softly. "What do they expect? If they come again, we shall hand them more death." He carried a scar or two from the battles before Three Rivers, and was somewhat touchy about missing that crowning event while abed with fever and possible sepsis that had, miraculously, retreated when a shabby-robed Kihon Jiao became involved.

The physician would be missed, but he was of more use in the palace. With the thought of the palace came Yala's face again, somber and weary under drenches of multicolored light from flame-flowers on a hot spring night.

At this hour, she might be taking tea in one of the Jonwa's sitting rooms, listening to the junior ladies' light conversation. Or she might even be visiting Kanbina, the two of them soft birds in a safe bower. The image was soothing, an anodyne for the sight before him.

A courier appeared at the far end of the courtyard, the bright crimson plume nodding upon his close-fitting helm. He spared the briefest glance at the display and skirted the assembly with a light but determined step.

Yala's letters would not come so. This was an imperial messenger. New orders, perhaps, or something else had happened. It was the latter prospect that pulled Kai's nerve-strings taut. "Send a fellow to bring him into the keep, Anlon. Unless it is a Red Letter, I am at business."

You do not look away from what you have wrought, Tamuron had said more than once, watching a broken army as the victorious one swept in pursuit, killing as they moved. *It is the measure of a man.*

So little? Kai had said, once, and the warlord—he had not been Emperor then—had fixed him with a dark, piercing sidelong look.

Very little, and yet beyond the capability of most.

It would be a Red Letter if Tamuron had died. And here Kai was, mired with the bones of an army, unable to return to his almost-father's pyre because he was a shield over the heart of Zhaon.

In more ways than one.

The messenger was escorted inside, and Kai settled more firmly upon his padded bench. A hot, uneasy wind flirted with awnings and stirred stray hairs, ruffled decorative fringe and mouthed bright armor. Gongs and trumpets flared outside the keep's low, ancient, single tower—the second day-watch was over, the third called to post and picket.

The whipmaster handed the sorrowful snake to his understudy, a lad of about fifteen summers who looked green at the work but set himself to it with a clenched jaw. He did not have much to do—the master had applied fifty of the seventy lashes due apiece for the first of their transgressions, setting fire to army tents.

The other hundred lashes, for the attempt upon the life of their general, could wait until tomorrow's dawn, if any of the traitors were robust enough to survive until then. If not, the corpses would be scourged, to further punish their shades.

When it was done, the shuddering lumps were hauled roughly away and two details called to clean the courtyard. Kai climbed the steps into the keep's drafty mirrorlit entry hall. The messenger had already unloaded his cargo and been taken to the field kitchen for something more substantial than the rai-balls they traditionally carried to eat in the saddle; the pile of dispatches and official correspondence held two surprises.

First was a triangular-folded letter with familiar, exquisite brushwork upon its outside. Perhaps Takyeo had merely added Yala's letter to an official bag before sending it. The second was a missive bordered with crimson ink, and its seal was Tamuron's.

Of course he longed to open hers first, but the red-bordered letter was far more concerning. He broke the waxen seal with a crisp sound and unfolded it as he paced his study, Anlon following to stack and sort the other correspondence into its own proper lanes and alleys, just like the tents outside.

The characters refused to make sense for a few moments. When they did, he tipped his head back, staring at the dusty rafters. Soon Anlon would be at the shutters, drawing them against the afternoon's sullen volcanic fury before the rain swept in, and the room would grow stifling.

"My lord?" His steward sounded alarmed. "My lord!"

It was not unexpected. Kihon Jiao had told Kai privately it would not be long, and if she lasted until autumn there would be celestial intercession instead of the medical arts to thank.

And yet.

My son, Kanbina had called him, proudly. Kai's own parents were ash upon a wind pawing at a barbarian-burned settlement, their guessed-at names carved upon an ancestral tablet he performed duties before with filial regularity. He had not known of her plan to petition Tamuron for the hurai granted to Zhaon's chief general, and was even more surprised when the Emperor agreed.

The circle of greenstone clasped his left first finger, the characters carved into sacred material clear and sharp. Of course she had not labored to bear him—but her courage, brushing that letter when she knew it would expose her to unwanted attention at a court that had all but forgotten her, shamed him nonetheless.

No doubt Yala's letter contained the details. And no doubt Yala was grieving, too. Kanbina had never learned *not* to be kind to creatures in need, whether they remained grateful or not. In that, she was like the Great Awakener himself.

"My mother," Kai heard himself say, quiet as a peasant facing utter disaster. "My mother is dead."

And he could not attend *her* pyre, either. Duty would keep him here, as useless as the flogged lumps, the evidence of their shame even now being scrubbed from the courtyard's wide, stony embrace.

PRODUCT OF MERIT

I was not sure you would see me," Fourth Prince Makar said, his hands clasped behind his back as he studied the bookshelf with deep instead of merely polite interest. He found the Jonwa's study restful, very much like his own with dark wood and clean lines, each book and scrollcase in its allotted place; much could be told about a man by the type of disorder he tolerated.

"No?" Takyeo, of course, kept himself under such rigid control it was almost impossible to find a stray hair. Even now, he was possessed of impeccable patience regarding a younger brother who had appeared without invitation or preliminary letter and whose errand could not be pleasant, coming as it did in such a time of mourning and tension. He had even called for tea, as if this was a planned visit. "Why not?"

"I thought you were retreating to the provinces." If the move had any chance of succeeding, either as feint or—even less possible—to grant Ah-Yeo a life unmolested by the dictates of policy and rule, Makar might even admire the brazenness of its execution. As it was...well, he had always found his eldest brother admirable in other ways.

If there was a sliver of likelihood that he could help his eldest brother remain alive, Makar was bound to at least attempt the feat. His arms ached from the morning's punishing practice with his preferred sword-tutor, his legs held a bruise or two from a weighted wooden blade, and he had taken himself to the Jonwa at the earliest hour for any visit with a firm step and a thoughtful mien.

"You start with business." Takyeo had aged visibly in the past few months, his face acquiring a novel and quite handsome leanness, but his smile—always deployed far less frequently than it should have been, alas—was just the same.

"Of course; it is a mark of respect." There was so little unmitigated truth a man could speak, and a prince even less, so Makar relished the opportunity. His nape was damp, more from the remains of a tepid, citron-touched bath than the day's gathering heat. "I know how you hate to waste time."

"Speaking to you is never a waste." Takyeo shifted in his chair. His leg had been well-nigh crushed; Zakkar Kai's pet physician was capable of miraculous things. "I have missed our conversations of late."

"*Learned men, come together and seek the Way.*" Makar's fingers gave a twinge. He had brushed that very sentence over and over, not stopping until his child-chubby fingers could perform it fluidly.

"Dho Xilung, an old friend." Takyeo did not have to search far for an appropriate answer of the same vein and exact number of Zhaon syllables. The game was a likewise friend, played between a patient elder brother and a precocious younger. "*Where the wise have congress, the world is elevated.*"

When Makar had started winning their matches, his eldest brother still played with good grace. It had been Takyeo who brought Makar brushes and exercise books of lined rai-paper when the boy was thought too young, and Ah-Yeo who had put his arm over a still-child Fourth Prince after the assassin came that terrible year in the citron-cloaked house of Hanweo.

You did what you must, Takyeo had said, gravely. *And you did well. You may have bad dreams, too. Those are natural.*

No one else had thought to tell him as much, assuming Makar's calm was a product of merit and his marked precocity, not the stunned, head-hanging exhaustion of a brutalized ox. "Ah, you have been reading the *Green Book.*" Makar could not help but smile, either, turning from the bookcase. His mourning-band glowed upon a blue silk sleeve; today he was not a scholar.

Takyeo nodded thoughtfully. He was not in full mourning, though perhaps he would have liked to be. "There is much within it upon the subject of grieving."

"Yes." Makar tucked his hands in his sleeves. Who had more cause to grieve than his patient, kindly eldest brother? The Khir princess had seemed docile and well-mannered, the type of wife any nobleman would be glad of. If Takyeo had not been a prince, they could have grown old in happy serenity. And Kanbina had been the only one of their father's mates who did not see a dead wife's child as an imposition or worse, a threat. "At least they are both beyond the reach of their enemies, now."

"At least that." Takyeo considered Makar for a long moment; he did not ask who his brother meant. That was another of Takyeo's fine qualities, the simple refusal to ask a question he already knew the answer to. "I know you, my brother. What have you come to ask of me?"

From anyone else, it would have irked Makar. From Takyeo, it was a blessing. "Would I have come merely to demand a gift?"

"No, but you would come to demand I swallow medicine." Takyeo's gaze turned to a wall-hanging—a restrained painting of the babu-jointed characters for *serenity*—giving his junior freedom from the weight of keeping a pleasant expression. "For my own good."

"And it did you good then, did it not?" It was extremely pleasing to be the person whose advice Takyeo took, no matter how long ago the event.

"I am in need of no medicine at the moment." His Eldest Brother's chin set, somewhat stubbornly, and that was a new thing. For his entire life, the man had been obliging and forbearing. It stood to reason he would reach the end of his patience sooner or later, but now was the worst possible time for the knot to be placed in the rope. "Do me a second honor, Makar, and tell me what you wish of me so we may move to more pleasant subjects."

"It is not what *I* wish." That was unadulterated truth as well. Were it left to Makar, Takyeo could retire to the countryside at will, and live the remainder of his life brushing scrolls and raising fine horses. "Mrong Banh and Zan Fein spoke to me. They ask if you will come to Council. Father does not, now. He does not even leave his bed." Makar was also not the only one to think it would not be long now.

Their imperial father's condition was grave, and Takyeo's position hardly secure. It was a configuration that could only mean disorder and despair.

Takyeo nodded thoughtfully, but it was not a movement of agreement, merely of acknowledgment. "So they wish to put the ox to plow, do they?"

"You are no ox, Eldest Brother." *But are you a snow-pard in truth? We have not yet seen your claws.*

Or, more disturbing, perhaps they had, and said claws were too small to pierce a single sheet of rai-paper.

"I feel stubborn as one." Takyeo's gaze did not alter, but he was not seeing the hanging, or even the wall it rested upon. "And if I were to visit the Council, it would be only temporary. I intend to leave Zhaon-An in a matter of days."

In other words, his decision was unchanged. Makar suppressed a sigh. "Some of your household have already left."

"To prepare the way." It was the phrase for every summer's corvée labor, smoothing the arteries commerce and travel both depended upon, instead of the more usual term for servants hurrying ahead to air out and refurbish neglected rooms. If it was a jest, it was an opaque one.

Makar half-turned, studying the books afresh. If Takyeo would grant him the grace of an unseen expression, he might as well return it. "Much as our fourth mother did."

"Is that what she's being called now? Not the suffering mouse in her bower?" The bitterness behind the words was harsh, and entirely new.

"So you know of the First Queen's venom." Of course, who in

the court did not? If Takyeo had merely given the *appearance* of unknowing, it boded well.

But not well enough.

"I have all my life, it seems." A polite understatement; Takyeo had been ever filial and long-suffering toward Gamwone. "Tell me, did *your* mother stir a step or raise a finger to help the Second Concubine?"

Why should she? There are more problems than yours afoot in Zhaon, Eldest Brother. Makar did not shrug. He could neither defend his parent as filial duty demanded nor rudely take exception to an elder sibling's partially justified comment, so it was best to simply step forward along the path. "We are not our mothers, Takyeo."

"I should hope none of us are our father, either."

Ah. So *now* Takyeo could be induced to speak of Father. "It could happen at any moment, you know. And when it does, he is beyond explanation or reconciliation."

"He has never been fond of either." A slight creak was Takyeo pushing against the desktop to aid his rising, and his cane tapped the floor as he stepped away from its shelter. "Very well, Maki. It pleases me to see things done thoroughly. But once Father..." The pause filled the study, brushed against flatbook-spines, and leached even Zhaon's wet summer heat from the room. So he could not make himself say it, after all. Interesting. "I intend to abdicate, and to retire to the countryside to live a blameless life."

"Is that where such things are found?" Perhaps wisely, Makar did not speak against the plan yet again. "I hope it is that simple."

"Nothing is simple." The cane tapped, the floor spoke softly under Takyeo's weight. It was amazing the wood did not splinter under the bitterness in his tone.

The Fourth Prince nodded. Perhaps there was hope after all. "You are wise to recognize as much."

"Makar, I would ask you something."

Good. "Then ask away." *Ask me for aid. Ask me to declare for you, ask me to give you a reason to stay, ask me what Kurin intends. I cannot help if you do not move, Takyeo.* But would Ah-Yeo recognize as much?

And if he did what Makar longed for him to, what would the repercussions be? Kurin claimed he slept easily at night, but no man who did spent so much time intriguing. Even Makar, safe for the moment, did his fair share. Very subtly, of course, but he was a prince and had his own eyes and ears in palace households, soft and retiring, only required to give a detail now and again in return for alloy sliver or small preferment.

If Kurin even suspected Makar's weight might be placed upon their eldest brother's side of the scale instead of being kept from the counting, not only the Fourth Prince but also the Second Queen would feel certain unhappy effects.

A brother was a brother, but a mother was more.

"What would you do?" Takyeo paused, continued. "In my position."

"Strategic retreat is part of my nature—perhaps that is from my mother." Makar freed a hand to stroke his shaven chin; his hurai was warm satin stone. The weight was a menace and a reminder, also a protection. Certainly his own sleep would be far more untroubled if the problem of Kurin were somehow addressed by their eldest sibling. "But surrender? No, that is not in my nature at all." *I did not think it in yours, either, no matter your forbearance.* Makar paused. "May I give you advice?"

"Of course." Whether Takyeo chose to follow it was another matter, but at least his tone was kind. "I asked for as much, Maki."

"Be careful of Kurin. I do not know quite what he intends, but…" That much was a lie, both of them knew very well what the Second Prince intended. And were Takyeo of a different temper, he might take the warning to its natural conclusion, and rid his impending reign of its closest, if not its greatest, danger.

"Kurin." Takyeo's cane tapped as he skirted his desk. "Is that indeed where the danger lies?"

Do you truly not know? "Danger lies everywhere." Makar now turned to face his brother, obscurely nettled. Either Takyeo was being deliberately obfuscatory or he suspected Makar of impropriety, and neither was a welcome mistake from a brother he, after all, loved.

"Do not mouth platitudes just at this moment." Takyeo's gaze was now sharp, and something moved behind pupils and iris, a depth rarely seen. In this moment, he looked very much like the Tamuron of Makar's childhood, and a breath of uneasiness touched the Fourth Prince's spine like a refined courtesan's fingertip, a cool, promising stroke. "If you know of something definite, now is the time to tell me."

"I do not absolutely know." The Awakened One once remarked you could not shake a man out of slumber who was only pretending it, and Makar did not like thinking himself capable of such internal untruth. Lying to others was a necessary skill; lying to one's own liver was perilous indeed. "I have suspicions." *Strong ones. Ask me how strong, Ah-Yeo. Please.*

"So do I." Takyeo shook his head and reached for the small bargong upon his desk. "Suspicion is not enough, Makar. Not yet. But where are my manners? I shall call for something to have with our tea."

The Crown Prince of Zhaon was required to give the appearance of such things as *honor* and *truth* and *justice*. The problem was, Takyeo believed in such things, and practiced them with the assiduousness of one born incapable of shameful actions. Makar's eldest brother was everything the sages said a ruler should be— kind, wise, full of merit.

What the sages said and what the world actually required were two very different things, even for those who found much utility in scrolls and flatbooks. "Please do not trouble yourself, Eldest Brother. I came only as a humble emissary upon Banh and that eunuch's business."

"If you wish to leave, you may. But I would like to have a meal with you, Makar, while we both have time."

Do you realize how little time remains? But Makar assented gracefully. He had done all he could, and hinted all he might while keeping his own lovely, beloved mother safe.

Now it was up to Takyeo to save himself.

WORK WITHOUT
FOOD

At night, the shores of the slightly smaller of the two great markets of Zhaon-An murmured with languid brothel-songs and the higher, sharper-pitched melodies of those selling other services. The Yuin was flushed and scrubbed occasionally like any city midden, but all things had their place under Heaven, and it was best to keep the poisonsellers, the knife-dancers, and the practitioners of other shadowed arts easily accessible for questioning.

Every good physician knew maggots only ate the dead flesh, cleaning away the rot so healthy tissue could be treated.

Suitably muffled in a long dark cloak despite the swelter of a summer night, a shadow passed along the edges of the Yuin as loose-haired boys and decorated girls leaned from their case-ments, importuning in high singsong. In his wake a second smaller shadow scurried, barefoot and apologetic. Bursts of perfume mixed with redolent sweat and the spice from the all-night stalls, noodles made from rai, mil, me-mil, and mixtures of the three soaking up frying oil and fat from what claimed to be meat and perhaps even was upon the more prosperous streets. In some stalls, the long thin Khir peppers provided heat, their harshness balanced by the lon-ger, round-bellied Zhaon gulao with their slow but deeper burning.

To work at night called for double the belly-filling a day required, and in summer the peppers forced the cooling humors to rise, slicking the skin with sweat and providing transitory relief. A makeshift stall selling long slivers of salted curltail-haunch over rai noodles smoked and sizzled as its proprietor, an old woman missing half her teeth, shook a knotted fist at the two Watch who had helped themselves to brimming bowls. The crests on their helmets bobbed as they grinned, slurping down the food—they must have strong stomachs, expecting such poor fare not to gripe them. But at least the old woman could go about her business for the rest of the night unmolested.

Or until the next group of Watch came along.

Turning sharply to his left, away from the fraying edge of the Yuin, the muffled man passed down a street of jumbled houses pressed together like pounded-rai cakes or meat-filled dumplings crowded into a steaming-basket. No torches or lamps hung over the doorways, but every pedestrian moved with purpose.

It wasn't wise to linger here.

Still, the cloaked man slowed, and his boots were of very high quality. He might have been approached for the purpose of relieving him of that footwear and any other desirable item had not the long, slightly curved shape upon his back, with its leather-wrapped hilt, silently dissuaded such a maneuver.

The man knew what he wanted, apparently. Or at least, he stopped at a certain door with a dagger-shaped character painted upon its lintel. His companion hurried forward to knock, though a short, imperative gesture said it wasn't necessary; the second, slighter figure all but cowered at the irritation the movement managed to express.

Inside, it was close and muggy, with only a coil of cleansing yeoyan-yao incense burning in a battered brass container. There was no bed, just a table with a low-burning, sputtering lamp of the kind known as *mother's eyeball* and a single sag-bottomed chair.

The slighter figure hurried to trim the lamp and turn it up, to arrange the chair, to do whatever might be required for the comfort of whatever rich man had bought her. His muffling cloak was hung on a handy though somewhat rickety peg near the door, which was swiftly barred.

With that done, the slight figure stood, vibrating with what might have been terror or anticipation, near the table.

"Take off your cloak," the rich man said, touching his topknot to make certain it was still in proper order. Its cage was simple, stiffened leather and the pin merely carved wood, but his dark clothing was very fine and had been noted more than once as he penetrated the Yuin. "There we are," he continued meditatively.

The girl—for such she was, a wide-eyed waif of no more than twelve winters—smiled uncertainly and moved to obey, slipping the rag that could only charitably be called a covering from her thin shoulders. A peasant lass if the work-roughened hands were any indication, her teeth were still fine, and her nervous darting glances around the room calmed somewhat as she visibly noticed the absence of a bed.

The rich man carried a small package, and as he unwrapped its cloth covering the girl's eyes widened. Balls of polished rai, cabbage in qur sauce, and a waxed container of steaming beef-buns. There was also a small stoppered clay jug with crushed fruit.

"You can't work without food," the rich man said, kindly, and indicated the meal. "Sit, eat. There's no tea, I'm afraid, but the fruit will serve. Well, go on." He made a little insisting movement, waving her for the chair.

It was perhaps not quite polite to sit while your superior was standing, but hunger won out. The girl bowed several times, stammered provincially accented thanks to her benefactor, and finally climbed into the chair. There were no eating-sticks, but *her* kind did well enough with their fingers, and well she knew it.

The buns vanished first, and she made a low happy noise like a curltail snuffling in its trough. The rich man smiled paternally, his arms folded over his chest and his back to the door, watching.

She was halfway through the cabbage when she halted and swallowed heavily, her stomach making its own comment in the form of a long resounding belch she set free, it being a mark of politeness to speak when one of your betters has fed you well.

"Is it good?" he inquired, kindly, his left thumb finding a divot upon his corresponding first finger where a heavy ring usually rested.

"V-v-very," the peasant girl stammered. "Though...though, my lord..."

"It's all right." The rich man's tone didn't change at all. He witnessed her sudden stiffness, heard the soft, grating sound she made, and made no move as the girl slid from the chair, curling on the filthy floor like a spiral-shell taken from damp ground meal and thrown into a hot pan.

When the gurgling and seizures were done, the rich man cocked his head. It was a good thing he'd taken the vial; this wouldn't do at *all* and furthermore was definitely not what he had originally commissioned. Perhaps his brother had intended something messily public. It certainly fit Sensheo's tastes, and if he had not thought to test the tool before using it, one or two crucial parts of his plans might have gone astray.

No, this was unpleasant but necessary, and now he knew the dimensions of a brother's treachery. They were utterly expected; he expected, as well, that a queen would soon see her chance to do a spear-wife's son a disservice or two.

The rai-pot, as the peasants would say, was boiling. All he had to do was wait.

"Ah well," the prince said, softly, as the death-rattle filled the peasant girl's throat. Who would have thought a few drops of colorless liquid in a beef-bun would have such an effect? "Greedy girl. You should have known better."

The sudden stink of death-loosened bowels was his only reply. He wrinkled his nose, stepping close enough to gather the rest of the buns—it wouldn't do to leave them lying about.

A few moments later the lamp burned steadily in a silent room, and Garan Kurin, muffled again in the long dark cloak, was gone.

Dry Lightning

Afternoon rose hot, breathless, and full of bruised stormlight. Zhaon-An seethed under smoke from cooking and other fires, hungry tongues kept shielded and contained. The palace complex, normally just as busy if slightly more well-regulated, lay under a pall of weary silence.

The eunuchs hurried along on their jatajatas, but with the peculiar trick of the ankles that made those clickclack sandals land soft as a feline paw. Courtiers and ladies-in-waiting did not gather in the pavilions or stroll like bright proud birds in the many gardens.

In the heart of the Kaeje—the original keep, built in the days of the First Dynasty—the hush lay even thicker in every corner, an almost physical weight. The mirrorlight was muted as if the antique, giant bronze shields used to bring the glow into the heart of living-space had been hung with gossamer cloth or moved just slightly on their oiled gimbals.

Under a light silken counterpane Tamuron lay supine, his eyes glimmering through almost-closed lids. Occasionally one of his fingers twitched and Zan Fein the head eunuch—his usual draught of umu scent much abated in the last few days, perhaps to save his master some irritation—would lean his pinkened ear close to the cracked royal lips to discern whether a command or simply a groaning exhalation was at hand. Ministers came and went, seeking this decision or the other; the Crown Prince had been prevailed upon to take his father's place in the great council despite his household's ongoing preparations for removal to the provinces.

The Second Concubine's funeral arrangements had altered that event somewhat, but gossip whispered that the loss of his foreign wife and his royal father's ruthless driving had forced that mild, patient prince to balk and turn aside like the snow-pard he had taken for his device.

Dry lightning played upon distant hills. There was no danger of fire yet; the drought-time of summer had not yet begun. The rai burgeoned in the fields, other crops stretching from black earth as well. It was the time of bent backs, of fighting weeds, of planting for the second harvest, of young animals frisking and their elders content merely to fatten.

The heart of Zhaon lay upon his back, his thinning hair combed by a bath-girl excused from other duties because her hands soothed the Emperor's temper. The suppurating lesions widened upon his body, but he had no will to scratch them, now. Once or twice he summoned his strength and called for Mrong Banh, who hurried to attend his lord. Their conversation was brief each time, and ever afterward no blandishment could induce the man to say what they had spoken of.

The storm lowered over the city like folded wings, and even the most hopeful or stupid of courtiers could not escape the knowledge that there was no recovery or last-moment rallying to a standard that would break an enemy's army. Their Emperor, strong in the saddle and matchless in battle, sank under the weight of his own failing body.

The Second Concubine had merely gone ahead to prepare a place for her lord.

THRIFTY STOCK

E ver afterward, Mrong Banh would think of that day with a shudder. It started with a headache so severe he gave up watching the stars lose themselves in daylight's skirts and tried to sleep, tossing and turning upon the narrow pallet that was the only bed he could stand when the riven-skull pain came. It lasted for hours, and eventually, when it receded enough that he was not blind, the astrologer poked his hair into an approximation of a proper topknot, ran his hands down the front of his wrinkled robe, and set off for the Artisan's Home. He could have gone to Kihon Jiao for a tincture of sleepflower to halt the pain, but that would require visiting Tamuron's bedside.

Mrong Banh did not wish to appear haggard and head-tender before his lord. The Emperor had his own failing health to steward, and would look pityingly at his poor astrologer. As much as it hurt to endure a great man's pity, it was even worse to see the great man laid low—especially when you had spent your life proud to be serving a master of such merit.

He was almost to the Home when he saw a knot of bright-clad court ladies in one of the gardens, so he stepped aside into a long colonnade and took a different route to avoid being hailed and asked for advice. Afterward, he wondered if Heaven had been

directing his steps, for at the end of the shadow-striped passageway were two familiar figures, one in bright blue and one in Khir
indigo, both with the pale bar of mourning upon their sleeves just
as it was upon Mrong Banh's.

It was the Crown Prince, leaning upon his silver-headed cane a
little more heavily than usual, and Komor Yala with her faithful
kaburei at her side, the girl whose adoring looks at her mistress
were much like a small, expensively bred dog's.

"—will not heal," Komor Yala said softly as Banh approached.
"Anh may go for a palanquin."

"It simply needs exercise." Takyeo shook his head slightly, and
brightened as his gaze fell across the astrologer. "See? Here is
Mrong Banh, and with both of you in attendance I may hobble at
a healing pace."

"Honorable Mrong." Lady Komor performed the slightest of
bows, far more merit than Banh had likely accrued with her. Still,
she was not the sort to bestow compliments where unnecessary,
and even Takshin spoke well of her. "I am attempting to scold the
Crown Prince into caring for his wounded leg; perhaps you shall
have better luck."

"*Ai*, not likely." Despite his tender head, Banh was pleased to be
greeted so. Nothing eased a man's pain like being considered useful. "He has been ignoring me since he could walk."

"I cannot ignore you, Banh. You nag too effectively." Takyeo's
smile held no pained shade, for once. His leg, it seemed, was not
the only part of him healing, even if at a spiral-shell's pace. "Tell
Lady Komor my leg is merely stiff, and will support me admirably
as long as we do not run."

"It would be no trouble to send for a palanquin," Lady Komor
began, and Banh had to hide a weary smile behind his sleeve.

"Ah," he said, hoping the inkstains on his cuffs did not show too
badly, "but should we send for one *I* might climb inside and ride
while my betters walk, and that cannot be borne."

"You do look somewhat pale." Lady Komor viewed him with a
pretty air of mild anxiety. "Are you ill, Honorable Mrong?"

"My head is somewhat tender this morn, and I did not even have the joy of drinking sohju last night to account for it. Never grow old, Lady Komor. It is a state full of many annoyances."

"You should marry." A somberly uttered jest, for Takyeo knew Banh's thoughts upon his own matrimonial prospects. "A wife would keep you young."

"Nag me into the tomb early," Banh muttered, with a quick glance at Komor Yala. She did not seem to take offense, even going so far as to raise her own sleeve to her mouth as if suppressing laughter. "Why, as long as I have you, Crown Prince..."

"Mayhap you should spear-marry." Lady Komor's eyes all but sparkled. A dark gaze was an honest one, the Zhaon said, but he did not find her pale one displeasing at all. "A scholar and a prince; a fine couple."

"Yes, but a spear-marriage's courtship is as full of annoyances as aging." Takyeo indicated the stairs through a very fine jewelwing-garden, masses of early flowers attracting the flutter-bright insects. "Whose turn it is to pour, who goes marketing for dinner—it is two generals without a single soldier, my lady, and *that* is a sad state of affairs."

Banh was actually feeling quite fortunate to meet them; plenty of courtiers would keep their distance seeing this company come over the rise. Lady Komor took very small steps, and he was almost irritated at her for doing so until he realized she was holding their pace to a minimum so successfully it was Takyeo who made one or two short, sharp hurrying motions.

Not at her, of course—a prince should never treat a lady so—but at Banh, who could be comfortably harried.

Consequently, mornlight had failed and the clouds settled their lid over Zhaon-An before they reached the Home. "I am bound for there." Lady Komor lifted her cupped hand, her fingers held gracefully together since it was ill-bred to point and jab at another's body or belongings.

"And I am for *there*." Mrong Banh indicated the apothecary's alley, with three fingers instead of a cup. "Well, Crown Prince? I am not so pretty to gaze upon over tea, but if we are forced to wait for Lady Komor there is a small shop for teaware that serves a quite fine cup of khang-eng, very good for the bones."

"I do have a chaperone." Lady Komor sounded very amused indeed. "And this may take me some short while."

"Women," Banh muttered, but Takyeo now looked slightly pained.

"I shall rest in Banh's teaware shop, then." Sweat glimmered upon the Crown Prince's forehead, and the two men watched Komor Yala glide away, her skirts moving sweetly and her head held high. "It would do me well to see her settled, Banh."

"No doubt she feels the same." Banh rescued a square of thick thirsty cotton from his sleeve and dabbed at his own damp forehead. "How is your leg?"

"The same as the last few times you asked after its health. Come, show me this teaware."

In short order the Crown Prince was settled in the small shop, the round proprietor all but expiring of satisfaction to have such an august customer gravely considering his stock while sipping silken-smooth khang-eng from the very western fringes of Zhaon. It was a matter of a quarter-mark for Banh to conduct his own business and make an attempt to haggle the price of a night-flower draught to an acceptable level—for though he did not lack alloy or even half-ingots, Banh came of thrifty stock and disdained to act above his station—and as he returned his only thought was of a tepid bath once he had swallowed enough tea to be polite.

Takyeo, his leg stretched before him and his elbow upon the table, brightened as Banh reappeared. The astrologer, however, halted, his eyes growing wide and his gaze fixing over the Crown Prince's head.

That was the only warning Garan Takyeo received, and had Banh been just a few moments later, or a few hard copper slivers thriftier, there would have been none. As it was, the Crown Prince spilled out of the chair, landing with a thump as the blade passed over his head with a whoosh and the assassin, his face muffled by a single sheer piece of dun cotton, raised the slightly curved onyashii to try again.

Smooth Another Temper

In the Artisan's Home, early afternoon and the pall of storm-light turned regular bustle into slow swimming against a river's heavy tide. "We could leave now," Dao said softly, leaning over the table. He wore a different robe today; faint traces of sweat showed upon his throat and forehead; did he hate this clutching, suffocating heat as she did? "You can even bring that *kaburei*, it is easy enough to free ourselves of such an impediment later."

Anh was hardly an *impediment*, and Yala had no intention of allowing Daoyan to treat her as one. "And you have a plan for leaving the city, not to mention riding north?" Yala could barely believe her ears. She had finally been able to arrange another visit, and seeing him again brought a swift sharp pain to her heart. She had to tell him of her intent, but how? "A plan for crossing the border, and then—"

"Come now, Yala. All things should be so easy as a pair of Khir deciding to leave an inhospitable city. Once we are over the border, I return you to Hai Komori, and no doubt your father will accept my offer for you this time."

She gazed upon the small glittering items upon the roll of velvet, different ones this time. Apparently his play at being a merchant was profitable enough, though a nobleman could only treat such a thing as a game. "This time?"

"Oh, I offered before." Dao's mouth turned down, and it was one of the few unguarded expressions she had ever seen him display. He did not glance about to see who was watching, either. "Bai laughed at me."

"Ah." She glanced at the door, where Anh sat upon a mat of coarse rush fiber waiting for her mistress. Close enough to guard Yala's honor, far enough away to gain some privacy. It was only natural that a Khir lady-in-waiting should wish to hear her own tongue spoken, and perhaps gain news from a merchant of her country. "I did not know that. Daoyan..." How could she even begin to tell him? *I have promised twice over to stay, once to my princess's shade and once to a Zhaon general.*

Of course the son of the Great Rider would not consider a weak woman's promise binding. Best not to mention Zakkar Kai at all, and merely say that Mahara's shade kept her in Zhaon-An until vengeance could be performed.

"Or perhaps you wish to leave tonight." He watched the door too, his grey gaze clear but troubled. "Simply *tell* me, Yala. We can be gone with very little trouble; I have come this far, have I not?"

"I do not doubt your capability *or* your willingness, Your Highness." What else could she say? There were more considerations, too. Daoyan should be in the city of the Great Keep; he was the only remaining son of the Great Rider. Her shock at finding him here had abated somewhat, and now she felt the chill of quite another set of considerations. "But I have made a vow, to stay for—"

"Is it a man?" His eyes narrowed, his nostrils flaring, and Yala swallowed a handful of irritation. It scraped all the way down, her temper already frayed from the Crown Prince's politely inviting himself along *and* the astrologer's sudden appearance. Now she was forced to smooth yet another nobleman's temper.

It did not help that he was partially correct, though Kai was not the overriding reason for staying in this terrible place. Instead of answering immediately, she studied the fall of nasty, bruised light through the doorway onto wooden floor brushed to satin sheen by many footsteps. Sometimes, ignoring impoliteness carried more sting than a rebuke, and she knew Dao well.

Or did she? She would never have thought him capable of leaving Khir behind, traveling to this horrible, suffocating pile of stone and lavishness, cooling his heels until she could plausibly meet him a second time. If anything, it was his willingness for the last that troubled her most.

"Someone in this palace paid for a death," she said, finally, turning her gaze to the hairpins and ear-drops displayed upon velvet pad, the small spindly table at her elbow a thin reason for yet another visit. She had to find the words that would make him see. "I would know who, Ashani Daoyan." It was impossible for her inflection to be more honorific—or more remote.

"And what would you do with such knowledge, Komor Yala? Serve vengeance with your maiden's blade?" He did not outright scoff at the thought, but it was perhaps close. Today his topknot-cage was fine-carved scentwood, just the sort of understated taste a merchant with pretensions would employ. "Leave that to her kin."

Would that I could. "You are her brother. Who should be in Khir, aiding the Great Rider as his only remaining son."

"Half-brother. *Bastard* son." There was no heat to the words, but a swift spasm of anger crossed his handsome features. Had he been born a little less comely and talented in the saddle, the nobles might not have been so sneeringly polite. "I know who and what I am. And I am unwilling to let you meet a similar fate to hers here. Were she still alive I would subtract you from her clutches soon enough—"

"Daoyan." Yala's bones turned to ice within her. The feeling was not *irritation*, precisely; it was much colder, and its edges were a *yue*'s gleam. "I chose to accompany your royal sister."

"You were *forced*. Even your father had not the hunrao to gainsay it, though he made plans with me soon enough after." Dao made a short sharp motion, brushing aside any maidenly objections. *I know best*, his tone said, *for I am male and I am a Khir noble, and both are due your compliance.* "What does it matter now? You will come with me."

Accusing her father of lacking hunrao was not something Yala could easily forgive, even if Dao was irritated enough to speak unguarded for once. "I do not—" she began, but halted, tilting her head. Anh had stiffened and was peering out the door, inquisitiveness in every line.

Shouting. Running feet. Ringing metal.

The Crown Prince. Yala's mouth turned dry. "Something is amiss," she finished, and rose swiftly, settling her skirts with a decided motion. "Anh? What is it?"

"Yala." Daoyan's hand flashed out but she avoided the maneuver with a half-turn. Was he mad? The merchant he was playing could not lay a finger upon a Khir noblewoman, not without severe reprisal. It was unlike him to forget such a thing.

Much about this troubled her, the thought that perhaps she did not know Ashani Daoyan as well as she thought most of all, but all else paled in comparison to this sudden hue and cry.

"My lady?" Anh, anxious, in Zhaon. She rose halfway from her crouch like a peasant girl craning to see what had invaded a field—a ruminant bent on chewing, a dog or padfoot searching for prey, or worst of all, a soldier intent upon food or leisure.

There were many dangers in the world, especially for a female creature.

"Come." Yala's hands were heavy with sweat, and her right dropped to her side. The urge to draw her *yue*, or merely to touch cross-hatched metal with her fingertips and derive some comfort, was all but overwhelming.

It was not ladylike to run, but she gathered her skirts anyway and hurried out the door, Daoyan left to shift for himself and Anh hard upon her heels.

A Festival Roast

The great pierce-towered capital of Shan rose above choking mist mixed with cookfire smoke; the morning was slightly cooler than afternoon would be. Still, upon every corner there were cheering peasants and tradesmen. Sparksticks crackle-starred, pale under foggy sunlight. The flame-flowers would bloom at and after tonight's banquet.

And Garan Daebo Sabwone was cold with sweat.

Shan did not require its royal brides to be pulled on a vast moving platform through the streets, dressed in a conqueror's or bridegroom's luxury. Instead, the First Princess of Zhaon was trapped in the hated bridal palanquin once more, scrubbed free of blood and with no sharp object inside, not even a fruit-knife or sewing pin. Perhaps it would have been worse to ride one of Shan's stupid horses through the cheering, strangling throng, enduring the tossing of paper money and pastefruit, the gazes of the common crowd.

She could not quite decide, so she sat and boiled with something uncomfortably like fear, dressed in heavy brocaded crimson nobody would see until the palanquin was peered into by a lord and that hateful merchant prince.

In a novel, she would change into a white bird, or a *real* prince would break her free of imprisonment.

At least her laces were properly tightened and her hair, braided and looped with multiple pins dangling clinking golden leaves, was well in place. Nijera had seen to it herself, cooing that this was a blessed day for the princess until Sabwone longed to slap her—or rise and run, screaming, in any direction that promised an escape.

There was none, so she gritted her teeth and remained silent. Perhaps they even thought her refusal to speak a maidenly reticence instead of furious terror. She could not even open the slatted window to gain some air; she had to sit here, again, simmering in her own sweat. Even the Khir princess hadn't been treated like this; she'd had a lady-in-waiting at her side, that ugly little ghost-eyed girl Takshin protected.

If Taktak was here he would be riding alongside the palanquin. *I would prefer to have him here, true.* Her future husband, a merchant brat with no feeling at all, taunting a poor girl who had opened her veins.

Just not thoroughly enough.

Maybe she could take a hairpin, and stab him. The thought was immensely cheering.

She did not even have a novel to pass the time, or a basket of fruit. Nothing but the robe, a few pillows, and the four wooden walls bearing down upon her as the palanquin lurched steadily toward doom.

The ride to the capital was a type of hell no sage or novel had ever brushed a description of, and this just one more insult to be borne until she could somehow escape. They watched her and sneered, those ill-bred lords of Shan, new ones arriving at pre-arranged stops and introducing themselves to her in their barbarian dialect.

Well, she would not learn it, or their stupid names. She would speak proper Zhaon only, for the rest of her days. She had so few weapons, would they grudge her even *that*?

The crowd-noise began to abate in increments, and the palanquin slowed—if that were possible, it was creeping like a spiral-shell or silver-smearing greasebug in a wet garden. She wished

Kurin were here, or even Sensheo—he had been fond of picking up tiny shelled things, admiring their homes before crushing them slowly, his dark gaze alight. *See, Sabi, it's easy. All you have to do is press in the right place.*

Nijera and some of the other ladies were learning the Shan dialect. No doubt they thought to catch themselves merchant barbarian husbands, when what they *should* have been doing was helping their princess. There were even strange rumors of something happening between Shan's capital and the border with Anwei, but Sabwone pointedly ignored *that*. What did she care if a few peasants were raided by bandits?

After the interminable suffering and step-by-step dragging, the end was somewhat anticlimactic. The palanquin halted, was set upon its wooden legs with a thump that jolted all through her. Sabwone shut her eyes, her hands crossed in her lap, the filigree sheaths over her smallest fingernails on either hand scratching at brocade. Dressed up and trussed like a festival roast, sold off to jumped-up merchants, betrayed even by her mother—oh, if it was the start of a novel, it would have been thrilling.

But it was not, and she was so small. And so terribly, utterly alone.

Sabwone's heart pounded. Next would come the banquet, which she would not see. They would all feast upon her degradation; when dark fell she would be trapped in a bedroom with a strange man and likely outraged. She had some idea of what the latter entailed, having seen the breeding of fine horses at some of the Daebo estates as well as illustrations in certain filched books.

She was afraid, and she had failed. Both were insupportable.

There was a courteous knock upon the palanquin's side. Sabwone kept her eyes closed. If she did not look, it would all remain unreal.

Wood slid upon greased runners. A relatively cool, mist-laden breath filled the palanquin, and she was abruptly aware of the smell of her own sweat, the tang of freshening incense from the bridal robe, and other less fetching bodily odors. At least she had been unable to eat, and to swallow more than a cupful of sweet tea before dawn.

"My princess," Nijera whispered, her shadow filling the aperture. "Courage, my princess."

Sabwone remained still, vibrating with that terrible, will-sapping fear. More shadows, blocking the light.

"It is her." A man's voice—a Shan lord giving the ceremonial statement, first in their barbarous dialect, then in proper Zhaon for her benefit.

"Good." *His* voice. Kiron of Shan, the man she was now supposed to bear heirs for. The filthy merchant who insulted her and spoke of bricking her into a tower. He said something else in Shan, and she expected him to insult her again before turning away and letting Nijera close the door.

However, he leaned in, and Sabwone's throat moved convulsively as she swallowed. Sweat upon her cheeks and forehead cooled under questing breeze-fingers, outside air creeping like a thief through a sleeping house.

"You are not riding to an execution," Kiron said finally, in his accented Zhaon. Did he speak to Takshin so? "Fear not, *ekanha*. You are safe, in good hands."

How dare he sound... sound so *kind*? As if she was a shrinking peasant maid, or a beast needing taming?

Sabwone's eyes flew open. She caught only a glimpse of him before he straightened and the door slid shut again.

The lord—one of those who had seen her in Zhaon now confirming she had not been exchanged for another, a false bride—said something short and dismissive in Shan, and Kiron's reply was muffled but still audible, delivered again in Zhaon.

"She is a mere girl, and far from home. It costs nothing to be gentle, Suron."

Their voices faded, and Sabwone writhed internally. Did the merchant pretender *pity* her? It was yet another insult she could not answer.

Still, her hands had ceased gripping each other so tightly, and when Nijera opened the side door again—once the maiden aunt had ascertained that the fabric walls on either side of the passage to the door of the wedding house were taut and no cracks or seams were available for an evil gaze to fall upon a vulnerable bride— Sabwone found that her aching legs were more than equal to the task of carrying her, if not for fleeing.

The worst was yet to come. Sabwone let Auntie Nijera fuss over the thin crimson veil, making sure the princess was muffled from head to toe. A triple string of golden beads depended from the headdress in front of her, ending at Sabwone's waist; the dangling shadow was an irritant as well. Her slippered foot met cool, gritty stone. She hardly saw the great slate steps she was hurried up, or the dark ironbound door that swallowed her whole. Darkness enclosed her, an entryway with wooden floors and stone walls, and the first surprise was how much it looked like any other palace hall at home.

Only now she was married, and there had been no prince or exorcist to save her after all.

ANGER NOT NEW

The world narrowed to a blade descending, Garan Takyeo helpless upon his back like a common garden insect. Mrong Banh, yelling like a battlefield general, had snatched up a chair and was menacing two of the trio of assassins; the third, masked as his counterparts, brought the blade down again as Takyeo, his hand finding the slim length of his cane, thrashed *under* the blow. His good leg shot out, catching the man just above the knee, and the cane's silver head described a blurred arc before it smacked the flat of the attacking metal, deflecting it another critical few degrees. *Up. Get UP.*

It was no use; his leg, protesting harsh treatment, was likely to fail him. Grappling was always his least favorite among the martial arts, though Takyeo had set himself to excel in it as he did all else.

Or at least not *embarrass* himself, and it was faintly amusing that it should be what saved him now.

The knee-strike staggered his attacker, and the man almost fell into the table. A good pot of khang-eng ruined, and for what purpose? To kill a man who wanted no part of what everyone else was chasing, after they had also killed his wife and lamed him in the bargain.

The anger was not new. What was new was his willingness to set it free, and Takyeo used every scrap he could find, his good heel thumping down and digging in as he sought to roll onto his side.

From there he could at least reach hands and knees so he was not spitted like an armorbug upon a pin.

"*Takyeo!*" Mrong Banh bellowed, the chair splintering as he sought desperately to keep the other two contained.

The assassin gained his footing and swung again, but something sailed overhead and shattered upon his topknot. Streams of boiling amber poured down the attacker's face, wetting his cotton mask, and a high, shattering battle-cry echoed through the teaware shop as a blur moved past Banh.

It was a Khir merchant in a dun cotton robe, but the man evidently had some training. He ducked under a wild swing, locked the second assassin's wrist and twisted the blade free. Another teapot sailed overhead, thrown with a great deal of force but little accuracy, and hit the first assassin's chest. It did not shatter, descending at high speed for Takyeo, who caught its handle with the speed of one who had been tutored in such reflexes from the moment he could crawl. He brought it around, smashing it upon the man's *other* knee, and was rewarded with a grunt of pain. The assassin's cloth mask, now soaked with tea, moved like a wet sail.

Metal clashed. The Khir merchant had the second assassin's blade and put it to good use, engaging the third and freeing Banh, who bolted across the shop for Takyeo. Just what the astrologer intended Takyeo could not say, and in any case it did not matter, for Komor Yala arrived at Takyeo's side, her right hand low and tense.

He had seen her at this work before, of course, placed before his foreign wife, Yala's sharp, ghost-eyed face thoughtless, serene as the Great Awakener's as that blade—dappled green metal, too short for a sword but too long for a knife—blurred in complicated patterns, driving away edged threats and always, always bending her a fraction out of harm's way.

She batted aside the curved shortsword, stepping farther into the arc of the swing in order to throw off the assassin's balance. Another pair of missiles appeared—teacups, shelved near the door, and later Takyeo realized it was Lady Komor's kaburei flinging them with scarcely concealed, gleeful abandon.

Komor Yala's slippered foot flicked out, deflecting the assassin's own kick, and Takyeo surged to his feet. His wounded leg buckled but he overrode the weakness, deciding it was no worse than having one limb taken up with a squirming younger sibling along for a game of drag-horse. Another teacup, this one fine-glazed raiku ware, crunched against the assassin's forehead, and Anh let out a country girl's whoop at a gorge-bird's fall.

Now he could unlimber his sword, with Takshin's laconic *you should go about armed, Eldest Brother* ringing in his head. As if his little brother thought he would do anything *but*, especially inside the Palace.

Just as the bright blade leapt free, though, Komor Yala let out a short sharp sound of effort and the assassin staggered back, a bright red necklace soaking into his throat-wrappings. The Khir merchant drove forward, bearing the second assassin's wicked-curved knife with its horn hilt as well as the sword taken from that same fellow, and in his movement was the fluidity of a man born to war.

Takyeo lunged, his wounded leg thankfully not buckling—not yet, at any rate. "Leave one alive," he cried in case Yala was disposed to listen, and how it burned that a woman, a *foreign* woman, was protecting him.

It was downright unprincely of him to allow it.

The assassin swiped wildly with his blade; Komor Yala bent back with the suppleness of a breathing reed, an acrobat's spine-curve move. Takyeo lunged again, meaning to drive the man into retreat, but a fiery nail tore into his side.

Out of practice, he thought, but the pain was from the third assassin, the one in the process of being unseamed by the Khir merchant. Blood flew, and the teaware seller, cowering in the ruins of a table, was screaming pointlessly.

The last assassin had flung one of his knives, and such was the fury upon Garan Takyeo that he did not notice until he had the one before him spitted, Komor Yala letting out a small wounded cry as she was shoved aside and went down *hard* in a tangle of indigo silk, her hairpin knocked askew.

The doughty merchant yelled something in Khir, more crockery shattered, and Takyeo's body decided it had endured quite enough. He spilled from his feet, curling to the left around the knife half-buried in his gut, and his wounded leg gave a flare of hot snapping pain before his head hit the wooden floor and he saw constellations.

CONSEQUENCES

Lightning stabbed the hills around Khir's Great Keep and its accumulated city; perhaps that was why the rumors flew from the stone halls of the noble quarter, through the artisans' and theater districts, across the great mass of those not yet starving but clinging to poverty's edge, and filled the slums. It even spread into the countryside past the city's fringes, where the rai was almost ready for first harvest, its long grains swollen and almost, almost ripe.

Nowhere was speculation more hushed or more rampant than within the Great Keep itself, where ministers came and went from the throne room, entering with apprehensive tranquility and leaving more often than not with the deep relief of those saved at the last moment.

It had been a long while since Ashani Zlorih, Great Rider of Khir, had called each minister to give account. Such was the Rider's prerogative, normally exercised only at the beginning of the reign but theoretically descending at any moment like the hooves of a war-trained steed. The Great Rider had also purged his personal guard of many who had divided allegiances—of course spring was the usual season for housecleaning and the greatest of the Khir had been otherwise occupied during that time, but still, ministers whose clients among the close-riders were suddenly forced into graceful retirement with the ancient gift upon the release of their service—a fine mare from the Great Rider's own stables—had exchanged many a long searching look since the beginning of summer's dry mountain-storms.

Some families who had not seen the Great Keep for generations had been called to present what sons had escaped or survived military service to Khir's ruler, and no few of those provincial nobles had been gifted with an iron stirrup to mark their acceptance into the ranks.

None, not even the great Domar clan, dared make any remonstrance. For Ashani Zlorih had grown quiet of late, and there was a steely glint in his clear grey Khir eyes that warned ministers who knew their business to hold tongue and wait for better hunting weather.

Chief among the wisely silent was Domari Ulo, who shook his head when approached—oh, carefully, to be sure, and with quite a few allusions to dignity, obedience, and loyalty that meant their exact opposite—by those unhappy at being removed from influence. *The Rider has his reasons*, the great head of the Domar clan would intone softly, and his slight smile led more than a few to believe the cat-faced, soft-walking, extraordinarily rich minister knew no few of those secrets—if not all, or at least more than his royal master.

After all, it was the head of Hai Domari who held the honor of negotiating with the dough-skinned, reeking envoy from the Tabrak, though that barbarian had lately begun to visibly wish himself gone from Khir. Unfortunately, even a stirrup-holder to the leader of the Pale Horde must obey a host's unwillingness to let a cherished guest embark again upon perilous travel.

So it was no large surprise when the great minister appeared in his rich subtle robe and the great seal of his office as if for a garden promenade, gliding into the throne room with a determined step. One or two of his clients hurried from the antechambers, bearing great envelopes sealed with scarlet wax pressed with the Great Rider's official seal, and if they did not stop to look at their patron it was only because the tidings were of such grave import as to forbid such a thing.

Perhaps an answer had been given to Tabrak, some whispered. Others held their fans before their mouths and said nothing.

The great hall of rule, its low padded throne-bench under the giant round stone calendar of the horse-goddess's chosen folk, held half its usual crowd. Scribes bent over long low tables along one side, the feathers in their scholar-caps bobbing as they brushed, stamped, sealed, and stamped again great decrees. They had been busy, of course, for Khir was in a ferment.

None wished for war again, of course. But the stain of defeat, and other reverses, must be washed away.

Domari Ulo paused at the prescribed stations, bowing perfunctorily at each. His obeisances had grown a little more careless of late, perhaps because there were whispers in certain corners that the line of Ashani had expended itself and a new Great Rider should be chosen.

A short while ago Hai Khir Ashani had been rich in heirs. The two legitimate sons were dead upon the battlefield at Three Rivers, disdaining to flee for their lives while the third, illegitimate offspring was dragged away by six strong close-riders sent for that express purpose.

And the Great Rider's only daughter, sent to Zhaon as tribute and surety for peace, was no more.

Gossip ran rank and rife upon *that* matter, too. And upon the new alliance with Tabrak, all but assured. The wisdom of giving such barbarians the honor of *alliance* was debatable, but using them as a butcher's blade to trim Zhaon's fat was a seductive notion indeed. The dough-skinned barbarians' new lord was rumored to be not of the stamp of his forefathers.

"Ulo." The Great Rider nodded as his chief minister halted before the throne. Close-riders gathered on either side of the dais and crowded its steps, some of them with the dazed look of the newly promoted, some familiar faces smiling with relief, their rank confirmed. Ministers were banished from the dais, gathered in a knot to Ulo's left around a man he almost frowned to see among them.

Domari Ulo cast a measuring look over the assembly, no doubt noticing quite a few of his protégés and clients were missing. "Great Rider of Khir." His bow at the dais's foot lacked nothing in depth or holding; to hurry through the stations of greeting your monarch could be permissible if you were simply eager to be in the presence that confirmed luck, wealth, and status to all below. In the august presence itself, decorum was safest.

Especially if your monarch was in a mood that could only be called *severe*.

With his obeisance accomplished, he straightened and waited to be beckoned up the stairs. Ashani Zlorih, however, stroked his cheek with blunt callused fingertips echoing the thickened ridges across his palm from reins and swordhilt. He was in full state, his dark silk robe figured with wheel-characters in bright crimson at hem, cuffs, and throat; the pointed slippers he wore were likewise heavily embroidered. A young scribe, the crest feather upon his hat trembling, knelt at the king's side holding a temporary desk piled with papers, inkstone, a few brushes gently swaying upon their stand, sticks of crimson wax ready to be pressed into service also vibrating as the leather strap about the lad's neck communicated his joy or fear at being so close to the ruler of his homeland.

Perhaps Ulo felt a sliver of unease then, for the king's personal secretary was his creature. Now, however, the young lad Ganreni Taoyan—member of a junior branch of the Domar, of course— dared not look at his benefactor, instead blinking at Ashani Zlorih with an expression best described as *penitent*.

"Did you think me unaware, minister?" The Great Rider said it softly, but his tone sliced through the mutter of scribes and the breathing of the assembled close-riders.

Silence fell through the Great Hall.

Domari Ulo affected astonishment, though it was probably closer to the truth than many other times his face had held the expression. "Unaware, Great Rider? Of what?"

"My daughter is dead." The king indicated the holding-desk, and the brushes upon it swayed as the scribe trembled afresh. The lad's left hand was bandaged, probably from some mishap on the training ground. Despite scribes needing flexibility in their fingers, it was unthinkable for a noble boy to *not* hold a sword; those who danced with brush instead of steel in their daily duties were to train twice as hard at sparring to make up for it. "My little Mahara, gone to Zhaon, is dead within a few moon-turns of her marriage."

It was no surprise, the news had reached them weeks ago. "My lord?" Ulo's perplexity was either wholly feigned or short-lived, so Zlorih bestirred himself, selecting an already sealed scroll from the pile upon the shaking desk.

The Great Rider handed the scroll to the close-rider at his right hand, a broad-faced youth with the clear grey eyes of a noble Zhaon but a crop of swelling pimples marring his temples and chin, speaking of sweat collected under a helm and blocking vital pores. It was probably an effort for Domari Ulo to remember the boy's clan—it was Kinreni Shonih, the oldest boy in the cadet branch that would take over Hai Komor.

Perhaps that was when Ulo thought upon Komori Dasho for the first time in a long while, the man found dead of old age near his fireplace, his seal missing and his iron neck finally bent. Perhaps Ulo was remembering Dasho's only daughter, sent to Zhaon with Ashan Mahara; no doubt he considered that girl a milksop bitch mouthing the same platitudes as her "incorruptible" father.

And perhaps, just perhaps, Domari Ulo began to feel uneasy at that moment.

The lord of Ashani, the Great Rider of Khir, made a short movement, and the close-riders at Domari Ulo's sides hurried to grab his arms. He shook them away, amazed at their daring, and froze when the Great Rider's voice thundered through the throne room, ruffling the banners hung overhead, every noble family and clan represented in needlework upon scraps of cloth.

"Accursed wretch!" Ashani Zlorih jabbed an accusing finger at his chief minister, the disdain in the gesture adding to the shock of its impoliteness. "My daughter is dead in Zhaon, and my last remaining son has disappeared as well. What say you to that?"

"Your Majesty..." Domari Ulo sank upon his knees, his robe's wide sleeves squirting through the clutching fingers of the guards. The bastard princeling had vanished, leaving only a short, exquisitely brushed message to his father—*I have other business.* "Your Majesty! What have you—"

"Hai Domari was raided this morning," Kinreni Shonih said, halting before Domari Ulo. His boots, worn within walls and roof in defiance of good manners because a close-rider to the ruler must ever be ready, made sharp crisp noises upon the steps. "Just as you left to visit your mistress for morning tea, Lord Domari. Much was found, including certain papers detailing a conspiracy against the Crown Prince of Khir."

Ashani Zlorih watched his chief minister turn yellow under the copper of his complexion, and the man's soft, richly oiled hands shot out, supplicatory. "My lord... my lord king... Great Rider..."

"Those who attempt to dye their hands with the Great Rider's blood face consequences," Ganreni Taoyan stammered, glancing uneasily at Zlorih. "The Zhaon have killed our princess, now the heir is in danger."

"Or already dead." Zlorih regarded Domari Ulo, his chin level. "Well, minister? Where is my son? And what do you know of my daughter's death?"

No doubt Ulo had thought his position unassailable. The forged papers detailing his "conspiracy" were thin proof at best, so Zlorih must move quickly now. Buried in the mass of spoil taken from Hai Domari might be a shred of some *other* proof, despite the stupidity of keeping such things to hand. Those who chafed at Ulo's prestige had been brought forward, and would be too busy picking the carcass to give their Great Rider much trouble. Any alliance with the flour-pale barbarians of Tabrak could be confirmed if that migratory nation moved against Zhaon as their envoy promised, or set aside as Ulo's traitorous pet project if necessary.

If *required.*

"Your Highness..." The chief minister's protest was a small croak, though no doubt he thought his cry of surpassing volume.

Ashani Zlorih was not the grieving father Ulo had grown used to, nodding assent as his chief minister suggested options or leaving certain matters in his minister's capable hands—chief among those matters, the sacrifice of a certain royal Khir girlchild. "Great Rider..."

"Chief Minister," Ashani Zlorih said, much more loudly than he needed to, and the hope rising on Domari Ulo's face was, for once, transparent.

And transparently crushed when another man, much more soberly robed, his topknot held in a cage of carved bone with silver hammered into its lines and with a pin of similar make, detached himself from a knot of ministerial spectators to Ulo's left, gliding on soft leather-soled, point-toed Keep slippers toward the dais, where he bowed with much grace.

"Great Rider, I am here." It was Khitani Udo, the Spider of Hai Akaleki himself. And now, instead of merely bloodless, Ulo's cheeks were almost pale as polished rai.

Almost, in fact, as white as the stinking Tabrak emissary who had been fêted and made much of for quite some time but was now confined to a safe, windowless, heavily guarded suite well within the Keep's stony arms. Domari Ulo had taken pains to be seen conferring with the barbarian upon this or that question, thinking it advantageous. After all, with a weak Great Rider robbed of heirs, much could happen in the land of Khir.

Especially if the Pale Horde came riding as they had many times before and a minister had reached a secret accord with an envoy. It was not necessary for such an accord to be more than suspected; the suspicion itself was useful.

Ashani Zlorih had let it happen, even encouraged it. Had kept his face set and unchanging as the great stone wheel-calendar hanging over his throne, had buried his plans within each other until they were ready—much as he had arranged for his beloved Narikh Arasoe's retirement from public life, her safety from assassins when her relationship with a man not her husband had become clear, and the education of their only son.

Ulo should have known, Zlorih mused, that no matter how pliant a Great Rider might appear, it was never wise to loosen his jesses even a fraction. Like a half-trained or a haggard hawk, the Rider could always bolt for freedom, and even if the bid was lost the ministers provoking it might not escape unscathed.

"I will leave investigation of this matter to you, Khitani Udo," Ashani Zlorih continued, "and expect to hear where my son is, living or dead, within a tenday. You have the commission to use any means necessary."

"Yes, Great Rider. I hear and obey." Khitani Udo did not glance at his former rival, but his satisfaction was palpable.

Perhaps it had not been wise to let the Spider remain among the living, and Ulo's head-meat no doubt raced with ways of remedying the error. If the Domari clan hall had been searched and the close-guard purged, who remained to be suborned or depended upon?

He was perhaps so occupied with the question he made no protest as Ashani Zlorih paused, waiting for the customary wailing protestation of innocence. When none arose, it was a relief—it would appear to the court that Heaven's thunderbolt had not missed its aim. The Great Rider made another short gesture. "Close-riders, take this filth to the dungeons. Chief Minister, I hold you personally responsible for drawing all secrets from it."

"I hear you, Great Rider," the Spider repeated unctuously, and perhaps that was what broke Domari Ulo, his court cap snatched from his head and his arms grasped by disdainful close-riders too young to have been caught in the morass of Three Rivers or ministerial influence. He began to wail brokenly as he was dragged from the throne room, and the scribe at the Great Rider's side trembled even more.

A clan did not live without its head, and even its junior branches might feel the weight of royal displeasure. But Ashani Zlorih merely glanced at the boy. "Who has yet to appear?" he asked, mildly, and the scribe hurried to check the list.

"The l-lord of Hai T-Toshani, G-Great R-R-Rider."

"Good." One royal hand waved, the heavy silver and greenstone ring of office upon its first finger glinting, and Khitani Udo hurried after the receding knot of close-riders bearing his unfortunate predecessor. What evidence Zlorih hadn't managed to forge the new Chief Minister would, if only for the pleasure of seeing his greatest enemy writhe upon the knife. "He should already be in the Keep. Send two close-riders to fetch him to my study, little scribe." His tone was almost fatherly; perhaps the scribe's name reminded him of his own son, vanished like morning dew.

The Great Rider rose, and as he passed all hurried to make their bows. A half-dozen of the new close-riders moved with him, raised unimaginably high for their age and minor nobility. Where else could loyalty be found, some would comment behind their fans— especially the ministers who felt no little satisfaction at Domari Ulo's fall? If a Chief Minister was found to be rotten, a Great Rider must be as severe as a father uncovering unchastity in a daughter or cowardice in a son.

Yes, Khir might soon be at war. All preparations spoke of it. But some few among the ministers wondered precisely whom they would ride against this time.

Let them wonder. The massive doors to the throne room opened and the calls of Ashani Zlorih's presence and passage began to reverberate through the Great Keep's high, cold, stony halls. He had room for future maneuver now, whether Zhaon asked for reinforcements or Tabrak for assurances against Khir's traditional southron foe. If he discovered whither his remaining son had vanished, he would have even more.

And if he discovered the boy was dead, Khir would find out its Great Rider still held a whip—and a few teeth left to bite with.

SPILLING SECRETS

The palace complex was full of fine gardens, but some of them held an air of benign neglect. This one had that particular advantage, being upon one of the less popular routes to the Kaeje's back entrance. "Gone to Takyeo the day before yesterday, I hear, and no doubt spilling all our secrets." Fifth Prince Sensheo, in bright venomous green silk with a glittering enameled topknot-cage, matched the rustling babu shade for shade. He studied a carven stone trunkbeast, its sides running with moss, mired in the center of a padflower-choked pond. No mourning band was upon his arm—of course, a junior mother's passing was regrettable, but not a tragedy. A senior mother's son was released from many of mourning's niceties, should he desire to be.

"He cannot spill what he does not know." Second Prince Kurin, his own armband glaring against a dark-orange sleeve, eyed his little brother speculatively. "How goes your betting lately?"

"I have decided the chariot I will back." Sensheo turned to his elder, his smile wide and guileless as if he was a youth caught stealing plums from Kanbina's garden again. The princes' last meeting had ended badly but no worse than many other childhood scraps, and it was silly to mention such a small matter. "And you?"

"I only wager as much as necessary." Kurin glanced along a colonnaded walk leading to the Iejo's bulk in the distance, and his expression did not change. "Ah, Makar! We were just speaking of you."

"Should I make a sign against ill-luck?" Makar paused, folding his hands into his sober brown sleeves. He was aping the scholar more and more these days, and even his gait had become ponderous. "I go to Father's bedside, Elder Brother." He nodded, coolly, at Sensheo. "Younger Brother. Mother missed you at breakfast."

"So formal. Tell me, does our Eldest Brother still intend to retreat with tail-between-legs?" Sensheo used the term for a whipped cur; it was faintly enjoyable to see Makar's gaze drift over his brothers' heads, circling and dipping to see if anyone was close enough to hear the ill-advised comparison of the Crown Prince to an offal-eating dog.

"Perhaps." Despite his roving eyes, Makar's expression betrayed nothing but faint distaste. "Where are you two bound? Will you visit Father with me?"

"Heaven knows I am there in spirit." Kurin delivered the platitude with his own gaze turned up to the stifling sky. In this light he looked sallow, and the burnt-orange silk of his robe, while expensive, did his complexion little good.

Still, they were not women, to show themselves to advantage in such light. A prince must be handsome, but appear uncaring of the arts used to make him so.

"As are we all." Sensheo restrained a smile, but not very successfully. Perhaps Kurin didn't even suspect the substitution of one small bottle with a soakwood stopper for another. It would be just like him to use the thing and then blame someone else when the effects were gaudy instead of subtle, and Sensheo could not wait for the occasion. "I, for one, hope Takyeo has the sense to run away. It will make everything easier."

"What nonsense are you speaking now?" Makar visibly wished he had taken another route to the Kaeje. Perhaps he had thought this path would give him time for the deep thought he pretended so frequently. "Our mother will—"

"Oh, *Mother*," Sensheo all but sneered. "You are brave, to hide behind her hem. Is she still worried about me?"

"If you visited her, you would know." Makar glanced at Kurin, and the message was clear: *Will you rein Sensheo's tongue?*

Sensheo almost wished him luck with the task. Soon enough he would be able to say anything he pleased, and the prospect filled him with a warm glow quite unlike summer's heat. "Go upon your way, then. We do not need your presence."

"I begin to think you do." His closest brother folded his hands within his scholar's sleeves. He should be wearing a court-hat instead of a topknot, if he would dress so drab. "Well, then, Kurin. Ask what you have placed yourself here to ask."

Sensheo suppressed a flare of irritation. How like his brother, to assume Kurin wished to speak to *him*.

Kurin, however, extracted a fan from his sleeve. A few lazy flicks of its carved scentwood fins stirred the breathless heat, and its decoration was a sinuous, elegant painted curve with a suggestion of scales. The snake was a lucky symbol, constantly renewing and kin to the great powers of fecund earth. "I wish to know if you are with me, Makar." He did not glance at Sensheo. "I know your brother is."

"Ah." Makar did not take his gaze from his little brother, and his mouth tightened. "Is he?"

So. Kurin *had* steered them here. Sensheo's irritation mounted, and he hoped it was not *too* apparent. "I wish what is best for Zhaon." There. Let them take that as they would.

"Have you done anything ill-advised lately?" Makar persisted. "I hope not, for I will not save you from yourself this time."

"You nag like a wife." Sensheo stroked his archer's thumb-ring. The heavy horn was satisfyingly solid. You did not, despite what some of the stupid said, have to meet your foe in the open. It was often more efficient to wait until you had a bow to hand. "Takyeo is weak, and he has no allies."

"Except Takshin. And Kai. And Mrong Banh, and probably that cursed head eunuch." Makar's hands did not move, but his tone suggested he was twitching a finger for each name on the list.

"Takshin is easy to distract and will go back to Shan anyway once he's given the proper inducement. Banh's an astrologer, he'll lick the hand of whoever's buttocks are firmest upon the throne. Zan Fein is a *eunuch*, and no threat." Sensheo's cheeks ached with the effort of keeping his expression neutral. "And Zakkar Kai… well, there are many dangers in an army camp."

"Again?" Makar studied him for a long moment. His sigh was a long-suffering elder's. "You," he said finally, "are a fool."

"Oh?" Kurin's eyebrows shot up and he regarded Sensheo with something like surprise, for once. "Ah, so that was you."

Which time? It was annoying; all the silver Sensheo had spent had still not gained him what he longed for. Still, what else was there to do but spend it? "The difference between us is that you sit and speak, and I *perform*." Sensheo relished the shock upon Makar's shaven, youthful features. His elder brother should have been a eunuch; he had the smooth cheeks and the creeping cowardice. "In any case it is unproven, and unprovable."

Makar sought to lecture him again. "And once he is gone, Khir will be emboldened. Not to mention others."

"Well, sooner or later they would anyway," Sensheo allowed. "But they are weak." After all, they had been vanquished by a foundling, Father's little dog.

"*Now* Khir is weak. Later they might not be so. *A dagger pointed at the heart of Zhaon*," Makar quoted sententiously.

Sensheo had heard Father say the same thing more than once, and it was just as craven now that his big brother was mouthing it. "By the time the horsefuckers decide they wish to test Zhaon again, there will be a strong son of Garan on the throne." He took care to gaze admiringly at Kurin while making *that* pronouncement. With everyone so worried about the First Queen's eldest son, a cautious man could lay his own plans in relative safety. "And Shan is married to us now. If Khir wishes to trade, they will have to swallow their pride and treat with us too. We can do without far Ch'han; Shan and the routes to Anwei are another question entirely."

"So, you have been paying attention to a few lessons lately." Kurin's expression was very similar to Makar's. The two elders gazed at each other now, as if they could not believe their younger sibling had outdone them at last. "And yet you say Kai has outlived his usefulness."

"You may argue he hasn't. But when Father ascends to Heaven, matters change." Sensheo settled his sleeves with a quick pair of tugs upon embroidered cuffs. "Jin may be sent off to head the armies, and Maki will be a minister, of course. *I* have no ambition, unless it is to rid Zhaon of weakness." It was a pretty way of putting it, if he did say so himself.

"I am heartened by your confidence." Kurin had evidently decided that was enough to speak about, at least in front of Makar. "But it grows warm, and Maki is right. We should visit Father." *Who knows*, his tone added, *when we will have another chance?*

"It will do him good to see three of his sons in accord." Makar did not stir a step, just yet.

"Considering his eldest will not visit." Kurin *tch-tch*'d like an old dowager auntie. "Somewhat unfilial of him."

"Who knows?" Sensheo was tired of listing Takyeo's inadequacies. Sometimes it seemed Kurin could think of nothing else, and did not see the other dangers. Then again, that was best for Sensheo's own plans. "Perhaps he even loved that foreign wife of his. And that foreign lady-in-waiting might encourage him." Why keep the skinny, ugly, ghost-eyed lady in his household, otherwise?

An awkward silence folded around them. Makar looked pained, and Kurin's cat-smile was that of a child watching a tiny jewelwing struggling upon a slowly piercing pin.

Sensheo might have continued reciting his argument for another few moments, but he was interrupted by a deep, frantic tolling. The largest bell in the palace complex shattered the storm-stillness, and the three sons of Garan Tamuron all turned in unison toward the sound, as if their gazes could pierce walls, gardens, the bulk of the

Kaeje, and fly past coverings to a body under a silken counterpane that had breathed its last.

So, Sensheo thought, as the bell continued its wild clamor. *And so.*

It begins.

Uncomfortably High Estimation

They had been hurried into the palace complex, far more deeply than Ashani Daoyan could have penetrated on his own without the cover of night. The place was a hive, and he could not even be glad of the chance to scout an enemy's inner defenses, for the lady he had come to rescue had not only proved recalcitrant, but their interview had been interrupted in most unsatisfactory fashion.

A dark, relatively cool hallway, a statue of two snow-pards snarling at each other and conjoined in their lower half, hallways with partitions on either side, and finally a sitting-room with every appurtenance of Zhaon wealth and taste swallowed their party, and he could not even speak to her.

"Who is *this* fellow?" The newest arrival—a scarred man in Shan black buttoned to the right, a greenstone hurai upon his left first finger and a kyeogra in his ear—looked to Komor Yala for an answer, but she was pale under her copper, holding her left arm as if it pained her.

"Narikhi Baiyan, at your service." Daoyan bowed in the style of a Zhaon merchant meeting a nobleman, something he had practiced much of late. It pleased him, though a little less than it had. It occurred to him this particular palace had to be the Crown

Prince's home—that prince had a snow-pard for his device, though he seemed sadly unfit for such an august creature's guiding spirit— and if Daoyan had known who the lamed bastard was, he might have finished the fellow off himself. "I know the lady Komor in some slight fashion." And if she was amused—or otherwise—by his choice of names, she did not show it.

"Indeed." The nobleman spared him a brief, courteous nod. That green ring meant princely status, and Daoyan racked his brains for this man's identity. Garan Tamuron had too many sons indeed. "She has been seeking a means of sending a message into Khir. That does not explain the teaware, though."

"My kaburei." Yala winced again, and from beyond the door rose a chorus of excited voices, a physician's ringing sharp and crisp as he barked orders for his patient's comfort. "It was all she could think of to do."

The kaburei in question, a girl with leather-wrapped braids huddled at Yala's side, was more worried about her mistress than any royal interlocutor. She kept trying to examine Yala's arm, but the lady gently, absently pushed her hands away.

The scarred man glanced at Daoyan, a dark, peasant-crafty Zhaon gaze evaluating him from topknot to toe with one swift sweep before returning to Yala. "Were you injured?"

"Not so much." Yala blinked. The strange, dazed look in her beautiful eyes was new, and not entirely welcome. "I fell, I think."

"That is not like you." The scarred man—ah, he had to be the Third Prince, and now Dao wondered if *he* was the reason Yala was not amenable to leaving immediately—stepped close to Komori Dasho's only daughter, and even dared to lay his hands upon her arm, fingers probing as if he had some medical skill. He turned her loose, however, and glanced up when the ratty astrologer, his topknot wildly askew and his robes spattered with blood, appeared in the receiving-room's doorway. "Banh? What news?"

"It is not good." The astrologer's head was hastily wrapped with pale bandages to match the mourning armband Yala wore. The questioning prince had his own mourning-mark, a blotch of death upon his restful black. "Jiao does not *think* a gut-channel was pierced, though. Lady Komor, come, let us tend to you."

"I am well enough." Yala pushed aside her kaburei's hands again, but the black-clad prince made a short, dismissive sound.

"Let her perform her duty, little lure." He sounded very accustomed to ordering Komori Dasho's daughter about, curse him. "Now, tell me again, what happened?"

"I was…" Yala blinked, and her gaze swam to Daoyan's. He willed strength into her, and was faintly surprised when she straightened, self-consciously, and let the kaburei fuss over her arm. "It is merely bruised, Anh. In any case, I was asking this merchant for news from Khir, and was about to solicit his aid in sending a missive to my father. We heard shouts, and the sound of battle, and of course—"

"Of course you ran straight for it." The prince shook his head, his kyeogra—what a strange figure, in Shan black and with that hoop—glinting. Who had gifted him the endless ring that would catch the ancestors' voices and keep him from the Great Fields before his time? Surely not— "And you, merchant. The guards say you fought well."

"*No man may do otherwise.*" Daoyan's hand itched for a hilt to lay upon, but such things were not allowed within Zhaon's palace complex. It made little difference, the best weapons were those taken from your opponents—as his cousin and a would-be assassin had so recently learned—but still, he disliked it.

"And you are learned as well." The Third Prince's lip-scar turned his every expression into a mockery. He was rumored to be a sharp, nasty sort indeed. "How interesting."

"My father made certain I was trained in many arts, my lord. I have had reason to thank him." Dao could have made the words far more sardonic, but he sensed this was not an opponent to treat lightly. "Naturally, I followed to give the lady what aid I could. In Khir, we care for our women."

"And you think Zhaon does not." The prince's dark gaze turned disconcertingly direct. "Of course, your princess was not safe enough here."

"Third Prince—" Yala murmured.

"It is *Takshin*, little lure." He spared her a brief, irritated glance, but there was a softness to the words that boded ill. Even if Yala had not encouraged, this man looked likely to press upon a field Ashani Daoyan had, until lately, been certain he owned. Or at least had a good chance of acquiring. "And I would know if this fellow is likely to cry *for Khir* and stab someone, if left to his own devices."

Dao's estimation of the Third Prince rose uncomfortably high. He had heard the rumors, of course—the boy sent to Shan and that land's mad queen returning scarred and difficult, held to be a sign of ill-luck wherever he was sighted. "There is precious little left of Khir to stab a man for," he said, carefully. "My devices are pretty baubles to sell and caravans to arrange, my lord. Such things were difficult enough before Three Rivers, and now impossible, so I traveled here where trade is easier."

"I could send a letter to my father through this honorable merchant," Yala said. "And perhaps receive a reply." *Do not argue*, her expression said—it was the very same as one a younger Yala had worn while planning mischief or misdirecting attention from Bai or even Daoyan himself so they could accomplish it.

So he subsided, sweeping yet another bow, but in *her* direction. "If I may serve you in any way, my lady Komor, you have only to say as much."

"At least you know your duty." The prince's tone, not to mention the twist to that marred mouth, was sardonic enough for both of them. "This will spread through the palace like fire. Banh—"

"Zan Fein?" The astrologer did not seem to notice his own shabby disrepair, and spoke much as an equal to this strange princeling. "He will wish to know."

"Indeed." The black-clad prince nodded sharply, a decision made. "Go, and send a messenger for Makar, too. He will help us keep order."

"A bruise only, for all I can tell," the kaburei murmured to Yala. "I shall fetch ointment, and some crushed fruit."

"And tea," Yala added, nodding to give permission. "Our friend Narikhi here has rendered service to Zhaon, and to me."

Did she mean it was her princess's husband she longed to stay for? Dao was on the verge of dragging the blasted woman away by her hair, but he swallowed impatience and anger both when she cast him a somewhat agonized look, as if apologizing for using his mother's clan-name.

What could he not forgive her? Yala had been raised and trained to duty, and she would fasten those sentiments upon their proper hook if he could merely get her away from this terrible place.

"By all means." The prince gave Dao another long, dissatisfied look, but dismissed him again to turn to the lady. "Stay in the Jonwa, little lure. I like not the thought of you dragged to the dungeons again."

Dungeons? And what does he call her? Dao's eyebrows shot up, but he was not given leave to question her more thoroughly, for there was another explosion of bustle in the halls and a strange, repeating bell-toll split the air, pealing wildly.

Now it was the Third Prince's turn to pale. He closed his eyes for a moment, his scars suddenly livid against skin robbed of humors by their contraction. "So," he murmured. "And so."

The astrologer staggered as if the blow to his head had only now penetrated his skull. He clutched at the doorframe, and a chorus of wailing rose somewhere in the palace depths.

"What is this?" Daoyan spoke in Khir, and had not meant to sound so alarmed.

Komor Yala shook her head, but comprehension visibly arrived a moment later. "It is their Great Bell," she said, and looked to the Third Prince. "Is it...?"

"My lord father," the Shan-dressed prince said tightly, "is dead. Stay *here*, Yala; it is safest thus. I will have your word upon it."

"Of course." Her chin lifted slightly. "The Crown Prince will need care."

"Good. In the meantime, go write out a reward script for this merchant fellow, and I shall seal it this afternoon. I would attend to such a matter personally, Honorable Narizh." He butchered the Khir name, and Dao wished his mother's clan heads were here to hear such a thing. "But that bell means death, and I am called upon." He turned upon his heel and strode away, catching the astrologer by the elbow and neatly directing the man into the hall, where a rising babble of exclamation washed at the walls.

This left Yala and Dao regarding each other over some few bodylengths of hot, still Zhaon storm-air. "You must return to Khir," she said, finally, the sharp consonants of their shared mother-tongue a comfort to hear. "It is *far* too dangerous here, and your royal father is no doubt worried."

"He did not worry before I was the only son remaining; he may make up for it now." Daoyan had no intention of being sent away before he had reached his goal.

"Dao. Please." Her pleading was sweet to hear; how often had he longed for her to ask for something, *anything* he could provide? "If you stay here *I* will worry for you—"

"I am to simply leave you in this place?" Of all the outcomes possible, that one was least to be borne. "I am unwilling, Yala." For once, he was not called upon to do what his father or his tutors demanded, and the freedom was far too pleasant to give up.

He had meant to prize her from the city and only then broach the subject of perhaps making their way in the wide world; Zhaon seemed created expressly to balk Khir desires in all ways, and for all of Khir's sons.

"What could I return to?" A mixture of sadness and fierce pride lit Yala's sharp features, and his breath drained away. He had never seen her thus. Her resolve was kept hidden as a *yue*, and while the loyalty to her princess made her even more attractive, it was also infuriating. "I am determined to seek out who paid for my princess's death."

"That is no task for you." And what, after all, could she find? He had pruned every branch likely to give sign of passage, as the saying went. Perhaps she wished to be cajoled—or perhaps, someone had been making advances upon a maiden's heart. They were notoriously weak, those organs, and she had been left here without brother or husband to keep her steps upon a narrow stripe. "Do not be difficult. Is there a man you seek to stay for?"

"What?" She colored very fetchingly. Women were honorless creatures, even his own *mother*. But his Yala was both proud and dutiful, the only woman he had ever— "My honor remains unstained, Dao."

"Good." He could not help the truth spilling from his lips. "Because if there is another, *I will kill him*."

"You would do better to return to Khir." Her color deepened, but she did not move to soothe his ire as she normally would have, or to further protest her own innocence. "You must, Dao. This is folly. If they somehow find out who you are—"

"What, they will marry me to a Zhaon princess and keep me in chains?" The idea had a certain appeal, though Zhaon women seemed overly obstinate and, quite frankly, mannish. At least if he was chained in a dungeon Yala would be duty-bound to aid the Great Rider's son, and once a feat of escape was accomplished she would be left with no alternative but to accompany him.

Then he would have everything he wanted after all. The idea held a certain attraction.

"Or worse," she said, steadily, and something about the quiet finality of the word in Khir made him halt, looking at the girl he had known all his life. "There is worse than we ever dreamed of in this land, Dao. Must I beg you?"

It was his turn to color, and he hoped the rising heat in his own cheeks was not visible. "You have never had to beg me for aught."

"Do not make me begin." Now she stepped close, and for the first time in their lives Komor Yala touched him, laying a hand upon his sleeve. "The Third Prince may be prevailed upon to give you safe passage through Zhaon's border; I trust you will have no difficulty in crossing the Khir guard-lines, should there be any."

No. "Yala—"

"Tell my father I intend to make my failure honorable by finding who in this palace paid for my princess's death." Her color had waned almost to paleness, and her eyes glittered sharp-clear and utterly honest. Her fingers bit with surprising strength. "You *must* survive, Dao, and return to Khir. Or all this is for nothing. I may even have time to brush a letter explaining matters to my father."

"You…" The word was ash in his throat. "I should carry you away with me now."

"And have them pursue us, thinking we are part of *that*?" She shook her head again, firmly, taking her touch away, leaving the spot upon his sleeve bereft. Her hairpin, its crystals disarranged, glittered sharply. Even disheveled she was incandescent, noble and stubborn as her beloved damoi, and Daoyan's breath threatened to leave him completely. "Come, I shall write out a reward. You must have money to travel."

"I care little for *money*," he retorted, stung at last and down to his very liver as well. "Will you not heed me, Komor Yala?"

"If you would speak sense, I would be silent as a maiden should be." *Now* she was sharp, a flush rising afresh. She had never spoken to him so before, and only once or twice to her brother when he had fretted her past endurance. "I *cannot*, Dao. Not until I know."

It beggared belief that she would balk him, but women had strange ideas. Daoyan swallowed his ire and bowed as a scolded merchant should, conscious of the open door. Some few in this heap might be able to speak Khir; caution was necessary. And she was correct about one thing, at least. Vanishing now would invite pursuit.

"Do not *bow*—" she began, and at least there was that. He was still regarded her friend, if not her prince, and now he had time to convince her. Waiting a few days for the Zhaon to begin tearing at each other's flesh over an empty throne was the more intelligent route, and so many in this hideous place were in the habit of hiring assassins it would be easy to clearly attribute Ashan Mahara's death to one of *them*.

In fact, he already had an inkling of how to do so; more than one army had been jostling upon that battlefield, and all of them had wished his half-sister's death. The princess's fate had been carved and unalterable the moment Three Rivers was declared a victory for Zhaon. Dao could even, were he in the mood, consider himself an avenging hand erasing disgrace upon his father's clan.

Just like stupid, dead Bao.

So Daoyan smoothed his expression and set about repairing whatever damage he had done by his insistence. "I am a merchant here, and you a great lady, Komor Yala. We must play our parts."

"Yes." Her hands returned to her sleeves, but a betraying tremble in indigo silk told him she was wringing them as her kaburei might a damp cloth to lay upon a fevered brow. "Come, then. I shall write you a handsome sum, and speak to the Third Prince for a safe-passage endorsement."

He followed in silence to a small letter-desk tucked in a corner of the receiving room and watched while she composed herself, shaking out her trembling fingers and listening to the hurry and worry of a great house enduring violent upset.

He had to push down a tide of not-quite-pleasant laughter, too. Garan Tamuron, Emperor of Zhaon, was dead, with his son and heir stabbed in the gut by Zhaon assassins. If Daoyan had not performed either deed, he could, at least, be amused and relieved at their advent.

It was only natural.

Yala selected a brush, breathing deeply to calm her hands. Her head bent, her nape gleaming slightly under a coiled nest of braids, and Dao studied the vulnerable, beautiful patch of skin. Soon enough he would carry Komor Yala upon his saddle to whatever destination he chose, marrying her in the old fashion. It would be an exciting journey, and once she was free of this palace's cursed influence she would obey him as strictly as ever she had her father and Baiyan.

With that prospect before him, Ashani Daoyan took a deep breath, arranged his sleeves, and settled himself to watch and wait.

THE GREAT BELL

The Second Queen of Zhaon pulled a tiny stitch tight, dispelling the urge to bite her lip with concentration. What was fetching in a maiden just learning to sew was not in a matron, or a queen.

The distant sound of the bell brought her head up. Lady Aoan Mau, her fingertips pattern-stained with suma in honor of her royal patroness, halted her steady plucking of a near-priceless antique sathron; several other ladies—sewing, practicing their brushwork upon whisper-thin sheets of rai-paper, pouring tea, speaking in low murmurs—were likewise startled, and a hush fell as they looked to their patroness.

Haesara listened intently, finishing the stitch with a one-finger knot. There was no reason for the Great Bell to toll so, unless...

"My queen?" Mau turned her head slightly. Nothing disturbed her round, placid face and even features for too long, and it was that serenity Haesara liked most about the woman. Not only that, but she was discreet, ruthless when necessary, and had exquisite taste. Her dresses were loose-sashed to draw attention to her grace, and her hair was often dressed low as well, with a carefully calculated air of almost-dishevelment. Upon another woman it might have been tiresome.

Or perhaps it was excusable only because Haesara enjoyed her so much. Mau was almost past the age of making a good match; it was selfish to hope she would not, and that a queen would not be robbed of her company.

Ordinarily Haesara might have murmured *something is amiss* and let the news reach her palace at its own speed. Today, however, she set aside her embroidery and rose, ignoring the soft susurration as her ladies hurried to follow suit. *Can it be? So soon?*

Her ladies gathered, reined dread and secret excitement rustling through heavy skirts and sweat-dewed foreheads. Soon would come the time of dry heat, the rivers slowly shrinking as the sun cast bolt after bolt into Zhaon's great bowl like a gambler who knew he could not lose.

But the lord of Zhaon, her most august husband, the man who had taken her from Hanweo and her home, would not see it.

"—and so *I* said, I think I could use it well enough." Jin beamed, his lean young face alight.

"Move your elbow." Luswone could not help but smile in return, a fractional curve of lips. This part of the Kaeje had been very quiet of late with Sabwone gone. Hopefully her daughter was over the border, safely in the care of her prospective husband. Of course she would not *entirely* relax until she had word that Sabi was past her husband's threshold... but it was comforting to think upon that prospect, and to be relieved of her largest worry.

Jin took his elbow from the table without missing a single step in his tale-dance. "I picked it up, and it's very like a xia pike; the blade is shaped *so* with a serration on the back side." His hands shaped the air.

"How very..." It sounded like a terrible thing, but he was alight with joy. Ever since his first weapons practice at four summers high he had loved the implements of cutting, bashing, bruising, and killing; for such a sweet-natured child, it was faintly unnerving.

But this was a world of such things; a son who enjoyed weaponry and a daughter married to a king were far from the worst insurance against becoming an impoverished dowager aunt hunching in an unlighted shack, like a few unfortunate crones she had seen in her youth.

"Terrifying, I know." Jin all but bounced upon his cushion. The table was laid for light luncheon; early, but then, Luswone disliked heavy meals in the damp season. Later, in autumn when the rains turned chill, it would be time for hearty midday fare to keep the stoves of the body supplied. Now that her children were older, she could, perhaps, allow herself some relaxation of her regimen—nia oil, cups of serenity tea morn and evening, every bite or sip measured and calculated. "But if used properly, a fighter can hold off three or more. It's amazing, *if* you're fast enough."

"And are you quick enough, my son?"

"Of *course*," he beamed.

Then I am content. "And this is different than the weapons you were so enchanted with at dinner not so long ago? The…with the balls, the round—"

"The uye-gua? Oh, yes. Very different. Those are flails, this is a spear. But a broad-bladed one. There are some with tassels, but that does not seem quite serious." Jin warmed to his theme, but his mother had ceased to listen. Another sound intruded upon their early luncheon, a deep sonorous tolling drifting through the open door to the verandah. Long strings of threaded nut-shells and beads swayed gently in the uncertain, fitful breeze to ward off insects.

Though that was a thankless and impossible task, rather like being a concubine to a warlord.

How strange. The bell—but Wurei-a Kanbina's pyre is past.

A spear of ice went through her, hairpin to slipper-toe. She rose, brushing the table as she did so. Plates and tea-cups danced, eating-sticks clattering, and later she would find a bruise upon her knee, her humors rising in defiance.

"Mother?" Jin outright gawped at her, his mouth irritatingly loose.

"Hush," she said absently, and the spear became a bony fist closing about her heart. She gazed down at her boy, the son she had finally brought forth after enduring sale to a conqueror, a daughter's difficult birth, and yet more visits from Garan Tamuron. The warlord had not been abusive, that much was true, but she had endured him much as a peasant would corvée labor, or clouds of flying spearmouth metuahghi intent on stripping entire crop-fields.

Her only recompense was the boy who sat staring at her, and now his brothers would consider him a threat. Especially Kurin, who was likeliest to win the coming contest. The Second Prince had been cruel even as a child, and with his mother whispering in his ear was likely to become even more so.

"Mother?" Jin whispered. "What is it?" Color drained from his cheeks; he looked very young again, the sweet boy who would climb into her lap and lay his head upon her breast to listen to her heart. *It speaks like mine*, he would say, and smile.

"It is your father," she said, numbly. Oh, it could turn out to be some other royal death...but she did not think so. "He is dead." *And now I must protect you, my son.*

Heaven grant she was equal to the task.

"You look like a nun in that rag." Mother clicked her tongue, but absently, for which Gamnae was grateful. She had a headache, and her mother's distraction over Kurin's behavior of late was a welcome reprieve.

"It is too hot to wear more," she murmured, hoping Mother would ignore her daughter *and* the pretty but very old summer gown of light blue silk. Her hope seemed to be answered, for Gamwone tilted her lacquered head and stilled, her resin-painted fingernails resting upon the small table where she had been occupied in writing letters. Brush, paper, inkstone, seal-wax, and an unlit candle; she would be at this chore for quite some while yet.

Which meant that if Gamnae was lucky, she could steal away. The only problem was where to find refuge. If she visited the Jonwa again, Kurin would find her afterward and ask about Lady Komor—oh, sometimes indirectly, other times with the smile that meant he knew she would tell him everything because otherwise there was worse than one of Sabwone's pinches or Sensheo's other torments to fear.

The worst was not even knowing what he *wanted*, so she could give it—or a facsimile—and make him leave her alone. Mother would only begin one of her tirades against Takyeo's dead mother if she found out, and that was uncomfortable but not outright awful.

Perhaps she could visit the Blue Tower. Mrong Banh was often stuffy and distracted, but he would show her how to make small figures from folded rai-paper and would allow her to sit in a corner with a scroll or an approved flatbook, one dry as dust but useful if she wished to hide.

Yes, Gamnae decided, the tower was the best place to hide today— but what was that *noise*? It was a tolling, over and over again, of the Great Bell. Its voice lingered sometimes in her bad dreams, because nothing good came of its ringing.

For a moment she thought Garan Wurei-a Kanbina's pyre had been a nasty dream, or that she had somehow forgotten to attend that event. That could not be true, though, for she remembered her pyre-gift—and she wondered if Kanbina was, despite Takshin's assurances, angry that something used instead of new had vanished into the flames.

Mother rose from her seat, arranging her skirts with quick flickers of her plump fingers, and tilted her head again. Her face lit with bright, almost youthful satisfaction, and Gamnae felt a faint swimming horror.

"At last," her mother said through clenched teeth. "Are we finally free?"

Gamnae then realized what the tolling meant. It was not an attack upon the city *or* another royal pyre, though one would follow in its wake. There was only one other reason the bell would ring upon a day not marked upon the great wheel-calendars as a festival or ritual meant to bring Zhaon and Heaven closer together.

No, it meant that Gamnae's ancient, eternal, remote, but always kindly father was gone.

She stood, hands clasped inside her sleeves despite the heat. She watched the First Queen close her eyes as if savoring an exquisite, expensive treat, and her stomach revolved.

Gamnae managed to reach her own quarters before bending and retching violently, but thankfully nothing escaped, and there were no servants to see.

A Holy Task

Any other man—noble or common—would leave his body in the care of his family or the nearest temple. The body of Zhaon, however, required special care.

"If it was poison, there is no record of such a toxin in any of the annals, or familiar to any physician or apothecary in Zhaon-An." Zan Iyue finished laying out the implements, and cast a nervous glance at his father.

Zan Fein was not a *physical* father; that avenue was closed to him. Still, he was responsible for those under his care, and Two-Face would forgive him for yearning after a role not ordained him by Heaven. At least, the head eunuch was relatively certain of forgiveness, so he simply gave a brief, eloquent glance of not-quite-assent and moved about his own work, soft slippers shushing over stone floor.

They did not wear their jatajatas in the innermost sanctum, for the hush was not to be broken by sharp instruments. At least it was cooler than aboveground, stone gathering icy humors from the earth itself; likewise, this space did not freeze in winter. Great vaults and ribbon-arches hewn from the blue northern mountains and set with a cement whose recipe had been lost in the Second Dynasty stayed an even, slightly chill temperature year-round.

The constancy was to be admired, if not always emulated.

Zan Kaian, round-faced as a woman and with a clear, sweet

voice often quietly ribboning into whatever popular tune had captured palace attention lately, looked pale and perspiring. It was not his first time attending to a body whose occupant could well be invisibly lingering, watching the preparations and ready to find fault—but it was the first time the body was of such high estate and merit.

The great seal of Two-Face, that god of thresholds, two-souled, eunuchs, and crashing gongs, frowned in flickering torchlight. No mirrors brought the sun's gaze here; this work was performed in earth's belly and lit only by the uncertain glow of bare flame.

"It was not poison. The physicians agree it was an illness, but not a communicable one. Perhaps a blockage of the humors." Zan Kaian glanced at his superior as well. It was a high honor to be Zan Fein's deputy, and to be chosen for this most solemn of tasks was indicative of high merit.

Like any pinpoint position, however, the seat was sharp and the fall considerable. "All evidence has not yet been viewed," the chief court eunuch murmured. "Careful, my chicklings. This is a holy task, and must be undertaken in solemnity."

"Yes, Head Eunuch," they chorused, like the good children they were.

Others would be washed at the House of Bees, but an Emperor must not be exposed to common eyes even in so holy a place as that dome with its carven spirals and channels cut into stone flooring to take effluvia away.

To unclothe the body of majesty, to gaze upon the frail dregs of one ascended to Heaven itself, was not a task taken lightly. The Garan Tamuron he was accustomed to was no giant, though his carriage made him seem so and his piercing eye seemed to lay bare all before him. In death he was reduced to normal dimensions, but the change was deceptive.

To offend an ascended Emperor's shade was a daunting proposition indeed.

He should have been concentrating upon the task at hand, but instead, Zan Fein's hands moved with reverential precision while the rest of him was occupied with something quite different. The Great Bell had sounded; the Emperor's queens, remaining concubine, and children were now alerted. The Golden, those bright-armored palace guards, were under the standards of a triumvirate so they did not unite behind a single leader and hold Zhaon hostage, but the danger lay elsewhere.

Tamuron's hair was thin and grey-streaked; Zan Kaian washed it lovingly with long, delicate fingers. He even hummed as he did so, but quietly, an old lament at the death of a father. The sleeping-robe Tamuron had worn as he slipped away was cut free with paired springblades, and Zan Iyue washed the feet and hands. There were not nails to trim; the bath-girl Tamuron had been so kind to kept the royal talons short and smooth so he would not scratch his blotched, itching skin.

No, the danger was that the Emperor's chosen heir had not yet shown the steel in his guts. In some men that glow never surfaced, in others only late; a prince's life was not hard enough to strike sparks from most, even if the prince had ridden to war with his father and acquitted himself well enough to earn a true device. The snow-pard was cunning, brave—and it hid its claws behind pads like a common house feline until the time was right.

Of course Garan Takyeo was the proper heir, but Zan Fein doubted he was the one who would eventually warm the throne. Rule required not only majesty but ruthlessness, and the eldest son had shown little of the latter.

The fact that his brothers were still alive, especially the Second Prince, was proof enough. *That* fellow left no stone unturned and no lip unlifted to shore up his own position. Even when a stripling he had proven himself both intelligent *and* vicious. And while the former quality was needed in any quantity a ruler could muster, the latter was best in moderate doses, lest it turn an emperor into a black stain bereft of Heaven's mandate.

It was a shame the Third Prince had no desire to rule, and a double shame that Zakkar Kai could not have been born to one of Tamuron's wives. Of course, the First Queen's long-term attention would have shaped either boy into something truly repugnant, and the Emperor, much as Zan Fein admired him, had largely let her blemish both her sons—Kurin by attention and Takshin by neglect. The Mad Queen of Shan had merely scratched what Garan Gamwone had already marred.

Many times Zan Fein had raged against the fate Heaven had decreed for him, but it seemed a blessing now to be observing the game instead of playing in deadly earnest. Whoever graced the Throne of the Five Winds would need his services, and he could simply let Heaven's many inhabitants decide who they favored.

And yet, Zan Fein thought as he arranged the linen for wrapping the body of a man who had in the end been struck down by a malady instead of an assassin's or fellow soldier's blade, such waiting carried its own risks. Who better than the disinterested observer, the silent watcher of the court's follies and the subtle voice weighing policy in deep discussions, the one Garan Tamuron turned to when answers were needed and the Art of the Tongue necessary to extract them—who better, after all, to look clearly at the competing princes, and decide which should be pruned?

His pride was perhaps overweening. Zan Fein set to mixing the unguents and resins to keep the body from bloating before it could be placed upon the pyre—and, not so incidentally, make certain the flames would devour flesh cleanly and utterly—and thought of which branch *he* would prune to keep the garden of Zhaon whole and healthy.

It was not until the work was done and the trio took the long weary climb up the servant's stairs—the body would be lifted as it had been lowered into this sanctum, by winch and pulley up into the small private shrine in the heart of the Kaeje, ready for its ceremonial procession to the pyre-ground—that he found other eunuchs waiting for him, their beardless faces drained of much color and excitement fluttering amid their sober robes and elongated fingers.

It seemed the game had already begun, and an opponent had taken the first move.

Zan Fein hurried for his bath, to wash the ill-luck and stink of death away. Then, he decided, he would visit Mrong Banh.

He did not like the astrologer, and was certain the feeling was mutual. Still, Honorable Mrong would have some ideas, if Zan Fein was truly to tilt the board.

DEEPLY WANTED

The Jonwa was full of activity, but what he wanted was not in his spare but very comfortable quarters *or* the small suite across the hall from the Crown Princess's sealed rooms. Nor was what he wanted in the gardens, walking desultorily with her head down and a kaburei hurrying to hold her sunbell, or being fussed over by said kaburei and a few young noble ladies after a terrible incident. Which left the sitting rooms, and the two larger ones were empty.

He did not scratch at the lintel of the third and smallest as was his wont, because when he glanced into the room it was empty except for Komor Yala at the partition to the verandah, facing the dry-garden. In a fresh green dress, she leaned against the doorway as if her legs were not quite certain, and her face was buried in her hands. Her slim shoulders shook.

There was nobody about, not even that kaburei girl who should have been attending her mistress. Takshin did not remember crossing the room; one moment he was peering from the hallway, the next there was bright green silk under his hands as he turned her— gently, so gently, afraid that if his fingers bit too deeply he would shatter something fragile.

A startled grey gaze met his. Her eyelids were reddened, and her nose—too sharp for beauty, as her face was too thin and the rest of her likewise edged instead of plump-perfect like her princess—bore pink at nostril-rims. Blotches stood out upon her cheeks, and a few stray hairs had escaped her braids.

His chest hurt. For a moment he thought she had, startled by his sudden appearance, stabbed him with that claw-toy of hers. Then he realized the pain was otherwise, and cupped the back of her head with one hand, callused fingers catching in smooth, silken braided loops. "Hush," he said, as he guided her into his arms. "Oh, my lady, little lure, hush. All will be well."

She fell into him like a tired stone into a well, and Takshin rested his chin atop her head as she shook with silent sobs. He would have preferred some sound to escape her, but she wept as if she was used to keeping such an act from inconvenient ears.

He knew that skill, and used it himself. He longed to deal with whoever had taught her such a harsh necessity.

"All will be well," he repeated, knowing she would not hear *him*, precisely, just a soft voice rumbling in a chest built for sonorous echo instead of graceful song. She sought to escape his grasp once, twice, then gave up and continued shaking.

He had not thought this morning that his Shan-style black long-shirt would soak up tears, but it was welcome. He was not quite happy she was distressed—but he could soothe her, and that was a duty he found he particularly liked.

Her storm did not last nearly as long as a summer downpour. He produced a small stack of folded rai-paper squares from his sleeve-pocket but did not turn her otherwise loose.

"I am s-sorry," Yala began, wiping at her nose with one of the squares. "I have r-ruined your tunic."

"I have others." His arms stiffened to draw her closer, but she leaned away. There was some awkwardness, but his strength told and she went still again, regarding him somberly, her chin tilted up and the color in her cheeks fading. She tried once more to step away, and since he had already made it clear he did not *have* to relinquish his hold, he let her go. "There is no shame in tears, Yala. Not for you."

"Do you ever cry?" She shook her head as soon as she asked, and dabbed at her eyes again. "No, I am sorry, Third Prince, I—"

"If you continue to address me formally I may break something in this room, Yala." He did not quite frown, but it was close. "And no, I have not wept since I was thirteen winters high. No..." He reconsidered. He did not quite wish to lie to her. Certainly there were things she must not know, for what woman would want to? But to *lie* to her was a different thing entirely. "That is incorrect. I wept once more, when the Mad Queen was finally dead and her pyre was embers."

Yala did turn aside then, and freeing her nose of tear-cargo was performed in the most ladylike way possible. He looked away at the shimmers of heat over the dry-garden, giving her time to attend the duty.

And, of course, since she was his little lure, she asked the question he expected least. "Did you hate her?"

"Of course I did." The truth did not even hurt as it passed his throat-stone. The Zhaon held it a pad of rai, but in Shan it was a rock. "That was why I wept. The feeling was... too large to be contained."

"So it must loose itself." Yala nodded, the spent paper squares wadded in her left hand. Her knuckles whitened. "I am selfish, Takshin. I weep not for your father or your elder brother, may he return to health, but because I am frightened, and alone, and—"

"You are not alone. *I* am here." It was so simple as to be laughable, but he would leap and jape like a street acrobat if necessary, to halt that devouring sorrow in her clear, foreign gaze.

"Yes. You are." Her shoulders came up again, like a kaburei's anticipating a heavy burden. "Am I wanted, then?"

"Deeply." His own private joke, she could not know he had already arranged for her safety—except his eldest brother had not yet brushed the endorsement quite yet.

Still, he had other methods if that one failed. Waiting was nothing new, and Takshin found he liked it when the end was so assured.

Oh, he could still halt, he supposed, but he had been set upon this path the first moment he saw her. Or perhaps the moment after. He could not tell, now, when it had started.

It seemed unprincely to try, as well.

"Is it…" She searched his face and he suffered it. What did she think he would seek her for, at this point? Probably something unpleasant, since the Emperor—the word *Father* was a step too far at the moment—was being washed and wrapped for his pyre and Takyeo was back in his bed again, this time not raving with fever or quietly ignoring everyone in the room, sunk like an ox in a mudhole.

No, Takyeo was dosed unconscious with nightflower while Kihon Jiao mixed pastes and unguents with a light touch, the shabby physician's expression as remote as his patient's but considerably more focused. Honorable Kihon had no time for amateurs and any visitor was likely to be unceremoniously disposed of with a curt word.

Where was Yala's kaburei, and the two noble girls? They should have been with her; she should not be left alone in the receiving-room, though her dress had been changed.

He was not quite sure of his temper if he found further evidence of their neglect. "Where are they? The Su girl, and the Hansei?"

"Fetching a list of necessary items for Honorable Kihon. I thought it wise to give them a task. Anh went with them and shall tell me who stops to gossip." Now she was brisk again, smoothing her flushed cheeks with her fingertips. "Lady Kue is overseeing the boiling of cloths; I suggested Steward Keh take this opportunity to bar the household to visitors and question every servant."

"Well done." Takshin should have thought to arrange such things, but he had been busy with his own tasks, including keeping Takyeo from thrashing before the nightflower took hold *and* setting the guard upon the Jonwa. The Golden he chose for that duty would not move until *he* released them, at least he could be certain of that much.

His cursed reputation was occasionally useful.

"I tried to think of more to do, but…" Her chin trembled, just a fraction, and he longed to take her in his arms again. Something—perhaps the tilt of her head—dissuaded him, and caution was called for.

"You have done more than enough." There was movement, curse it, in the hallway. So much patience, so much waiting for her to arrive at a matter he could solve, and now they were to be interrupted. She was disheveled, he was not much better, and for a moment he toyed with the idea of leverage. "Your kaburei should be here to attend you, but no matter. We shall send for some tea to settle your nerves, and—"

"Takshin. And Lady Komor." A familiar voice—and there were only one or two visitors who would pierce the Golden cordon around the Jonwa.

Thankfully, it was Mrong Banh, his topknot pulled tight and his face pitilessly worn under bright, storm-tinted afternoon mirrorlight. He had aged all at once from the round, smiling youth of Takshin's childhood into an elder, and there was even a hint of grey in that hurriedly redone topknot.

"Honorable Mrong." Yala recovered quickly, and Banh's gaze was that of a soldier who had survived a disaster, seeing not what was before him but some other, catastrophic scene.

"Oh," he said, absently, and smoothed his hands down his robefront. They were inkstained as usual. "Yes. There you are." As if they had accosted him in a garden.

A distant rumble of thunder broke the hush outside. Somewhere in the palace women were wailing, and the sound rasped at Takshin's nerves. It was not right, for Banh to look so...

So *lost*.

"Come in." How strange. Usually looking at wounded, wandering creatures filled him with a sharp irritation, the urge to strike quickly and put an end to the witlessness. Was this, instead, what pity felt like? "Sit down, and you too, Yala. You look ready to fall over. There must be tea, and both of you must eat." And now he was a maiden-auntie with children in her care, fussing over tea and cakes when the world had shifted underfoot.

"Eat?" Komor Yala blinked, and some sense returned to her clear, ghostly gaze. Her hand did not relax, though, and she squeezed the rai-paper with its cargo of weeping a little more firmly. "Of course.

Yes. I shall attend to that. Sit down—and this time, Takshin, *please* use a cushion, at least."

"As you command, dear lady." He bowed, and the faint trace of her distracted smile was a balm. "Come, Banh. We are commanded to mannerly seating. It is official, then, is it not?"

"It is." Banh looked about him like an eggfowl searching for a lost chick. "But...how is Takyeo? I came as soon as I...I should have seen..."

Takshin gestured at a pretty triangular table and its attendant cushions. "Come, Banh. Sit." It was...strange, to hear himself sound so gentle. Komor Yala swayed for the door, a noblewoman's soft, indirect step, and there were a few drops upon her skirt after all.

They were not blood but evidence of her tears, so Third Prince of Zhaon—or whatever he was now that the ordering of the world had slipped a peg or two—set his jaw, and ignored them.

For now.

WHATEVER
MATERIAL
AVAILABLE

I t would have been better if the girl would weep, but Garan
Daebo Sabwone—now Suon Garan-a Sabwone, though Nijera
thought it unlikely she would sign her name thus—was dry-eyed,
pale, and very quiet. Her tension manifested itself in small ways,
though she did not slap at her ladies' hands anymore and she ate
barely enough to keep the furnace of her own life stoked, not nearly
enough to fuel new growth.

At least the wedding night had passed without incident, and the
king seemed, all things concerned, rather gentle with his new bride.
Nijera had feared the worst upon *that* front after the palanquin epi-
sode, but some of her subtle, thankless work among the lords of
Shan who attended their ruler was bearing a return or two. They
were well-disposed toward *her*, at least, and a lady-in-waiting who
was so conspicuously virtuous and loyal had some small authority
that could be exercised to smooth her superior's way.

The great palace of Shan was not nearly as pleasant as Zhaon-
An's complex, but it was large, the walls were solid stone, and it
had some fine gardens; besides, there were a great many new
hangings and pleasant gifts brought to the queen's apartments,

a connected series of rooms around a tiny, gemlike green court-yard bearing the marks of trimmed-away neglect and more than one strange cabinet. It was the custom here to gift a royal bride for many days after her advent, perhaps to ease the shock of transition.

Mirrorlight brightened as Nijera pulled the curtains aside, her heart beating quickly. Every time she performed this duty she was afraid she would find the girl supine and lifeless amid rich tangled cloth upon the great round bed. Sabwone had huddled there the first morning, large-eyed and with tearstained cheeks, though there was evidence upon the sheets of consummation and the king had lingered to drink traditional, honey-thick kouri and hold the cup to his new wife's own mouth for a token sip. He had even, handsome young thing that he was, attempted to cajole her into drinking more.

Sabwone submitted, but she did not *speak*. The girl's silence was worrisome. She seemed to have turned from spoiled brat to wilting reed all but overnight, as if a malignant spirit had crept into her body through sliced wrists and wrapped about her liver, crouching there to devour her humors and block any chance of conceiving an heir.

"A bright good morn has risen." Nijera greeted the bed and its occupant, and set about her morning tasks. "My queen, would it please you to have breakfast? There is walanir, and jaelo tea."

"Very well," Sabwone said, colorlessly, pushing herself up upon her elbows. The king had left before dawn rose stinging pink in the east, and there were unsettling rumors flying through the court. Not from Zhaon, thank Heaven's great congress of shining gods *and* the Awakened One, but from the west and south. Even Lord Suron, who visited daily to make certain the new queen's ladies had all they required and pass a few pleasant words with Nijera herself, bore a faintly anxious tilt to his rather large nose.

That was another worrisome item—the nobles of Shan were reluctant to send their maidens to the palace for service to the new queen. Given the rumors of the Mad Queen's practices—whispered of even within Zhaon's borders—it was not entirely surprising, and yet it was a slight to Nijera's lady.

And that, Nijera found, she did not like at all, especially when the girl was so wan and lifeless. The palace had three housekeepers, and the one responsible for the queen's quarters was an iron-mouthed stick with a leather sudo hanging from her belt. She had not plied it upon any of Nijera's junior ladies but once or twice looked as if she longed to, and Nijera was already seeking alternatives to that dame.

It would be easier if Sabwone would take up some of her responsibilities. And yet, the girl looked so...

Well, she looked *lost*, frankly, and somewhat stunned by married life. How had First Concubine Luswone not prepared her child for this? It was not meet to think ill of a royal concubine who had after all plucked Nijera from drudgery and placed her so high, and yet.

She bent to check the coil of freshening incense under her queen's morning dress; the smell, a reminder of Zhaon, was a blessing.

"Auntie?" Sabwone said, a tiny whisper from the bed. It was the first time she had called her poor cousin thus, and the presumed closeness would have been very welcome under other circumstances.

"Yes, child?" She should not speak so, but habit was very strong. Her inflection was very honorific, though, and it really was not a task to be gentle.

Not when a brat had been so humbled. It was uncharitable of Nijera to think so, but she was past the age of attributing noble motives to herself where none existed.

"How long..." Sabwone had pushed herself up to sit upon the bed, hugging her knees. Her sleeping-shift was wrinkled, and her hair was mussed almost completely from its nighttime braid. "I mean to ask, how long do you think *he* will visit? Father never visited Mother so."

Ah. Nijera circled the dress-stand, making certain all was as it

356 *S. C. Emmett*

should be. "Not that you remember," she said, finally. The girl was safely married now, and could be spoken to of things a maiden must not hear. "Until his ardor cools, I suppose. Until you are well with heir, such visits are to be wished for."

"It is unpleasant." Sabwone darted her small glances, gauging her lady-in-waiting's reaction in quite uncharacteristic fashion. "You are lucky, to escape it."

"I am told it can be quite pleasant indeed." Nijera rather doubted it, but there were songs, rumors, and certain treatises an unmarried aunt of certain age could filch and read without fear of too much damage to reputation.

"For men." The queen hugged her knees. Her wrists were still bandaged, nia oil rubbed into the healing slices every evening to prevent scarring. "They are all beasts."

"He is not cruel." Nijera paced to the bed, her own skirts making a low, decorous sound. "And you are a queen now. It is not so bad."

Sabwone rested her chin upon her knees. Her cheeks were hollow, and her very fine dark eyes had shadows underneath. "Queen of what, though?" But she shook her head, strings of hair come loose and raveling over her bare shoulders. Shan sleeping-shifts had no sleeves and were much shorter than Zhaon's modest gowns. "I wish I was home."

"That is only natural." Had the girl been like this during the journey, Nijera would have thought much better of her. As it was, now she seemed only very young and very small, and it was unpleasant to think Daebo-a Luswone had not prepared her daughter as thoroughly as possible, for whatever reason.

Well, a maiden aunt was left to work with whatever dress-material was available. This was no different. "Come, my queen," she continued. "Let us morning-bathe you, and attend to your breakfast. Then we shall dress you, and perhaps you might like to see the palace?"

"Hardly a palace," Sabwone scoffed, but her arms had tensed upon her knees. "You hate me too, don't you."

I could have, very easily. Nijera suppressed a sigh. Hatred was best reserved for larger matters than spoiled children. "Of course not. You have been a frightened cat, though, and your claws have gone where they do the least good." The proverb was no less true for being banal; Nijera paused, searching the girl's face for any sign of her former temper.

"Claws." Sabwone's hand's loosened, and she examined them with an air of bemusement. "I wish I had some."

A rustling at the door was junior ladies preparing to enter and attend to their queen. Nijera's heart hurt, a sudden swift stab of something close to longing. The look upon Suon Sabwone's face was one she herself must have worn a long while ago, hearing the news that her own marriage was set aside due to her father's fall from ministerial grace.

Even the Emperor shits in a pot, as the kaburei proverb went. High position was no guarantee of happiness, or even of a tolerably comfortable life. It was best to learn as much early and thoroughly, make your peace with what station Heaven had decreed for you, and set yourself to endure. That Sabwone had not arrived at such a conclusion spoke ill of her parents, though certainly the Emperor of Zhaon and his concubine were far above such things as Nijera's private opinion.

This princess-turned-queen, however, might not be past influencing. Nijera's was a position of deep trust, and the child would remember who was patient with both her spite *and* her sadness.

If she did not, well, Nijera had survived being set aside once, and could no doubt do so again.

"Now what would you do with those?" She smiled, and held out her hands. "Come, my lady queen. Let us ready you for the day. You are to rule the king's heart, and that will not happen if you are too weak to speak."

"I do not want his heart." But Sabwone brightened slightly, and clasped her auntie's hands, letting herself be drawn from the bed. "But I suppose I should see this palace of theirs. It is not like home."

It would be useless to admit that Nijera liked Shan much better. Here she was a chief lady, not a useless poor cousin, and at least her days were full of effective action. "No," she murmured, a loyal agreement. "It is not. But we may make it a home, my queen. Come, into your slippers; there is much to be done."

A Smooth Transition

The Jonwa's largest receiving-room had a table that matched its stature, but its partition-door to the similarly largest of its gardens was firmly drawn closed. Mirrorlight, that soft maidenly dependent upon the sun's glow, bathed it in soft radiance, gilding every edge and cushion.

"This is grim indeed." Garan Makar settled his hands inside his brown silken sleeves and glanced worriedly at Mrong Banh. "How many assassins?"

"Three. Held off by a kaburei throwing crockery, a foreign woman, and an astrologer." Takshin found some little levity in the story. At least, he gave every appearance of doing so, with a sardonic twist to every word. "Not to mention a foreign merchant. In any case, Honorable Kihon is not certain a gut-channel has been breached. It does not smell worse than any other wound."

"Heaven is with us." Mrong Banh was ashen, and his hands were almost fists, escaping that status only because he was not, after all, of a very warlike spirit. "I should have seen—"

"If astrologers could see everything, it would leave little for kings to do. Or exorcists." Makar exhaled, sharply. "And . . . Father."

"I am told he was fast slipping into slumber before rousing. He gave a great cry, and blood poured from his mouth." Mrong

Banh darted a glance at Lady Komor, who sat, pale and straight-spined in bright green silk, her own hands folded decorously in her lap. Takshin did not seem to think such a personage should be excluded from this meeting, and though Makar gave the foreign lady-in-waiting one or two considering glances, he did not demur. "There was . . . there was nothing to be done."

"That is the truth of it," Zan Fein said from the doorway, gliding into the room upon a draft of umu scent too strong to be anything but freshly applied and closing the partition behind him with soundless grace. "My lord Third Prince, my lord Fourth Prince, Honorable Mrong—and I know of you, Lady Komor, though we have not been introduced. Please pardon my interruption, and my boldness in speaking to a lady."

Komor Yala looked, Mrong Banh thought, faintly bemused. "You must be Honorable Zan Fein," she parried. "It is a pleasure to meet one spoken of so highly by Honorable Mrong." She even handled the astrologer's name with less difficulty than some of his countrymen.

Zan Fein bowed. He wore embroidered slippers instead of his jatajatas, of course, but even in the distinctive clicking sandals he could move very quietly when he wished. Had he been waiting in the hall, choosing a proper moment for entrance?

Banh wouldn't put it past him.

It was Fourth Prince Makar, however, who said what Banh—and no doubt Takshin—was thinking. "And to what do we owe this honor, Zan Fein? You have come from the deep places of the palace, no doubt."

"Nothing has been left undone. But yes, I have stolen away from my work because we are faced with an extraordinary situation, and I have come seeking wisdom from those most likely to possess it." His beneficent smile, just a faint curve of lips, did not change in the slightest.

Komor Yala stirred, but held her peace. Instead, she watched Third Prince Takshin, perhaps to garner some indication of why he wished her at this particular meeting.

Banh thought it very likely Takshin was not as calm as he appeared, and that the foreign woman was something in the nature of a talisman. Or the crushed herb felines derived a mild intoxication from, both small granary-hunters and larger wild creatures of that clan.

Of course, she had been present during the attack as well, and might have noticed some small clue.

"He starts with a compliment," Takshin said to empty air. "Well, it must indeed be dire."

"Merely remarking upon merit is no compliment, Third Prince." The head eunuch even looked *pleased*, like a tutor with a good student, before his gravity reasserted itself and he glided for the table.

"Honorable Zan," Lady Yala said, clearly but softly, "will you sit? There is tea. It will do you good."

"I am honored to be asked, Lady Komor." Zan Fein lowered himself upon a heavily embroidered, circular cushion. "You have a reputation for grace and for politeness; it is pleasant to find a rumor so close to truth."

"Or terrifying," she murmured, and glanced at Takshin again. Now she was wondering if she would be called upon to pour tea for the eunuch, but Banh solved the problem by turning the still-steaming teapot's handle for the newcomer and choosing a fine white slipware cup. It was very strong huchin, that tonic for shattered nerves, and Zan Fein did not demur.

The silence turned painful. Lady Yala's nose-rims were pink and her eyes reddened; despite that, she was utterly composed. Still, a faint line was discernible between her eyebrows. One could see an echo of the somber girl she must have been in Khir's cold Northern arms. Or perhaps she had once been merry and laughing as Jin, and time pressed the blitheness out of all.

Did none of them know how to start? Ships without rudders, caught upon a great current. "I take it there are disturbing signs," Mrong Banh finally said, heavily.

"There have been disturbing signs for years." Zan Fein's nose hovered over the teacup. How he could smell even huchin through his umu perfume was beyond Banh. "I wish to make certain they do not turn to disturbing realities. Tell me, Honorable Mrong, how badly is the new Emperor wounded?"

Of course, Takyeo had not been called for thrice or acclaimed yet, or sat upon the low padded bench of the Throne of Five Winds, or presented with a huge seal carved with the characters of his chosen reign-name or with the second hurai for his right hand to match the princely one on his left. The great ceremonial coat had not been placed upon his broad shoulders, and he had not spent the night in the small innermost chamber of the Kaeje, rising at dawn to light the ceremonial taper. That flame would go from hand to hand, coal to coal, chunks of burning added to peasant fireplaces or to a candle in noble houses that all other lamps, briefly extinguished for the occasion, would be lit by.

Garan Takyeo was still the new Emperor, and he lay drugged with a hole in his guts and a half-healed leg.

"Honorable Kihon does not think a bowel-channel was pierced," Takshin repeated, but his expression was grave. "Even if it is not, Kurin will not wait."

An uncomfortable silence filled the receiving-room. Finally, Zan Fein sighed, shifting slightly upon his cushion. "At least we did not have to say so," he said, his gaze resting upon Mrong Banh, two commoners in a room of nobles.

"There is some comfort in that." But the words were ashes upon Banh's tongue. He remembered boy-Kurin, a rather sweet but exacting child, before his mother's constant, steady poison, drip by drip, wore into material that was not yet obdurate. Now the Second Prince was a sealed flask, and who could tell what mixture filled him? "But this is not his work. At least, I do not think so."

"It does not have to be," Zan Fein pointed out. "I would indeed say it does not matter."

"If Kai were here…" Makar laid the thought delicately upon troubled air. Thunder grumble-groused in the far corners of Zhaon, lightning stabbing at low-hanging cloud-bellies but letting loose no torrent.

Not yet.

"The Head General would ensure a smooth transition, yes." Zan Fein inhaled the steam from his cup again.

"Especially if he brought a few detachments along." Takshin's expression turned sardonic. "And I thought you would take convincing."

"The threat from Khir is temporarily less than that of palace strife." Makar, now that the idea had been broached, was turning to the question of *how*. "But Kai will not know of this until he is told."

"And by the time dispatches leave the city the matter will already be decided, one way or another." Zan Fein shook his head.

"A letter will not reach him?" Lady Komor murmured hesitantly, her gaze downcast. Of course in Khir women did not speak much, and much less in such august company. She studied her lap as if much of interest was to be found there.

"It is Lord Yulehi's half of the year." Takshin's tone was unwonted gentle, addressing her. He even said his uncle's name without a snarl. The yearly splitting of influence between chief ministers was not a new tradition in Zhaon, and Tamuron had wisely forced his queens' clans to abide by it. "My cursed uncle will have the city sealed, on the pretext of avoiding unrest."

"I would not be surprised if Zhaon-An was already sealed. It is a difficult question." Zan Fein regarded Mrong Banh, who for once did not mind such scrutiny. "Even the mews and coops will be watched, lest someone tie a silk scrap to a bird's leg."

"Leave that to me," Takshin said. "I shall undertake to send a message to Kai. What are *you* prepared to do, Makar?"

"What can I do, other than stand guard?" Makar cupped his own tea in his fine scholar's hands, his hurai clinking softly against clay passed through hardening fire. "Sensheo will not listen to reason, and is likely to be an annoyance simply because he possesses the capability to do so."

"That is true." It answered one of Banh's deeper questions— why, precisely, Makar was *here* instead of with Kurin having some version of this same conversation. If there was a balance among Garan Tamuron's sons, the Fourth Prince was the fulcrum, and he lost nothing by letting his younger brother commit a folly in the Second Prince's favor.

As long as that folly was not *too* great. And he also wondered why Zan Fein, of all people, would so openly declare favor for Takyeo. Relations between the Crown Prince and head eunuch were cordial, certainly, but hardly warm.

Of course, relations between Zan Fein and *anyone* were never overly warm. The head eunuch belonged to the Emperor, and now Tamuron was dead.

Troubles came fast and thick now, not least of them the fact that Heaven had only hinted of this great upset. The Second Concubine's passing had been expected for years, but Tamuron's... was not, though the stars spoke of a newcomer in the near future. Heaven must have made a quick decision or taken especial care to veil itself, and such a precaution in the vaults overhead spelled much tumult for the kingdoms below.

"Is it likely Khir will attack?" Makar's gaze now settled upon Lady Yala, who had not raised hers from her lap. Her dress, bright green silk, was different from the indigo Banh had seen her in that afternoon; its cheerful color was likely only a matter of it being the first to hand. She had still taken time to re-tie her mourning armband, and attention to such a detail spoke well of her.

The silence lengthened until Lady Yala raised her head, as if she could hardly credit being asked. Her cheeks had drained of color, and the crescents under her eyes were bruise-dark. "I hardly think it so," she said, slowly, aware that she of all of them knew Khir best, if not the temper and thoughts of that land's great ruler. "Three Rivers robbed Khir of many sons, I cannot think my country eager to lose yet more. Yet my princess's... misfortune is a powerful inducement to action, no matter how ill-considered." She touched her teacup with a fingertip to gauge its temperature. "My father would often say the Great Rider is not a hasty man, but a thorough one. If Khir has not marched by now, perhaps they do not mean to."

Did she know of Kai's shinkesai? Banh studied the woman, wishing she was not so discreet. A rather odd idea on the nature of Kai's feelings toward a certain lady-in-waiting occurred to him, and hard upon its heels, another arrived about the exact provenance of a body with its fingers marred left upon the First Queen's steps early in spring. He longed for some quiet time and perhaps a dish of cabbage to chew while he sorted both notions and accorded them their proper weight, but this was an emergency.

"Misfortune indeed," Makar said, darkly. "It comes upon us now like a pale horde."

Banh suppressed a shudder. Tamuron had thought it likely Tabrak would indeed come riding, and meant for his eldest son to meet the threat if he could not. If the newcomer in the skies was *that* collection of filthy, dough-skinned rampaging murderers, they would descend like metuahghi, those numberless insects with their bright carapaces and habit of traveling in crowds to suck entire provinces dry of crops.

"Let us worry for Takyeo first and the Tabrak insects later." Takshin still regarded Lady Komor, who had returned her gaze to her sleeve-wrapped hands against her thighs. It was almost painful to see a woman so straight-backed but hollow-cheeked. "My lady, you have endured much today. Perhaps you may inform Lady Kue and Steward Keh that we have guests, and retire for well-earned rest."

"Forgive me, Third Prince, but I shall not stay." Zan Fein set his cup down. "A short visit to inform my lords the Second and Fifth Princes of the progress made in preparing their august father's ascension is in order."

"Oh, indeed." Makar turned his own cup a quarter, perhaps to avert further misfortune. "Perhaps I shall go with you when you inform Kurin and Sensheo, not to mention Lord Yulehi, of the preparations."

"And I as well," Mrong Banh added hurriedly. It was not that he did not trust Makar, he told himself, or that he grudged Zan Fein the chance to play Kurin's chess-board as well as Takyeo's.

It was only, precisely, that he did not, and he did. Banh's lord was dead, and now his children, beloved as each one was to an astrologer who might never have descendants of his own, were of varying quality. He could admit as much, even if it pained his heart.

Was this what fathers felt?

Still, Makar and Zan Fein had both come here first, if only to feel where the ground was most solid. Such a statement, subtle as it was, would still be noticed—and both of them would know as much.

If Takyeo survived, and Kai could be reached...

"Very well." Takshin's bitter little smile was entirely habitual, or it could have been that he was thinking exactly what Banh was. "I shall pass your regards on to Ah-Yeo."

"Do." Makar paused. "Should he wake, Taktak..."

"I shall tell him you stopped to enquire, Maki." Takshin's smile was lazy and ferocious now. "Go, now, scatter like chaff, all of you."

"I shall return to watch over Ah-Yeo," Makar promised before he left, and such was his somber mien Mrong Banh believed him.

WORDS FOR
SATISFACTION

There were many words for satisfaction, but Binei Jinwon, Lord Yulehi, was at the moment seeking to choose exactly the correct term for waiting many long years, smiling and scraping, until a hated enemy expired. It was an exquisite feeling, and one he wished to savor.

Even his royal nephew's highhanded behavior of late faded in importance next to that feeling. And it was impossible not to admit that Kurin seemed to have all matters well in hand.

His clan-niece, her round, soft face blotched, was busily weeping into her embroidered sleeve, but whether from relief or sheer glee was difficult to tell. Notice of the attempt upon the Crown Prince—now the putative Emperor, if he survived, which was of course to be devoutly wished for in public—had reached them in the person of a breathless Golden who supplemented his regular pay with running small errands for Second Prince Kurin.

In the normal way of things, Kurin would be Crown Prince until Garan Takyeo produced an heir, but *that* knot had been neatly cloven of late, and there was time enough to attend more thoroughly to the prospect if the spear-born whelp survived. At the moment, there were more pressing concerns.

"If only we could be certain," he murmured, gazing into his teacup. "The Fifth Prince does not seem very...thorough."

"He has his uses." Kurin had already changed into pale mourning. Hasty of him, but also very filial. The boy's topknot was pulled not-too-tight, and even its cage was bleached, carven bone, with a bone pin. "Mother, perhaps you should withdraw."

Binei Jinwon heartily agreed—there was much to be discussed—but Gamwone lifted her tearstained face and stared at her son. Her pupils were swollen, her eyes black as moonless night. She said nothing; her full lower lip quivered.

"There, there." Jinwon patted her free hand, laid along the table like a discarded rag. The filigreed shield upon her smallest fingernail glinted as mirrorlight wavered; he wished with a sudden vengeance that she would take herself to some inner room and weep in honorable peace instead of this...display.

At least the daughter was performing as a woman should.

It was time to think of a suitable match for *that* girl. The work of guiding a clan, even if a young relative wished to take the brunt of it, was eternal, and there was no thanks or relief to be found for the ceaseless striving until one's name was carved upon a stone urn to be closed in a decent tomb. At least Gamnae did not seem as ambitious as her mother.

Though, of course, it was too soon to tell.

His niece snatched her plump paw away. "How utterly predictable," she hissed. "Send Gamwone out so the men may dispose of her." Her upper lip curled, and her nose wrinkled. "Have you forgotten, uncle, who made your present position possible?"

"Mother—" Kurin began.

"And *you*." That terrible black gaze swiveled in her son's direction. "*You* have forgotten the labor I had in birthing you, and the care I gave when you were a sickly, puling little thing." Her chin trembled for a moment, and she focused on Binei Jinwon again. "You would have *nothing* if not for me, either of you. *I* lay under that warlord for the good of our clan, *I* produced the sons he needed, *I* fought for both my clan and my sons when none else would. I have endured rival after rival, insult after insult, and now he is gone and *you* wish to insult me as well?" The blotches on her cheeks were not grief, it appeared, but rage.

Of course Binei Jinwon's own family was merely a junior branch of the Yulehi; the main branch was gone with Gamwone's father. Who was probably viewing his daughter's current behavior with much distaste, if anything Jinwon remembered about the man was correct.

"You have made great sacrifices—" he began, meaning to soothe, but Gamwone laughed, a loud, bitter sound cutting straight through his sentence like a cavalry charge through lightly armed peasants.

"Shut up until I ask you a question," she barked. Even Garan Tamuron would not have used such words, or that tone. "And you, Kurin. This is how you repay your poor mother? I labored a day and a half to birth such an ungrateful child."

Such was a woman's lot; did she expect a prize? "Your lord father—" Binei Jinwon began.

Gamwone scuttled forward, moving upon her knees, a maneuver performed so often it was thoughtless-quick. Her hip hit the table they gathered round in a stifling-close Kaeje room, and the flat of her hand struck Lord Yulehi's cheek.

She had *slapped* him.

Silence fell. She settled back upon her haunches, and Binei Jinwon's chin, pushed aside, almost touched his shoulder. He stared at a wall double-muffled with tapestries, and the thought of returning the blow circled his thoughts once. Only a lifetime of keeping his humors reined halted him.

That, and Garan Kurin's flat dark gaze when his uncle turned back to the table. "Oh, Mother." Kurin sighed and shook his head slightly, dissuading his elder from further action. "That was ill-advised."

"You little—" Binei Jinwon began.

"I told you to cease your speaking, you poisonous toad," she hissed. Her hair, lacquered as it was, had come undone over her temple, and a tendril touched her ear. "Perhaps it is *you* who have taught my son to be ungrateful."

"I am the head of the clan—" he began, but Kurin lifted a hand.

"Uncle." The honorific held quiet but undeniable command. "Mother is right."

Both now-widowed queen and clan head stared at him. Gamwone's mouth had slackened slightly, and Jinwon's felt just as loose.

"You are head of the clan only because you enjoy Mother's support, you know," the arrogant princeling continued, and his uncle considered the utility of striking them both for one terrible moment. "And I must be filial, of course. Come, Mother." He opened his arms, beckoned, and Gamwone, with a faint coughing sob, moved again upon her knees to lean against her son's strength. The young man met Binei Jinwon's gaze over her dark, disarranged hair, and while he stroked and smoothed, his expression gave his uncle to understand that this was a necessary detour.

So Jinwon arranged his features, only half mollified. His nephew wished to have the ruling of the clan, but from behind a curtain— oh, it rankled, but not nearly as much as his throbbing cheek.

Gamwone sobbed into her son's mourning-robe, and Jinwon's nose twitched slightly. He kept his face carefully clean of disdain, though, or at least, so he hoped. There was much to do in order to ascend the summit; the ill-advised—but hardly unwelcome— attack upon Garan Takyeo was fortuitous, but its effects would be lost if they did not move carefully and quickly.

Oddly, as his uncle watched, Garan Kurin smiled. It was a wide, sleepy grin of patent goodwill and good nature, and he found himself smiling back with a minister's unerring instinct for placating a greater authority.

"The Palace and the city are closed," Kurin continued, as he stroked his mother's hair. "To guard against unrest, of course. I want the police to comb the Yuin."

Such a move was unprofitable at best, adding as it would to the unrest instead of tamping it. "For what?"

"Anything. It is no doubt a hotbed of sedition, and those bought to serve treasonous ends often rest there. There must be nothing left, uncle, that produces any...unflattering details. Of any sort, from *any* Yulehi. Do you understand?"

He knows. Or, what does he know? Enough? Too much? Binei Jinwon's own intrigues, and the small arrangements for his own profit or position, were to be swiftly curtailed. Loose ends should, indeed, be tucked away, tidied, or outright snipped. Binei Jinwon regarded the weeping mother and her smiling son, a chill finger touching the base of his spine. Until a few short weeks ago, he had ever considered Kurin bright enough but far too lazy to head the clan *or* arrange for his own ascent.

But there was the small, heavy chest in one of the storerooms of his estate in the Noble District, with its cargo of ingots and papers. And now, Kurin was plainly telling his ministerial uncle that no intrigue was to be countenanced unless *he* ordered it.

If Binei Jinwon, a seasoned survivor of both Garan Tamuron's ascent and the many dangers of court life, had misread the boy so badly, what else had he overlooked?

What had all of them failed to see?

COULD HAVE BEEN CRUEL

There was a great deal of pain, but of course, there had been his entire life. Takyeo's eyelids drifted open. The night-flower essence blunted the sawing in his guts and the fiery metal bar in his leg, but nothing could eat the deep, biting, abiding shame of never quite being princely enough.

"How is he?" someone said softly. The voice was Takshin's, but unwonted gentle indeed.

A cool hand touched Takyeo's fevered brow. A pale smear of unbleached silk resolved into a woman's indistinct shape, a breath of jaelo cut the medicinal odors and sharp reek of a body sweating under the cart-wheels of inescapable pain. "The same," a soft voice said, with the consonants each holding a sharp finality. Had his Khir wife returned to visit his bedside?

No, it was Komor Yala. He blinked again, and another face lifted over the lady's shoulder. The physician, his scanty beard untrimmed, blinked bloodshot eyes and scrubbed his sensitive fingers against a scrap of cotton. "I cannot tell," Kihon Jiao said, heavily. "The fever is not well, but it could simply be the body's attempt to rid itself of ill humors. I like not how the wound looks."

Takyeo's lips were cracked; he stared at Komor Yala, who studied his face and reached for a table at the bedside. "Only sips," she said softly, and Takshin, a black blot with a golden gleam at one ear, lifted his eldest brother's slack shoulders while Yala held the cup. A small amount of blessed coolness trickled down Takyeo's throat, and the nightflower wished to drag him down into welcome darkness again.

He denied it. "Tak...shin," he croaked as his brother laid him down. "How bad is it?"

"Bad enough." At least one of his brothers could be relied upon not to coat the bitterness with sweetened rai. "One moment, Ah-Yeo. Physician, what medicine remains?"

"I could try cinnabar," Kihon Jiao said, somewhat reluctantly. "But it is powerful as nightflower, and dangerous."

"Well?" Takshin's raised eyebrow stated he feared little danger, but at least he was not attempting to frighten the physician. No doubt he thought the man made of stern stuff, or simply liked him.

"I shall send for some." Kihon Jiao looked past Takshin at the bed and its occupant. "If his fever intensifies, or he begins to convulse, call me quickly."

"Indeed." Takshin nodded his accord, and the physician retreated.

"You are in mourning again," Takyeo whispered. "Who has died?"

Komor Yala's lips pursed, and though she said nothing, her glance told him clearly.

If he had the strength to stand, Takyeo might have staggered. As it was, he simply waited as she set the small earthenware cup of fresh water upon the small table and returned to smoothing the sheet over his chest, pushing bits of sweat-soaked hair from his forehead, and generally applying her neat, chilly fingers to his comfort. She had cared for Mahara like this, if his wife had ever been ill; her manner bespoke much familiarity with such operations.

So. Father was...dead. *Zhaon has so much regard, he has no need for mine*, Takyeo had said, and while he was not incorrect, it still closed upon his throat like a mailed fist.

The world spun away, returned changed in the space of an

eyeblink. Takshin, most likely too busy as of yet to attend to dressing himself in mourning, was murmuring near the door with Kihon Jiao, and Yala closed her pale, exhaustion-ringed eyes for a moment. Takyeo studied her face again, then cleared his throat.

She stiffened, and those pale grey irises flowered as her lids lifted. "Forgive me," she murmured in her fluid, slightly accented Zhaon. "More water?"

"No." The word was a dry husk of itself. "Kai. Zakkar Kai." If the general could be reached and brought to the city, it would alter the wildly swinging balance of events. Those who would raise their hand against a Crown Prince would find an Emperor supported by the God of War's beloved son a different proposition indeed.

"Still with the Northern Army." Faint color bloomed in her cheeks, and worry creased between her dark, arched eyebrows.

"Ah." The nightflower wrapped him in deceptive languor, but he denied its weight. Father was dead. The linchpin of Zhaon broken in half, and now that weight descended upon Takyeo's shoulders. Though he suspected he would break too, he had not quite yet—and therefore must do as he was trained. "The… assassins?"

"Dead." The slight color, fetching indeed, had fled her cheeks.

"Cease worrying, Eldest Brother." Takshin shut the door behind the physician. "All is well in hand, as long as you do not take more fever and destroy even your fine constitution. I have almost solved the problem of how to reach Kai."

Komor Yala stirred. "It is very simple," she murmured.

"Do not—" Takshin began, but her chin dropped and as her head bowed and shoulders curved inward, he paused.

Wonder of wonders, someone had finally halted the prickliest of Garan Tamuron's sons. Takyeo cleared his throat again; the water seemed to have lodged somewhere inconvenient. "It seems," he husked, "that there is a solution you will not countenance, Takshin. Pray continue, Lady Yala."

"One rider," she said, to her pale-clad lap. Noblewomen changed their dresses often, but this was excessive; she should not have to bear such things. "Swift and light, someone who may be trusted and will not be missed during the…" She darted a quick glance at Takyeo, continued. "The funeral. Someone Zakkar Kai will not disregard."

Put that way, it was indeed obvious. "Who could disregard *you*, my lady?" Takyeo's throat was now slick with something hot and foul, but he took care to speak gently. "I bless the day you were sent from Khir."

"No." Takshin had found his voice again. "I will not allow it."

"Is it my trustworthiness you doubt, or my ability?" Yala shook her head. Her hair was dressed very simply, in the manner of a woman whose servants were too old or too busy to attend to such a duty. Of course she had retrieved her mourning-robe herself, as soon as an opportunity was presented.

A foreign lady in a violently upset court would do well to wear whatever was prudent.

"It is the danger," Takshin said, and made a short, sharp violent movement, as if he wished to pick up one of the implements scattered across the physician's table and hurl it. "If anyone should go—"

"You are needed here, to guard the Crown Prince—the *Emperor*," Yala said, firmly. Not only could she gain the last word upon Taktak, but she could also interrupt him without fear, it appeared. "If you vanish there will be gossip."

"You and that claw-toy may protect him." Takshin's chin set stubbornly. Of course he could not be certain of her feelings; if he were, he would not have asked for the marriage endorsement.

Or perhaps he would, simply to be doubly sure. A man who trained himself to want nothing was dangerous when the dam finally broke.

"And who will protect Honorable Kihon, should the Emperor turn ill?" Yala's gaze rose, and she searched Takyeo's face. Perhaps she hoped he would disagree, and it was unprincely of him to be grateful enough *not* to. But her quiet bravery in even suggesting this course called for his own. "Or Honorable Mrong, or Fourth Prince Makar, or—"

"Makar may go hang," Takshin muttered. "Takyeo, I need only a few moments to think of a better solution."

"You have not yet," she said, quiet but inflexible. "Time is our enemy, Third Prince." The honorific sounded almost tender. Takyeo wished they would be silent for a moment so he could rack his nightflower-fogged mind for a better solution as well, but he suspected none would be forthcoming.

"Lady Yala." He tried to stir upon the cushions, but his tender belly, riven by an assassin's blade, reminded him such a motion was unwise. "I would ask why you are willing to undertake such a difficult task for a prince of a foreign land."

Takshin made a short, rude noise and turned, ostensibly to examine a hanging illustration scroll of a prong-horned deer native to the Salt Wastes, brushed in midleap. The Jonwa was not silent— feet hurried in the corridors, and the Palace beyond seethed, a vast unsound as familiar as Takyeo's own breath. If Komor Yala was disposed to lie to either of them, this was an ideal moment.

But he did not think she would.

Finally, Komor Yala answered. "You could have been cruel." Her fingers knotted together. "To my princess. I expected as much."

"If I had not married her, she might yet be alive." He searched her expression for any flicker of ill-feeling that would show she knew, or secretly hated him for it.

"Perhaps." Now she regarded him steadily. "But she would wish for me to help her husband, Garan Takyeo. Her shade watches from her tomb, and I would not have her shamed."

Was it that simple? It mattered little, Takyeo was all but helpless, and Yala very well could have let the assassin have his way. It was not right for a foreign woman to save his life *or* risk herself in the proposed fashion. His father would use any tool to hand, ruthlessly, and Takyeo had ever judged him harsh and unfeeling for doing so.

Was Father's shade watching *him*, now, hovering a little distance over their heads? What would he think of this? A fine jest, the survival of a Zhaon emperor dependent upon a Khir noblewoman.

"Then go with my blessing," he said, heavily. Takshin turned from his perusal, and his little brother's gaze was hot and dark with accusation. "I can write no letter, I am too weak."

"Takshin will write it." She half-turned upon her seat, gazing at the Third Prince, and Takyeo had the exotic experience of seeing his brother's features smooth themselves, the change as sudden as an arrow set loose. "Will you not? And I must have a horse, a map, dried meat and fruit—"

"Very well," Takshin said. "If you wish this, little lure, then I will see it done." His jaw had set, and his scars paled.

"And I shall owe you even more of a debt." She smoothed pale cloth across her knees; she could not ride in mourning, but Takyeo thought she would not mind the lack.

Takshin's response was a mutter that might have been a terrible word, half-throttled in deference to her station before he set his shoulders and bent to the work at hand. "Go to your chambers and gather what you need. Make some shift for your kaburei; I have half a mind to flay her for inattention."

"Anh may be trusted, my lord." Yala rose with swift grace, but she did not withdraw. Instead, she approached Takyeo's little brother, and held out her hands.

Takshin stared at her remotely for a few heartbeats; finally, he clasped her fingers, and a muscle flickered in his cheek. Then he turned her loose, not ungently. "Go."

Her presence remained though she quit the room, a light breath of jaelo and a reminder of grace. Takyeo and Takshin regarded each other. The nightflower essence was a warm wrapping along every aching limb and a heaviness in his chest, but the new Emperor of Zhaon held his brother's gaze.

"If she is harmed," Takshin said softly, "I shall hold you responsible."

"One more burden to bear." He settled against his cushions. Whether Father was watching or not, this was Garan Takyeo's decision alone, and he had made it. "If I survive this, Takshin, you will hate me too."

"Of course not." But Takshin's gaze did not alter. "I must call for paper and brush, Ah-Yeo, and Kihon Jiao will return. I shall send for Banh, too. There is no reason not to start tonight."

A Good Wife

Misty mornings gave way to bright, piercing, clear, hot days, and the afternoon storms common in Zhaon did not come this far south. Instead, they arrived well after dark, and sometimes thunder shivered the air even inside the stone palace halls. Perhaps the Shan could sleep through such a display, but it proved impossible for Sabwone unless exhaustion closed her eyes on every third night or so; the days were a perpetual blur of bright exhaustion, heat, and strangeness.

Still, there was reason to be cautiously hopeful. Nijera had turned into a quite biddable thing once her mistress found the proper means of addressing her. Still, the rumor-whispers had turned into hurrying, significant looks, and the racket of booted feet was audible even in the royal consort's chambers where Sabwone spent most of her time attempting to embroider, walking in the parsimonious garden—a *single* garden, where she had been used to several—and stretching her ears to gather what rumor she could in their cups. She could even demand—oh, she couched it as a wistful request, to be sure, since now they thought her a wilting stem—novels, and no bar was put upon her reading now that she was married. There was even walanir with every meal, and Nijera no doubt prided herself upon obtaining it as Sabwone played the part of a silk-mouthed princess abjectly grateful for any small crumb.

If she had known this was the course required, she would have employed it much earlier.

Best of all, the king was called away with some regularity, and three entire nights without enduring Suon Kiron's fevered thrusting and sweaty grunting upon her person almost made Sabwone feel her old self again.

Almost.

That afternoon, though, she was deep in a thrilling tale of two noblewomen and a prince who had been stolen as a baby by an exorcist when sudden intense activity flooded the short hall outside her sitting room. She glanced up, restraining the urge to tuck the novel under a convenient pillow, and discerned that a visit from her royal jailor was indeed at hand. She bent her head to the flatbook again, characters swarming like ants before her suddenly blurring eyes.

Why would he not leave her *alone*? He had what he wanted when it was dark, why did he bother coming to vex her now?

Her ladies scattered like longneck eggfowl, Nijera directing them in a hurried undertone to fetch tea and small pastries for the lord of this place. Sabwone ignored it as much as she was able, and Kiron of Shan stalked into the room with the softness of a junglepard. He even wore boots into her presence, this pretender, as if he was Zakkar Kai come fresh from some victory or another to report to her father.

Well, Sabwone did not think very highly of anyone who brought mud indoors, but who cared what she disliked at the moment?

"My lady *ekanha*," he greeted her, and Sabwone took care to lay aside the book properly before arranging her hands in her lap and pretending to attend, demure and docile, to his ridiculous accent. His Zhaon was *quite* amusing; an actor in the Great Theater of Zhaon-An would no doubt play him as a roly-poly parvenu in an ill-fitting jacket with a great drooping mustache and a dialect so thick every common tradesman and peasant would hold their sides with laughter.

She realized she was smiling slightly, and composed herself. Of course, with her chin so far down, nobody could see.

"Speechless again?" Kiron loomed over her, and her hands tightened in her lap. Nothing said she had to do more than listen, and he was welcome to think her overcome with admiration or fear. "I shall make certain to tell your brother I have tamed you."

If you like. She longed to return to her book, but he must have some purpose. Sabwone sat and seethed, the hatred bright and sharp inside her vitals. If she *did* carry an heir, would he leave her alone? It would be nice to have a baby, perhaps, a child to raise, someone who would love only her.

And if it was a daughter, she wouldn't send her haughtily away as her own mother had. No, she would raise a daughter quite differently indeed.

Soon Kiron waited for a reply, but she did not grant him one. After a short while he sank down, as one of the ladies—Gonwa Eunwone, a much-junior cousin of the falcon-eyed Lady Gonwa and her eternal heaven tea—hurried to find a cushion. It must have been uncomfortable to sit so with his boots on, but he managed, and once settled he waved the girl away.

She went willingly, a tiny slip of a thing in a very ugly primrose cotton dress edged with black silk, which no doubt she thought was rather fetching but would earn her endless ridicule at any *proper* court.

"You are trying very hard to ignore me." The king of Shan sounded amused. "I might even take insult, *ekanha.*"

That word again. Did she care what it meant? Nijera was studying the Shan dialect, no doubt Sabwone could find out if she wanted to.

She did *not*. She studied her knuckles instead, and thought of a knife. A very sharp one, not meant for peeling fruit. She would have to choose her time carefully, of course, but there were instances, both in history and novels, of an insulted woman freeing herself from a tormentor or two.

Very fine instances indeed. In fact, Sabwone was willing to admit that her first mistake had been not using such a tool upon a man rather than her own soft wrists.

"In any case," he continued, as the ladies fluttered just out of earshot, "you shall have to do without me for some short while."

Good. Sabwone raised her head slightly, now gazing at his hands. Callused at fingertip and across the palm, they were quite fine, and if they had not belonged to such a man she might even have liked them.

"There is trouble between here and Anwei." Kiron settled himself more comfortably upon the cushion. "Do you know of the Tabrak, wife?"

A direct question, and one she could not avoid. Sabwone let her gaze rise still farther, to his chin. He had a fine jawline, she might admit, and like his hands she might have liked it except for its bearer. He *looked* handsome indeed, but his lack of any proper breeding meant he was more a laborer than a prince, and she was trapped beneath him.

"Barbarians," she said, flatly, taking care to make her Zhaon as soft-lisping as any Palace lady. Some few of the ladies imitated her way of speaking, sounding very much like the First Queen's companions; others let the burr and buzz of Shan creep into their speech like the little harlots they were. No doubt *those* would find husbands among the merchant pretenders here. "They come like storms, pass through and melt away; they are said to have skin pale as polished rai, and to eat babies when they have slaughtered their parents."

"She speaks." His chin changed shape, he was *smiling*, the wretch. "And of such pleasant things."

"You *asked*," she flared, before she could stop herself. "Should I lie?"

"There she is." His hands lay upon his knees, loose and easy. Even at night, they did not bite her very badly. She bore no bruises, not upon her outer skin. "I think I might grow to like you yet, wife. In any case, it seems they have ideas above their station, these *yaman*, and I am to kill them."

Unless they kill you. The prospect cheered her. If he died against some bandits—it was, after all, what merchants did—what did that leave for her?

A queen had ruled Shan before.

Her interest piqued, Sabwone raised her gaze, studying his face. Slightly triangular, clean-shaven, with a narrow nose and eyes deeply folded, he was not entirely objectionable. In fact, were she to dream of a proper prince, he might look very much like this, leather half-armor and all. If he was uncomfortable sitting in its sausage-case, it did not show.

"That pleases you, does it?"

Sabwone longed to tell him it did, deeply, but it would ruin the image she had spent weeks carefully cultivating. "*A wife should not be pleased at her husband's departure*," she quoted, and his dark eyes lit from within.

He actually laughed, this pretender, a merry bark very much like Takshin's when he returned from this hellish, threadbare place. "And she is well-read, to quote Zhe Har to me. Well, will you bid me goodbye, and wish for my safe return?"

If I must, but I'd rather not. "A good wife should." She fastened her gaze over his right shoulder. Auntie Nijera was at the door, listening to one of the Shan lords—the large-nosed one, Suron, who barely glanced at Sabwone except to sneer. Now he was speaking rapidly but in a low tone, and several ladies had drifted closer to listen to his tidings. He was in leather half-armor too, and Sabwone thought it quite possible the maiden aunt had set her sewing-basket to catch his needle.

Well, after being passed over by a nobleman *and* a merchant, she was no doubt desperate. It served her right, too. They made a comedic pair, him long and lean and her a round eggbird. At least both of them were ugly, they could match that way.

"Then do so. You have behaved quite well, Sabwone of Shan." But Kiron's expression hardened, and so did his tone. "I will leave the city in your care, as is traditional. If anything goes ill, the council will appeal to you for decision."

"What?" She could not hide a start. A council? Appealing to *her*?

"Our queens are not kept immured, as in the North." Suon Kiron leaned forward slightly. "Continue to do well in this, and we may yet find some accommodation between us. Would that please you?"

What would please me is to return home. And yet, this was intriguing. Sabwone realized her expression was perhaps singing too loudly, and composed herself. "It would please a good wife, would it not?"

"So they say." He nodded approvingly. "I shall take my leave this afternoon. You will come to the palace steps so all may see you bid me farewell, and know who their mistress is while I am gone."

Her jaw threatened to loosen, and a hot satisfied tongue uncurled in Sabwone's belly. "Truly?"

"Oh, the old men will take care of everything. You must simply sit and smile prettily, *ekanha*, and wait for your husband to return."

Sabwone could not help herself. She smiled, and no doubt those who watched avidly to sense discord between the newlyweds would be disappointed. "Oh, yes," she said, and kept her hands firmly clasped. "I shall do as you ask." She watched him depart, and her liver, somewhat stunned these past few weeks, had regained its proper place within her.

It would be no trouble at all to attend this council.

And, she thought grimly, *we shall see what a queen may do in Shan.*

SAFE AS A FOAL

Asmall, disused storeroom in the Jonwa held a lamp, a hurriedly undraped table, and a quantity of shrouded furniture standing silent witness to three hushed figures. "I do not like it." Banh rubbed at his face, stubble bristling against his palms, then picked up the brush and bent again to his work. "Lady Yala, you are brave, but—"

"Your disappearance would be remarked as well." The lady accepted a small bundle from her kaburei, who was deathly pale, her leather-wrapped braids trembling as much as the rest of her. "The guards at the Palace gates, and at the city—"

"The Third Prince will take you from the palace to the North Gate." Mrong Banh chewed at the inside of his mouth, added another mark to the map on the broad sheet of sturdy paper made from pressed rags instead of noble rai. "I gather he has his own methods, and a horse for you as well."

"He is most resourceful," she murmured. In the trousers and Shan tunic—one of Lady Kue's, and much too long for her— instead of her riding habit, she was a child playing dress-up. It was almost shocking to see her in such ill-fitting clothing. "Now, Anh, when asked where I am—"

"I am to say you are ill with grief. And I shall bring your meals to your room, and..." The girl glanced at Mrong Banh, who nodded encouragingly, careful not to splotch the map. "My lady, I *cannot*."

"You must eat from the dishes, so my absence is not discovered," Lady Yala said, in that particular tone of soft command. "It is only a few days."

"What of the young ladies?" Anh's fingers quivered as well; she bent to checking and retying the laces on Lady Yala's outer tunic. "They will ask."

"The Third Prince will have Lady Kue keep them occupied while I am 'ill.'" She sounded like she doubted the ease of that task and shook her head slightly, testing two braids running in parallel. It was an odd hairstyle, especially as the ropes hung free down her back instead of being pinned. Her boots were indigo leather, a remnant of her riding-habit, so at least her feet would remain dry. "Did you find what we require?"

"Certainly, and I stole it from the storeroom with no trouble at all." Anh's cheerfulness returned, albeit somewhat muted. "My lady, is it really..." She stole a glance at her mistress's face, and the picture they presented—brave lady, faithful servant—was touching. If the kaburei was literate, no doubt this was novel-worthy excitement. "I wish I could go with you. I could cling to the saddle."

"No, my Anh, I must travel very swiftly indeed. *You* will be quite occupied in helping the Third Prince and Honorable Mrong."

The kaburei shook her head much more vigorously than her lady. "Great lords should not let you go alone." But she did not say it very loudly, and said lady gave a quelling glance, all the more sharp because she so rarely employed such a measure.

"I do not like this plan either," Mrong Banh said. "But it is for Takyeo, Lady Yala, and I owe you a great debt for the attempt."

"You are kind, Honorable Mrong." She smiled at him, and Banh's cheeks were unwonted warm.

"You will please do me the greatest honor of addressing me as *Banh*, my lady, now and evermore. And if there is anything a poor astrologer may do for you, consider it accomplished. Come, look at the map."

Her shoulder almost touched his as she bent close, a breath of jaelo from her bath much nicer than Zan Fein's perfume. "There is

Zhaon-An, and there is Zakkar Kai. At…Tienzhu Keep." She indicated with a well-manicured fingertip, her accent turning the name
almost into a stand of cedars instead of a plum orchard, and he nodded.

"Indeed. You are in luck, the North Road will take you very
near; this is Haeso, where you must strike north and east. The
great bridge will warn you, mind that you cross and *then* turn away
from the Road. Follow the river for an hour's trot, then turn north.
There should be cart-roads for the army foragers, and any peasant
will be able to tell you where the old keep is." What else could he
tell her? "Beware of any rider upon the Road, and when you reach
the army, do not leave the saddle until you see Kai." The thought of
soldiers ringing a defenseless lady was chilling, and the plan held so
many risks it was hardly worth undertaking.

And yet, having seen Komor Yala and her greenmetal blade, he
thought it likely that she would sell herself dear if any importunate commoner, armed or not, ventured too close. "I will think of
a thousand things to warn you of once you leave," he finished, staring dully at the map. It was a poor, hurried piece of work indeed.

Lady Yala ducked through the strap of a sturdy leather and cloth
marketing-bag, settling it diagonally across her body. She studied
the map, and pointed at a particular character. "Ku-ri-he-on-guah."
She sounded out the phonetic script. "What lies there?"

"Kurheong. A very large town; if you see their gates, you will
know you have gone too far east."

"Ah, very useful." She smiled, momentarily pleased, then
sobered. "And it is wooded through here, and here is the ravine I
must enter to reach the keep. You have a fine hand, Honorable, and
an even finer brush."

He mumbled something self-deprecatory, heat rising to his
cheeks, and her returned smile was rain to thirsty earth. At least
the dry season was approaching and she might not be caught in a
downpour if her luck held.

A flicker of motion at the doorway was the Third Prince easing past the partition, and Banh pressed his hand to his galloping
heart. "Takshin! Make some *noise*."

"I enjoy testing your liver, Banh." But there was no smile upon Takshin's scarred, remote face, set as if he contemplated an unpleasant duty. "If we delay much longer dawn will force us to waste another day. Have you all you need?"

"If not, I shall have to make do." Lady Yala took a deep breath, and Banh suspected she was not as calm as she appeared. "I am in your hands, Garan Takshin."

Banh busied himself with blotting the map and rolling it securely, clipping it into a small scrollcase, and handing the result to the lady, who accepted it gravely with both hands.

"Then you are safe as a foal under its dam, my lady." Takshin nodded at Banh, gave a dark glance to the suddenly pale kaburei, and let the lady precede him through the door. "I need not threaten you," he announced to the air over the kaburei's head, "or tell you the consequence of an inadvisable word, do I?"

"Of course not." Banh almost waved the ink-freighted brush at him; there was no use in frightening the poor servant. "She is canny and brave, our lady. She will arrive in good order and we will speak lightly of this in years to come, with Takyeo laughing loudest."

"May you be right," was Takshin's parting reply, and then they were gone. Banh sagged at his table, and the kaburei girl breathed part of a prayer to the god of servants.

Mrong Banh hoped, very badly, those august beings were listening.

Earning Extra Slivers

Leaving the Palace was a minor trick indeed; the larger was returning unremarked. Sixth Prince Garan Jin, his head humming pleasantly from sohju and his leg bruised from a brutal drillyard practice that morning, was considering his options when two shadows dropped over the wall, the larger landing with the ease of one trained in the lightfoot and the other slim, slight, and graceful though it lacked such a closely guarded skill.

He watched as both figures—the smaller one muffled with a head-wrapping, the solicitous larger with a hilt protruding over his broad-muscled shoulder—kept to the shadows along the skirting, pausing to allow a pair of Golden to march past with servants carrying lanterns. The guard schedule seemed unusually heavy tonight.

And why shouldn't it be? The world had cracked in half. Leaving the Palace to drink had seemed a fairly reasonable reaction, all things considered, especially after news of the attack on Takyeo spread like fire. Now Ah-Yeo was immured in the Jonwa, and nobody knew how badly he was wounded or where. Father's body was being wrapped and prepared; even Mother, busy with arrangements, had little time for him.

It occurred to Jin through the sohju's haze that these could be assassins or other mischief-makers, escaping after a long day's work. Jin drifted after them, using the lightfoot himself, but they rounded a corner not too far away and he had to hurry or lose sight of their indistinct shadows.

He was very nearly stabbed as he rounded the corner in a rush, and only a short, horrified exclamation stopped the blade-point pricking at his throat. "Jin?" Takshin snarled, his breath carrying a hint of alcohol—so even *he* had needed a little bolstering. "What are you doing *here*?"

"It is the Sixth Prince?" Lady Komor pushed down the cloth muffling the lower half of her face, but those grey eyes were unmistakable. "Oh."

"I almost killed you." Takshin sighed, and his hand upon Jin's shoulder gentled. The knife—a short, curved Shan blade, very nice indeed—vanished. "Well, little brother? Are you part of this?"

"Part of..." Jin blinked several times. What, under Heaven, would *these* two be doing out at night, and dressed so strangely? "Where are you going? What's happened now?"

"Nothing." Takshin never looked particularly merry, but tonight he was positively dour. "Forget you saw us, or I swear I will—"

"Sixth Prince Jin." Lady Komor's hand rested upon Takshin's shoulder, and it seemed that small appendage was stronger than it looked, for it halted Taktak as surely as a chain at a watchdog's throat. "We are engaged upon a particularly pressing matter, and require your silence. It is for Takyeo."

The constellation assumed quite a different shape inside Jin's head. "Oh. You're going for Kai." It was the only thing that made sense.

Takshin tensed, but Lady Komor nodded. "Yes." Short, and simple—she had much presence of mind, this lady, and Jin liked that about her. "And if you are discreet, we may have the General here in a short while. Please let us pass, and say nothing to anyone."

He was nettled at the caution. "I never told anyone about the Market, did I?" he pointed out. "Let go of me, Takshin. Is that a Shan dagger? It's curved."

"Little longtail." Takshin almost shook him, but at least the hurtful gleam had left his elder brother's eyes and he was not one to pinch or slap like Sensheo. "Go home and sleep. This is not for you."

"Are you sending a rider? You are, you have to be. They have the mews and cotes watched, the Golden are muttering about having to stand guard for *birds* now." A fabulous idea struck him. "I could ride. I could ride faster than anyone."

"You are needed for the funeral, Sixth Prince." Lady Komor, as usual, sounded kind. "Leave the rest to us."

"But you'll need to get through the gates, and I can—"

This time Takshin *did* shake him, but not very hard. "Do you think I have not considered the gates?"

Jin wished he wouldn't interrupt, but such was the way of elder brothers. "Oh, the posterns are open, but that's not the trouble. There are guards posted on every highroad a few bowlengths from the walls. Stopping everyone and examining their papers."

Takshin regarded him in the dimness, tense as a drillyard opponent with a new weapon to master. "And how do you know this?"

"I was drinking with some of the city watch; they like earning the extra slivers for additional guard duty." Jin had the satisfaction of seeing Takshin's expression change once more through the gloom, and Lady Komor stilled, her hand still upon his shoulder. Normally Taktak would have shaken away such a touch. "How badly is Takyeo hurt? Let me *help*."

"You may indeed help." Perhaps Lady Komor's slim fingers squeezed, for his third-eldest brother finally let go of him completely as she spoke. "But it will be in the manner you like least, Sixth Prince. By being discreet, keeping your ears sharp, and bringing anything strange you see or hear—no matter how small—to me or to the Third Prince. Will you do so?"

"Of course." He would never have admitted it, of course, but his liver swelled within him at the thought of being useful, especially to a *lady*. She wasn't like the other court dames, certainly, even pretty Su Junha, who didn't even deign to glance at him though he was a prince. "I still think I should ride for Kai. Are you sending a Golden? I can—"

"*That* matter is attended to." Lady Komor straightened Takshin's sleeve, gently as a noblewoman with a leashed frillbird, and let her hand drop. "Time is short, my lord Third Prince."

"Too many people know of this," Takshin hissed. "Mind you do not open your lips, Jinjin."

"*Pft.* I keep all sorts of secrets, *Taktak.* Lady Komor." He managed a bow in her direction, and was gratified at hers in return. A few moments later they were gone, and Jin stood in the shadows for a moment, thinking.

It was good someone was riding for Kai. He would want to be here for the funeral. And...Takyeo was wounded. It must be bad, for both Takshin and the lady to be so grave. Jin understood assassins—he was, after all, a prince, and there were those who wished to remove such creatures for their own ends.

But for Takshin and Lady Komor to be so secretive, while Takyeo was hurt...

It occurred to Jin, not for the first time but with sudden sharp clarity, that the assassins might not have been hired by a noble family with ambitions or a commoner with a grudge against his betters. It was a horrible, hideous idea, but perhaps one of his brothers had done something...

Well, something downright unfamilial.

The shadow of that thought had earlier driven him outside the Palace as a reflex, for he did his best thinking while moving stealthily at night, every nerve alive and aware. Yet its implications had robbed him of any enjoyment in sohju, and now it robbed him of the will to move from his hiding-place for a few more moments while he considered things he had never been given much reason to think about before.

He was very young, certainly. As the baby of the family, he did not have much to fear. Unless...unless something happened to Takyeo. Something not merely dangerous, but permanent.

If Father could die, Garan Jin realized, his eldest brother could, too. Why, anyone could. Even Sabwone. Even his mother.

Even his own young, and heretofore presumably immortal, self.

Finally, cold though the night's warmth made scaling the Palace walls a sweaty proposition, Sixth Prince Jin glanced about him guiltily, and went upon his way.

CEASE SUCH ACCOUNTING

The little longtail-cub was correct; a moment's work to crack a dozing guard's head with a dagger-hilt and they were free to ease through the postern of the North Gate, but a few bowlengths in the distance lanterns gleamed and a soft warm breeze freighted with the smell of rich black earth sighing during its sleep carried men's voices to Takshin, Komor Yala, and the Tooth. Lady Komor had not remarked upon the nobleman's estate he led her to *or* its stable, beyond giving the defaced pillars before the princely home a curious glance.

One day he would tell her why he had ordered those characters rubbed out. Perhaps when she was brought to the door of that very residence in a red-and-gold palanquin, accompanied by celebrants and wailers, beating gongs and all a bride's paraphernalia. But not now.

She rubbed the Tooth's nose; the large, cob-headed grey bred for Palace guards and princely mounts was usually deeply mistrustful but apparently liked her enough to suffer it. Of course, she was Khir, and their horse-goddess was profligate with the rider's gift. The Tooth was war-trained, and would do what he could to keep his small rider in the saddle.

"I should go instead," Takshin said again, without any real hope of it occurring.

"You are needed here, to guard the Crown Prince." With her hair pulled back, high-braided down each side of her head, Yala looked much younger. There was the shade of the girl she must have been, and he wondered if she had been a merry child. "I shall reach the Head General, or die trying."

Do not say such things. "You are not *allowed* to die, little lure." Takshin's hands ached. He leaned back upon his heels, trying to ignore the cold blade in his guts at such a prospect. He wanted to touch her shoulder, smooth her half-cloak's darkness over the lovely curve, but instead he turned away and made certain the saddle-girth was tightened properly. "He is a warhorse, and will fight should they seek to pull you from the saddle."

"You have told me that twice." She smiled, but the worry-line was deep-graven between her eyebrows. "I have the map, and dried meat and fruit, and my *yue*."

Takshin lost the battle with himself; his left hand curved around her waist and he pulled her close. He rested his chin atop her head, and for a moment, with her slenderness fitted against him, the restless fury retreated fully instead of just accepting a cage in his liver. "Stay to the side of the road. Be wary, and swift. Strike to kill, if you must."

"You sound like my brother." She did not seek to pull away, though. "I shall protect my honor, never fear."

It is not your honor I worry for. And *brotherly* was the last thing he felt, though it would give him an advantage in advancing his true cause. "When you reach Kai, do as he commands." The very idea choked him, but she was safest thus. At least Kai was . . . honorable. "I will come to you, if it goes ill here."

"You must stay with the Emperor, Takshin. To the very end." Now she freed herself from his grasp, but gently. "I will help him for my princess's sake, but you are his brother."

It was useless to tell her that he saw death sitting upon his eldest brother's face, and had already turned his head-meat to the question of what would happen after Takyeo succumbed. Again, his self-control failed. He leaned forward, pressing his lips to her forehead. Her skin was just as soft as in his dreams, and the fire spilling through him from that contact just as sweet.

Startled, she drew away, nearer the Tooth, who flicked an ear at the strangeness of humans. "Third Prince—"

"It is *Takshin*. You will address me thus." Takshin laced his fingers. She did not need to, but she put her boot in the cradle, and he lifted her to the saddle with a little more force than necessary. "Be careful."

"And you, Third Prince."

It hurt. "Yala."

"Takshin." This time she smiled before pulling muffling cloth up, settling it over mouth and nose to keep both free of dust. She gathered the reins, and the Tooth, sensing something even more untoward than tonight's disruption of routine, tensed. "I owe you a debt, for this."

Would she never cease such accounting? "There is no debt," he replied, thickly.

She must have smiled again, for the corners of her pale eyes crinkled. Yala touched her heels to the warhorse's sides, her knees clamping home, and even in the dark he could see her sinking into the saddle. A bright, fierce pain pierced him from crown to sole as he watched her hold the Tooth to a trot, hopping from grassy verge to the Road's paved surface. Excited, eager to be gone, the Tooth flicked his tail, and when Yala's back stiffened the horse lunged forth into a canter. She melded with the motion, all fluid grace, her cape wrapped close, and Takshin's breath refused to seat itself properly in his chest as he ran for the wooden wayfarer's shed looming indistinct to the right. It was a moment's effort to spring to the top of the wood-pile, then he gained the roof. The bow he had retrieved from his estate in the Noble District unlimbered, an arrow nocked with habitual ease, and his breath came tearing-hard as he cast a dark-adapted glance over the battlefield.

There is no debt. What an idiot he was. He *should* indebt her, to keep her close. And she thought him *brotherly*. He might have laughed fit to scream at the thought, were he alone and without fear of being overheard.

Torches glittered. A cry went up, and he drew to his ear. Let fly, and pulled another arrow free. Again, aiming for the shadows clustering before a grey warhorse cantering upon the road's pale sleeve. Lanternlight danced and spun, and the idiots had built a bonfire as well.

They were fine targets for one used to hunting Shan bandits and long-ears under a wan half-moon, indeed.

She leaned over the horse's neck, making herself as small as possible, and Takshin let another arrow fly. One of the shadows reaching for her fell, and another arrow whistled before he was conscious of drawing. He rained death from the sky to protect a fleeing mirage.

Half a dozen men were upon the Road. None lived, struck down as a grey horse passed.

Takshin finally lowered his bow. He had the remaining hours of darkness to clear a few more of the bastards from other roads spinning away from Zhaon-An, then he had to return to Takyeo. Banh could not gainsay an assassin, and had other duties to attend to once day rose.

If she was grateful, he could...no, he wanted her freely, of her own will.

But, Garan Takshin realized, listening to the hoofbeats fading on a cruel-sharp autumn wind, it did not matter. He already had the lady's regard in some small fashion, and she did not dislike him.

A desperate man took what he could, willing or no.

No Waiting Gaze

Rhythm of canter and jolt of hoof-fall, *thunk-thunk-thunk*, weightless, *thunk-thunk-thunk*. The grey was eager; Yala let the first flush of speed pass and reined him, her knees and slight weight a single straw upon a river's surface. Placed correctly, even a grassblade could change the course of the mighty, mythical Yantuan deep in Ch'han's heart.

She could only hope she was so dropped, at the correct junction.

The night wore on; they bypassed towns and rode through ungated villages, each a symbol upon Mrong Banh's map firmly held before her mind's eye. Walking to cool, cantering when urgency grew, it was not until dawn painted the eastern horizon that the realization struck her.

For the first time in her life, Komor Yala was completely alone.

Not only that, but another man had been within arm's length of her, had even pressed his lips to her forehead. Like any mistreated creature, Garan Takshin gave his affection in spates if he could be induced to trust at all.

He reminded her so very much of Baiyan, though her brother had hardly been ill-treated. They were both given to fierce gestures when the strict control they held themselves to was fractionally loosened. She could not countenance another reason for his behavior, could she?

It was much safer to reminisce of her damoi.

Thinking of her brother and fierce, extravagant gestures led her to yet another quandary: Ashani Daoyan. It beggared belief that he had arrived in Zhaon-An at all. He had not spoken much of Mahara before they were interrupted—perhaps because the grief was too fresh, though they had never met. Ashani Zlorih had not wished for his daughter to know her bastard brother, fearing the contamination of her honor.

Now Yala wondered about her own. Was it quite unstained? She did not *think* she had acted incorrectly...and yet the kiss upon her forehead burned quite differently from Zakkar Kai's soft touch. Garan Takshin's fingers had pressed just short of pain, and his arms around her did not feel at *all* brotherly.

It would pain her to lose the Third Prince's regard, she admitted. Surely there were other reasons for his behavior.

Perhaps it was only that he was unused to anyone showing loyalty to his beloved Takyeo. It certainly seemed that Garan Tamuron's first son, without a royal mother to shield him, needed aid—and he had the gift of inspiring loyalty through kindness.

Dao would see it was impossible to lever her from the palace, and even more impossible for her to return to Khir in his company. If she could have induced him to ride for Zakkar Kai—but explaining why a mere merchant would risk such a thing was beyond her power in the short time they possessed, and in any case sending the Great Rider's son to Khir's greatest enemy was folly of the highest order.

Her heart ached for Dao, arriving in a foreign city to find out his sister had been murdered. Though Daoyan lacked nothing in the way of luxury or training while growing up, with his brothers wary and his father distant he was always so alone.

Still, it was madness for him to have left the Great Keep, and that the lunacy had endured for long enough to bring him to Zhaon-An was a troubling sign indeed. Perhaps this ride, bruising and dangerous as it was, would give her some solution; she would have much time for uninterrupted thought.

It was strange to be without even a servant, no waiting gaze to weigh upon her decorum, no possible chance of gossip, nothing but the road and the strengthening daylight. Glimmers showed behind the fields on either side, peasants well underway on the day's work of tilling, sowing, reaping, repairing, laboring to bring forth the rai that made all else possible.

Just after the sun showed a thin crimson nail-paring upon the eastron horizon she turned slightly off the road, working parallel to its ribboned length behind a screen of summer-crowding saplings the peasants used for thin, flexible poles. There were several dusty footpaths where those who did not quite wish to be seen or pay a toll edged along, and she saw nobody for a long while though hoofbeats resounded beyond the screen and there was an occasional grinding of cart-wheels. Before the heat rose too high she found a small, secluded glade some ways from the road, picketed the horse—Takshin had not thought to tell her his name— and chewed a bit of dried meat and leathery dried umju, washed down with clear water from a nearby, almost-overgrown rill. Later in summer it would probably be a swamp-dried hole, but now it was a welcome coolness.

Birds sang as she settled her back against a spreading two-year lyong tree bearing full leaf, mellifluous shade rustling like a well-kept garden. Had they missed her at the palace? Hopefully not, if Anh was quick and Lady Kue could keep Hansei Liyue and Su Junha busy with other matters.

It was so strange. She did not have to keep her feelings submerged and her face a pleasing blankness; there were no letters to worry over or sewing to fret at her fingertips, no tea to order or etiquette to remember. The leisure might have been pleasant if she did not feel so exposed.

No father, no brother, no husband, no servant, no other noble lady to watch—did she truly *exist*, sitting under this lyong with hot, grainy eyes, her only company a grazing beast?

At least the horse saw her, but he paid no more attention than to his own tail. And quite a fine tail it was. He was a little ungainly, true, but she could see why Takshin had chosen such a mount—there was speed and strength in his lines, functionality instead of slender-legged but impractical beauty.

Perhaps the Third Prince felt the same way about her. It would be a relief, but a pang passed through her at the thought.

Yala finished chewing, rested her forehead upon her knees, and fell into a light doze. She would stiffen and climbing back into the saddle would be a misery, but she dared not move again until dusk. In a short while she would lead the horse to the rill and let him drink, then picket him securely.

Come twilight, there would be hard riding.

LOVELY GIRL

There was much to be done, even if her mistress was gone. The important thing was that nobody learn of her absence. Anh hurried down the sloping passageway, her head full of secret pressure, counting upon her fingers to make certain she remembered. The torment of possibly overlooking something critical when so much depended upon one tiny kaburei would keep her from sleeping tonight, she was sure.

There was a nobleman approaching, bright cloth glimpsed from the corner of her eye pushing her to the side and into a reflexive bow before she realized only someone of very high station would be wearing silk and bowed yet more deeply. When he halted, she wondered briefly at the event, but then he spoke, and a thin cool finger of dread slid down her spine.

It was one of the princes, for his robe was not merely lined but entirely silk, and unbleached besides. She did not dare to glance at his face, and his tone was slightly familiar. "And who is this lovely girl?"

There was no help for it, she had to answer. "Anh, Your Highness." Heat filled her cheeks—why on earth would such a person wish to speak to *her*?

There was nothing good in being noticed by Fifth Prince Garan Sensheo. The kaburei gossiped among themselves, of course, and they painted him as an exacting master who was not exactly careful where his sudo landed. His steward was a thin-mouthed creeping fellow who frequented the baths and had the habit of pinching some of the attendants, and his housekeeper, a round matron with a collection of iron hairpins, punished any infraction real or imagined. To be given to *his* household was almost as bad as being selected by that old dry stick Yona to serve in the First Queen's.

Almost.

"*Your Highness.*" He mimicked her address. "You know who I am, of course."

"Glorious Fifth Prince Garan Sensheo." That was the proper address, was it not? The new Emperor had not been acclaimed and the succession had not been reordered, but if she had erred...Her hands shook, cold and damp. All her humors were contracting into her liver, and she wasn't sure if the bravery stored there was enough to carry her through *this*.

"And she is intelligent, too. Tell me, lovely girl, whose kaburei are you?" It was a song currently popular among the bathing attendants, both in Zhaon-An and the Palace itself. He even lilted it; he was said to have a fine singing voice.

"Lady Komor Yala's, Glorious Fifth Prince." Anh longed to run away, but that was the worst possible move. Open disobedience was treason, and her lady was not here to ameliorate any penalties.

"Ah, the Khir girl." As if he did not know very well who Anh's lady was. "And are you serving her well? We would hate to have a Zhaon kaburei shame us before a guest."

Dull hatred bloomed deep under Anh's liver, and she did her best to bury it. Her face was set in hard mud, the accommodating smile of a peasant girl well used to indignity. "I serve well, Glorious Fifth Prince."

"Oh, please, simply *Fifth Prince* will do." An indulgent smile stretched his well-fed lips. "Where are you from, lovely girl?"

"A...a village," she hazarded, and her arms began to tremble too. He wanted her to betray Lady Yala in some fashion, and Anh would *die* before she did such a thing. Still, if she was not very careful, some omission on her part might perform the betrayal despite her.

"Well, of course." A thin thread of irritation crept into his jollity. "I didn't think you were born in the Palace."

What would Lady Yala say? "I was not blessed so, no." For a moment Anh was frightened of her own daring. But the Fifth Prince merely nodded, a movement glimpsed at the very edge of her vision, as if she had said something profound.

"And where is your lady today, lovely girl?"

So that is what he wants. Fortunately, Anh knew what to say. "Abed, Glorious Fifth Prince. Sick with grief."

"I did not think she and the Emperor were close."

No, for the Second Concubine. Anh realized the trap just in time, and kept her mouth shut. An indiscreet word here might raise gossip that Lady Komor mourned more for a concubine than for the Emperor. Instead, she kept her gaze fast upon the floor—solid wood, polished by set after set of hurrying feet. How many times had she been in this passageway, and she'd never looked down to see where her toes would land?

"Well." The prince tucked his hands in his sleeves, a tiny movement glimpsed in peripheral vision. "Convey my wishes for her complete recovery to your lady, little Anh. What a charming name. Would you like another syllable for it?"

I know my place. Anh shook her head, hurriedly. "I have not earned manumit, Glorious Fifth Prince."

"I'm not sure the Khir know about manumit. You'd best ask your lady. You could spend your entire life with leather on your braids."

That wouldn't be so bad. Not if it was in her lady's service. A kaburei took pride in a master or mistress of any quality, for it reflected well downstream. "Yes, Glorious Fifth Prince."

"If you change your mind, I could ask Lady Komor for you. She seems the tenderhearted sort."

If he made an offer for her...oh, surely Heaven would not allow such a thing to happen. Anh's mouth was dry. She folded even deeper into her bow. "An h-honor," she stuttered. "Great p-prince."

Perhaps he even took pity upon her. "Well, you'd best be about your business. If Lady Komor says yes, you might be manumit soon, lovely girl. Would you like that?"

I don't know. "I...I cannot tell, Glorious Fifth Prince." She wondered if she was dismissed enough to scuttle away. Her hands were sweating enough to fill a teacup. She had the idea, unwelcome indeed, that the Fifth Prince might maneuver Lady Komor into a position where Anh *had* to be given away, and then what would become of her?

"Think about it. I'm a very tenderhearted sort, too. Well, go on. I'll see you again."

Anh hurried away, her heart thumping and her liver uneasy in its seating.

She wished, suddenly and vengefully, that her lady was not *quite* so highly placed or well-regarded, for then today would be an ordinary day and this devouring fear would be a stranger to her. But that was a useless thought, and she had more than enough of the useful kind to crowd her head-meat and keep her moving.

Upon Our Consciences

The dovecote was warm and full of murmuring as well as the sour smell of birdshit; he was glad of the jatajatas keeping his feet clear of the sticky floor. At least the cages were constructed so none of the soft grey birds could splash his robes, so long as he took a modicum of care. "*All* of them?" Kurin tongue-clicked like a disapproving dowager and shook his head. "The North, East, and South gates?"

"There's no telling who slipped out." A faint edge of bitterness clung to Binei Jinwon's tone. He was taking the news of his sudden demotion from head of the clan very well, all things considered, but still bore watching. "Arrows and knifework. Someone knew what they were about."

Kurin rolled a scrap of silk tightly around the wooden sliver; he slid the last message into its case. Normally a cotewatcher would tie the straps to the birds' legs, but this was a delicate time in the Palace; the Golden watching this particular hutch were under the command of a fellow whose family was much beholden to Garan Kurin—especially the youngest sister. "Of course, news of Father's ascension to Heaven is useful to any number of parties."

"Yes, but why kill the barrier-guards?" His uncle lifted his ministerial robe slightly, like a lady crossing a bridge over a swollen stream. "What is the message?"

Was the man simply speaking to hear himself bleat? Kurin kept at his work; it required nimble fingers and a tranquil heart. Winged things could sense dismay or irritation, and it weighed them down. "Very simple: *We know*."

"Know what?"

"That is precisely what they hope we are wondering, Uncle." How was it, Kurin mused, that an elder, supposedly wiser, did not grasp what was stupidly, simply obvious? Head of the clan, indeed. It was a wonder the Yulehi were not extinct if this was the quality of their head-meat. He was grateful to his lord father for granting him a fraction of Garan, in that case. "Whether or not a message left, we are meant to wonder, and let the matter work upon our consciences."

"Assuming we have such appendages." Uncle twitched his mourning robe away from a cage. He and Mother were well matched, both querulous in their own way. "You are sending quite a few, nephew. Are you certain that is wise?"

Are you certain it is wise to yammer at me so? Kurin's temper was not frayed yet, but it could easily become so. "Yours is not the only matter I am attending to, Uncle."

"*My* matter?"

"Of course." Kurin longed to shove the fellow outside, perhaps with a clout to the ear, but such behavior was beneath him at the moment and inefficient besides. Binei Jinwon was still a useful tool, and one did not lay such aside until one was forced—or until one had another to hand. "You are Yulehi clan head, a nephew upon the throne is to your advantage, is it not?"

"Certainly." Uncle regarded him sourly. "And I shall be blamed if we are found out?"

"Of course not." *Only if it suits me.* Kurin tied the first few cylinders, neatly and thoroughly, a trick he could perform one-handed. Each fat grey bird submitted patiently, knowing its place in the great scheme of the Middle World. He suspected at least one of the directions now starred with dead men was a feint, but which one? Impossible to tell, events were moving quite quickly. He had only one of the Golden commanders, but that was enough if the ministers decided Kurin's was the wind to turn their sails to, like the great Anwei junks plying the eastern seas to far N'hon and even farther to the strange, wild coast of northern Ch'han.

"So much bother." Lord Yulehi's nose wrinkled. Of course, unlike the mews where the fierce hawks slumbered waiting for the hunt, this was no place for a nobleman. "You would think the commonborn spear-whelp would simply die, and save us the trouble."

"Careful, Uncle. That is my Eldest Brother." Yes, it would be quite amusing when he finally rid himself of this puffed-up festival bladder. He already had made certain preparations in that direction, but now was not the time. For one thing, he needed this fellow to help with his mother, who was in an excess of feeling—it could not be called *grief*, but the exact name for it escaped Kurin at the moment. "Common mother or not, we share a father, and that is all that matters. Cau Luong was very clear upon that point, was he not?"

At least the clan-head—more a painted screen set before the real power, as in stories of the Second Dynasty—had stopped flicking his robe about like a courtesan. "I have not your learning, Second Prince."

Nor any of my other fine qualities. Kurin rolled another scrap, inserted it into a cylinder. "Then you must trust that he was. In any case, there is more than one group needing some manner of direction at the moment, and I am here to provide." He finished tying the last of the tiny scrollcases, exhaling softly as his fingers threatened to cramp. His hurai was too thick for this work; when finished he slipped it back upon its finger with relief. "And I wish to know exactly where one or two people are, and whether they mean to come to Zhaon-An."

"Chief among them General Zakkar, I presume."

"Not chief," Kurin lied. Perhaps his uncle would even believe him. "But it would not hurt to know, and we have made arrangements for that, you and I. Shouldn't you be discussing duty and pleasure with that Geh fellow?" The second Golden commander would be a welcome addition to Kurin's camp, and where two of them went the third would follow.

Lord Yulehi shook his head. It was amazing, how a grown man could bridle like a girl told of marriage. "He is recalcitrant."

A girl, bridling—he wondered if Sabwone, his favorite, clutching, clawing little sister, was happy in her own new home. The palace was certainly less interesting without her, but she would be a decided irritant at this juncture. Poor thing, but women were meant for marrying, and Shan was now even more certain as an ally. "We might require his services later, uncle." Patience, Kurin told himself, was essential. He had worked too long and too subtly to risk a misstep now. "You are to overcome his recalcitrance."

"You sound like your mother." Perhaps his uncle meant it as an insult.

I doubt that very much. She would not be half so polite. "She is preparing for the funeral," Kurin murmured, and hoped it was true. Gamwone was weeping into any bolster she could find, and alternated between bewailing that she was now left alone and vengeful mutterings as if Father were still alive. He did not envy Gamnae the duty of staying at her side to ameliorate the worst excesses; he suspected his sister would be all but useless in that capacity anyway.

"You do not seem to be grieving, nephew."

Oh, the man was *definitely* feeling some injury to his pride. Which was unfortunate. Kurin halted, his gaze coming to rest completely upon Binei Jinwon. "Are you implying that I am guilty of something, or merely unfilial?"

"Neither," Lord Yulehi said hurriedly. "I was remarking, with admiration, upon your stoicism. It is a quality much admired in a king."

"But in an Emperor?" Kurin's smile was rather gentle, but it would have made his little sister—or even Sixth Prince Jin— frantically wish to be anywhere else. One of the birds mantled as if it thought itself a hawk, and something splattered upon the floor.

"What is an Emperor but a king of kings?" Now Lord Yulehi's forehead held a faint sheen of sweat, which was somewhat gratifying except for the fact that it could simply be from the stuffiness of the confined space. The drowsing birds reeked of feathers and ordure; it was almost impossible to believe such rancid beasts could fly.

"Indeed." Kurin decided he had done all he could at this particular juncture. It was time to let the small, stupid winged things do *their* duty. "Come, let us give freedom to these poor feathered peasants."

When they left the dovecote, Kurin found his robes were in quite good repair, unlike Lord Yulehi's. But the larger surprise was a gleam in the fleeing shadows of rising dawn, a hard dart of light from a gold hoop caught upon his younger brother's ear.

"Takshin." Kurin did *not* bow a greeting. In any case, he was the elder. The morning was sweet outside the cote's stink, and Takshin's scarred face largely unreadable. "You are up and about early."

"As are you." He did not wear mourning except for an armband, Garan Tamuron's third son, and his arms were crossed over his chest as he lingered in the shade under creeping starvine, its buds swelling fruitlike. When they bloomed it would be a wall of tiny white and purple flowers upon twisted, knotted, gnarled branches, a marriage of decoration and usefulness. "Send that puppet away, Kurin. We have much to discuss."

If it bothered Lord Yulehi to have another nephew speak of him so, it did not show upon his broad, sweating face. He bowed to Kurin, lingering a little at the bottom of the motion, and turned his shoulder in Takshin's direction. "I take my leave, my lord." He no doubt intended it to be a crushing insult, but Takshin's dark, level gaze did not alter in the least.

Kurin lifted the woven-osier lid, released the birds; the explosion of feathers coughing from the carry-cage was like dyed silk shaken in a weaver's courtyard. He also let the minster amble out of earshot, restraining the urge to roll his eyes at the older man's obvious ear-pricked lingering. "No wonder the clan fell to our father," he said finally, and was rewarded by a single glimmer of startled amusement dancing far back in Takshin's pupils.

"Don't let *her* hear you say as much." It seemed Taktak could not speak of their mother without loathing filling his tone. Unfilial—but understandable, Kurin thought.

Very understandable indeed. "Lecturing your elder, how utterly like you. Come, walk with me, and tell me what you want."

"I want something?" An eyebrow lifted, and Takshin turned the scarred side of his face for his brother's viewing, a movement so habitual he no doubt was unaware of performing it.

He had not moved to deny Kurin the release of his messengers, though he clearly knew very well what they might be carrying. Which was surprising, but Kurin knew better than to hope.

"You would not be posed so elegantly in the shade if you did not, my preening eyebird." Kurin also knew better than to think his prickly little brother had finally seen sense, but there were no Golden or other witnesses about. Of all the things he had expected today, this was not one, and that was faintly troubling as well as interesting.

Most interesting *indeed*. He made doubly sure his robe was free of any importunate stains, scraped a boot-toe against the wooden slats placed for such an operation, and continued in the most pleasant tone possible. "You will not be the only man approaching me today, Takshin, so let us be quick."

Uneasy Dreams

Midday came and went, and the furnace of Zhaon simmered. Even in the shade of a thick copse Yala was uneasy; the horse, however, barely flicked an ear. He seemed quite content to nap in the shade, occasionally pulling mouthfuls of rank, luxurious weeds. A nearby meadow-clearing held the ruins of a burned-out cottage, and perhaps it was that marker of ill-luck that kept Yala alert when she should have been resting as much as possible.

Just as the sun reached its summit the horse raised his almost-misshapen head, ears intent and his muzzle dripping with clear cool streamwater. The wind had veered, and brought with it the sound of hoofbeats. A party of at least eight, going at a steady pace, but she was far enough away that the horse would not utter a greeting to others of his kind.

She hoped they were not chasing her. Was this what a bandit felt upon hearing any footfall, hoof or human? The urge to rise, tighten the horse's saddle-girth, and strike for the road was overwhelming, but she put her forehead back upon her knees and breathed deeply, dispelling impatience. The long-ear that broke cover was the one the hawk stooped upon; she would have to be cannier than a puff-tailed, quivering bit of meat.

Were she in the Jonwa, she would be writing letters, waiting for Anh to bring lunch and a pot of strong tea. Then, perhaps sewing in the receiving room, if there were no polite calls to be made—and with Kanbina turned to smoke and dust, there was nobody who would invite her save perhaps Gamnae, who would be busy with other matters.

Of course Takshin might scratch at the lintel and make some manner of cutting remark about laziness or scribbling women, or deliver an edged compliment about the pretty picture she made sewing with Su Junha or Hansei Liyue. Or, were she wandering in the garden with a sunbell, she would feel a gaze upon her and raise her chin to find the Third Prince somewhere in the vicinity, carefully not studying her in return.

She could still feel his lips upon her forehead, and smell him—a tang of leather, hot sharp metal, and he favored twigs of highly fragrant unjuo in his bath, apparently. The curve of her lower back still burned where his fingers had pressed, pushing her against his chest.

She thought of the relief, when she had turned away from a metal-sheathed post, to find he had stepped between her and the whip-strike. And how he had laid her *yue* in her palms afterward.

If she had not already promised Zakkar Kai…

Enough. She should think of something useful. Something *safe*, and that word could not describe Third Prince Garan Takshin in even the most fevered of imaginings.

Would Takyeo really become Emperor? It seemed impossible, though he was next in succession. Yala's head hurt, a swift lancing pain as the horse returned to grazing.

Perhaps it was merely the successive shocks of the past few days that made her liver shift so within her and her thoughts take such unaccustomed turns. She did not want to find herself honorless, but the uninterrupted exercising of head-meat she had been eager for was transforming her into a wandering cloudfur, its head full of strange startlements and ruminating stupidity.

Twice more that day she heard commotion upon the road, but she was far enough away and had no fire, safely cradled in shade. There would be much coming and going whether they were searching for her or not. And who would look for *her*? She was a pebble, not even trapped in a shoe.

Finally, when the heat was worst, she fell asleep at the foot of another spreading lyong tree, and her uneasy dreams were full of rustle and the thunder of pursuing hooves.

Understand
Each Other

I must confess, I am somewhat surprised." Kurin tucked his hands into his sleeves, halting to enjoy a dry-garden vista full of thorny succulents and riverine stones. "I thought you firmly convinced of Takyeo's ability."

"Ability is not the question." Takshin took a firmer hold upon his temper. No doubt the Second Prince had been sending busy little messages to other conspirators, perhaps even those who would wish to hunt a lone rider on a large, ugly grey horse. He could only hope the Tooth's ill temper and Yala's quick wits would keep them both a shade at the edge of vision, gone when a man glanced again. "It is simply that he would hesitate to have *your* head struck off for treason."

"While I labor under no such constraints." At least Kurin looked amused, and halfway complimented. He was already in pale mourning, too, and though he had been in the cote for some while no effluvia daubed his hem. He had ever been lucky. "It seems I spoke better than I knew. What do you want, Taktak my younger brother? What is your price?"

There was no help for it, so Takshin set his jaw and braced his stirrups. "A marriage endorsement." In Shan, the reins would be held in a man's teeth as he galloped for the enemy, an operation he had never seen fit to employ. A horse should know what to do by knee-pressure alone, and he valued his ivories as much as an old man missing half of them might. "Leave it blank, and send it to me."

"Ah." Kurin's smile widened. The morning heat was collecting in corners, and the dust was already thick. "Who is the lucky lady? One of the court wenches, perhaps?"

Did Yala have enough water? Was the horse fit, or had he been lamed? So much could go wrong. "Mock me, and I shall withdraw my offer. You'd be a fool to."

"What exactly are you offering?" Kurin's lazy tone warred with the gleam in his gaze, sharp interest like a merchant turning a bright bauble this way and that, wondering at its worth.

"The same thing I offered Takyeo." It was a lie, of course. He would disdain to bargain with his eldest brother; he served there precisely because he wished to.

Because it pleased him, where so little else did.

"And what is that? A surly, stomping sneer every now and again?" Kurin's expression suggested he knew very well what his brother was offering, but wished to hear him say it.

So Takshin swallowed the bitterness and did what he must, gazing across the dry-garden's clipped, trained wilderness. "A blade you do not have to worry is turned against you." Hot air glimmered above the stones, an illusion several sages held was water trapped and trembling at the edge of becoming steam.

"What stops you from sinking the blade into my back now, dear brother?"

What, indeed. The consideration that striking Kurin down now would rob Takyeo of some legitimacy, since nobody would believe he had not ordered the death, obviously did not cross his brother's mind.

Besides, if Takshin did so and Ah-Yeo succumbed, the throne would fall to Makar, who was a far more dangerous adversary. Takshin knew Kurin's desires but was uncertain of Makar's, and there was little time to plumb the latter.

"Shan." He had to give Kurin an answer he would believe. "Or more precisely, I am little threat if handled correctly. I was adopted; I may no longer succeed Zhaon's throne. And whoever sits upon that overdecorated bench will find me very useful indeed."

Kurin was half convinced, but the bait needed more sweetening. "And my surety is...?"

"You are a merchant, to be needing one?" The insult was calculated to keep the conversation upon its channel, and away from Yala. If Kurin suspected exactly where his little brother would spend the marriage endorsement, half Takshin's advantage was already lost.

It was always best to hide what one could, and as long as she was not named directly during this conversation he could consider her unthreatened by his elder brother. Should that change, legitimacy could be damned and he might strike a few more heads from their shoulders too, just to be certain. Oh, Takyeo would dislike it later, if Heaven somehow looked down and decided for once to perform as it ought. He could always take Yala to Shan; Kiron would enjoy her and Sabwone would only need one short, sharp lesson before she left anything of Takshin's strictly alone.

"Now who is mocking?" The Second Prince—or perhaps Crown Prince when the succession was formally ordered, if Takyeo continued to draw breath that long—rubbed at his chin, his hurai glinting as Takshin's own. "It's a reasonable question, Taktak."

"Well, Rinrin, you have nothing but my word. That should be enough." The sun was above the bulk of the Iejo's back, this garden clinging like a perfume ball to a courtesan's belt. He had other matters to attend to, no doubt Kurin did as well, and for a moment Takshin envied the thorn-spiked plants whose only duty was to grow where they were placed.

On the other hand, they were at the mercy of a gardener's shovel, while Takshin was sharp enough to cut the hand seeking to uproot him.

"A flimsy assurance." All things considered, Kurin was far more intrigued than his little brother thought he would be, which spoke to any number of things, not least the fact that his mother's eldest son was playing catch-the-kite like the rest of them.

Which hinted perhaps he had not been responsible for the attack in the Artisan's Home, narrowing the suspects indeed. Takshin set that particular thought aside for later brooding. "Have I ever failed in a promise before?"

"You flung an arrowhead upon a table and promised to hold Mother accountable for any attack upon Ah-Yeo." Kurin settled his hands inside his sleeves despite the heat, and Takshin was almost, *almost* certain he had accomplished his aim.

"And who says I do not?" He simply had not yet had time to bring their mother to account for this latest attempt, which might be laid at her partition after all if Kurin was truly innocent. No doubt the First Queen of Zhaon thought she would escape her younger son's wrath, but if Shan had taught him anything, it was how to wait. "Do you wish me to retract that promise?" It would curdle, but...

It would be worth it. *I owe you a debt, for this.*

"Oh, certainly not." Kurin's smile broadened, rather like a feline who had studied enough birdcage locks to be satisfied he could attempt breaking one. "Not at *all*, my beloved younger brother. Very well. Go away, I must think this over. Should I decide to engage your particular...skills, you shall receive a letter from me bearing the endorsement."

"Well enough." Takshin turned away, paused. His fingertips ached to touch the gold hoop in his ear as an exorcist might tap at a good-luck charm, but that would be a banner raised upon a hill for any enemy to see. "I do not need to warn you to be discreet."

Kurin's laugh was full of genuine goodwill. "Oh, certainly not. We understand each other, little brother."

At least, I understand you. If Kurin was indeed blind to Takshin's affections, so much the better, but he did not think it likely.

It was not treason, he told himself. He saw Death crouching upon his eldest brother's face, but while Takyeo lived, Takshin would protect him. There were, however, others to protect as well.

Perhaps he should even visit a temple and beg a god or two—or even the Awakened—for some mercy, like a peasant belly-crawling for patronage.

It did not matter. He would lower himself to whatever was required to keep Komor Yala safe—and to keep her close, he would do much more.

Long-Ear,
Flushed

Waking alone was just as disorienting as riding until dawn, but perhaps Khir's horse-goddess had visited while she slept, for as soon as Yala opened her eyes she knew what the cobheaded grey's name was. It had a certain fittingness. "*Gunzheu,*" she murmured in Khir, with the particular ending-inflection that meant a proper name instead of *any* archer, and the horse flicked an ear in her direction, opening one mild, doze-heavy eye. "It suits you, my fourfoot cousin."

The horse regarded her with amused insouciance, rather like his owner. Yala uncurled, stretching, and winced several times. At least there had been no downpour, the stifling clouds were but a pall in the distance.

In short order she had shared a bit of dried fruit with her fourfoot friend and was in the saddle again. He was more than willing, and as a hot, dry dusk fell, Yala felt somewhat sanguine about her task.

Unfortunately, as she cantered through an ungated village shortly after midnight someone must have seen her, for a huntinghorn sounded high and trembling upon the night wind, and the sound of gongs burst the night's taut dark drum-head. She could not afford to think it some other alarum, unconnected to her presence.

The long-ear is flushed, she thought grimly. *Now let us see how well the hunters ride.* She chirruped to Archer, and her knees tightened. He was responsive as a fine brush, veering off the road into the screen of ragged bushes, and she spread Mrong Banh's map before her internal eye again.

There was a distressing amount of distance between her and the character representing Kai. She would have to cut a sapling soon, sawing with her *yue* to gain a thin, flexible rod.

Just in case.

Teeth clenched, jaw aching, Komor Yala bent over Archer's neck and urged the horse on, testing his responses. He obeyed with good grace, and she hoped he was as amenable as his master could sometimes be.

Corrections and Chastisement

Her eyes stung, and so did her nose. For once, she was not buried in a round, stifling, swathed room. Instead, the First Queen of Zhaon had settled upon a square cushion, her plump elbow in unbleached silk upon the polished wood of a low table, and gazed over a lacquered, ankle-high balustrade at one of the Kaeje's many gem-bright gardens. A square teapot of Uewo make steamed, its thin, expensive walls seeming barely strong enough to contain the liquid within. Two cups of the same make stood ready, but the guest was late and Gamwone stared at fluttering jewelwings as well as the zipping jumjeos with their heavy carapaces held aloft by blurring transparencies.

All was in readiness. She did not shift, staring at the green and the bright flowers. At least she was not cold; summer haze vibrated over the rustling babu. A water-clock *thik-thock*ed in the near distance, standing sentinel over a clear pond; crimson and blue petals scattered upon a hot wind. The rains had moved to the evening hours, but the garden still steamed.

She had wept all she thought necessary, and nobody cared enough to listen to her raging. Now, she was laying plans. Gamnae was in her rooms, no doubt weeping for her father—she was useless, and young, but still a valuable piece for a mother whose own son was behaving terribly.

Even though Kurin had chastised Binei Jinwon. That fat curl-tail, *daring* to speak to her so—she still felt his cheek stinging her palm, and how satisfying had that been?

Very. As satisfying as seeing her coming guest bow and scrape would be. Garan Gamwone was a force to be reckoned with, and though Kurin was headstrong, she was still his mother. The mother of the next Emperor, if all went well.

It *had* to go well. She would not accept any other outcome.

Finally, there were hurrying footsteps in the hall behind the papered partition. She turned her head a fraction, knowing she would be seen in the proper attitude of grieving, poetic contemplation when the servants and guest entered. It was necessary to give the right impression, and she wondered who would cling to her guest's skirts today. Bringing out another cup or two was a way to drive home that she was a powerful patroness, and a generous one if her few strictures were followed.

Or if you were useful enough. Especially while so much else was...uncertain.

Her fingertips wandered over the small ceramic bottle in her left sleeve, its round belly crossed with warning zigzags. Yona had procured it, as she did so much else; it was Yona who had brought the news that Tian Ha, erstwhile prime physician to the First Queen of Zhaon and consequently much consulted about the court for small ailments or large, had finally expired.

Consequently when the partition slid along its groove, she wore a very slight smile, which she hurried to replace. But the expected guest did not appear; instead, Yona, in unbleached cotton that turned her sallow, her mouth a tight thin line and her cheeks somewhat paler than usual, bowed deeply before half-rising, crossing the threshold heel-to-thigh in the peculiar manner of a teahouse server bringing a bill to a patron too illustrious to be faced afoot.

"Lady Gonwa is late," Gamwone murmured, returning her attention to the garden's smear. Under the green and the carefully snip-arranged branches, there was soil teeming with worms, maggots, and other wriggling things.

"Glorious First Queen of Zhaon." Yona settled herself just inside the now firmly closed partition, arranged her hands correctly, and bowed again, far more deeply. "Lady Gonwa sends her regrets. Her niece is ill, and she...she cannot attend...there is a gift, of course, but..."

Oh yes, there would be a *gift*. Gamwone stared at the garden, its beauty reduced to a green blur with vermilion and blue dots. Down among the roots the nasty things crept, and to be a queen was to crush them under a decorated jatajata's wooden slats. A noble daughter married to a warlord learned to fight with what weapons she had.

So the court ladies, like the idiot creatures they were, were waiting to see which quarter the wind would finally hail from. "The niece," she said, softly. "Eulin. A big, provincial girl. Sent to that *horsefucker* princess, to bow and scrape." Gamwone examined her nails, the smallest on each hand protected by a filigree sheath. And to think she had arranged herself out here, knowing Lady Gonwa's liking of tea taken upon a garden porch. "Yes?"

"Yes, that one." Yona did not repeat Gamwone's vulgarity, having no shield of nobility to render it piquant instead of ill-bred. "But she is not in the Jonwa; Lady Gonwa brought her back to the city estate after the foreign princess was...well."

After she was murdered. Oh, they would probably lay that one at Gamwone's door, too. They blamed her for everything, when they were not scrambling to insult.

The fact that she *had* contracted an impresario to bring one or two petty annoyances to bear upon the Emperor's firstborn brat from his dead spear-wife had nothing to do with it. In the first place, it was to be expected since one who could not avoid an assassin was not a noble; in the second, after all, the tradesman of the Shadowed Path had not succeeded.

Perhaps she should have availed herself of more. A hundred of them, and sooner. Maybe someone else would finish him off while he lay in the palace that should have been her own son's, and afterward it might rankle that hers was not the hand sending the spear-born brat into his pyre.

"Oh, don't cower there," she said, sharply. "Come closer, Yona."

The chief lady-servant did, upon her knees—the traditional way of approaching an angry superior. It irritated Gamwone even more—she had arranged herself prettily in order to convey a great favor upon the chief of court ladies, been rudely snubbed even though she was in deep mourning for her husband, and now Yona was acting like her mistress was going to call for the sudo.

Though there were many of the articles hanging in the tiny closet Gamwone had set aside for corrections and chastisement. It appeared they all needed reminding of just who she was.

"Your Gracious Highness." The honorific address for Zhaon's First Queen—first among equals, the saying went, but what a lie—had at one time soothed the lady so addressed. Now it irritated her, hearing Yona laboriously pronounce the syllables without the burring of her provincial accent.

"Come, come." She waved a plump, beringed hand, smooth silver-edged greenstone clasping her left first finger, a heavy creamy band on her third right. Lady Gonwa's guest-gift, in a pretty silk-wrapped box with its bright orange cotton bow, was to hand in a sewing basket near Gamwone's side. "Perhaps I should give this to *you*. Certainly you're better company."

"Your Majesty honors her handmaiden." But Yona did not move farther forward. On another day her caution would have pleased Gamwone as being a proper due.

Now it was a reminder that she was utterly isolated. The summit was a lonesome place, especially with everyone below you shaking the ladder, and even the thought of her lord husband in his tomb after dying like a creature caught in a thick black pool of pitch could not fend off the dreadful uncertainty.

"Closer, Yona." Her tone brooked no disobedience, and her fingertips drifted across the warning zigzags in her sleeve-pocket again. She had meant to deal with this small matter after tea, feeling the flush of victory—she had, after all, outlived Garan Tamuron and was the mother of his only *real* heir—but now was as good a time as any. "There. Now, pour me a cup of tea."

Yona did as she was bid, her sleeve trembling slightly.

"Listen, my servant." There were ways to make that collection of syllables sound fond, and Gamwone used one now, half-lisping the sibilants. "We must look after each other, two women alone in a great house, must we not?"

"Yes, Your Majesty." Yona's profile held an echo of the girl she had been, before her mouth turned thread-thin while guiding the crops of house-servants grown younger and younger in order to make them more tractable, reliable, *safe*. Their freshness, however transitory, showed her age. "I am your faithful servant."

"Good. Now, do you remember that bath-girl my late husband…" Gamwone paused, not just from the shame of it—a *bath-girl*, all very well for a moment's dalliance, but the selfish man had to express a *partiality*—but also from the sure instinct that it was best not to state what she wished too clearly, even now.

Besides, a good servant should anticipate without overstepping, and if Yona needed a lesson, Gamwone would provide it *after* this matter was cleared up.

"Dho Anha," Yona murmured, because of course a great lady like the First Queen should not have to remember such a trifling detail. "Still at the baths, Your Majesty. Grieving, no doubt, as are we all."

And no doubt wanting to replace one royal customer with another. Kurin had been seen in her company more than once lately, and it had pleased her before the game had changed. Now it was time for severity. They were wily, clutching beasts, those bath-girls, and Gamwone must keep her son safe, must she not? No matter how headstrong he—temporarily—proved to be.

"No doubt," she agreed, dryly, and slipped the vial from her sleeve-pocket. She set it upon the table, just at the very edge, where Yona could not help but see. "Do they all eat together, those lice?" The derogatory term for those who scrubbed others' flesh was old and not quite noble, but again, Gamwone's position was so high, she might as well call things what they truly were.

Had not the King of Heaven created much of Zhaon itself by using every item's proper name?

"I do not know," Yona said, quietly, almost as if she feared an explosion. "But perhaps...some wine? Or some sweets in a pretty box..."

"Too easily traced." Gamwone made a short, irritable motion. Yona's hand obediently leapt out, arrested itself halfway to the vial, and she glanced at her queen, hurriedly lowering her dark, somewhat bloodshot eyes. "Find another method."

"But, my queen..." Yona fell silent as Gamwone turned her head slightly, eyeing her servant, whose hand still hovered in midair.

"Well?"

"The physician...the Emperor...and there is already much gossip..." Yona had gone chalky, her lips a most unbecoming shade.

"The *Emperor*? They are laying even that upon my steps." It should not have surprised her; Gamwone tapped the long, resin-laden second fingernail of her right hand against her lips. "I do not care for gossip, chief servant. You will find a way."

"Yes, my queen." Yona's fingers flickered and the vial vanished. She dropped her chin, staring at the table, and Gamwone picked up her teacup. The liquid steamed gently; she had always liked the sweeter teas. "Shall I have lunch brought to you, or...?"

"Yes, but not here. In the crushflower-papered room, and there must be sweetbroth for Gamnae. We must keep up her strength during this—"

"She is visiting the Second Queen, Your Majesty." Yona's throat must have had something lodged in it, or perhaps she feared Gamwone's response to the news. "Our lord the Second Prince sent her there this morning, after breakfast. To offer comfort."

Oh, that brat. But Gamwone smiled; she could afford to be generous now. Tian Ha was gone, Garan Tamuron was gone, soon Garan Takyeo would be gone, and the bath-girl too.

She wondered, idly, why she had not bestirred herself like this before. It was too ridiculous, her fearing discovery for so long; after all, Tamuron had done nothing and now he could do nothing to her ever again, especially if she engaged an exorcist or two to keep her house steps well-cleansed. She would do that, once the excitement died a little and Kurin, her beloved Kurin, was safely upon the throne. He would come to appreciate her a little more once he had warmed that seat some while.

And meanwhile, the spear-wife's brat would succumb. He was no *proper* Emperor, leg-crushed and abed.

"Oh, very well," she said, magnanimous. "I shall enjoy my tea alone, then there will be lunch."

"Yes, my queen." Yona bowed again, deeply, and heel-thigh retreated from the presence of her superior. The vial had vanished into her own sleeve, and thinking further upon the matter was not necessary now that it was all arranged.

The partition slid shut, and Gamwone gazed upon the garden. They were held to be healthful, but she preferred embroidered flowers. Those carried no dirt.

Those who ruled had to accept a certain amount of filth. It was duty, and she had ever borne hers, had she not?

She sipped her tea, listening to the muffled scurrying in the hall. Yes, despite Kurin's little rebellions and the Gonwa bitch's attempt to insult her, Garan Yulehi-a Gamwone was now feeling very calm indeed.

Bring Our
Messenger Home

Wearing unto a bloody sunset, the day passed as any other except for late or missing dispatches, which normally arrived regularly as a heartbeat. Kai was not overly worried; sometimes a rider met misadventure, and a stack of correspondence waited for him anyway. The reorganization of the Northern Army was not quite a delicate task, but it was a time-consuming one, and he had to drive himself twice as hard as the lowest soldier.

A general always did.

Thankfully, the attempt upon him had not been met with indifference or worse, suppressed glee. Instead, his soldiers had clamored for the offenders to be given to them in the old fashion; those who resented not being able to vent their fury contented themselves with spitting upon the corpses—or performing other, less polite acts.

There were condolences to sort—carefully brushed from Jin, proper and scholarly but with an unsteadiness to their characters that spoke of true feeling from Makar, from Takyeo with a postscript that Kai was much missed, and even Takshin had taken time to brush one. Kai read them, setting aside the ones from court ladies, ministers, or those who were likely to be only formulaic. Every one would have to be answered by himself or Anlon, and small gifts sent to thank the writers for their kindness.

Two letters from Gamnae, of all people, another from Takshin—why would he bestir himself so?—and three from Yala. Did she miss him so much? A warmth quite separate from the day's sweat and dust poured through him, and he almost forgot how his skin was crawling with the need of a bath. Breaking the seal on the first of Yala's three letters was a pleasure, sharp anticipation filling his belly.

It was a pleasant enough missive, except for a postscript asking what incense his late mother liked, so it could be taken to her tomb. There was some message he could not decipher hiding between Yala's lines, and he wondered if Kanbina's passing had been... tranquil.

Kai settled a little more heavily upon his chair, staring at a lady's exquisite brushwork but seeing a thin face instead, with large dark lustrous eyes and pain-hollowed cheeks. The toxin hidden in some food or drink years ago had damaged internal organs; it was a wonder she had clung to life so long, a late, fragile jewelwing upon a frost-etched autumn leaf.

Well, Kanbina was safely beyond the reach of any misfortune now.

He reached for Takshin's letter, despite Yala's unopened missives temptingly close. He would have to ration their sweetness.

Takshin's hand was fine, though his characters somewhat spare. Kai read with mounting alarm, his teeth aching as they sought to grind, chewing at impatience—a bitter dish, and one he hated. The most common character for ill news was tall like the pierced spire of a Shan temple, but to Kai, its lower half had always looked like a lump in the throat. Like the one which bobbed when a man spoke, a strange insurance against lies—not very effective—or choking, which might have been mildly comforting if one could be certain of just how it worked.

Of course Takshin would be the one to send, quietly and plainly, an account of Kanbina's last words. It had arrived later because he had arranged for it to be privately carried, as he explained in the last few lines, and Taktak did not wish his friend and brother unaware.

A thorny mercy, like any from that quarter.

"My lord?" Anlon hesitated at the door, and afterward cold sweat would drench Kai, because he almost waved a hand and told the man *not now*.

The habit of conscientiousness was worn too deeply, but he was not particularly gracious. "What?" he barked, and his steward did not quite quail.

But it was probably close. "There is a rider," Anlon said. The bandage was hidden under his tunic and half-armor; his wound was well on its way to healing. "Waving a yellow standard with the characters for *snow-pard* painted upon it, and being chased."

For a moment Kai was not certain he had heard correctly; then he sprang from his chair. "My boots," he said, briskly, "and the long-eye. Archers to the wall, and mounted archers ready to bring our messenger home."

What else, under Heaven, had happened while he was away? He should have refused to leave the capital—but how could he? Tamuron was not merely his Emperor but also his friend, and he had trusted the man through worse than this.

It was not until he reached the keep's high, ancient wall and trained the tube of the long-eye upon faraway figures dancing through a wavering curtain of summer heat reflecting the last gleams of a long and unsatisfying day that he realized just how ill the news was likely to be.

A slight figure, wrapped in muffling cloth upon what was indis-putably a war-trained grey meant for princes and the Golden, clung to the saddle with sweet natural grace as at least half a dozen other figures urged their own horses—a motley group, two bays, sev-eral indeterminate lathered cobs, and one fine deep-chested black mare—like hounds after a fulvous brushtail. The standard was a message-flag from Takyeo's time at his father's side fighting Khir before Three Rivers, a particular victory in the snows of a moun-tain pass.

And as Kai watched, it was almost torn from the lone rider's hands as one of the pursuers urged their beast closer.

The silk tore and the standard fluttered, a jewelwing's graceful death trampled under shod hooves. The lone rider still retained the stave and dropped the reins, rising with that fine, natural grace. Even though the grey pounded and careened underneath, the rider was steady, small adjustments of one born into the saddle keeping him upright. He leaned slightly and the flexible sapling whipped; the pursuer who had ripped the silk free tumbled from his own saddle and Kai's mouth was sour.

The spear of ice in Kai's guts knew before he did. There was only one slim, short being under Heaven's great arching halls he had ever seen ride like that, bending supple as a hau tree's flexible branches. A blurring bolt—they had horsebows, the beastfucking bastards—flickered past.

It cannot be.

But it was. His eyes were not deceived, nor was his liver, though it turned cold too and settled crossways inside him.

"My horse." Zakkar Kai handed the long-eye to his second adjutant, the somewhat dour Gua Yuen, and strode for the stairs. "My *horse, now!*" The repeat was a bellow, and he began to run, his boot-heels all but striking sparks from old stone eroded by the elements and the repeated passage of mail-shod feet. "Now, or I will have every last one of you whipped! Open the gate! *Move!*"

SMALL BUT
DEFINITE

To be a physician was always to fight a losing battle; Kihon Jiao's teachers had been extremely clear upon that point. The body, both physical and subtle, was not imperishable though the shade might survive for a long while if one's descendants were properly filial. The Awakened One spoke of a state beyond life or death, but that was not a physician's matter.

Yet sometimes Kihon Jiao hoped it was indeed true, and that certain of his clients—by no means all of them—would achieve such a status. To attend the body's many imbalances and improprieties uncovered a great deal most would like to keep hidden, from cowardice to infidelity, and it was best to be an impartial observer.

Or so Jiao had always thought until this moment, as he palpated the wound with gentle fingertips and tried not to notice his royal patient's sudden loss of color and great clear drops of forehead-sweat.

"You do not have to say," Jiao said, flatly. This Jonwa bedroom had become familiar, its spare luxury speaking volumes about the palace's most high-ranking occupant but now cluttered with the tools and impedimenta of the medical trade. "I can see it hurts."

"Quite a lot, too." Garan Takyeo was braver than his father, that much was certain, and that was very brave indeed. The wound did not *look* like much, but now it was clear it *had* breached a gut-channel. Rot was settling itself in the vitals, where food was turned into shit.

And that, no matter how Kihon Jiao worked, was almost certain death.

"Most men would scream, were I to touch them so." Jiao tried an encouraging smile, but it felt unnatural upon his frozen face. The consciousness of impending failure packed his throat with dry cotton. "My lord…"

"You do not need to say, either." Takyeo's eyes half-lidded, their pupils large with nightflower's screen keeping the worst of the agony at bay. "I can feel it crawling through me. When it reaches my liver—"

"I may reopen the wound." Jiao considered the body before him, seeking to lay aside everything as transitory as *feeling* and see the problem logically. "Express the foul matter, and perhaps sew the tear. There is nightflower laced with omyei to keep you from feeling the event, and cinnabar to flush the wound."

"Strong medicine." Takyeo exhaled softly. "Do as you please, physician. I shall endure it."

"You sound like your father." Jiao realized it was an inadvisable thing to say, but hoped his audible admiration would outweigh such impertinence. At least this patient did not seem of the stripe to order an only halfway insolent physician flogged, even after health was miraculously re-achieved.

"A fine…" Takyeo paled even more and coughed, his belly rippling. The sound was broken in half by a swallowed moan of pain, and there was a scratch at the door. "A fine compliment, Honorable Kihon. Thank you."

"Don't feed his liver so, it will explode." The Shan-black leanness of Garan Takshin stepped catfoot into the room and glanced mildly at Kihon Jiao. "And what are you about, physician?"

"I am at my work, Third Prince." *Perhaps you should be about yours, whatever that is.* Jiao took his fingers away and twitched his patient's bed-shirt back into place over the muscled abdomen. It was a criminal thing, to mar a man so finely made.

"Takshin." The Crown Prince—Emperor now, though he had not yet been carried to the throne room—smiled, and it hurt to see the effort he expended to cover evidence of agony. "How goes it?"

"Oh, Kurin thinks he owns me now." The Third Prince did not glance at Jiao, who retreated to the table to tug thin, fine kidskin gloves upon his hands and mix the cinnabar paste. If he could express the foulness from the wound, sew whatever channel had been cut, and replace it with the astringency...risky, very risky, but it could work.

At least his patient was willing to try. Jiao could do no less, though failure might cost him his own head. He might almost welcome it, seeing a patient so manifestly meritorious slip away.

"He should know better." Takyeo suppressed a cough, and paled even further at the resultant wave of pain. His pupils ate his irises, and the sick-smell in the room was almost as thick as the reek of herb, paste, tincture, and unguent. "You are not to be *owned*, Taktak."

"Oh, not by him, at least." The Third Prince's grin was just the same as ever, a pained baring of teeth holding little true amusement but a great deal of that quality the Khir called *hunrao* and the Zhaon termed *oxhoof*, the refusal to retreat though the battle was lost. His gaze had settled on Jiao, who bore it patiently as he measured and ground. "What is our plan now?"

Amazingly, the new Emperor attempted a laugh. "Honorable Kihon will clean me out, stitch some innards, pack the wound with cinnabar and other similarly strong things, and sew my outside like a festival bladder. I shall be a medicinal pillow before long."

"I shall put you in a theater-flower's bed." Takshin's gaze did not alter either, but Jiao's hands were steady. He had been watched by far harsher critics. "And what chance has this of working, physician?"

As much as anything else, at this point. He wished, not for the first time, that he could use a comforting lie. Unfortunately, this particular patient did not wish for such softness, and Jiao had always disdained to engage in such frippery. Skill and truth should speak for itself, though the man who used both was often passed over for those of lesser merit. "A small one. Small," he amended, "but definite."

His own arrogance was a burden no less than his patients' pain.

"And—I must ask, Ah-Yeo—you are determined upon this treatment?" The Third Prince addressed the new Emperor, whose smile was just as strained as Jiao's felt.

"Completely, Taktak. Before I consign myself to it, though, I wish for you to bring me paper, an inkstone, and a brush." The patient did not shift upon the bed, but his attention turned elsewhere, a general marshaling dispositions. "There are a few matters I must settle."

"Ah, I visit as a brother and am turned into a kaburei, running to fetch." The scarred man rolled his eyes as a young boy might, and Takyeo's laugh was for once unforced, even if the pain strangled the sound halfway through.

A flicker of something dark and wounded crossed the Third Prince's face, a transitory flash like flame-flowers. Jiao finally dropped his gaze to the cinnabar paste, careful to keep his own bare wrists free of any stray droplet. Cinnabar was hungry; it ate certain diseases whole. The trouble lay in calculating the dosage so its appetite did not consume the patient as well.

The Third Prince knew his eldest brother was likely to die, and it pained him. All at once Jiao's own feelings about the scarred man were different too. You saw what they were made of, these fragile creatures upon whom the whole of Zhaon depended for good or for ill. Excellence and nobility aside, they were merely men, just like peasants and kaburei. Some good, some bad, most indifferent—but these two, Kihon Jiao thought, were worth serving as far as his skill would allow. Like Zakkar Kai, whose concern for a man of much lower rank and willingness to trust Jiao's shabbiness had led the physician to the very heart of the settled world.

The Third Prince strode to the door, calling for paper, inkstone, and brush; Takyeo's gaze met Kihon Jiao's. The truth was there, graven with suffering-lines upon the new linchpin of Zhaon.

So. He knew he was about to die, too. And yet he faced it a great deal more calmly than many Jiao had witnessed.

The physician bent to his work again. It was no use to set oneself against an accomplished thing. Yet his patient was not dead *yet*, and while he ran the course, the physician could not do otherwise.

YALA'S RIDE

Dry indigo scarves filled the westron horizon, muffling the falling disk of a setting sun. Under other circumstances, it would have felt more like playing kaibok and less like impersonating a long-ear chased by hounds. Perhaps she might even have enjoyed the ride, but Komor Yala was far too busy to feel anything other than high fierce exhilaration fueled by complete terror.

Archer, understanding they were pursued and that his rider did not wish to be, longed to run flat-out. Yet she held him just a touch under that supreme effort, her weight telling him what she wished. At least he was willing, perhaps thinking it a grand game with new friends. Yala bent away from a cavalry hookblade seeking her midsection as another bolt hummed past. She swung the sapling she had sawn through with her *yue* early that morn after a long night spent riding dodge-a-kite with the men after her now, felt its long springiness whip across a man's face. They were wolves and she a stag, fleet but tiring and armed only with her *yue*—useless at a gallop unless she wished to open her own throat to save herself from dishonor—and the whipping staff with pale yellow silk-knots still clasped to its frayed length.

It was marvelously flexible, though, and it probably stung when she slashed at another fellow grown too importunate, reaching as if he thought he could drag at Archer's reins. The horse tensed under her, but Yala's knees and calves clamped since she stood in the

stirrups as if she was about to draw and loose at a long-ear in swaying grass; Archer merely laid his ears even more flat and turned a
fraction as she wished him to.

"*Hai-yohai!*" she yelled, the traditional cry of a hunter whose
hawk had not gone awry, and struck again with the long whiplike
sapling, transferring it to her left hand and dispelling the urge to
cower against Archer's neck. She was a bigger target for the bowman, of course, but the keep was so close—she recognized it as the
sun sank in a lake of blood to the west, shadows bringing every
edge into sharp relief. At least she had not missed the town or the
great bridge, though she had lost much time that entire weary day
by avoiding these men.

Another bolt whickered past. She had driven off the two closest; a distant horn sounded. She hoped it was the keep, and hoped
further that they had seen the standard before it was torn from the
sapling. Had she time or supplies to properly sew, it would not have
dared slip loose.

Archer bunched and lifted, sailing over a planting-ditch. Great
clods of black Zhaon earth spattered, flung by shod hooves, and
there was the ravine she was to follow to the keep had she not been
under siege herself. The decision was instant—she aimed for the
broken ground on its eastron side and Archer shot forward, his gait
changing to a strange floating gallop. He could not make such an
effort for long, and the scree on the slope might cause him to turn
a hoof.

Then I will have to take a horse from one of them. She dropped
again into the saddle, the sapling held back and ready in her
left hand. There was no time for prayer or beseeching, her head
filled with the strange running thunder of the best kaibok games
played with Komori Baiyan in her youth, all her skill and strength
stretched to the limit as their lathered horses pressed neck to neck.

Archer slowed the merest touch and took the slope with the
surefoot grace of the cloudfur's mountain cousins, those shag-
coated beasts with curving horns and hooves that looked too delicate to bear them up sheer cliffs. A rattle, another whining bolt

chip-splintering off a boulder, and they gained the top of the rise just as more horns sounded, *definitely* from the far-off keep with its red Zhaon flag fluttering from the tallest spire.

They have seen us. Or they have seen something.

Again she held Archer back; that queer floating pace was new, and she did not wish him to call upon his last reserves just yet. This horse was worth far more than any Zhaon probably suspected; intelligent and amenable, he would want for nothing in the North. He would be cosseted, run at the hunt to keep him sharp, and bred to the finest, fleetest mares his owner could afford.

The other riders had the advantage of fresh mounts and that cursed bowman. Yala risked a short sharp glance over her left shoulder and saw three silhouettes at the top of the ridge. Now she saw, also, why Banh had cautioned her to follow the ravine; the road running through was sheltered. Eschewing that cover, she was now a moving piece upon a chessboard, laid bare to unfriendly eyes.

Not that it mattered.

Thunk. Something hit just above the floating ribs on her right side, driving her onto Archer's neck. Yala snatched at the reins; for a moment it didn't even hurt and she thought perhaps a kaibok ball had glanced off and away. Then the pain began, a spear buried in her back, and her knees clenched upon Archer's heaving sides. *Not yet, my lovely, my beautiful.* You could call a horse whatever you wished, and utter all manner of blandishments without any impropriety whatsoever.

She barely realized she was speaking aloud, or more precisely, screaming in Khir as she never had since well before the weight of decorum settled upon her and the dowagers began the long process of training a girlchild into a noblewoman.

After the first jolt, the pain was a hungry fangmouth beast; she risked another glance and found the man upon the black mare far too close. The sapling slid; it threatened to squirt free like a kaibok cup-mallet struck from an unwary hand.

But Yala was a good player, and had only let go with one hand to catch with the other. Flexible lyong wood whipped free and the pain sank its teeth up her ribs, seizing her entire right side with a monstrous cramp. Another rider might have been unseated, but Yala was *Khir*; she swung, the sapling struck at the man's pock-marked face and was torn from her grasp.

She screamed an obscenity she had heard Bai mutter more than once and folded tightly over the grey's neck. He was lathered now and each hoof-fall was a fresh knife in her back, but Yala tightened her knees again, falling into his rhythm, and leaned into his jolting, jarring gallop like silk piled in a rocking basket.

"*Now*," she called into the wind roaring past her face, stinging eyes and cheeks since the muffling cloth meant to hide her features and the fact of her femaleness was likewise lost. "*Now, my beauty, my Archer, my love! Fly! Fly!*"

There was a heartbeat of hesitation, as if the grey did not quite believe she was giving him leave. Then he gathered, an arrow upon the string, and leapt forward in a great rush with that same strange, floating gallop.

Komor Yala could do nothing but hold the reins, keep herself to the saddle like a thornburr upon a woolen skirt, and hope.

Pinned
Jewelwings

The great palace of Shan, so much smaller than Zhaon-An's sprawling complex, was nevertheless taller and set upon a promontory besides. Her legs ached from the stair-climbing, but this spire commanded a view for many a li—spreading houses and streets, rolling fields, orchards, mirrorlike paddies, and in the near distance, smoke as the hamlets put to fire and sword lay shuddering under their conquerors. Burning vapor rose in columns; when the wind shifted the smoke was overlaid with a sweetness of roasted curltail and fried hair as well as spoiled food and far more noxious vapors.

The barbarians had fired everything outside and driven streaming refugees against the closed gates. The ministers and lords who could afford to were fled to the uncertain safety of the provinces, but those pedestrians or peasants too slow to reach Shan's capital safely had been pinned like jewelwings in a collector's book, and much of the horde—a mass of tiny figures clinging to horses and their vast wagon-train of supplies and captured spoils—had turned their attention to consuming a banquet, like large black ants at a nestful of xiahiao hatchlings.

So this was the Tabrak, the ghostly raiders said to eat babies and spit pregnant women upon spears, lifting their bodies to rot in the sun. Maybe this creeping segmented beast had even eaten her merchant-pretender husband, though the prospect gave Sabwone little comfort indeed at the moment.

They did truly look like beetles, from this height. Instead of the regimented boxes of a Zhaon army or the Golden performing their drills upon a palace square, horses and riders milled about, tents and cooking fires arranged in a haphazard but dense cloak at the city's blackened but still temporarily unbreached walls. Metal glinted only here and there; they did not wear bright armor but leather and fur.

"My lady," Nijera said nervously, trembling and huffing from the effort of clearing stair upon stair, "we must think of your escape." Her hair was dressed very simply, her hairpin a small half-moon of glowing shell.

"Escape?" Sabwone had chosen her favorite dress this morn, the babu-patterned silk with a tight, bright yellow sash. It might be the last gown she ever wore, if the walls fell today. "My lord husband left me the city; I cannot give it to these barbarians." *It almost makes the Shan look civilized. Why, they probably even eat their horses.*

A deep thudding from the second-largest city gate announced that some of the raiders were not occupied merely with plunder and rapine but now with forcing their way into the winding streets full of moaning, mounting fear. It was only a matter of time, and the palace itself, walled and set upon its crowning point, would not be far behind. The great black palace gates were timber, and however hurriedly braced, they would not hold forever.

"They can barely hold the walls. The food stores are burning, we shall starve." Nijera's hands wrung at each other as her mistress's did, and neither woman was aware of the motion. "Please, my lady. I have made some small arrangements—"

The first intimation of disaster had burst into the queen's quarters in the form of a junior eunuch who bethought himself to chivalrously spread the news among oblivious females before looking to his own safety. Sabwone barely begrudged him his flight; Kiron had been gone for a good sixteen days and her attempt to join the council of lords left behind was an abject failure; they ignored her as her own parents had, and she saw little use in attempting to scream them into submission just yet. Now even they were gone; nothing remained in the palace but old retainers and weeping women. The walls were held by whatever men could be found under the round, oft-smiling lord named Buwon; he had little time for her, busy as he was with kicking those reluctant to do their duty to the battlements.

At least he had visited once and urged her to leave. No few of Sabwone's supposed ladies-in-waiting had taken the offering, fleeing through drainage tunnels in the company of junior eunuchs and cowards who could still hold a pike.

And you, my queen? Buwon had muttered the words in somewhat formulaic fashion.

"You may leave if you like." Sabwone repeated her answer. "I am a princess of Zhaon, Aunt Nijera. I will not flee these mongrels."

What princess of Zhaon could say otherwise? It was like a novel, but no book brushed upon rai- or pressed-paper ever spoke of the smell, or the way one's knees went weak with fear. Well, she had been swimming in a bath of terror since being dragged from home; it was nothing new.

Lord Buwon had regarded her for a long moment, his round face free of any smile. No doubt he had been one of Kiron's creatures roundly unimpressed with her from the beginning. *Then we will not either*, he had said, finally, and bowed—he had not upon entering, but perhaps taking his leave was more a relief to him.

What else could she have done? Flee like a kaburei, like a cowardly merchant's daughter? The disaster was total, and struggling would avail her naught. She had learned as much since receiving the news of her impending marriage; at least if the horde swept through and beheaded her she would not have to suffer the merchant pretender or any of his ilk again.

The thought that she might suffer worse, like a barbarian conqueror heaving and grunting atop her, was not to be borne, so she set her wits to two things—climbing to this highest point, and finding some means of doing what she had failed to in the palanquin.

Should it become necessary.

"Stupid girl," Nijera muttered, but Sabwone pretended not to hear. Why had the woman bothered to stay?

"You should have left," she said, but softly. What did it matter? What did *anything* matter? Of course the walls would not hold. Perhaps someone, anyone, would be riding to the rescue, and if they arrived in a timely fashion she would not creep back into the palace with a peasant's ingratiating smile.

No, Sabwone would have proved her worth, even to this collection of jumped-up merchants. Wouldn't her mother be forced to admit her daughter had been right to rail against this marriage?

The wind veered again, bringing that sweetish smell of roasting. She realized what it had to be all at once, and though she had not wanted any breakfast her gorge rose. The new queen of Shan gripped at the stone sill of this tiny window in the highest peak of her beleaguered palace like a scroll-illustration of Hae Jinwone in the Blood Years, and raised her chin.

She was Garan Sabwone, the daughter of the conqueror of Zhaon, and retreat was impossible. It was somewhat of a surprise to find her own bravery, though it was more mere distaste for the cowardice of others and the desperate desire to prove that she was not, after all, the spoiled, vapid brat they thought her.

At least this was something even Father could not ignore. They had packed her off to Shan, now they would be sorry.

If Suon Kiron somehow miraculously returned before the palace gates were shattered by the barbarian flood, she would deal with him roundly.

If not... Garan Daebo-a Sabwone eyed the casement. A slim girl could just fit, she decided. She might have to turn sideways, but that was no hardship.

I will show them all. Yes, if the miracle did not come, she would not wait.

She had always wondered what it would feel like to fly.

LONGTAIL AND KITTEN

After five days of no afternoon downpour it was official—the drought time of summer was upon Zhaon. Uncertainty rose like dust, not yet choking but definitely present, collecting in corners while incense burned in house-shrines, prayers rising for the shade of the old Emperor and the health of the new. Disturbing rumors raced from Zhaon-An like a lone light rider crying aloud at a gallop in every village square.

Still, stormclouds massed over the city that afternoon, and Garan Gamnae did *not* hunch her shoulders as she swept down a colonnaded garden path. A ghost of cool, water-scented breeze fluttered her pale mourning sleeves, ruffled her braided but unpinned hair, and her mother's voice was still ringing in her ears.

You will not visit that son of a commoner, Gamnae. I forbid it.

Well, Mother forbade plenty of things, but it was not *right*. It was not right at all, like the empty space upon Kanbina's pyre. Mother said Kanbina was a creeping little mouse, but the Second Concubine had always patiently steadied young Gamnae's hand upon the teapot while pouring, and was not at all angry when a child dropped a precious, breakable thing. Later, of course, Mother was furious when she found out about the visits, so they stopped except for those politeness utterly demanded.

Now Gamnae wished she had been braver.

She climbed the steps to the Jonwa's large door, and set her chin. Still, neither Golden on the stairs or at the door itself gainsaid her.

Perhaps she was expected after all.

Inside, it was cool, somewhat dim, and very much as usual. The snow-pard statue's paired snarling looked less fierce, more like an old friend, and Housekeeper Kue appeared with a bow, her eyes red-rimmed but her Shan tunic neatly buttoned and tied. "Second Princess," she said, softly. "It is good of you to visit."

"I...I wish to see my Eldest Brother, please?" She had practiced the command endlessly inside her head as she walked, now it burst out as a request instead.

"Yes, of course." At least Lady Kue did not look disdainful. Rather, she seemed slightly relieved. "They are all with him."

They who? Gamnae followed the housekeeper's steady gliding, wishing it was Komor Yala greeting her instead. *She* would remark softly upon something or another that would help Gamnae find her bearings, but the Khir lady was ill with grief and abed. Perhaps Gamnae could force a visit upon her, too, and...what? Reassure herself that someone else she liked was not about to die?

If Father could die, what hope was there for the rest of Zhaon? Mother had stopped alternately weeping and raging, but she was dangerously absent-minded, often staring into the distance with an unsettling half-smile playing about her full lips. Kurin was also absent but in a different way, busy with whatever important matters he could find. Gamnae was not supposed to leave her mother's side and would certainly be punished—and yet, it seemed worth it, or at least it had this morn when she had prevailed upon her close-servant to fetch her jatas.

The housekeeper indicated a door and stepped through, bowing, to announce Gamnae, who smoothed the front of her skirts with a quick nervous motion and tucked her hands in her pale mourning sleeves. She stepped through, head high, and found herself in an unexpected crowd.

Jin was at Takyeo's bedside, hunching upon a three-legged stool and holding their Eldest Brother's hand. Sensheo was near the verandah door, gazing onto a water-garden with a set expression as if he hated both pungent medicinal odors and faint breath of rot. Which wasn't surprising, Gamnae smelled it too, but a noble was never supposed to remark openly upon such things except as a witty aside.

Makar was busily brushing something upon paper at a small letter-desk, his own mourning garb straight and severe as a schol-ar's, though of much better quality. And there was Kurin, his topknot caged in scrubbed white bone with a bone pin, exam-ining Gamnae as if he had plans for punishing her disobedience after all.

It was Takshin who stepped to her side and offered his arm. *He* was not in mourning, save for a strip of unbleached linen around his left arm, and his gold earring gleamed mellow. "Good," he said, as if he had invited her. "You're here."

"I...I heard..." Gamnae could not look away from Takyeo's pale, drawn face. He looked much older, old as Father, even, and his abdomen was heavily bandaged. The shabby physician Kihon Jiao was busy at a table, mixing and grinding, and Gamnae longed to clap a hand over her mouth so the last part of the sentence would not slip free.

"You heard I was dying," Takyeo said, in a thin, reedy voice so unlike him it gave her the shivers. "Rumor is, in this one case, undeniably correct."

It was one thing to suspect, another to hear it confirmed, and yet another to see him wasted and pale like this, great circles under his eyes and his lank hair spread upon his shoulders, where often a laughing, very small Gamnae had sat and pounded upon his top-knot, crying for her brother-horse to gallop. "I..." Gamnae gulped, and Takshin's hand settled over hers in the crook of his elbow. He did not squeeze hard or warningly, but applied a brief, bolstering pressure.

She never would have believed him capable of such gentleness.

What would someone who knew how to handle this say? "I heard," Gamnae heard herself state, dismally. "I did not believe it. You can't die, Ah-Yeo."

"All men may accomplish such a feat," Makar murmured from his place. It was probably a learned allusion, but Gamnae darted him a look that should have broken the inkstone. "I have made four copies, Ah-Yeo, and am starting on the fifth."

"Very good. Come." Takyeo beckoned Gamnae, and she realized that the smell—the bad part of it at least—must be coming from him. "I would hold your hand for a short while too, Naenae."

It had been a long time since anyone except Jin called her that. Sabwone was missing, too. She would have been at the garden door with Sensheo, making observations in the haughtiest possible tone to cover up her own fear. And Kai would have been at Takyeo's side, ever watchful but ready to smile encouragingly.

As long as she was seeing the missing, she might as well add Father, but he would have ordered them all from the room so his first son could rest. Still, he would have had a gentle word and a pat on the hand or head for Gamnae, though she had long outgrown the latter.

She approached the bedside; there was another three-legged stool cuddled close to Jin's. Her sixth brother's chin was set and his mouth was a thin line, but his lips wobbled slightly as he glanced at her.

It was a relief to find someone else felt like crying, too.

Takshin settled her upon the stool with great care, even bowing close enough to mutter, "A welcome sight, Gamnae, well done," in her ear. Which threatened to break the tears free as well. Did he not know that he was supposed to be insulting, so she could be annoyed?

The smell was indeed very bad, and thin red lines were crawling up Takyeo's chest along his veins. He was sweating, and when he took her hand his grasp was loose bones inside a thin, fever-hot skin sack. "You two," he said affectionately. "A longtail and a kitten." The words broke halfway, and his breath was sour too.

"I do not purr," Jin said, and Gamnae elbowed him.

"You're the smelly longtail," she muttered, just loudly enough for Takyeo to hear.

Eldest Brother's laugh was cut short as he winced. "*Ai*, even merriment hurts. Listen, I am ceding you Guahua and Jin, Haeniu. They are next to each other, but you must not fight."

"We never fight," Jin said.

"Not where you can hear us," Gamnae added, mildly enough. So, she was to be the absurd little sister, and ease his mind.

Plenty of things were beyond her power, but this, at least, she could do. The two estates he mentioned were fine ones, and no doubt Mother would be pleased—but Gamnae was, just at the moment, not quite ready to accept such a gift.

The corners of Takyeo's eyes crinkled, but he did not laugh again. It probably hurt too much. "You must promise to help each other, when I am gone."

"Stop it," Jin said, fierce and low. "Stop. You can't. Please, Ah-Yeo."

She longed to elbow him. "When you are recovered we will tease Jin about this."

"Certainly. But not too much." Takyeo squeezed her hand again, gently, and lifted his left hand to reach across his chest and pat at hers. The hurai slipped upon his first finger; he had lost so much weight in so short a time.

The tiny movement of that greenstone band stabbed her chest. Her liver, probably half the size of anyone else's to match her failed courage, was spinning in place like a child's top.

"Guahua will also provide a fine living for you should you choose not to marry," Takyeo continued, brisk and businesslike though his voice was a cricket-whisper. "Promise me you will consider the notion."

Choose not to marry? Well, Sabi had gone to be a queen, and Mother would not let Gamnae do any less. Still...Takyeo was *dying*, and when your eldest brother was so close to joining the ancestors, what could you say? "I promise I shall consider," she said, numbly.

"Good." Takyeo's gaze unfocused and he sagged upon the pillows, both his hands grasping hers.

Jin seized them, so hard his knuckles whitened and her own hurt. "Ah-Yeo? Ah-Yeo!"

"The pain is very bad," Eldest Brother said softly. Gamnae's throat closed to a pinhole in heavy silk, the kind it took an iron thimble to force even a thick, very sharp needle through.

"Physician?" Takshin appeared, and reached to work Jin's fingers free, also loosening Gamnae's. "Do not break their fingers, Jin."

"I'm *not*." Jin stood, his hip bumping Gamnae almost off her stool, and shoved blindly past their third-eldest brother. He stamped for the verandah door and Sensheo, who for once only ignored him instead of turning with a cutting remark.

The physician bustled up, and held a cup to Takyeo's dry, cracked lips. "Nightflower and omyei." His tone was matter-of-fact, and the announcement was to stave off any question of what he was giving to his patient.

Gamnae all but gaped. With *that* brew flowing inside his humors, Ah-Yeo should be unable to speak at all.

"Come." Takshin plucked at her shoulder. "You may attend Makar, and hand him what he requires to seal the paperwork."

"Must I?" she whispered, but obediently let him draw her away. "And Lady Komor? Is she better? I must visit her."

"Not today," Takshin said, and his expression was so forbidding she almost quailed.

Almost. After all, she had disobeyed Mother, and *she* was far more terrifying than Taktak.

"I thought you would be weeping," Makar said by way of greeting. "Sit there."

At least *he* was always the same. Takshin glanced over Gamnae's shoulder at what the Fourth Prince was writing, nodded, and returned to Takyeo's side.

"I am stronger than you think." Gamnae settled, rolled up her sleeves in case she had to touch the inkstone, and watched him wield the brush. The room still smelled awful, but she made up her mind not to care.

And she made up her mind to consider any marriage carefully indeed.

THE RETURN

O ne last cloudburst hovered over Zhaon-An after several dry days, and those in the labyrinthine streets watched the darkening sky nervously. The Palace held its breath, eunuchs hurrying on strangely hushed jatajatas; ministers visited each other and spoke in hushed tones behind their fans; lesser and junior civil servants watched their masters allying and breaking alliance while the work of sealing, stamping, and minor policy decisions went on. The great administrative apparatus was not quite smitten and brooding like an anthill without its guiding intelligence, but it was very close.

So uncertain was the Palace that a small band of riders almost passed through the main gates unchallenged. At the last moment they were hailed, and their leader recognized as he barked a single command.

The Golden drew aside.

The riders passed all aclatter through two baileys and past several gardens, arriving at a long flight of stairs meant only for human feet. Their leader, the crest of his helm floating upon the strengthening breeze, again did not hesitate but urged his great grey mount up the slope; the horse, only slightly hesitant, did as he was bid.

They trotted to the stairs of the Jonwa itself; the leader dismounted with a creak of leather and a half-muffled curse, striding for Emperor Takyeo's door. The two Golden on duty, caught between the imperative to let none but a prince pass and the green-stone hurai flashing upon the visitor's finger, drew aside, and he stripped his helm as he plunged into the dimness. Even the mirrorlight was muted, and a rumble of thunder roll-rattled like clay weights inside a kettle.

So it was that Zakkar Kai returned to the bedside of Emperor Garan Takyeo, whose reign lasted less than a moon-cycle. The Emperor, dosed with a prodigious amount of nightflower and omyei, did not wake to see his old friend but slipped the moorings of physical life as infection—and the hunger of the cinnabar his wound was packed with—drained his humors and snuffed his kind, princely life.

It was also Zakkar Kai who carried the news that one of the men attempting to keep the news of his beloved battle-father's death and the new Emperor's need from reaching him was alive, and had spoken the name of his royal patron.

Garan Sensheo.

TEN THOUSAND YEARS

T his is very disturbing." Kurin stroked at his chin. The Jonwa hallway resounded with hurrying feet; deeper in the palace customarily given to the Crown Prince's use wailing began as female servants took up their traditional task at their master's ascension to Heaven. "Things are uncertain enough as it is, we cannot begin killing each other."

Easy for you to say. Kai's eyes burned and his hindquarters still felt the bounce and jolt of galloping to reach Takyeo in time. Takshin was gazing at him every so often with a strange expression; he hoped the Third Prince did not think Kai had tarried. Mrong Banh, his topknot so askew it was more of a bird's nest, sat at Takyeo's bedside, and the astrologer's hand was caught in a corpse's cooling claw.

For the first time, Banh looked elderly; he did not greet the new arrival. Tears gleamed upon his cheeks as his jaw worked over and over, his lips twitching faintly as if he prayed or addressed the newly fled shade with his inner voice. The body upon the bed lay, a silent and uncaring witness.

Takyeo's shade would linger to hear those last admonishments, perhaps, and that was the only faint comfort Kai could find in the situation.

"It wasn't me," Sensheo repeated, spreading his hands. He did not even look surprised at the accusation; a smirk lingered at the corners of his full lips. "I have no idea."

"He was very clear upon whose behalf he had been paid," Kai repeated. His hand ached for a hilt; it took more strength than he liked to keep it clear. Takyeo's face was grey and slack; lines graven by suffering easing bit by bit as flesh lost the heat of living humors. "And the triggering command, brushed upon silk and tied to a messenger-dove's leg, was explicit enough."

Takshin's gaze swung toward Kurin. Kai willed him to speak if there was anything to say, but the Third Prince held his silence. He stood with his hand easy upon the hilt of a curved Shan dagger with a flawed ruby in its hilt, and his readiness was the coiling of a viper before the strike.

"I don't suppose there is proof other than the word of a common bandit," Sensheo sniffed. Pale mourning did not suit him, and his topknot-cage was vermilion lacquer upon dark wood. "Who could have been paid by anyone at all, I might add. Why would *I* wish to kill Takyeo? It makes no sense."

"It makes far more sense for you to attempt upon Kai," Kurin supplied with a shrug; Kai's gaze swung to him. "What? It is well known he hates you."

"Be that as it may." Kai did not fold his arms. His right hand ached, ached. Even his *shoulder* hurt with the urge to draw and to strike. "If not Sensheo, who? Who would you have me believe the impresario of this performance, Kurin?"

"There is no shortage of suspects." Kurin folded his hands inside his sleeves. "But, if I may venture an observation, Sensheo is simply not intelligent enough, nor forward-thinking enough, to send more than a cheap assassin or two, Kai."

Sensheo did not bridle at the comment, merely gazed at the doorway as if he expected reinforcements.

"Then who *shall* I consider?" Kai almost added a few uncomplimentary terms common among angry soldiers, locked them in his throat with an effort. A small voice very much like Takyeo's own echoed inside Kai's head, urging calm. Perhaps it was truly the shade of Tamuron's eldest son, cautioning him against murder before a fresh corpse of a loved one. Such a thing was terrible indeed—but not as terrible as what had already occurred. "Who would move to forestall news that Takyeo summoned me? I could have been here days ago, if not for—"

"You mean you've left the Northern Army, while Khir re-arms upon our border?" Kurin clicked his tongue, thoughtfully. "Unwise."

Kai's face set itself in granite. Gamnae, sitting near the small letter-desk, pressed her fingers to her mouth. Next to her, Makar kept brushing, steadily and softly, his head bent. He had taken his topknot-cage out, and his hair lay loose upon broad shoulders, a mark of extreme grief. Still, he kept at his work, and though a tremor passed through his shoulders his wrist and fingers held their steadiness.

He was brushing the third copy of Takyeo's will, now that the paperwork of the individual bequests was written, signed, witnessed, and sealed. It was just like Ah-Yeo to attend to both matters, and just like Maki to perform the brush-duty.

Jin, his back against the wall, stared from one brother to another, his mouth loose and his eyes glazed. His fingers rose, plunged into his hair, and he ripped at his topknot blindly. "We shouldn't fight." Perhaps he thought he was screaming, but all he produced was a throat-cut whisper.

"This is not the fight," Kurin observed. Tension had invaded his frame, and he kept his gaze upon Kai's. "This is where we find who has won."

"Won what?" Kai's hands knotted so tightly the bones groaned. Tamuron, dead. Yala, pale from bloodloss, thrusting a bloodstained letter into waiting hands, her hair raveling over a pillow while she repeated her message over and over as if she did not quite believe she had reached him after all. And now Takyeo, his breath stolen and his fingers too thin for his hurai, a sacrifice laid open upon a smoking altar while a priest chanted for fortune or omen. "Death, and more death. That is all that has been achieved today."

"Stop," Gamnae moaned, the piping of a small bird caught in a trap. "He will not go quietly if you all…"

"He is beyond any of us." Kihon Jiao had not moved from the bedside, and the man's face was etched with sleeplessness as well. He had visibly driven himself to extremity to save his royal patient, and now might be wondering what would become of him. His hand had descended to Mrong Banh's shoulder, and the knuckles whitened under spatters of herb-paste and other marks as he squeezed to grant the astrologer some mooring against this current. "If you must wrangle, go to some other room."

"Mind who you speak to, *physician*." Sensheo all but sneered.

Kai's hand leapt for his snarling sword-hilt, closed tight, and sweat greased his entire body. Takshin met his gaze, and the Third Prince shook his head.

Just slightly, just enough. *Not now*, that small motion said, and repeated less loudly, *I am with you, but not now.*

"Enough!" Kurin freed his hands from his sleeves and spread them, a short, sharp motion. "You have arrived, Kai, so be it. A full investigation shall be made, and all proofs examined. But for right now…" He glanced at the bed, and his throat-stone bobbed. It was the only mark of emotion he showed, beyond the paleness under his copper. "For right now," he continued, softly but with great force, "we shall act as brothers should. And you, Sensheo, will be under house arrest until this…allegation…is thoroughly investigated."

"I can agree to that," Takshin said, heavily. His gaze had moved to Sensheo, and his scars were livid against paleness. "And if you do not, little brother, I will *make* you."

"I will not—" Kai began, but Makar looked up from his steady brushing.

The Fourth Prince's eyes were wet, and so were his cheeks. "*Enough!*" he bellowed, and Gamnae started with a wounded little cry.

Mrong Banh finally spoke, surging upward and staggering the physician back two steps; his voice was a terrible brazen trumpet.

"Go *elsewhere* with your bickering and your threats." He rounded upon them all, and the tears upon his cheeks were bright under the choked mirrorlight. "The best of us is dead; will you continue wrangling until the rest follow?"

Kai's hand fell from the hilt. Jin, trembling, slumped against the wall, wringing his hands and looking very young, strings of hair falling in his face as his topknot-cage bounced upon the floor, free at last. Takshin's hand fell upon Sensheo's shoulder, fingers biting cruelly, and the younger man started but said nothing, the color draining from his face.

"The Emperor is dead," Kai said, heavily. He stared at Kurin, and a muscle flickered in his cheek.

"May the Emperor live ten thousand years," Kihon Jiao replied, formulaic, and scrubbed at his face with his tincture-dyed hands. If he longed to weep like Makar, or as Gamnae now began to, it did not show.

A Delicate Time

A cortege of Golden receded into the distance; a shield-square of those bright-armored palace guards stayed at the high, very expensive gate to the Fifth Prince's estate outside the Palace walls, often described as a jewel in the heart of the Noble District. The guards did not step onto the grounds; it was Makar, his hair still loose against his shoulders, who accompanied his mother's younger son to the bright-polished white stairs before a pile of expensive blue stone and immense ceduan timbers.

"I do not see why I should suffer this." Sensheo all but sulked, gesturing the door-servants away with a short, sharp movement. His steward was not in evidence, but that worthy would come running as soon as news reached him of his master's advent. "For all I know, *you* arranged the whole affair to—"

"Stop being a child." Makar's hands ached. So did his eyes, and his heart. He spared barely a glance at the entry-hall, graced by a heavy, indifferently executed but no doubt very expensive statue of a horse's front half seeking to struggle free of the unfinished lower half, green veins in the white stone glowing under a pillar of mirrorlight. The carver should have turned the beast's head at a more pleasing angle. "The investigation will reach no conclusion, and after a decent amount of time you will rejoin the world. For right now, keep your mouth sewn shut and your intrigues to a minimum."

"You *did* arrange it." Sensheo's lower lip stuck out. He rounded on his elder brother, and he had not the grace to remove his topknot-cage. He had not even the grace to pretend at grief, and his idiocy was making it very easy for Kurin to trap not just him but all of Hanweo if Makar could not find some means of slowing its spread. "Does Mother know? Or did she help?"

The weariness was far more than physical, and Makar's shoulders bowed under it. "Neither of us arranged anything. It's far more likely Kurin did this to deflect attention." *And very neatly, too. I expected him to pin a rai-slip upon your shoulder, but not in this particular fashion.* All in all, they could be grateful their now-eldest brother had not been more thorough, though Sensheo, with his particular genius for missing the point, would not see the matter thus. "We must think, Sensheo. This is a delicate time, and I cannot have you bumbling about."

"Bumbling? You—"

One moment Garan Makar was slump-shouldered, standing tired and almost defeated at the threshold. The next, he had Sensheo's robe-front knotted in his fists and had driven his younger brother to the wall between two spindle-legged tables holding paired Ch'han vases—expensive only because of the cost of dragging them step by step from that far land, not for any aesthetic consideration—with bright crushflowers painted upon their vulgar sides.

"Shut. Up," Garan Makar hissed, and his face contorted terribly. "Suborning soldiers in the Northern Army? You *idiot*. Your attempts to kill Kai have gone too far, and I will not save you this time. It is a wonder he hasn't guessed and extracted your coward of a liver."

Sensheo struggled and sought to strike again.

Makar slapped his fist away with contemptuous ease. "You have not practiced lately, brother. It shows." He brought a knee up, and sank it where it did the most good.

The Fifth Prince—oh, once Kurin ascended the throne and ordered the succession their titles would change, and Makar was almost too exhausted to consider the prospect—promptly wheezed, and every inclination he may have had to fight drained like water through the westron sand-wastes. Makar propped his mother's second son against the wall and waited for him to catch his breath.

He did not like losing his temper. He especially did not like that his stupid, silly, graceless younger sibling had provoked the event.

"Now," he said, when Sensheo had ceased to moan imprecations. "Stay in your house, little brother. Leave the arrangements to me, and I will see you freed soon enough. But you must cooperate, and I warn you now, should Kai find enough evidence of your recent indiscretions, I will not lift a finger to gainsay him."

The scholar prince turned upon his heel, left his brother to rearrange his untidy clothing, and exited what was now Sensheo's prison.

For Garan Makar was called to show his support and filial reverence by aiding Banh and Zan Fein with arrangements for the enthronement ceremonies, and he would have to move carefully to keep himself—and his mother—from the First Queen's endless petty vengeance or Kurin's simple, thorough tidying-up.

ASCENSION IN PEACE

The palace boiled like a yeast sponge or a rai-pot, the ferment not spilling free but nevertheless chattering a lid upon its rim. Garan Kurin, his hands shaking—small tremors imperceptible from outside, and strenuously ignored from within—stood in the middle of the room he slept in when he visited his mother's part of the Kaeje.

It was not as congenial as his own estate outside the complex walls, and the clean mourning robe placed upon its stand, a coil of freshening incense slowly perfuming its folds, was alternately a leering shade and a prosaic piece of cloth. But the room was convenient, and was furthermore exactly where he was expected to be, changing his sickroom-contaminated clothing before the great machinery of custom and ritual came to drag him to the place he was born to occupy.

First would come the eunuchs, sober and dark-robed, and Kurin would send them away. Next would come the court ladies, wailing, lingering upon his mother's steps in their grief for an Emperor they had not time to applaud the seating of. Some of them might even have liked Takyeo personally, but when it became clear Father would not countenance a marriage to a mere Zhaon girl, the mothers had turned their sewing-baskets to catch other princely prey.

After that the Golden would come, and pound specially shod spear-butts upon the stone steps and broad avenue before the First Queen's part of the Kaeje, producing a rolling thunder. They would do this between one watch-gong and the next, the exhausted consigning their spears to fresh hands at regular intervals. It was considered lucky for a Golden to partake of this ceremony; there would be no shortage of performers. The night would pass with that noise and various other ceremonies, while Kurin prayed for guidance—or appeared to—before a hurriedly prepared altar with both his father's and Takyeo's names painted upon wooden stele.

Finally, in the morning, a group of notables and beggars—the former richly robed and selected by formal Court lottery, the latter counted through the traditional northern gate of the palace complex and eager for the feast that would be served them as dusk rose—would take their stations and begin their cries for him to come out. *That* was when Kurin could appear in mourning, making the traditional signs of refusal thrice more before being lifted on a litter borne by a few husky Golden and taken to the chambers of state in the southeast part of the Kaeje where the ceremonies would begin. Just a few walls separated him from the small stone room, hastily cleaned of his father's belongings, where he would spend tomorrow night in prayer to Heaven to make him fit to steer Zhaon's course.

In all reality, he would lie awake in the dark for a short while, considering various moves and countermoves, before dropping into the black well of well-earned sleep.

Quite different from how Sensheo would spend his evening hours for the next few days, Kurin presumed. A slight smile lingered upon his lips as he smoothed the sleeve of the fresh mourning-robe. His mother's few male servants crowded the hallway, waiting for the call to aid in dressing. One or two of the junior close-maids would arrange his hair, and he had a visit from his mother to look forward to as well.

A hidden pocket of the robe worn to Takyeo's death-room held a small, heavy object. He drew the small porcelain vial taken from another brother's sleeve on a hot dusty day free, and gazed at its rough, unglazed belly, its soakwood stopper.

Yes, Sensheo was probably in a lather. His little brother's many intrigues, some clumsy, others approaching subtlety only by accident, were more often than not at cross-purposes with each other. The fellow simply did not know how to *wait*, and that was the most necessary skill of all.

Easy enough to make the men guarding Zhaon's egress points think they were serving one prince when in fact they served Kurin's ends, and doubly easy with the use of a few impresarios— thoughtfully arranged by his uncle, who would be attended to in some little while—to make the hired riders think they had discovered a great secret about their shadowy patron.

The question of just what to do about Sensheo lingered in Kurin's head-meat; he paced to the partition that would reveal a low porch and one of the Kaeje's many gardens if he slid it aside.

He did not. These few moments of unguarded, unwitnessed thought were probably the last he would have for some time.

This particular tincture was not what he had sent Sensheo into the Yuin to fetch, but it would do. Using it, and pointing yet another damning finger at the most usefully idiotic of his brothers, was satisfying to contemplate—but did he want that chess-piece taken from the board so soon?

Someone had been sent to fetch Kai, and it galled Kurin not to know precisely *who*. A Golden, most likely, one beholden to Takyeo or to Kai himself. It wasn't like his dear, departed eldest brother to make such a move—no, the act of sending a rider had Takshin's characters plainly stamped onto its surface. Had the rider been sent before or after Taktak offering his services? His Shan-adopted little brother was indeed a blade to be pointed in a safe direction, and Kurin looked forward to finding out which court lady had caught that prickly pard's eye.

He suspected the Khir girl, which was deliciously fitting indeed. It would send their mother into convulsions of rage, and in that event Takshin's chosen lady had best beware.

Or maybe the marriage endorsement was a feint. At least Taktak, like Makar, never disappointed. And at least either of them were too wise—or in Taktak's place, too utterly removed from the line of succession by adoption—to move against their new Emperor.

Well, Makar was probably more *indolent* than *wise* on that front. And Jin, of course, was no threat.

Not yet.

"Kurin?" A soft scratching at the hall partition. Of course Mother would not leave him alone to contemplate his ascension in peace.

Garan Kurin, soon to be Emperor of Zhaon, tucked the unglazed vial into the sleeve of the robe waiting patiently upon its stand. His smile, for those few moments, was almost that of an orange-ruddy brushtail, and his exhaustion-heavy eyes glimmered. It made him quite handsome; he adjusted his hurai, his sickroom-tainted robe, and touched his topknot before striding across the chamber to the partition, halting feline-soft and listening to his mother breathe.

"Kurin?" she repeated, querulously. "My beautiful eldest, are you there?"

For the love of Heaven's many gods, leave me alone. *For once, for just once, leave me alone.* The thought submerged as soon as it crossed his head-meat, a reflex so swift it barely caused a ripple. Only a shadow of irritation remained.

He stood very still, breathing through his slightly open mouth, ready to lay a hand upon the partition and stop its opening. Mother was a problem he could not solve just yet.

He knew the solution. It was clear, and yet...

In any case, he told himself, he had a few moments remaining of blessed solitude and quiet. The smile faded. Kurin stared at the partition, breathing deeply and bracing himself for what came after a man had won a victory that opened new vistas instead of halting the war.

His father, warlord and peerless general, might not be quite proud of his second son. But what took a warlord to create would need a different manner of lord to consolidate, and Garan Kurin was made for the task.

"Kurin?" his mother breathed again. "Oh, my beautiful boy, please, answer me."

I will, Mother. Thoroughly, and in my own good time. He stood where he was, digging his toes through soft palace slippers into mellow-varnished wooden floor, and waited for the inevitable.

PITY OR
REVULSION

The Jonwa was strangely silent except for brief bursts of wailing in its depths as grief loosened the voice of a kaburei or other female servant. The sound traveled through corridors absent of their master, and this small room was a bubble of peace amid the buffeting.

"A glancing blow." Yala's lips were dry-cracked, and the great hollows under her pale eyes glared at him as she clasped her hands before her. Her hair, free of all braid and hairpin, was a river down her back; nobody had noticed one of Zakkar Kai's dun-cloaked fellow riders with an indifferently wrapped topknot being carried into the hallway and slipping a slim arm over a kaburei's willing shoulders, vanishing into a side-passage. "Nothing more. I am well enough."

"You must eat," Anh fussed. "And have crushed fruit, and a proper bath, and—"

"Then be about your work." Takshin exhaled sharply as the girl hurried for the door, carrying the muffling cloak. Now freed of its heavy length, the hastily found tunic Yala wore showed. Cut for one of the smallest of Zhaon's soldier-sons, it was still too large, and tightly belted. The trousers, hastily hemmed, were also baggy enough to swallow her. "Where, and how, little lure?"

"My side." Yala moved, stiffly, to a cushion near her writing-desk. Takshin strode across the room and caught her elbow, helping her sink without her usual grace. "Here." She indicated her lower back on the right, wincing as the movement pulled strained and sliced muscle. "Honorable Kihon has examined; he pronounced it cleaned well and sewn well enough, though not with a noblewoman's skill. The physician at the keep was rather in a hurry."

Takshin knew very well who had sent riders north to keep word from reaching Kai. They had come close enough to grant him a nightmare or two; he should have planned better. He should have gone himself, no matter if he would be missed or not. As it was, Takyeo's condition had merely been a fire delayed by a ditch, but they could not have known as much when she was sent.

He should have, though. His own failure was a hot-metal wad in his throat, a sword in his vitals as well.

A coronation and two funerals would proceed. Custom would enthrone an Emperor and free two bodies, father and son, from the clutching of physical life at once. He should have felt grateful, he should have felt *liberated*, for without Takyeo to keep him nailed in Zhaon-An he could go where he pleased.

Instead, there was only a raw aching inside him. Her bravery, her daring, and his own actions—all for nothing.

Well, not quite. He sank down upon the cushion next to hers, his legs finally deciding they could bend. "I will never risk you again." He heard his own weariness, and the finality of the statement.

"I risked myself." Yala's hands folded decorously, though they rested against rough cotton instead of a silk skirt. There were red marks upon her soft palms, and a harsh-looking scrape across her knuckles.

He could not help himself. Takshin reached for her right hand, scooped it delicately from her lap. She did not resist him, merely gave a startled but somewhat apathetic glance. She was too fatigued to gainsay him, which was all to the good.

"And I failed," she said, dully. "Again. Had I been swifter—"

"No." He did not squeeze as he longed to, grinding small bones together to halt whatever else she would blame herself for. There was no gentleness in him, but at least he would avoid harming her in that fashion. "You did all you could, Yala. There is nothing more. Listen to me."

"I am listening." She did not seek to pull away, which was for the best, since he would not have let her and she deserved forbearance. "I am merely very tired, my lord Third Prince, and would very much like to have a bath, and to rest."

"Soon." He turned her hand over, examined her palm. The rein-marks glared at him, and he could not stab or bludgeon them. "Did the Tooth bear you well?"

"The tooth? Ah." A faint smile crossed her wan face. He could not even appreciate seeing her hair unbound, a sight normally granted only a brother or husband. "His name is Archer, and yes, he is a fine beast. If not for him I would be full of arrows, and resting in a ditch besides. He is the best horse in Zhaon, my lord."

"Then he is yours." The thought of her broken and tangled in a peasant's water-channel frayed his temper even further. "And, Yala, there is one other thing which is yours, and will be given to you. Can you guess?"

"I should not accept gifts." Her mouth trembled slightly, and that small quiver was another spear to his liver. "I did not bring him in time, Takshin. Even to bid the Crown Prince farewell."

"You brought him at the right moment," Takshin lied. "Here." He dug clumsily under his Shan longshirt's main side, drawing thick unsealed paper free of the internal pocket. "Read."

It was awkward; she had to use her left hand since he would not relinquish her right. She opened the sheets and glanced through the inmost one, her eyebrows drawing together. "You are to be…" She glanced at him, obviously gauging whether felicitations were in order, but returned to reading, with palpable, weary puzzlement. "It is unfinished." She smelled of heat-haze, dust, and the sourness of hard riding, but a breath of jaelo clung to the mix, drawing it tight with a silver thread. "The bride's name is missing."

"I did not know what characters you would choose." *And I was afraid you would say no. But now you will not.*

In fact, she *could* not. With Takyeo gone, she was forced to find whatever safety she could.

Garan Takshin had, at long last and irrevocably, won something he wanted.

"This is the Crown Prince's hand, and his seal." All the breath seemed to have left her, for her voice was a mere whisper. "He… brushed this? As he was…"

The wishes of the dying could not be disregarded. It was hardly fair, but then again, life itself did not play upon a level board, and with Takyeo gone he was forced to do what he could to gain her safety.

"He wished you cared for, Yala. And I am not so bad." The other endorsement, Kurin's careful brushwork and heavy seal, was hidden in Banh's tower, still the safest place for any treasure a son of Garan Tamuron might need held. If the new Emperor made any trouble about a marriage endorsed by his predecessor, Takshin would win anyway. "Am I?"

This was not how he had expected the interview to go. He should have waited, but he was utterly unable to. Patience might bring a man all he needed, but it had its season, and that time was past.

"My lord…" She touched the stamp at the bottom—Takyeo's device, closely akin to the banner from the storerooms she had taken to announce her presence to the keep—with a trembling fingertip. Her nail was cracked and broken, and it hurt to see. "I do not know what to say."

"Simply say, *yes, Takshin*." Nothing more was required. "And I will do the rest." *Unless there is someone else you prefer. In which case, speak his name so I may kill him, and quickly.*

But he swallowed that truth, as he had so many others. There was no need to voice it.

Still Yala hesitated. She searched his face; he suffered once more that probing, delicate glance. He hated to be looked at, hated the flash of pity or revulsion at his scars.

But her clear gaze was free of either. She studied him as she might a horse or a character upon a scroll, searching for meaning, and he longed to show her the curves or straight lines, angles or dots she wished most to see.

"My father—" she began, tentatively.

"Is *not here*, Yala, and you are unlikely to see him until Khir and Zhaon reach an agreement. It could be years, and another war in the meantime." The hunt was over, he had the creature caged, and it would take much to free its bright fragile plumage from his grip. He could lose much else and remain uncaring—it was, after all, a matter of pride. This one small, simple thing he would keep. "And would he grudge you a prince? Do you dislike Zhaon I shall take you to Shan. Or to your own father, and woe to the Khir who raises a blade to me. This I will do for you, little lure, if you ask it." *And more. Simply ask.*

"Takshin..."

"There is little I would not do simply for your asking." He could have closed his eyes, the sweetness of hearing her pronounce his name in such a fashion almost too piercing to be borne. "You must know as much by now. Agree, Yala. It is best."

Why would she not simply agree? And yet he did not mind, for it was part and parcel of *her*, the hesitation.

"Is it?" Her shoulders softened. She leaned toward him like a hau tree's roots craving wetter soil, like a crushflower's head following the sun. "I do not know what is best, or what is right. I am weary, Takshin, and I long for rest." Her voice broke, soft Zhaon much less accented now, but with the shade of Khir riding sharp-hoof behind the words.

"This is right." He let the words carry his own certainty. "I am ugly, and abrupt, and I have little grace. But I will protect you. I am far from the worst fate for a Khir woman so far from home."

"You are not ugly," she said, with a firmness that almost convinced him she believed it. "And in any case, I am as far from beauty as possible, especially now."

He could have told her otherwise, but that was a task for a poet or a courtier, and he disdained both roles. "Ah, laying a silk thread for compliments, are you?" Still…he could learn to, if it would ease her. "Very well, I shall give you one or two. Daily. Especially after you marry me."

A thin, pale smile touched her lips, and Anh's return led to her seeking to reclaim her hand. Takshin, however, did not let go. "Answer me," he said, softly so the kaburei halted in confusion near the doorway would not hear. "Tell me *yes, Takshin.*"

"Yes." A flush rose to her cheeks, and the smile faded. Well, she was naturally somber. Soon enough she might forget as much, if he could settle her in an estate with a fine library, somewhere they would be undisturbed by fellow princes and their machinations. "Takshin—" There was more she wished to add, but he did not let her.

Not when he had what he willed. After all, she might reconsider—though a woman who visited her princess's shade daily was not one to slip the chain of a dying Emperor's wish.

Takyeo had been kind to her. Takshin was not made for kindness, but he thought he might well learn, with such a tutor.

"Very well." Now he set her free, and reached for the inkstone and the stand of clean brushes. "Fetch an ink-dish, and water," he told the kaburei. "A few characters, Yala, and I shall leave you to rest."

"Must I…" She stared at her hands, perhaps ashamed of the welts, bruises, and scrapes no noblewoman should ever have to suffer. "Must it be now?"

"Yes." Victory would make him indulgent, but just now he had to insist. "Now, Yala. And then I will keep you safe, as Takyeo would wish."

It was not a lie, he told himself. Takyeo *would* wish Yala cared for as soon and well as possible; he simply had been too occupied with other matters to say as much openly. Now it was too late, and if Takshin did not take this chance one of Kurin's games—or Sensheo's clumsy maneuverings—might place her at risk.

He did not relax until, with a firm wrist and probably aching fingers, Yala brushed five careful, exquisite little characters in the Khir fashion upon the endorsement.

Once blotted, the paper returned to his pocket, and he could afford to retreat. But only to the doorway, where he watched the kaburei fuss, with many a careful, solicitous tongue-click, over his future wife.

NONE OF YOUR ANTICS

T he Kaeje rustled with hurried footstep, whispered news, and lively speculation, but the First Queen's chambers were deathly still. The eunuchs had come and been sent away; next would come the howling upon the steps.

"My son." Gamwone opened her arms. She had attended to her hair; it rose lacquered upon her head in its usual fashion. Her dress was undyed mourning silk but her two hairpins glittered with falling gold beads in flagrant defiance of custom and propriety. "My brave, beautiful son."

"So now I am beautiful, hm?" Kurin gave a weary smile, but did not move to embrace her. Gamwone threw her arms around him instead and received a perfunctory pat upon her back before he held her at arm's length. "Not a disobedient little boy?"

"Oh, you have always been my favorite." A trembling smile, and she patted at his arms, his cheeks, his chest. He allowed it, though he frowned. "And now my boy will be Emperor. My lovely, canny boy."

"Yes, Mother. Come to tea." If she would simply behave, he could be done with this in short order and move to more pressing matters.

He did not think it likely, but a good son gave his mother every chance.

"Tea?" Her soft, plump hands fluttered delicately. "Oh, I couldn't possibly. There is so much to do—the coronation, the procession, so many details."

"That is Zan Fein and Mrong Banh's province, Mother, not yours." It would be singularly unwise to grant her any public task at all. "Come, and sit with me. We must speak."

"Oh, certainly, certainly...will my uncle be here?" She sobered, and the shadow of imperiousness crossed her still-beautiful face. Her slippers shushed as he herded her toward the sitting-room. "He should come to pay his respects."

"Lord Yulehi is otherwise engaged upon an errand or two, Mother." He indicated the door and let her precede him, closing the partition with a decisive click. "You need not lift a finger. There is, in fact, nothing for you to do, except one simple thing."

Now she turned to face him, tucking her hands in her sleeves, a tremulous, disbelieving, somewhat predatory smile bunching her cheeks and showing her fine teeth. "Oh? And what is that, my love?"

Kurin wished this task already accomplished. It was by far the most distasteful of the day's duties. "Be silent, and cease your intriguing. I am not Father or Takyeo, Mother, and I will not have you disturbing my affairs with—"

"Oh, so this is how it is?" Gamwone stiffened, and the gold beads swung upon her hairpins. The double-hung walls closed around Kurin, and he could hardly breathe. Even the table had rounded corners, and no doubt she would wish them padded with cotton. "I place you upon the Throne of Five Winds, and you think you may order me about?"

"You did not place me anywhere, Mother." His quiet should have warned her that his temper was thinning, but he attempted to explain anyway. Not that he held any great hope she would comprehend. She seemed singularly unfit—but that was a woman's nature, and he must be filial. "I was born for this, and have achieved it. And I am telling you, there will be none of your antics from now until you join Father."

"You *dare*—"

"Mother." He stepped close; his fingers sank into her soft, plump upper arm, and he squeezed. Sabwone would have recognized the look upon Garan Kurin's face, and Gamnae too; either of them would have retreated to avoid what came next. So would Jin, and to a lesser extent, Sensheo.

Without Takshin or Lord Yulehi, though, Sensheo had nothing—and so did Kai, who could suspect all he liked as long as he performed his function. There was no profit in the Head General seeking to unseat Kurin, even less for Makar, and Takshin, by far the most unpredictable, was safely out of succession and had, besides, something he wanted very badly from Kurin's own hand.

All in all, it was neatly accomplished, and now his other plans could begin to arrange themselves. He merely wished this over before the wailing began.

"I have overlooked your behavior for long enough," he continued, giving her a small, rattling shake to make certain he had her full attention. Her skirt swung to match her beads, and she gasped. "I am a dutiful son, but I am also Emperor, and you will behave as befits your station. Is this in any way unclear?"

The trouble was, Father had let Mother do largely as she pleased. Perhaps he had even loved her in his own distant, warlord fashion. Still, Kurin did not intend to let her ruin what he had wrought, in *any* small fashion.

His short rest was over; he had returned to the battlefield. The small lump in his sleeve, unnoticed by servants come to dress their master, was at once a comfort and a dragging weight.

"You," Gamwone hissed. Her pupils swelled, much as Takyeo's had under the influence of strong analgesic. "You are just like him. All my struggling, all my suffering, and you do not care."

"I care, Mother." Could she not grasp as much? "You will have everything you have ever wanted, as long as you leave intrigue and statecraft to me." Women might run a house, but a kingdom was a different matter entirely. "I am a loving son."

The hangings upon the walls watched with bright, cushioned

indifference. Garan Gamwone drew herself to her round, full, inconsiderable height, though her arm was still trapped in his grasp. "I *birthed* you," she began, dangerously quiet. If he let her continue she would not cease until she had battered someone into quiescence, even herself. Or Gamnae, who had endured enough today.

Kurin stepped forward, his hand sliding to her wrist, and turned her. It was simple for a prince used to the drillyard to overpower a lone, soft woman. Before she quite realized it, her arm was twisted behind her back in a hold Zakkar Kai would have recognized— and Jin as well, whom he had patiently taught to deploy it. It was the manner in which a wrestler or a soldier held a civilian who was not to be harmed but also not allowed any intransigence. "Come," the new Emperor said, and tightened the hold when she inhaled to begin crying aloud. "You will have a cup of tea, Mother. Strong enough to suit even you. It will be slightly medicinal, and you will behave, or I will *make* you."

"How *dare* you—" she began, but the fight left her like air escaping a festival bladder, and she sagged in his grip as he propelled her through the partition and down the hall, not caring if servant or guard saw.

Garan Kurin had also taken, from the table littered with medicines and other paraphernalia in Takyeo's room, two vials of nightflower and omyei. One rested within his sleeve now, for he had suspected it would be necessary.

"You have no allies, Mother. Only me." What a wonder, that she had not realized as much. "You should consider that, and do all you can to keep me content."

Yes, things were about to change immensely within the great palace of Zhaon. Kurin could hardly wait.

Outside the First Queen's part of the Kaeje, upon wide white steps, women's voices rose in the ancient song of grief.

THE MOON
WISHES IT

The morning was clear and fine, albeit with a promise of awful, dust-choked heat later. The night's rain, falling upon thirsty, groaning black earth, had tamped the worst of the dust, but enough remained to coat the throat and irritate the eyes. Anh said it would only grow worse.

The dry time was upon Zhaon. Late last night, from one watch to the next near dawn, a thudding had worked its way through the entire complex like a dull heartbeat. It was the Golden, beating their spears against stone, and now a new Emperor was enthroned. That morning, the Jonwa had received flame from the heart of Zhaon. Lamps were relit, other fires kindled, and the Palace kitchens were humming again.

Yala folded her hands. They were freshly oiled, nia and attar rubbed into the aching spaces between her fingers, and her broken nails had been likewise lovingly attended to by Anh as Yala soaked in a warm bath, disliking more heat but almost groaning with relief at the easing of her muscles. "I cannot say otherwise," she said, desperately. "The Crown Pri—the *Emperor* wrote it, and I cannot refuse his dying wish. Please understand. I am sorry, Kai."

"Takyeo arranged it, did he?" Zhaon's Head General wore pale mourning, and there was a fire in his deep-set eyes few had seen before. A dragon watched over his shoulder, but its roar seemed less a battle cry than an anguished snarl. At least he was not shouting, but his slight stagger when she had finally managed to speak the news pierced her from heart to liver, and everywhere else. "I cannot blame *him*; I told him nothing. Perhaps I should have."

"I..." Yala could not say it. Or could she? "We could, perhaps..." It stuck in her throat. Was she seriously contemplating betraying her honor, and for the Zhaon who had all but ground Khir under a mailed heel? "I would go with you," she said, finally, through the obstruction. "Wherever you willed, Zakkar Kai. My...feelings...have not changed."

The surprise was not in hearing the words leave her mouth. It lay, instead, in the fact that she meant them, and had dared to say as much clearly.

She was an honorless woman after all.

"And do you feel nothing for Takshin, then? It is a pity, he seems..." Kai's hands were fists in his own lap, but no solicitous care had been taken with his rein-blisters or small scrapes. Calluses scratched as he spread his fingers, rubbing them against mourning-cloth.

The color of death was everywhere, this summer.

"No," he finished. "Forgive me, Yala. I spoke from bitterness, and I would not subject you to it."

"Should I have said I preferred you? I was..." She could not blame her own weariness. She was a coward, in truth as well as deed, for the time to speak was before she signed the endorsement.

How could she have denied Garan Takyeo's solicitousness, though? Her princess's husband, while he lay dying wracked with a gut-wound, had still thought to arrange matters as well as possible for a simple lady-in-waiting. It was utterly impossible to refuse.

Then again, it was only permission, not the actual marriage herself, was it not? That was a craven thought, and likewise was the idea, occurring to her this morning as she stared at her chamber ceiling before Anh stole in, alerted by the change in her mistress's breathing from sleep to waking, that perhaps Garan Takshin would not leave her alone in Zhaon-An while he was off fighting Zhaon's wars as Zakkar Kai would obviously be called to do.

"No." Kai continued gazing at his hands, much as Yala had while trying desperately to think of another solution, much as she had while attempting to find the words to place these tidings in. "Takyeo was wiser than us all. Takshin has had little enough his entire life. You will provide him some rest, and that is much to be wished for."

Now her chest cracked. He said it so lightly, as if it did not matter. Perhaps he had merely been amusing himself, before.

"Oh." It was all she could think of to say. It was beneath her to suspect indifference on his part. Was her honor truly so frail? Had she acceded to Daoyan, she might be honorless in a different way, now. Taken from Zhaon and placed upon his saddle—and oh, how, under Heaven, was she to give this news to *him*?

Perhaps she would be spared that; hopefully he had already left Zhaon-An. If he had not...

The iron control of years spent under the watchful gaze of Hai Komori's aunties stiffened her spine, pushed her shoulders back, and denied the burning in her eyes, the spear in her chest.

The wound upon her back, cleaned and bandaged by Anh's careful fingers, hurt far less than the rest of her. She would never play kaibok again without thinking of the solid impact, the pain all through her, the blood as she fell from the saddle into waiting soldiers' hands. Gasping out her message, over and over again, and Kai's face rising from the fog of agony, set and pale.

They sat in silence, lady and general. Yala's nose was full, and she lifted her hand to wipe at her cheek.

Zakkar Kai's callused fingers arrived first. He brushed away the tears, and she could not help herself. She caught his hand, cradled it in both of hers, and squeezed as hard as she could.

"Yala." A small, broken word. It was not right; Zakkar Kai, the beloved of the God of War, should not sound so throat-held. So *lost*. "I will only say this once."

Oh, Kai. She nodded, and waited for fresh pain. He was well within his rights to curse her, to call her faithless, even to strike her, and Yala would bear it.

There was nothing else to do.

"Should you ever..." Kai let out a long, shuddering breath. When he continued, it was softly but with great force, each word edged no less sharply than the blade upon his back. "Should aught happen to Takshin, or should he treat you ill, all you must do is send me word. Tell me, *the Moon wishes it*, and I shall come for you no matter what. I will leave any battle, any station, I will ride as you did, and I will do whatever is required." His chin dipped as he peered at her, and she found she had not the courage to watch his face.

Yala nodded, staring at her lap. The tears were rising again, and she doubted she could stanch their flood.

"Tell me you understand," he said, low and urgent. "Please."

She nodded again. "I ... I understand."

"Good." He drew his hand free, not ungently. "And now I must leave you, my lady, or I will be tempted to do what I should not."

"Kai." Wrung out of her, his name fell between them, a wounded bird. She could not even bear to look upon him, now.

"Yala." He rose. "Above all, do not risk yourself like that, ever again."

On that point, you and Takshin are more alike than you know. "I cannot promise," she whispered. Any prospect of ease or rest, of tranquility or the lack of danger, had fled with the smoke of Mahara's pyre. The successive shocks piled upon her until she could not move, could not *breathe*.

"I cannot make you." He turned, and strode for the door. "But Takshin might."

Then he was gone, and Komor Yala, alone in the empty Jonwa receiving room, buried her face in her hands and, finally, wept without restraint.

Even that brought no relief.

A Message

Garan Tamuron and his eldest son were laid upon pyres side by side, and the new Emperor honored both father and eldest brother by carrying the spitting everflame torch himself, step by slow step, to the oil-drenched wood as the Great Bell tolled. Some might have expected the second, smaller pyre to refuse the kiss of cleansing flame carried in such a hand, but it caught with no difficulty and the more superstitious among the Court were relieved.

It was a time for sorrow—Garan Tamuron had reunited the Land of Five Winds, after all—but also a time for rejoicing, since a new Emperor was now solidly upon the throne and life could settle into its normal rhythm again.

The dry season meant work tending to aqueduct and canal, guarding growing rai, planting second crops, and though business with Khir was still strangled, it had been so for many a year and there was always Anwei to trade with instead. The new Emperor was also likely to teach the northern horselords a lesson or two in respecting their betters—or so many at the Palace, in the city, or among the civil servants in small town and village stated, more or less openly and more or less confidently.

From Shan there was no news until a single lean rider furred with reddish hair and with skin the color of mourning presented himself at the gates of Zhaon-An's great palace complex upon a dry, dust-choked afternoon some few weeks into the new reign.

Led past garden upon garden, through richly appointed colonnade and brightly mirrorlit passages, the visitor was brought to a
receiving-hall and left to cool his barbarian heels—still in their
boots, for he had menaced the servants responsible for ensuring
no profane shoe stepped inside the Kaeje with a flash of discolored
teeth through the reddish beard choking the lower half of his face.
The visitor stank, too, far more than the brightness of some of his
clothing—the remnants of a Shan noblewoman's colored rain-cloak,
for one, and similar inappropriate scraps—should have allowed. A
man who could dress in something other than drab was presumed
to have the alloy sliver necessary for the bath-house, after all.

The knee-high box the pale-skinned intruder carried stank just
as badly, though it was wrapped in rich damask silk.

Finally, the visitor was ushered into Zhaon's greatest hall, and
bowed—in unpolished fashion, but respectfully enough—after he
had presented the leaden medallion and scroll of pounded-rag paper,
thick and heavy, that passed for his credentials to a waiting eunuch.

"And who is this, standing before me?" the new Emperor said,
with a faint, ironclad smile. Perhaps his hind end had not yet
become quite accustomed to long hours upon the throne listening,
hearing, and deciding, for he shifted slightly as he took in the barbarian from booted toe to fuzzy top.

"Turik, stirrup-holder to Aro Ba Wistis of the Horde, greets
Zhaon." The Tabrak straightened from his bow. "I bring thee a gift,
oh lord of Zhaon." His accent burred and butchered its way through
the syllables, but they were still largely decipherable. "And a message."

"A gift? Quite kind." The new Emperor gestured, and the box
was brought to the steps before the throne, laid carefully. "I have
not asked your lord Aro for tribute, Turik, but I shall view his bauble." He handled the strange names passably well, but then again, a
monarch should be peerless in learning as well as war.

"Not tribute, lord of Zhaon." Either he had not taken the time
to learn proper address to the Emperor, or he was deliberately
insulting—but the Emperor merely smiled, graciously, and gestured for the silk-wrapped box to be opened.

It had ridden many weary leagues, bumping against a saddle; now, a eunuch's nimble fingers teased at its wrappings. Zan Fein, standing among others of his dark-robed kind at the Emperor's left hand, murmured to a much younger, very somber eunuch who hurried away, his jatajatas hushed instead of announcing their name.

The barbarian stood, grinning stolidly, and the wooden box was cunningly designed to fall open once its lid was removed. The sides thumped down upon the stair, and one of the ministers—Lord Yulehi, still in his half-year of primacy, newly confirmed by his very filial nephew—let out a short, coughing sound of disgust.

"The gift is this, oh lord of Zhaon." The stirrup-holder's rotted teeth showed even more as his lips pulled back, a grimace of high amusement. "We have brought one of your fillies home, to replace one lost by another."

Kurin stared at the thing upon the steps. Its ear-drops, still held by blue ribbon, were familiar, as were the two hairpins thrust through a nest of sadly bedraggled braids. He knew the jewelry, and even though the features were blurred they were still perfectly recognizable.

The Emperor's gaze rose to take in the barbarian again. "Sabi," he said, blankly.

"And the message from Aro Ba Wistis is thus," Turik said, in loud, careful Zhaon. "*We are coming.* Shall I repeat it?"

"No." The new Emperor had gone pale. There was a rustling, a thumping of footsteps, and the Golden guards, warned by Zan Fein's messenger, burst into the hall. The four attendant upon the throne leveled their spears, and several ministers cried out in disgust and disarray as they recognized the thing contaminating the steps. "Sabwone. *No.*"

The Tabrak was still laughing when they bore him away to the dungeons, and Garan Sabwone's head, flesh sloughing from its cheeks and its eyes, not to mention the back of the horribly collapsed, crushed skull, leered at her now-eldest living brother.

To Be Continued…

The story continues in ...

BOOK THREE OF THE HOSTAGE OF EMPIRE

Coming December 2021

Acknowledgments

Thanks are due to Sarah Guan, without whom there would be no series; Nivia Evans, whose endless patience has oft kept a writer from utter despair; Angeline Rodriguez, whose organization has made miracles possible; Mel Sanders, for too many things to count; Miriam Kriss, who worked very hard to make this possible; and Lucienne Diver, for shepherding a weary word-wright through the final gates. A heaping share of gratitude is also due to the sensitivity readers—anonymous at their request, but never forgotten—who kindly and firmly showed hurtful lacunae in the manuscript, as well as those whose scholarship kept the author from numerous errors. Any remaining blunders or flaws are simply and solely my own fault.

Much gratitude goes to my children, who think it's amusing to share their distracted parent with imaginary people, and several friends, online and off, who commiserate and celebrate as the occasion calls for.

Finally, my very dear Reader, let me as usual thank you in the way we both like best, by telling you yet another story . . . as soon as I recover from this one.

extras

orbit

meet the author

S. C. EMMETT is a pseudonym for a *New York Times* bestselling author.

Find out more about S. C. Emmett and other Orbit authors by registering for the free monthly newsletter at orbitbooks.net.

if you enjoyed
THE POISON PRINCE

look out for

THE WOLF OF OREN-YARO

Chronicles of the Bitch Queen: Book One

by

K. S. Villoso

Born under the crumbling towers of her kingdom, Queen Talyien was the shining jewel and legacy of the bloody War of the Wolves. It nearly tore her nation apart. But her arranged marriage to the son of a rival clan heralds peace.

However, he suddenly disappears before their reign can begin, and the kingdom is fractured beyond repair.

Years later, he sends a mysterious invitation to meet. Talyien journeys across the sea in hopes of reconciling their past. An assassination attempt quickly dashes those dreams. Stranded in a land she doesn't know, with no idea whom she can trust, Talyien will have to embrace her namesake.

A wolf of Oren-yaro is not tamed.

CHAPTER ONE

THE LEGACY
OF WARLORD TAL

They called me the Bitch Queen, the she-wolf, because I murdered a man and exiled my king the night before they crowned me.

Hurricanes destroy the villages and they call it senseless; the winter winds come and they call it cold. What else did they expect from my people, the Oren-yaro, the ambitious savages who created a war that nearly ripped Jin-Sayeng apart? I almost think that if my reign had started without bloodshed and terror, they would have been disappointed.

I did not regret killing the man. He had it coming, and my father had taught me to take action before you second-guess yourself. My father was a wise man, and if the warlords could've stopped arguing long enough to put their misgivings behind them, he would have made them a great king. Instead, they entrusted the land to me and my husband: children of that same war they would rather forget. The gods love their ironies.

I do regret looking at the bastard while he died. I regret watching his eyes roll backwards and the blood spread like a cobweb underneath his wilted form, leaking into the cracked cobblestone my father paid a remarkable amount of money to install. I regret not having a sharper sword, and losing my nerve so that I didn't strike him again and he had to die slowly. Bleeding over the jasmine bushes—that whole batch of flowers would remain pink until the end of the season—he had stared up at the trail of stars in the night sky and called for his mother. Even though he was a traitor, he didn't deserve the pain.

More than anything, I regret not stopping my husband. I should have run after him, grovelled at his feet, asked him to stay. But in nursing my own pride, I didn't give him a chance. I watched his tall, straight back grow smaller in the distance, his father's helmet nestled under his arm, his unbound hair blowing in the wind, and I did nothing. A wolf of Oren-yaro suffers in silence. A wolf of Oren-yaro does not beg.

Almost at once, the rumours spread like wildfire. They started in the great hall in the castle at Oka Shto when I arrived for my coronation, dressed in my mother's best silk dress—all white, like a virgin on her wedding day—bedecked with pearls and gold-weave, with no husband at my side. My son, also in white, stood on the other side of the dais with his nursemaid. Between us were the two priests tasked with the ceremony— a priest of the god Akaterru, patron deity of Oren-yaro, and a priest of Kibouri, that foreign religion my husband's clan favoured, with their Nameless Maker and enough texts to make anyone ill. They could pass for brothers, with their long faces, carp-like whiskers, and leathery skin the colour of honey.

My husband's absence was making everyone uncomfortable. I, on the other hand, drifted between boredom and restlessness. I glanced at my son. He had stopped crying, but the red around his eyes had yet to disappear. It was my fault—on the way to the great hall, he asked for his father as any two-year-old would, and I snapped in return. "He's gone," I told him in that narrow corridor, where only the nursemaid could hear. "He doesn't want us anymore." The boy didn't understand my words, but the sharp tone was enough to send tears rolling down his cheeks, a faint reflection of how I had spent the night before.

Now, Thanh rubbed his eyes, and I realized I didn't want to wait a moment longer. I turned to the priests and opened my mouth. Before I could utter a single word, the doors opened.

"Crown her," my adviser said, breaking into the hall. His face had the paleness of a man who had looked into a mirror that morning and seen his own death. His sandals clicked on the polished earth floor. "Prince Rayyel Ikessar left last night."

You could hear the weight of the words echo against the walls. In the silence that followed, I thought I could make out the rising heartbeats of every man and woman in that room. Not a day goes by that I am not reminded of what was lost to my father's war; even bated breaths could signal the start to that old argument, that old fear that I, too, may one day plunge the land into blood and fire once more.

Eventually, the Kibouri priest cleared his throat. "We must delay until the prince can be found."

"This day was approved by our order, set in stone years ago," the Akaterru priest replied. "It is a bad omen to change it."

"Every day is like any other," the Kibouri priest intoned. "You and your superstitions..."

My adviser stepped up the dais to face them. Both priests towered over him. His mouth, which was surrounded by a beard that looked like a burnt rodent, was set in a thin line. "Warlord Lushai sent a message this morning, congratulating Jin-Sayeng's lack of a leader. He will march against us by tonight for breaking the treaty if we do not crown her."

I didn't bother to pretend to be surprised. "Rayyel is hiding there, I assume," I said. It was such a bald-faced move: put me in a situation where I could not do anything *but* create trouble. Throw the wolf into a sea of sick deer—whatever will she do? Warlord Lushai once considered himself my father's friend, but daring me to make trouble in front of the other warlords was one step too far.

My adviser turned to me and bobbed his head up and down, like a rooster in the grass.

I gritted my teeth. "Get that crown." I didn't want to give them a reason to think I wasn't fulfilling my end of the bargain.

The Kibouri priest was closer to it. He didn't move.

"My lords," I said, looking at the warlords, the select few who were not too ill or infirm or couldn't find the right sort of excuse to avoid the coronation. "You agreed to this alliance. You all signed it with your own blood. Do you remember? Years ago, you all cut your arms, bled into a cup, and drank from it to mark the joining of Jin-Sayeng as one. Not even Lord Rayyel and I have the power to stop this."

There was a murmur of assent. A whisper, not an outcry, but I went with it. I turned to the priests. The Akaterru priest had already dropped his head, eyes downcast. The other eventually forced his knees into a bow.

They took the smaller crown. It was made of beaten gold, both yellow and white, set on a red silken headpiece. My father had it made not long after I was born, commissioned from a famous artisan from some distant town. I stared at it while the priests began their rituals, one after the other. I could have done without the Kibouri, but I didn't want to risk offending the Ikessar supporters in the crowd.

They crowned me with reluctance. No spirits came to crest a halo around my brow or send a shaft of light to bless the occasion. In fact, it was cloudy, and a rumble of thunder marked the beginning of a storm. I wondered when they would discover the body, or if they already had and were just too afraid to tell me.

Even after I became queen, the rumours continued. I was powerless to stop them. I should have been more, they said. More feminine. Subtle, the sort of woman who could hide my jibes behind a well-timed titter. I could have taken the womanly arts, learned to write poetry or brew a decent cup of tea or embroider something that didn't have my blood on it, and found ways to better please my man. Instead, Rayyel Ikessar would rather throw away the title of Dragonlord, king of Jin-Sayeng, than stay married to me.

It changes a woman, hearing such things. Hardens your heart. Twists your mind along dark paths you have no business being on. And perhaps it wouldn't have mattered if I hadn't loved Rai, but I did. More than I understood myself. More than I cared to explain.

—————◆—————

I don't like to talk about the years that followed. Even now, pen in hand while I splash ink over my dress, I find it difficult to recall anything past the cloud of anger. All I know is that five years passed, quicker than the blink of an eye. I was told the anger could do that. That it could rob whatever sweetness there was in the passage of time, add a bitter tinge to the little joys in the life of an unwanted queen. "Will my father come?" my son would ask on his nameday without fail. Each year he would grow taller, stronger, more sure of himself, and each year the question would lose a touch of innocence, be more demanding. "Will my father come?" Soft eyes growing harder, because we both knew that wasn't what he was really asking anymore. *When will he be home? Why did you send him away? Why didn't you stop him?*

And each year, I would struggle to find an answer that wouldn't make the courtiers turn their heads in shame. They knew I couldn't have thrown him out—I didn't have the power to lord over the heir of the most influential clan in Jin-Sayeng. Yet I could not allude that he abandoned his duties. I could say it easily enough to the Oren-yaro, but not in court—not in front of his family's supporters. As if the weight of the crown wasn't heavy enough, as if I wasn't spending every waking hour fending the warlords off each other, off of me. After centuries of Ikessar Dragonlords, I was the first queen of Jin-Sayeng, and all the difficulties didn't bode well for my rule.

In late summer of the fifth year, I returned after an afternoon riding my horse through the rice fields, where I had been surveying the damage caused by last year's storms. There was very little a monarch could do about such things, but it gave people strength to see me, or so I liked to think.

Arro stood by the gates, waiting. I slowed my horse to a walk. It was always amazing how I could predict the future simply by my adviser's expression. If it was going to be a good week, he often greeted me with a smile, his eyes disappearing into the folds of his face. That meant most provinces had paid their taxes, there were no land disputes (or at least none that people had lost their heads for), and every single warlord was accounted for.

He didn't smile now. His lips were flat—not quite a frown, as if he wasn't sure he wanted to expend his energy all that way yet. I dismounted from the horse, allowing a servant to take her back to the base of the mountain to the stables. Arro wiped his hands on his beard and held out a letter, which had been opened. No doubt it was checked thoroughly by the staff, in case someone tried to poison me by sprinkling dust on the inside of the scroll that I might later inhale. The Ikessars loved to use such tactics—I had even lost a great-uncle to it during the war.

"What's this?" I asked, just as my dog Blackie appeared between the trees. I whistled, and he bounded to me, ears flopping while his tail wagged so fast it felt at risk of falling off. I patted my tunic before taking the letter.

I read it once, and then a second time. I could feel my heart pounding, my mouth growing dry. I wanted to ask if this was a dream. It must be. I had so many others like it before. The details were always different: Sometimes it would come from a messenger, his horse slick with sweat. Sometimes it would be a falcon with a note attached to its leg. Sometimes a hooded Ikessar would come bearing gifts before revealing himself to be my husband, years changed and begging for my forgiveness. In each dream, I had fallen to my knees and wept with joy. It felt odd that I now couldn't muster any emotion beyond cool detachment.

I looked back at Arro and found my voice. "What do you think?"

"The man who abandoned his position, who abandoned *you*, has no right to demand a meeting on his terms, let alone in a place as far as Ziri-nar-Orxiaro. I smell a trap."

"He insists that it is a safe place for us to meet. Anzhao City would be on neutral grounds, away from the warlords' meddling."

"Easy for an Ikessar to say," Arro grumbled. Blackie came up to rub along his leg, and he pushed the dog away in disgust. He tugged his rice hat back into place. "Take my advice, my queen. Ignore it. The man disappears for the better part of five years and then thinks that you will come running to him after a mere *letter*? Such arrogance."

I was silent for a moment. "The warlords..." I started. "A good number of them supported the Ikessars."

Arro snorted. "They did. And so? They are content with whispers in the dark. None have dared challenge your position."

"Not yet," I said. "Whispers in the dark are still danger-ous. Did we not learn that in the days of the Ikessars' rule? They can roust the people, put ideas where they don't belong. All it takes is one warlord to decide he's had enough and get two more to agree with him. The rest will follow, and I will be yet another failed Dragonlord in this damned land's history."

"It's like trying to take control of a pack of dogs. Just bark louder than the rest."

"And you know a thing or two about dogs, do you, Arro?" I asked, watching him try to avoid Blackie's pestering tongue with a measure of amusement. Finally, I took pity on him and whistled. The dog returned to me. "The other warlords do not challenge me because Rai left of his own accord. They can say whatever they want... They have no proof I put a sword to his back and bullied him out of my lands. But it doesn't mean it will end there. Lately, they have turned to openly blaming me for his actions, and if word gets out that Rai wrote to me and I refused to answer, they will think I meant to hold on to the crown by myself. The idea of a wolf of Oren-yaro on the throne still frightens them."

Arro looked like he wanted to argue, but one of the things I appreciated about him was that he saw sense even when he didn't agree with it. He tucked his hands into his sleeves. "I will convene with the others," he said. "We will have to investigate this letter before we can make a decision."

"Of course," I said. "But this is the first time in years that Lord Rayyel has agreed to talk to us. Regardless of our personal opinions, he remains of importance to the royal clans. Don't do anything drastic—I will not have him frightened into silence."

He nodded, wiping his hands on his beard yet again. It was an affectation of his, a Zarojo mannerism. Arro had grown up in the empire, brought over to serve my father a long time ago—I would've thought he'd have jumped at the chance to visit his home after so many years.

I went up the flagstone steps leading to the garden, Blackie running in circles around me. I was doing a remarkable job at keeping calm. Only when I reached the fountain did my knees buckle. I sat on the edge, listening to the water bubble and the frogs croak.

"I told you to declare war on the bastards five years ago," a voice called from the gate. I looked up to see my father's general striding past the rose bushes. He must've been there when they first opened the letter. Although I knew it was a precaution, it irritated me that I was always the last to know, that other people were always making decisions for me. Taking a deep breath, I got up to face him.

Unlike Arro, Lord General Ozo never tried to hide his displeasure, especially his displeasure at *my* ruling.

He threw a staff in my direction, giving me only a split second to catch it before he charged with bamboo sticks, one in each hand. I stepped back and met his attack. Ozo was a big man, covered in hard muscle that had yet to go to fat, despite his age. Bamboo against bamboo clattered together. I staggered back.

"War," I repeated. "I told you before, Lord General Ozo. We don't have the resources."

He slapped the back of his head with his hand, his arm tattoos a deep black against his sunburnt skin. "I'm the one with the soldiers. I'm the one who can tell you we can crush the bastards if you just gave the order."

"And I'm your queen," I said as I tried to jam the end of my staff into his head. Just once, it would be satisfying to see his nose break.

He sidestepped, twirling the sticks in his hands. "Some queen. Your footwork alone..."

I bristled as I fixed my feet. "Is that insubordination?"

"That's honesty," he snarled as he charged me a second time. I spun on my heel, my staff slamming into his gut. But he only laughed it off. "This land is teetering on the brink of destruction because you can't make up your mind about what to do with that husband of yours." He continued to attack. "The other warlords laugh at you behind their cups. The peasants think you weak. You want to see the bastard? Order me to set fire to his holdings, and he'll come riding back to save his clan. I'll cut off his head, then."

"He's still your Dragonlord," I gasped, barely keeping up with his assault. I didn't know where the man still found the energy. He was old, too old to be sparring in broad daylight.

Sweat poured down his face as he finally grabbed my staff, dragging me up to him. "Uncrowned, like his uncle before him," he said. "I won't submit to it. He's no king of mine. And *you* won't be queen for much longer if you don't make a decision. You forget that *you're* Dragonlord, too." He spat on the bushes, a healthy globule that trickled down the leaves. My poor gardener was going to be livid. Then he pushed me away.

"Must this end in war?" I asked, relaxing my stance. "If I can find a peaceful resolution..."

"A peaceful resolution?" he asked incredulously. "*You?* You're Warlord Yeshin's. Yeshin the Butcher's daughter. The land will never allow *you* peace if you don't crush them under an iron fist first. You want our people to listen to you instead of their warlords, their clans, their families? Put them on a tight leash. Strangle their necks if you have to."

"Says Yeshin's general."

Ozo sniffed, flicking his sticks from side to side. "Or you can walk willingly into this trap for the sake of seeing your sorry sack of a husband and bring shame to the Oren-yaro. After everything your father has sacrificed, you would do this to him. And for what? The man has been nothing but trouble to Jin-Sayeng!" He lunged. The right stick smacked against my face before I could lift the staff to protect myself.

My skin prickled as I twirled the staff, jabbing him on the side. "You would say that, Lord Ozo," I hissed as I pulled back to jab him again. "You hate his clan."

"Hundreds of years under his clan's rule has brought us nothing but sorrow." He rewarded my efforts with another blow to my head. I reared back, shaking, and he gave a small grin. "You're the one with every reason to hate them. Their incompetence killed your brothers."

"Brothers I've never met," I grumbled, wiping my jaw.

"They were good men, and the Ikessars took them from us. Before your father's war, we had a Dragonlord who chose to wander the world instead of rule. And *his* father before him…" He spat again. "Shoddy rule after shoddy rule, and now this. Now you have the chance to prove to Jin-Sayeng we don't need the bastards at all."

My fingers tightened around the staff. "We don't, Ozo. But this alliance was my father's decision."

"A sorry excuse for an alliance. I've never seen an alliance where the other party slinks away and refuses to do their part for half a decade. And if you *do* decide to go to the empire, what then? Do you know how corrupt their cities are? Their officials won't help you. As far as they're concerned, Jin-Sayeng is a land of penniless peasants, and they wouldn't be wrong. And all you've got is that cracked halfblood adviser of yours, and Captain Nor. Nor's Oren-yaro, at least—I don't doubt her capabilities, but she's not Agos."

"Don't start this, General. Not again."

He lowered his sticks. "He was the best guard captain my army had produced, and you threw it all away for nothing. Don't come running to me for help if you get in trouble." He started to walk away.

"Not another step, General," I said in a low voice.

"You've got a sword. Put me in my place if you want to stop me," he snarled.

I dropped the staff and drew my sword.

He turned his head to the side and laughed. "Now what? Cut me down."

"Don't test me."

"But I am," he said, laughing. "I am, and you're failing. You hesitate. You always do, pup, and I'm sure when the time comes, you'll hesitate with *him*, too. Your lenience will be the death of us all." With a wave of his hand, he walked off. If he was anyone else, I could've had him executed on the spot, but...he was still a lord. An elder. In many ways, his authority eclipsed mine.

My fingers trembled as I watched him disappear around the bend, the same way my husband had done all those years ago. *War.* The word twisted inside my gut. General Ozo had wanted it declared the eve of the coronation. War would bolster Oren-yaro rule...if we won it. We had the largest army in the land, but that meant nothing if the others united against us.

"Mother."

A second voice, one that most days would have calmed me. Today, it filled me with dread. I sheathed my sword, wiped my face, and turned to my son.

"I heard what the general said," Thanh breathed. He hesitated. "Is it true?"

"You really shouldn't be eavesdropping on grown-ups."

He cocked his head to the side, the way he always did when I called him out for things and he understood he'd done wrong, he'd just rather not dwell on it. I believe my father would've called it something like discourtesy. Defiance. I merely found it amusing. "But are you really going to see Father? You're going to bring him back?"

Up until that moment, I hadn't been sure what I was going to do. A part of me was inclined to set the letter aside. I had done it before. After Rayyel left, it took a whole month for his first letter to arrive. It was an angry letter, full of his misgivings about our relationship. I left it inside my desk, refusing to read the rest of it. I had hoped he would send another soon, that time would ease the anger, would allow us to speak without throwing barbed words at each other.

That *soon* became five years. The letter in my hands was his second.

"If I do go to Anzhao," I said, "I can bring you back a book, or a falcon. I've heard they breed such beautiful falcons in Anzhao City. A white one, perhaps. And they have these little dogs..."

"I want my father," Thanh said, his voice growing stern.

I stared at my son, at the way he held himself, firm jaw, straight back, more pride and dignity than most adults I've known. My beautiful boy, seven years old, aged by his father's absence in a way I couldn't have anticipated. I had watched him turn from that chubby-cheeked toddler calling impatiently for his papa to this calm, quiet child who could no longer recall his father's face. Do you know what it feels like to see your son looking back at you, waiting for an answer that would soothe away those hurts, all those years of crying for his father in the night? To know that your words could crush his hopes and dreams in an instant? The boy could break me.

I held my breath and spoke before I could even really think it through. "So I will," I said. "I'll bring your father back, even if it's against his will. I promise. We'll be a family again."

If they were lies, they were such beautiful lies. The rush of relief in his eyes sealed the deal.

I've never known a life outside politics.

I *have* been told that monarchs can have hobbies. The last true Dragonlord, Reshiro, kept butterflies. But then again, he was an Ikessar, and only Ikessars would find interest in that sort of thing.

My words to my son ringing in my ears, I returned to my chambers to try to find that first letter. It was gone. The drawers contained other things—a rattle from when my son was an infant, various brushes and empty ink jars. Old books. A wrinkled piece of brown paper I had folded several times over for my son—it had been a boat, and then a hat, and then a frog that could jump if you pressed its back. No letter. It was odd; I was sure I had left it there.

I returned to the new letter and read it a third time. My husband's words were flat and empty, precise, as if he were asking to meet with any other official. He addressed it to my full name and ended with his, with no hint of emotion anywhere. As if I was nothing. Not his wife, not the mother of his son. Not a woman he loved.

You would think that last part wouldn't sting anymore. I had considered the possibility enough times in the past—years of silence could do that. He didn't love me anymore. He never loved me at all. But I knew thinking like this was wasted energy. I could unearth all my memories of him and turn them over in my head until I came close to madness, and I would still come to a different conclusion every time. That look in his eyes as he helped me down the steps when I was heavily pregnant with our son—was it devotion, or was it abhorrence over my weakness? Whenever he held my hand, was it because he wanted to, or because *I* wanted him to?

That old irritation returned. Assurance was not something I had ever received in my marriage, and it would be foolish to expect it now. I could just as easily shove the letter into my desk again and forget about it for another five years. Life was complicated enough as it was. Rayyel left us. Twist the words however you want; he was the one who walked away.

I sat on the edge of the bed and looked through the window. Out in the courtyard, I spotted members of the Queen's Guard busy with their daily exercise, the light drizzle cloaking their sinewy forms. Their faces were blank, determined. I doubted that expression would go away even if you threw them naked into freezing snow.

Unfaltering, dutiful, and loyal to a fault—these tenets are why the rest of Jin-Sayeng have labelled our people *wolves of Oren-yaro*, a term that started as an insult. These wolves, they like to say, these bloodthirsty beasts, these savages who would stop at nothing. But far from taking offense, we decided to adopt the title, bestowing the name *wolf of Oren-yaro* on all who fall under the shadow of our province. As a people, we embrace these tenets, regardless of clan, regardless of caste, setting us apart from the rest of Jin-Sayeng. It has created a unity never before seen in these lands. We know it. The others know it. It is why the Oren-yaro are as feared as they are revered; the strength of our resolution has toppled realms.

Let me tell you a story. A long time ago, five hundred and twenty-six wolves of Oren-yaro died protecting Shirrokaru, the Jin-Sayeng capital and Ikessar stronghold, from warlords who rebelled. The rebels numbered over three thousand. By the end of the assault, all our soldiers lay dead except for one: Warlord Tal aren dar Orenar. He stood in the middle of that battlefield, covered in the blood of friend, family, and foe, and held his position for over two days in case the enemy dared to return. When the Ikessar lord came to view the slaughter, Warlord Tal was still able to throw his sword aside and bend his knee before he died.

I had no intention of bending my knee, not to the man who had broken *his* vows. But I thought of Warlord Tal, for whom I was named, as I watched my soldiers out in the courtyard. I watched them go through the motions, their voices drowned by the torrent of rainfall, and thought that if Warlord Tal could do it—if he could fight a battle in the face of defeat and then stand strong between those corpses for the sake of never giving up his post—then I could do my part. I could learn to swallow the silence and face my husband again.

if you enjoyed
THE POISON PRINCE

look out for

THE MASK OF MIRRORS

Rook & Rose: Book One

by

M. A. Carrick

Nightmares are creeping through the City of Dreams....

Renata Viraudax is a con artist who has come to the sparkling city of Nadežra—the City of Dreams—with one goal: to trick her way into a noble house and secure her fortune and her sister's future.

But as she's drawn into the elite world of House Traementis, she realizes her masquerade is just one of many surrounding her. And as corrupt magic begins to weave its way through Nadežra, the poisonous feuds of its aristocrats and the shadowy dangers of its impoverished underbelly become tangled—with Ren at their heart.

1

THE MASK OF MIRRORS

Isla Traementis, the Pearls: Suilun 1

After fifteen years of handling the Traementis house charters, Donaia Traementis knew that a deal which looked too good to be true probably was. The proposal currently on her desk stretched the boundaries of belief.

"He could at least try to make it look legitimate," she muttered. Did Mettore Indestor think her an utter fool?

He thinks you desperate. And he's right.

She burrowed her stockinged toes under the great lump of a hound sleeping beneath her desk and pressed cold fingers to her brow. She'd removed her gloves to avoid ink stains and left the hearth in her study unlit to save the cost of fuel. Besides Meatball, the only warmth was from the beeswax candles—an expense she couldn't scrimp on unless she wanted to lose what eyesight she had left.

Adjusting her spectacles, she scanned the proposal again, scratching angry notes between the lines.

She remembered a time when House Traementis had been as powerful as the Indestor family. They had held a seat in the Cinquerat, the five-person council that ruled Nadežra, and charters that allowed them to conduct trade, contract mercenaries, control guilds. Every variety of wealth, power, and pres-

514

tige in Nadežra had been theirs. Now, despite Donaia's best efforts and her late husband's before her, it had come to this: scrabbling at one Dusk Road trade charter as though she could milk enough blood from that stone to pay off all the Traementis debts.

Debts almost entirely owned by Mettore Indestor.

"And you expect me to trust my caravan to guards you provide?" she growled at the proposal, her pen nib digging in hard enough to tear the paper. "Ha! Who's going to protect it from them? Will they even wait for bandits, or just sack the wagons themselves?"

Leaving Donaia with the loss, a pack of angry investors, and debts she could no longer cover. Then Mettore would swoop in like one of his thrice-damned hawks to swallow whole what remained of House Traementis.

Try as she might, though, she couldn't see another option. She couldn't send the caravan out unguarded—Vraszenian bandits were a legitimate concern—but the Indestor family held the Caerulet seat in the Cinquerat, which gave Mettore authority over military and mercenary affairs. Nobody would risk working with a house Indestor had a grudge against—not when it would mean losing a charter, or worse.

Meatball's head rose with a sudden whine. A moment later a knock came at the study door, followed by Donaia's majordomo. Colbrin knew better than to interrupt her when she was wrestling with business, which meant he judged this interruption important.

He bowed and handed her a card. "Alta Renata Viraudax?" Donaia asked, shoving Meatball's wet snout out of her lap when he sniffed at the card. She flipped it as if the back would provide some clue to the visitor's purpose. Viraudax wasn't a local noble house. Some traveler to Nadežra?

"A young woman, Era Traementis," her majordomo said. "Well-mannered. Well-dressed. She said it concerned an important private matter."

The card fluttered to the floor. Donaia's duties as head of House Traementis kept her from having much of a social life, but the same could not be said for her son, and lately Leato had been behaving more and more like his father. Ninat take him—if her son had racked up some gambling debt with a foreign visitor...

Colbrin retrieved the card before the dog could eat it, and handed it back to her. "Should I tell her you are not at home?"

"No. Show her in." If her son's dive into the seedier side of Nadežra had resulted in trouble, she would at least rectify his errors before stringing him up.

Somehow. With money she didn't have.

She could start by not conducting the meeting in a freezing study. "Wait," she said before Colbrin could leave. "Show her to the salon. And bring tea."

Donaia cleaned the ink from her pen and made a futile attempt to brush away the brindled dog hairs matting her surcoat. Giving that up as a lost cause, she tugged on her gloves and straightened the papers on her desk, collecting herself by collecting her surroundings. Looking down at her clothing— the faded blue surcoat over trousers and house scuffs—she weighed the value of changing over the cost of making a potential problem wait.

Everything is a tallied cost these days, she thought grimly.

"Meatball. Stay," she commanded when the hound would have followed, and headed directly to the salon.

The young woman waiting there could not have fit the setting more perfectly if she had planned it. Her rose-gold underdress and cream surcoat harmonized beautifully with the gold-shot peach silk of the couch and chairs, and the thick curl trailing from her upswept hair echoed the rich wood of the wall paneling. The curl should have looked like an accident, an errant strand slipping loose—but everything else about the visitor was so elegant it was clearly a deliberate touch of style.

She was studying the row of books on their glass-fronted shelf. When Donaia closed the door, she turned and dipped low. "Era Traementis. Thank you for seeing me."

Her curtsy was as Seterin as her clipped accent, one hand sweeping elegantly up to the opposite shoulder. Donaia's misgivings deepened at the sight of her. Close to her son's age, and beautiful as a portrait by Creciasto, with fine-boned features and flawless skin. Easy to imagine Leato losing his head over a hand of cards with such a girl. And her ensemble did nothing to comfort Donaia's fears—the richly embroidered brocade, the sleeves an elegant fall of sheer silk. Here was someone who could afford to bet and lose a fortune.

That sort was more likely to forgive or forget a debt than come collecting…unless the debt was meant as leverage for something else.

"Alta Renata. I hope you will forgive my informality." She brushed a hand down her simple attire. "I did not expect visitors, but it sounded like your matter was of some urgency. Please, do be seated."

The young woman lowered herself into the chair as lightly as mist on the river. Seeing her, it was easy to understand why the people of Nadežra looked to Seteris as the source of all that was stylish and elegant. Fashion was born in Seteris. By the time it traveled south to Seteris's protectorate, Seste Ligante, then farther south still, across the sea to Nadežra, it was old and stale, and Seteris had moved on.

Most Seterin visitors behaved as though Nadežra was nothing more than Seste Ligante's backwater colonial foothold on the Vraszenian continent and merely setting foot on the streets would foul them with the mud of the River Dežera. But Renata's delicacy looked like hesitation, not condescension. She said, "Not urgent, no—I do apologize if I gave that impression. I confess, I'm not certain how to even begin this conversation."

She paused, hazel eyes searching Donaia's face. "You don't recognize my family name, do you?"

That had an ominous sound. Seteris might be on the other side of the sea, but the truly powerful families could influence trade anywhere in the known world. If House Traementis had somehow crossed one of them . . .

Donaia kept her fear from her face and her voice. "I am afraid I haven't had many dealings with the great houses of Seteris."

A soft breath flowed out of the girl. "As I suspected. I thought she might have written to you at least once, but apparently not. I . . . am Letilia's daughter."

She could have announced she was descended from the Vraszenian goddess Ažerais herself, and it wouldn't have taken Donaia more by surprise.

Disbelief clashed with relief and apprehension both: not a creditor, not an offended daughter of some foreign power. Family—after a fashion.

Lost for words, Donaia reassessed the young woman sitting across from her. Straight back, straight shoulders, straight neck, and the same fine, narrow nose that made everyone in Nadežra hail Letilia Traementis as the great beauty of her day.

Yes, she could be Letilia's daughter. Donaia's niece by marriage.

"Letilia never wrote after she left." It was the only consideration the spoiled brat had ever shown her family. The first several years, every day they'd expected a letter telling them she was stranded in Seteris, begging for funds. Instead they never heard from her again.

Dread sank into Donaia's bones. "Is Letilia here?"

The door swung open, and for one dreadful instant Donaia expected a familiar squall of petulance and privilege to sweep inside. But it was only Colbrin, bearing a tray. To her dismay, Donaia saw two pots on it, one short and rounded for tea, the other taller. Of course: He'd heard their guest's Seterin accent, and naturally assumed Donaia would also want to serve coffee.

We haven't yet fallen so far that I can't afford proper hospitality. But Donaia's voice was still sharp as he set the tray between the two of them. "Thank you, Colbrin. That will be all."

"No," Renata said as the majordomo bowed and departed. "No, Mother is happily ensconced in Seteris."

It seemed luck hadn't *entirely* abandoned House Traementis. "Tea?" Donaia said, a little too bright with relief. "Or would you prefer coffee?"

"Coffee, thank you." Renata accepted the cup and saucer with a graceful hand. Everything about her was graceful—but not the artificial, forced elegance Donaia remembered Letilia practicing so assiduously.

Renata sipped the coffee and made a small, appreciative noise. "I must admit, I was wondering if I would even be able to find coffee here."

Ah. *There* was the echo of Letilia, the little sneer that took what should be a compliment and transformed it into an insult.

We have wooden floors and chairs with backs, too. Donaia swallowed down the snappish response. But the bitter taste in her mouth nudged her into pouring coffee for herself, even though she disliked it. She wouldn't let this girl make her feel like a delta rustic simply because Donaia had lived all her life in Nadežra.

"So you are here, but Letilia is not. May I ask why?"

The girl's chin dropped, and she rotated her coffee cup as though its precise alignment against the saucer were vitally important. "I've spent days imagining how best to approach you, but—well." There was a ripple of nervousness in her laugh. "There's no way to say this without first admitting I'm Letilia's daughter…and yet by admitting that, I know I've already gotten off on the wrong foot. Still, there's nothing for it."

Renata inhaled like someone preparing for battle, then met Donaia's gaze. "I'm here to see if I can possibly reconcile my mother with her family."

It took all Donaia's self-control not to laugh. Reconcile? She would sooner reconcile with the drugs that had overtaken her husband Gianco's good sense in his final years. If Gianco's darker comments were to be believed, Letilia had done as much to destroy House Traementis as aža had.

Fortunately, custom and law offered her a more dispassionate response. "Letilia is no part of this family. My husband's father struck her name from our register after she left."

At least Renata was smart enough not to be surprised. "I can hardly blame my gra—your father-in-law," she said. "I've only my mother's version of the tale, but I also know *her*. I can guess the part she played in that estrangement."

Donaia could just imagine what poison Letilia's version had contained. "It is more than estrangement," she said brusquely, rising to her feet. "I am sorry you crossed the sea for nothing, but I'm afraid that what you're asking for is impossible. Even if

I believed that your mother wanted to reconcile—which I do not—I have no interest in doing so."

A treacherous worm within her whispered, *Even if that might offer a new business opportunity? Some way out of Indestor's trap?*

Even then. Donaia would burn Traementis Manor to the ground before she accepted help from Letilia's hand.

The salon door opened again. But this time, the interruption wasn't her majordomo.

"Mother, Egliadas has invited me to go sailing on the river." Leato was tugging on his gloves, as if he couldn't be bothered to finish dressing before leaving his rooms. But he stopped, one hand still caught in the tight cuff, when he saw their visitor.

Renata rose like a flower bud unfurling, and Donaia cursed silently. Why, today of all days, had Leato chosen to wake early? Not that fourth sun was early by most people's standards, but for him midmorning might as well be dawn.

Reflex forced the courtesies out of her mouth, even though she wanted nothing more than to hurry the girl away. "Leato, you recall stories of your aunt Letilia? This is her daughter, Alta Renata Viraudax of Seteris. Alta Renata, my son and heir, Leato Traementis."

Leato captured Renata's hand before she could touch it to her shoulder again and kissed her gloved fingertips. When she saw them together, Donaia's heart sank like a stone. She was used to thinking of her son as an adolescent scamp, or an intermittent source of headaches. But he was a man grown, with beauty to match Renata's: his hair like antique gold, fashionably mussed on top; his ivory skin and finely carved features, the hallmark of House Traementis; the elegant cut of his waistcoat and fitted tailoring of the full-skirted coat over it in the platinum shimmer of delta grasses in autumn.

And the two of them were smiling at one another like the sun had just risen in the salon.

"Letilia's daughter?" Leato said, releasing Renata's hand before the touch could grow awkward. "I thought she hated us."

Donaia bit down the impulse to chide him. It would sound like she was defending Renata, which was the last thing she wanted to do.

The girl's smile was brief and rueful. "I may have inherited her nose, but I've tried not to inherit *everything* else."

"You mean, not her personality? I'll offer thanks to Katus." Leato winced. "I'm sorry, I shouldn't insult your mother—"

"No insult taken," Renata said dryly. "I'm sure the stories you know of her are dreadful, and with good cause."

They had the river's current beneath them and were flowing onward; Donaia had to stop it before they went too far. When Leato asked what brought Renata to the city, Donaia lunged in, social grace be damned. "She just—"

But Renata spoke over her, as smooth as silk. "I was hoping to meet your grandfather and father. Foolish of me, really; since Mother hasn't been in contact, I didn't know they'd both passed away until I arrived. And now I understand she's no longer in the register, so there's no bond between us—I'm just a stranger, intruding."

"Oh, not at all!" Leato turned to his mother for confirmation.

For the first time, Donaia felt a touch of gratitude toward Renata. Leato had never known Letilia; he hadn't even been born when she ran away. He'd heard the tales, but no doubt he marked at least some of them as exaggeration. If Renata had mentioned a reconciliation outright, he probably would have supported her.

"We're touched by your visit," Donaia said, offering the girl a courteous nod. "I'm only sorry the others never had a chance to meet you."

"Your visit?" Leato scoffed. "No, this can't be all. You're my cousin, after all—oh, not under the law, I know. But blood counts for a lot here."

"We're Nadežran, Leato, not Vraszenian," Donaia said reprovingly, lest Renata think they'd been completely swallowed by delta ways.

He went on as though he hadn't heard her. "My long-lost cousin shows up from across the sea, greets us for a few minutes, then vanishes? Unacceptable. Giuna hasn't even met you—she's my younger sister. Why don't you stay with us for a few days?"

Donaia couldn't stop a muffled sound from escaping her. However much he seemed determined to ignore them, Leato knew about House Traementis's financial troubles. A houseguest was the last thing they could afford.

But Renata demurred with a light shake of her head. "No, no—I couldn't impose like that. I'll be in Nadežra for some time, though. Perhaps you'll allow me the chance to show I'm not my mother."

Preparatory to pushing for reconciliation, no doubt. But although Renata was older and more self-possessed, something about her downcast gaze reminded Donaia of Giuna. She could all too easily imagine Giuna seeking Letilia out in Seteris with the same impossible dream.

If House Traementis could afford the sea passage, which they could not. And if Donaia would allow her to go, which she would not. But if that impossible situation happened... she bristled at the thought of Letilia rebuffing Giuna entirely, treating her with such cold hostility that she refused to see the girl at all.

So Donaia said, as warmly as she could, "Of course we know you aren't your mother. And you shouldn't be forced to carry the burden of her past." She let a smile crack her mask. "I'm certain from the caterpillars dancing on my son's brow that he'd like to know more about you, and I imagine Giuna would feel the same."

"Thank you," Renata said with a curtsy. "But not now, I think. My apologies, Altan Leato." Her words silenced his protest before he could voice it, and with faultless formality. "My maid intends to fit me for a new dress this afternoon, and she'll stick me with pins if I'm late."

That was as unlike Letilia as it was possible to be. Not the concern for her clothing—Letilia was the same, only with less tasteful results—but the graceful withdrawal, cooperating with Donaia's wish to get her out of the house.

Leato did manage to get one more question out, though. "Where can we reach you?"

"On the Isla Prišta, Via Brelkoja, number four," Renata said. Donaia's lips tightened. For a stay of a few weeks, even a month or two, a hotel would have sufficed. Renting a house suggested the girl intended to remain for quite some time.

But that was a matter for later. Donaia reached for the bell. "Colbrin will see you out."

"No need," Leato said, offering Renata his hand. When she glanced at Donaia instead of taking it, Leato said, "Mother, you won't begrudge me a few moments of gossip with my new cousin?"

That was Leato, always asking for forgiveness rather than permission. But Renata's minute smile silently promised not to encourage him. At Donaia's forbearing nod, she accepted his escort from the room.

Once they were gone, Donaia rang for Colbrin. "I'll be in my study. No more interruptions barring flood or fire, please."

Colbrin's acknowledgment trailed after her as she went upstairs. When she entered the room, Meatball roused with a whine-snap of a yawn and a hopeful look, but settled again once he realized no treats were forthcoming.

The space seemed chillier than when she'd left it, and darker. She thought of Alta Renata's fine manners and finer clothes. Of course Letilia's daughter would be dressed in designs so new they hadn't yet made their way from Seteris to Nadežra. Of course she would have enough wealth to rent a house in West-bridge for herself alone and think nothing of it. Hadn't Gianco always said that Letilia took House Traementis's luck with her when she left?

In a fit of pique, Donaia lit the hearthfire, and damn the cost. Once its warmth was blazing through the study, she returned to her desk. She buried her toes under the dog again, mentally composing her message as she sharpened her nib and filled her ink tray.

House Traementis might be neck-deep in debt and sinking, but they still had the rights granted by their ennoblement charter. And Donaia wasn't such a fool that she would bite a hook before examining it from all sides first.

Bending her head, Donaia began penning a letter to Commander Cercel of the Vigil.

Upper and Lower Bank: Suilun 1

Renata expected Leato Traementis to see her out the front door, but he escorted her all the way to the bottom of the steps, and kept her hand even when they stopped. "I hope you're not too offended by Mother's reserve," he said. A breeze ruffled his burnished hair and carried the scent of caramel and almonds to her nose. A rich scent, matching his clothes and his carriage, and the thin lines of gold paint limning his eyelashes. "A lot of dead branches have been pruned from the Traementis register since my father—and your mother—were children. Now there's only Mother, Giuna, and myself. She gets protective."

"I take no offense at all," Renata said, smiling up at him. "I'm not so much of a fool that I expect to be welcomed with open arms. And I'm willing to be patient."

The breeze sharpened, and she shivered. Leato stepped between her and the wind. "You'd think Nadežra would be warmer than Seteris, wouldn't you?" he said with a sympathetic grimace. "It's all the water. We almost never get snow here, but the winters are so damp, the cold cuts right to your bones."

"I should have thought to wear a cloak. But since I can't pluck one from thin air, I hope you won't take offense if I hurry home."

"Of course not. Let me get you a sedan chair." Leato raised a hand to catch the eye of some men idling on the far side of the square and paid the bearers before Renata could even reach for her purse. "To soothe any lingering sting," he said with a smile.

She thanked him with another curtsy. "I hope I'll see you soon."

"As do I." Leato helped her into the sedan chair and closed the door once her skirts were safely out of the way.

As the bearers headed for the narrow exit from the square, Renata drew the curtains shut. Traementis Manor was in the Pearls, a cluster of islets strung along the Upper Bank of the River Dežera. The river here ran pure and clear thanks to the numinat that protected the East Channel, and the narrow streets and bridges were clean; whichever families held the charters to keep the streets clear of refuse wouldn't dream of letting it accumulate near the houses of the rich and powerful.

But the rocky wedge that broke the Dežera into east and west channels was a different matter. For all that it held two of Nadežra's major institutions—the Charterhouse in Dawngate, which was the seat of government, and the Aerie in Duskgate, home to the Vigil, which maintained order—the Old Island was also crowded with the poor and the shabby-genteel. Anyone riding in a sedan chair was just asking for beggars to crowd at their windows.

Which still made it better than half of the Lower Bank, where a sedan chair risked being knocked to the ground and the passenger robbed.

Luckily, her rented house was on Isla Prišta in Westbridge—technically on the Lower Bank, and far from a fashionable district, but it was a respectable neighborhood on the rise. In fact, the buildings on the Via Brelkoja were so newly renovated the mortar hadn't had time to moss over in the damp air. The freshly painted door to number four opened just as Renata's foot touched the first step.

Tess made a severe-looking sight in the crisp grey-and-white surcoat and underskirt of a Nadežran housemaid, but her copper Ganllechyn curls and freckles were a warm beacon welcoming Renata home. She bobbed a curtsy and murmured a lilting "alta" as Renata passed across the threshold, accepting the gloves and purse Renata held out.

"Downstairs," Ren murmured as the door snicked shut, sinking them into the dimness of the front hall.

Tess nodded, swallowing her question before she could speak it. Together they headed into the half-sunken chambers of the cellar, which held the service rooms. Only once they were safely in the kitchen did Tess say, "Well? How did it go?"

Ren let her posture drop and her voice relax into the throaty tones of her natural accent. "For me, as well as I could hope. Donaia refused reconciliation out of hand—"

"Thank the Mother," Tess breathed. If Donaia contacted Letilia, their entire plan would fall apart before it started.

Ren nodded. "Faced with the prospect of talking to her former sister-in-law, she barely even noticed me getting my foot in the door."

"That's a start, then. Here, off with this, and wrap up before you take a chill." Tess passed Ren a thick cloak of rough-spun wool lined with raw fleece, then turned her around like a dressmaker's doll so she could remove the beautifully embroidered surcoat.

"I saw the sedan chair," Tess said as she tugged at the side ties. "You didn't take that all the way from Isla Traementis, did you? If you're going to be riding about in chairs, I'll have to revise the budget. And here I'd had my eye on a lovely bit of lace at the remnants stall." Tess sighed mournfully, like she was saying farewell to a sweetheart. "I'll just have to tat some myself."

"In your endless spare time?" Ren said sardonically. The surcoat came loose, and she swung the cloak around her shoulders in its place. "Anyway, the son paid for the chair." She dropped onto the kitchen bench and eased her shoes off with a silent curse. Fashionable shoes were *not* comfortable. The hardest part of this con was going to be pretending her feet didn't hurt all day long.

Although choking down coffee ran a close second.

"Did he, now?" Tess settled on the bench next to Ren, close enough that they could share warmth beneath the cloak. Apart from the kitchen and the front salon, protective sheets still covered the furniture in every other room. The hearths were cold, their meals were simple, and they slept together on a kitchen floor pallet so they would only have to heat one room of the house.

Because she was not Alta Renata Viraudax, daughter of Letilia Traementis. She was Arenza Lenskaya, half-Vraszenian river rat, and even with a forged letter of credit to help, pretending to be a Seterin noblewoman wasn't cheap.

Pulling out a thumbnail blade, Tess began ripping the seams of Ren's beautiful surcoat, preparatory to alteration. "Was it just idle flirtation?"

The speculative uptick in Tess's question said she didn't believe any flirtation Ren encountered was idle. But whether Leato's flirtation had been idle or not, Ren had lines she would not cross, and whoring herself out was one of them.

It would have been the easier route. Dress herself up fine enough to catch the eye of some delta gentry son, or even a noble, and marry her way into money. She wouldn't be the first person in Nadežra to do it.

But she'd spent five years in Ganllech—five years as a maid under Letilia's thumb, listening to her complain about her dreadful family and how much she dreamed of life in Seteris, the promised land she'd never managed to reach. So when Ren and Tess found themselves back in Nadežra, Ren had been resolved. No whoring, and no killing. Instead she set her sights on a higher target: use what she'd learned to gain acceptance into House Traementis as their long-lost kin...with all the wealth and social benefit that brought.

"Leato is friendly," she allowed, picking up the far end of the dress and starting on the seam with her own knife. Tess didn't trust her to sew anything more complicated than a hem, but ripping stitches? That, she was qualified for. "And he helped shame Donaia into agreeing to see me again. But *she* is every bit as bad as Letilia claimed. You should have seen what she wore. Ratty old clothes, covered in dog hair. Like it's a moral flaw to let a single centira slip through her fingers."

"But the son isn't so bad?" Tess rocked on the bench, nudging Ren's hip with her own. "Maybe he's a bastard."

Ren snorted. "Not likely. Donaia would give him the moon if he asked, and he looks as Traementis as I." Only he didn't need makeup to achieve the effect.

Her hands trembled as she worked. Those five years in Ganllech were also five years out of practice. And all her previous cons had been short touches—never anything on this scale. When she got caught before, the hawks slung her in jail for a few days.

If she got caught now, impersonating a noblewoman...

Tess laid a hand over Ren's, stopping her before she could nick herself with the knife. "It's never too late to do something else."

Ren managed a smile. "Buy piles of fabric, then run away and set up as dressmakers? You, anyway. I would be your tailor's dummy."

"You'd model and sell them," Tess said stoutly. "If you want."

Tess would be happy in that life. But Ren wanted more.

This city *owed* her more. It had taken everything: her mother, her childhood, Sedge. The rich cuffs of Nadežra got whatever they wanted, then squabbled over what their rivals had, grinding everyone else underfoot. In all her days among the Fingers, Ren had never been able to take more than the smallest shreds from the hems of their cloaks.

But now, thanks to Letilia, she was in a position to take more.

The Traementis made the perfect target. Small enough these days that only Donaia stood any chance of spotting

Renata as an imposter, and isolated enough that they would be grateful for any addition to their register. In the glory days of their power and graft, they'd been notorious for their insular ways, refusing to aid their fellow nobles in times of need. Since they lost their seat in the Cinquerat, everyone else had gladly returned the favor.

Ren put down the knife and squeezed Tess's hand. "No. It is nerves only, and they will pass. We go forward."

"Forward it is." Tess squeezed back, then returned to work. "Next we're to make a splash somewhere public, yes? I'll need to know where and when if I'm to outfit you proper." The sides of the surcoat parted, and she started on the bandeau at the top of the bodice. "The sleeves are the key, have you noticed? Everyone is so on about their sleeves. But I've a thought for that...if you're ready for Alta Renata to set fashion instead of following."

Ren glanced sideways, her wariness only half-feigned. "What have you in mind?"

"Hmm. Stand up, and off with the rest of it." Once she had Ren stripped to her chemise, Tess played with different gathers and drapes until Ren's arms started to ache from being held out for so long. But she didn't complain. Tess's eye for fashion, her knack for imbuing, and her ability to rework the pieces of three outfits into nine were as vital to this con as Ren's skill at manipulation.

She closed her eyes and cast her thoughts over what she knew about the city. Where could she go, what could she do, to attract the kind of admiration that would help her gain the foothold she needed?

A slow smile spread across her face.

"Tess," she said, "I have the perfect idea. And you will love it."

The Aerie and Isla Traementis: Suilun 1

"Serrado! Get in here. I have a job for you."

Commander Cercel's voice cut sharply through the din of the Aerie. Waving at his constables to take their prisoner to the stockade, Captain Grey Serrado turned and threaded his way through the chaos to his commander's office. He ignored the sidelong smirks and snide whispers of his fellow officers: Unlike them, he didn't have the luxury of lounging about drinking coffee, managing his constables from the comfort of the Aerie.

"Commander Cercel?" He snapped the heels of his boots together and gave her his crispest salute—a salute he'd perfected during hours of standing at attention in the sun, the rain, the wind, while other lieutenants were at mess or in the barracks. Cercel wasn't the stickler for discipline his previous superiors had been, but she was the reason he wore a captain's double-lined hexagram pin, and he didn't want to reflect badly on her.

She was studying a letter, but when she brought her head up to reply, her eyes widened. "What does the *other* guy look like?"

Taking the casual question as permission to drop into rest, Grey spared a glance for his uniform. His patrol slops were spattered with muck from heel to shoulder, and blood was drying on the knuckles of his leather gloves. Some of the canal mud on his boots had flaked off when he saluted, powdering Cercel's carpet with the filth of the Kingfisher slums.

"Dazed but breathing. Ranieri's taking him to the stockade now." Her question invited banter, but the door to her office was open, and it wouldn't do him any good to be marked as a smart-ass.

She responded to his businesslike answer with an equally brisk nod. "Well, get cleaned up. I've received a letter from one of the noble houses, requesting Vigil assistance. I'm sending you."

Grey's jaw tensed as he waited for several gut responses to subside. It was possible the request was a legitimate call for aid. "What crime has been committed?"

Cercel's level gaze said, *You know better than that.* "One of the noble houses has requested Vigil assistance," she repeated, enunciating each word with cut-glass clarity. "I'm sure they wouldn't do that without good cause."

No doubt whoever sent the letter thought the cause was good. People from the great houses always did.

But Grey had a desk full of real problems. "More children have gone missing. That's eleven verified this month."

They'd had this conversation several times over the past few weeks. Cercel sighed. "We haven't had any reports—"

"Because they're all river rats so far. Who's going to care enough to report that? But the man I just brought in might know something about it; he's been promising Kingfisher kids good pay for an unspecified job. I got him on defacing public property, but he'll be free again by tonight." Pissing in public wasn't an offense the Vigil usually cracked down on, unless it suited them. "Am I to assume this noble's 'good cause' takes precedence over finding out what's happening to those kids?"

Cercel breathed out hard through her nose, and he tensed. Had he pushed her patience too far?

No. "Your man is on his way to the stockade," she said. "Have Kaineto process him—you're always complaining he's as slow as river mud. By the time you get back, he'll be ready to talk. Meanwhile, send Ranieri to ask questions around King-fisher, see if he can find any of the man's associates." She set the letter aside and drew another from her stack, a clear prelude to dismissing him. "You know the deal, Serrado."

The first few times, he'd played dense to make her spell it out in unambiguous terms. The last thing he could afford back then was to mistake a senior officer's meaning.

But they were past those games now. As long as he knuckled under and did whatever this noble wanted of him, Cercel wouldn't question him using Vigil time and resources for his own investigations.

"Yes, Commander." He saluted and heel-knocked another layer of delta silt onto her carpet. "Which house has called for aid?"

"Traementis."

If he'd been less careful of his manners, he would have thrown her a dirty look. *She could have* led *with that*. But Cercel wanted him to understand that answering these calls was part of his duty, and made him bend his neck before she revealed the silver lining. "Understood. I'll head to the Pearls at once."

Her final command followed him out of the office. "Don't you dare show up at Era Traementis's door looking like that!"

Groaning, Grey changed his path. He snagged a pitcher of water and a messenger, sending the latter to Ranieri with the new orders.

There was a bathing room in the Aerie, but he didn't want to waste time on that. A sniff test sent every piece of his patrol uniform into the laundry bag; aside from the coffee, that was one of the few perks of his rank he didn't mind taking shameless advantage of. If he was wading through canals for the job, the least the Vigil could do was ensure he didn't smell like one. A quick pitcher bath in his tiny office took care of the scents still clinging to his skin and hair before he shrugged into his dress vigils.

He had to admit the force's tailors were good. The tan breeches were Liganti-cut, snug as they could be around his thighs and hips without impeding movement. Both the brocade waistcoat and the coat of sapphire wool were tailored like a second skin, before the latter flared to full skirts that kissed the tops of his polished, knee-high boots. On his patrol slops, the diving hawk across the back of his shoulders was mere patchwork; here it was embroidered in golds and browns.

Grey didn't have much use for vanity, but he did love his dress vigils. They were an inarguable reminder that he'd climbed to a place few Vraszenians could even imagine reaching. His brother, Kolya, had been so proud the day Grey came home in them.

The sudden trembling of his hands stabbed his collar pin into his thumb. Grey swallowed a curse and sucked the blood from the puncture, using a tiny hand mirror to make sure he hadn't gotten any on his collar. Luckily, it was clean, and he managed to finish dressing himself without further injury.

Once outside, he set off east from Duskgate with long, ground-eating strides. He could have taken a sedan chair and told the bearers to bill the Vigil; other officers did, knowing all the while that no such bill would ever be paid. But along with stiffing the bearers, that meant they didn't see the city around them the way Grey did.

Not that most of them would. They were Liganti, or mixed enough in ancestry that they could claim the name; to them, Nadežra was an outpost of Seste Ligante, half tamed by the Liganti general Kaius Sifigno, who restyled himself Kaius Rex after conquering Vraszan two centuries past. Others called him the Tyrant, and when he died, the Vraszenian clans took back the rest of their conquered land. But every push to reclaim their holy city failed, until exhaustion on both sides led to the signing of the Accords. Those established Nadežra as an independent city-state—under the rule of its Liganti elite.

It was an uneasy balance at best, made less easy still by Vraszenian radical groups like the Stadnem Anduske, who wouldn't settle for anything less than the city back in Vraszenian hands. And every time they pushed, the Cinquerat pushed back even harder.

The busy markets of Suncross at the heart of the Old Island parted for Grey's bright blue coat and the tawny embroidered hawk, but not without glares. To the high and mighty, the Vigil was a tool; to the common Nadežran, the Vigil was the tool of the high and mighty. Not all of them—Grey wasn't the only hawk who cared about common folk—but enough that he couldn't blame people for their hostility. And some of the worst glares came from Vraszenians, who looked at him and saw a slip-knot: a man who had betrayed his people, siding with the invaders' descendants.

Grey was used to the glares. He kept an eye out for trouble as he passed market stalls on the stoops of decaying townhouses, and a bawdy puppet show where the only children in the crowd were the pickpockets. They trickled away like water before he could mark their faces. A few beggars eyed him warily, but Grey had no grudge against them; the more dangerous elements wouldn't come out until evening, when the feckless sons and daughters of the delta gentry prowled the streets in search of amusement. A pattern-reader had set up on a corner near the Charterhouse, ready to bilk people in exchange for a pretty lie. He gave her a wide berth, leather glove creaking into a fist as he resisted the urge to drag her back to the Aerie for graft.

Once he'd passed under the decaying bulk of the Dawngate and across the Sunrise Bridge, he turned north into the narrow islets of the Pearls, clogged with sedan chairs. Two elderly ladies impressed with their own importance blocked the Becchia Bridge entirely, squabbling like gulls over which one should yield. Grey marked the house sigil painted onto each chair's door in case complaints came to the Aerie later.

His shoulders itched as he crossed the lines of the complex mosaic in the center of Traementis Plaza. It was no mere tilework, but a numinat: geometric Liganti magic meant to keep the ground dry and solid, against the river's determination to sink everything into the mud. Useful... but the Tyrant had twisted numinatria into a weapon during his conquest, and mosaics like this one amounted to emblems of ongoing Liganti control.

On the steps of Traementis Manor, Grey gave his uniform a final smoothing and sounded the bell. Within moments, Colbrin opened the door and favored Grey with a rare smile.

"Young Master Serrado. How pleasant to see you; it's been far too long. I'm afraid Altan Leato is not here to receive you—"

"It's 'Captain' now," Grey said, touching the hexagram pin at his throat. The smile he dredged up felt tired from disuse. "And I'm not here for Leato. Era Traementis requested assistance from the Vigil."

"Ah, yes." Colbrin bowed him inside. "If you'll wait in the salon, I'll inform Era Traementis that you're here."

Grey wasn't surprised when Colbrin returned in a few moments and summoned him to the study. Whatever Donaia had written to the Vigil for, it was business, not a social call.

That room was much darker, with little in the way of bright silks to warm the space—but warmth came in many shapes.

Donaia's grizzled wolfhound scrambled up from his place by her desk, claws ticking on wood as he trotted over for a greeting. "Hello, old man," Grey said, giving him a good tousling and a few barrel thumps on the side.

"Meatball. Heel." The dog returned to Donaia's side, looking up as she crossed the room to greet Grey.

"Era Traementis," Grey said, bowing over her hand. "I'm told you have need of assistance."

The silver threads lacing through her hair were gaining ground against the auburn, and she looked tired. "Yes. I need you to look into someone—a visitor to the city, recently arrived from Seteris. Renata Viraudax."

"Has she committed some crime against House Traementis?"

"No," Donaia said. "*She* hasn't."

Her words piqued his curiosity. "Era?"

A muscle tightened in Donaia's jaw. "My husband once had a sister named Letilia—Lecilla, really, but she was obsessed with Seteris and their high culture, so she badgered their father into changing it in the register. Twenty-three years ago, she decided she would rather be in Seteris than here...so she stole some money and jewelry and ran away."

Donaia gestured Grey to a chair in front of the hearth. The warmth of the fire enveloped him as he sat down. "Renata Viraudax is Letilia's daughter. She claims to be trying to mend bridges, but I have my doubts. I want you to find out what she's really doing in Nadežra."

As much as Grey loathed the right of the nobility to commandeer the Vigil for private use, he couldn't help feeling sympathy. When he was younger and less aware of the differences that made it impossible, he'd sometimes wished Donaia Traementis was his mother. She was stern, but fair. She loved her children, and was fiercely protective of her family. Unlike some, she never gave Leato and Giuna reason to doubt her love for them.

This Viraudax woman's mother had hurt her family, and the Traementis had a well-earned reputation for avenging their own.

"What can you tell me about her?" he asked. "Has she given you any reason to doubt her sincerity? Apart from being her mother's daughter."

Donaia's fingers drummed briefly against the arm of the chair, and her gaze settled on a corner of the fireplace and stayed there long enough that Grey knew she was struggling with some thought. He kept his silence.

Finally she said, "You and my son are friends, and moreover you aren't a fool. It can't have escaped your notice that House Traementis is not what it once was, in wealth, power, or numbers. We have many enemies eager to see us fall. Now this young woman shows up and tries to insinuate herself among us? Perhaps I'm jumping at shadows . . . but I must consider the possibility that this is a gambit intended to destroy us entirely." She gave a bitter laugh. "I can't even be certain this girl *is* Letilia's daughter."

She must be worried, if she was admitting so much. Yes, Grey had suspected—would have suspected even if Vigil gossip didn't sometimes speculate—that House Traementis was struggling more than they let on. But he never joined in the gossip, and he never asked Leato.

Leato . . . who was always in fashion, and according to that same gossip spent half his time frequenting aža parlours and gambling dens. *Does Leato know?* Grey swallowed the question. It wasn't his business, and it wasn't the business Donaia had called him for.

"That last shouldn't be too hard to determine," he said. "I assume you know where she's staying?" He paused when

Donaia's lips flattened, but she only nodded. "Then talk to her. If she's truly Letilia's daughter, she should know details an imposter wouldn't easily be able to discover. If she gives you vague answers or takes offense, then you'll know something is wrong."

Grey paused again, wondering how much Donaia would let him pry. "You said you had enemies she might be working for. It would help me to know who they are and what they might want." At her sharply indrawn breath, he raised a hand in pledge. "I promise I'll say nothing of it—not even to Leato."

In a tone so dry it burned, Donaia began ticking possibilities off on her fingers. "Quientis took our seat in the Cinquerat. Kaineto are only delta gentry, but have made a point of blocking our attempts to contract out our charters. Essunta, likewise. Simendis, Destaelio, Novrus, Cleoter—Indestor—I'm afraid it's a crowded field."

That was the entire Cinquerat and others besides...but she'd only stumbled over one name.

"Indestor," Grey said. The house that held Caerulet, the military seat in the Cinquerat. The house in charge of the Vigil.

The house that would not look kindly upon being investigated by one of its own.

"Era Traementis...did you ask for any officer, or did you specifically request me?"

"You're Leato's friend," Donaia said, holding his gaze. "Far better to ask a friend for help than to confess our troubles to an enemy."

That startled a chuckle from Grey. At Donaia's furrowed brow, he said, "My brother was fond of a Vraszenian saying. 'A family covered in the same dirt washes in the same water.'"

And Kolya would have given Grey a good scolding for not jumping to help Donaia right away. She might not be kin, but she'd hired a young Vraszenian carpenter with a scrawny kid brother when nobody else would, and paid him the same as a Nadežran.

He stood and bowed with a fist to his shoulder. "I'll see what I can discover for you. Tell me where to find this Renata Viraudax."

Follow us:

f /orbitbooksUS

🐦 /orbitbooks

▶ /orbitbooks

Join our mailing list
to receive alerts on our
latest releases and deals.

orbitbooks.net

Enter our monthly
giveaway for the chance
to win some epic prizes.

orbitloot.com